Also By Allison:
The Dragon and the Double-Edged Sword (The Stones of Peragros Book 1)

Coming Soon:
The Stones of Peragros Book 2

More to be announced soon. Find her at linktr.ee/allison_ivy

REWARD

As the author of *Inked in Blood and Memory*, I'm offering anyone reading this the opportunity to earn a cash reward by showing this work to any literary agent, publisher, or producer who extends an acceptable contract offer to me. The reward is 10% of any initial book advance or option contract for film, capped at a maximum of $10,000.00 USD. Additionally, if you know of any international publishers, I'd love to hear about their proposal to translate *Inked* into different languages.

Why offer this incentive?

- Over 98% of works published are introduced to publishers through direct connections rather than unsolicited submissions.

- Reading is inherently collaborative, needing not only the author's words but a reader's imagination. This reward allows readers to play a role in launching the career of an author they appreciate. And I will be forever grateful for your help.

Our objective is to introduce this work to professionals in the publishing and film realms. I'm often in awe of just how small the world is. Somewhere out there, you are reading this and know of someone who may enjoy this work.

If there are individuals within your network involved in publishing or film (agents, editors, executives, avid readers, librarians, bookshop owners, etc.), it is my hope that you will pass along this book to them.

Please forward any leads, opportunities, or introductions via the provided email address below.

Thank you sincerely for your assistance.
Allison Ivy
allison@allisonivybooks.com

INKED IN BLOOD AND MEMORY

ALLISON IVY

INKED IN BLOOD AND MEMORY

Copyright © 2024 by Allison Ivy

All rights reserved. No part of this book may be used or reproduced in any manner whatsoever without written permission except in the case of brief quotations embodied in critical articles or reviews.

This book is a work of fiction. Names, characters, businesses, organizations, places, events and incidents either are the product of the author's imagination or are used fictitiously. Any resemblance to actual persons, living or dead, events, or locales is entirely coincidental. I did not trap people in this book.

For information contact: allison@allisonivybooks.com
https://allisonivybooks.com

Cover art by Triff/Shutterstock.com, Liu zishan/Shutterstock.com, Einheit00/Deviantart.com, and Black-B-o-x/Deviantart.com
Book Formatting by Derek Murphy @Creativindie
Proofreading by Samantha Gove at Raven's Wing Editing Services
Requiem Font created by Chris Hansen/Livin Hell, 2004.
Scene breaks by Giuseppe Ramos D
Chapter art by Jordan from Skritch's Images & Gambar Kunde harahap
Teacup with a Flower and Cattail Plant Silhouette by Valentyna Smordova
Maine Coon, Teddy Bear Toy, Vintage Snake, Howling Wolf, Wedding Dress, Picnic Basket Drawing, Magical Vintage Book, and Book Drawing by Georgi Marchev
Graveyard Halloween Background by Dikas Design
Antique watch and Mask of Feathers art by nellivalova
Minotaur Mythology Mascot, and Candles on White Linocut by Martin Malchev
Cocktail sketch illustration. by Pretty Meerkat
Metal Chain Illustration, A Knife Illustration, and Isolated modern house on fire by blueringmedia

Paperback ISBN: 979-8-218-47849-0
Hardcover ISBN: 979-8-218-48962-5
First Edition: December 2024
10 9 8 7 6 5 4 3 2 1

For J.P.
Thank you for talking me through the plotholes.

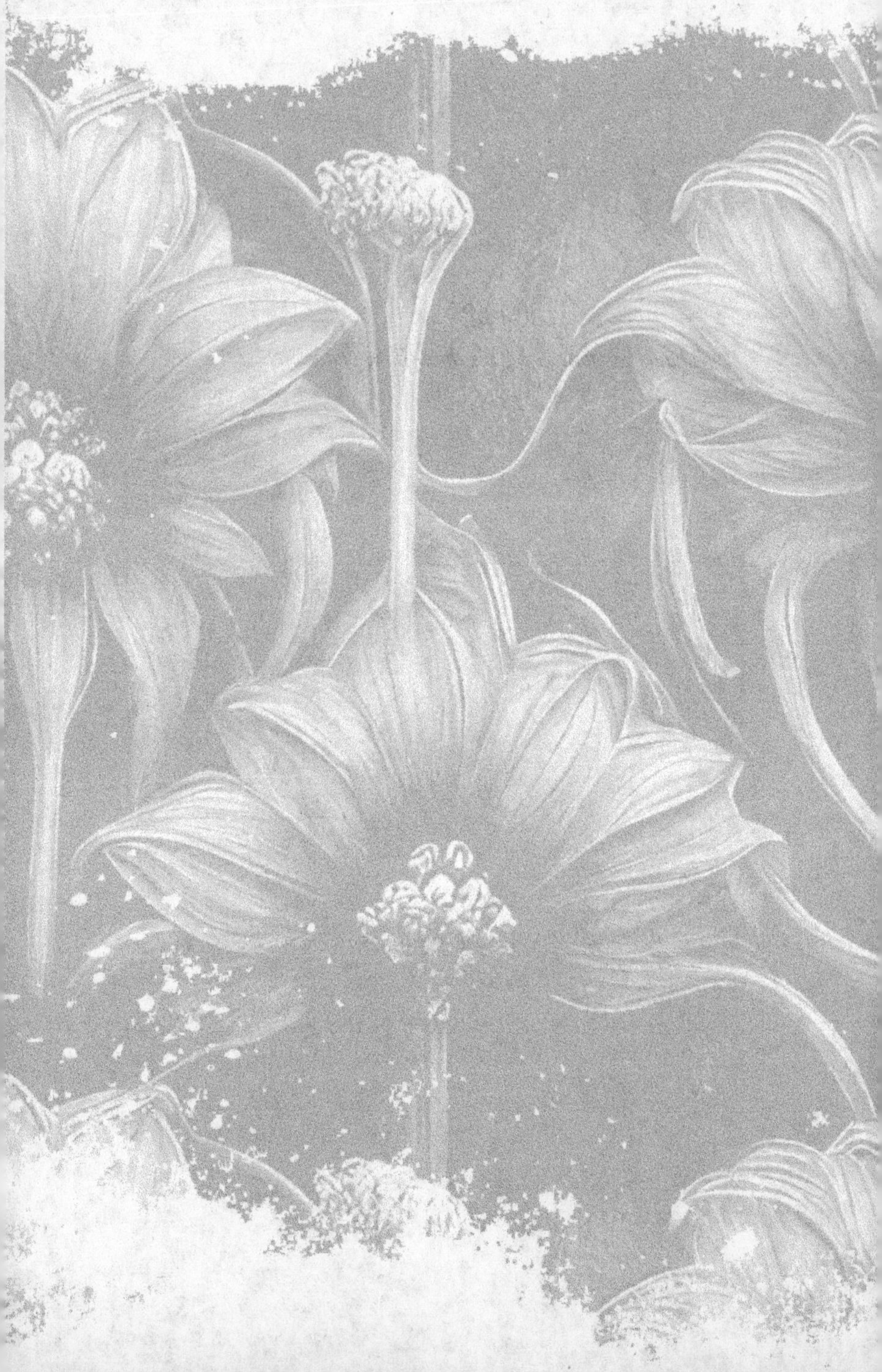

CHAPTER ONE
LY THI REN

You never forget your first ritual sacrifice. So why had I? That seems like something you'd remember. It's not something most American families gather for.

Hey, Má. Could you pass the rau răm? Oh, and what time is the sacrifice tonight?

And yet, I had forgotten. I had forgotten the little things, too. My mother's laugh, her abrupt chortles that often devolved into giggles. My childhood nickname.

We eat pho the night our own parents sacrifice one of my best friends. It's weird what sticks with you after years of trying to forget. We eat in silence, though I haven't yet realized the reason for the solemn mood. My nine-year-old brain doesn't quite grasp the idea of "sacrifice." I can't wait to wear my new ceremonial cloak. I begged my parents to let me wear it through dinner, but they refused.

"It's too special," they say. "You don't want to ruin it, do you, con gái?"

No, I don't want that. Still, my eyes wander to the piece of clothing that hangs on the coat tree next to the front door. The intricate symbols fascinate me. The only other place I've seen them is on the book. Not just any book. The book.

I get to see it on special occasions during the four months out of the year our family guards it. The other eight months are split between two additional families. My best friends', Sophie Vanguard and Jeremy Berg-Nilsen.

We'll join them later for the ceremony or the "thanksgiving," but not that Thanksgiving. We are not pilgrims, but our three families are special. Chosen. And today, Jeremy is the most special.

"Ông xã, are you sure this is the only way?" Má squeezes Ba's arm.

Ba remains quiet for so long I almost ask him if he's heard Má. I'm not sure what she means by her question or why it's gotten even quieter than before.

Ba answers before I speak. "It's too late to back out. Maybe we could have years ago, but not now. This is how we keep our family safe." He kisses my mother's hand and stands to clear the plates.

I knit my brows together. Why are they so serious? It's like they're sad. But it's the day of the thanksgiving. They should be happy.

Later that night, I beam proudly in my cloak with the strange symbols, relishing the feel of the velvet hem between my fingertips. Incense burns in a corner, permeating the air with a smoky aroma that I've always hated, but it reminds me of the days we celebrate the four equinoxes.

The adults hug and talk amongst themselves excitedly. All but Mrs. Berg-Nilsen, Jeremy's mom. She stands against the wall, keeping to herself. Her long blonde hair covers most of her face, but I can tell her cheeks are wet.

I ponder this as I sit cross-legged on the antique rug with Jeremy in his family's living room. We sip Capri-Suns and talk about what we think will happen in a few minutes.

"Happy birthday, Jeremy," Sophie says after arriving with her parents and barreling through the adults' legs. She holds a cloak that matches mine out behind her as she runs like she's a superhero or a bat and plops down on the rug between us.

"Thanks, Sophie," Jeremy mumbles, staring at his Capri-Sun.

Of the three of us, Sophie is the most frenetic. I think that's the word Ba used. The adults are always hiding the sugar from her. She channels her chaotic energy for good most of the time. At school this past week, a couple kids from our grade cornered Jeremy. Sophie took me by the hand and came to Jeremy's aid, not letting up until the kids backed off.

"Why is your mom crying?" I ask Jeremy.

His eyes move from his drink to his shoes, and he tugs at the laces. "Dad says she's happy, but she won't look at me."

"Grownups are weird," I say, watching Jeremy's parents lead the rest into the kitchen.

"I think I did something real bad," Jeremy says.

The door swings closed, and I'm on my feet, ignoring Sophie's questions and drawn to the conversation happening behind the closed door.

I dare to push it an inch and peer through the crack where I have a view of Jeremy's mom.

"There has to be another way," she says while barely containing her sobs. Her tears come faster now as she gasps for air.

My eyes widen. Her words are eerily similar to Má's. "Are you sure this is the only way?"

I've never seen an adult cry, and I never thought Mrs. Berg-Nilsen could cry. She's the happiest adult I know, always saying how important it is to look on the bright side. To see her cry shakes me up, and I'm struck by the wrongness of this thanksgiving. Isn't this a happy day?

Someone clutches Mrs. Berg-Nilsen's right hand from across the table, stroking it with their thumb. Mr. Berg-Nilsen, I guess. "You know there isn't, sweetheart. We have no choice."

Sophie's mother, Dr. Sylvia Vanguard, chimes in. "If there was any other—"

"What do you know, Sylvia?" Mrs. B. snaps. "It's not your child. No, you and Roger had a daughter, and so did Lien and Đài."

The sudden change in her voice makes me flinch. I don't know why. I'm not the one being scolded.

"We've sacrificed in our own ways," Sophie's mom replies.

"Not your own flesh and blood."

"This was the deal we made, Caroline," Sophie's mom continues. "We need to see it through."

4

The door creaks, and I gasp reflexively. I hadn't realized my palm still rested on the door. The kitchen falls silent until someone steps in front of my view and yanks the door open all the way. It's my father.

"Ren, you know better than to eavesdrop," he says. "Go back to your friends."

As I turn to obey him, Dr. Vanguard speaks again. "We should start to prepare anyway. It's almost the minute of his birth."

I return to my spot on the rug with Sophie and Jeremy, feeling the weight of the heavy cloak on my shoulders more than ever.

"...And afterward, maybe we can have a sleepover and play Haglen Brook Bandits," Sophie is saying.

Jeremy nods enthusiastically, but I am no longer excited. Something in Mrs. Berg-Nilsen's voice has made me sick to my stomach. I've never heard that kind of tone in an adult before. A mix of anger and fear. The room in front of me blurs, my eyes losing their focus as I replay what I've heard.

Out of the corner of my eye, I notice Jeremy and Sophie trying to get my attention. With effort, I pull myself out of my thoughts and focus on Jeremy's words.

"What were they talking about?" he asks.

But I don't have a chance to tell him. All six parents emerge from the kitchen. Mrs. B slips outside as the rest approach us.

Something clenches in my stomach. It's only years later that I'll be able to pinpoint the feeling—dread.

Sophie's father is the one who holds out his hand. "Jeremy, take my hand, son."

Jeremy moves to go, but I grab his wrist, a sudden panic in me that even I don't quite understand. "No."

Jeremy narrows his eyes at me in confusion as Má speaks up from behind Mr. Vanguard. "Let go of him, Ren," she says firmly.

Sophie touches my leg. "What's wrong?"

I stare down at her and then look at the six people around us. Whatever they want to do to Jeremy, there is nothing I can do to stop it. I'm a kid with no real power. I'm not even sure I need *to do anything. But that sick feeling lingers in my gut.*

But Má and Ba wouldn't let anything happen to Jeremy. And Jeremy's mom and dad love him. Adults are to be trusted. Especially Má and Ba.

Reluctantly, I let go of Jeremy, trusting the adults, and Sophie's dad leads him by the hand to the center of the room.

Má motions for Sophie and me to join the other adults. Sophie rises and takes my hand to lead me over, but my feet are planted on the thin rug. The weight of her hand barely reaches me.

"Are you okay?" Sophie asks, stroking my thumb.

I shake my head. "Something's wrong," is all I can say. "I can feel it."

I can tell Sophie wants to ask me to elaborate, but Má moves behind us to usher us the rest of the way. She breaks us apart, taking my left hand and Sophie's right as we join the circle. Ba grabs my right hand, and Sophie's mom instructs her daughter to grab her elbow.

Sophie leans behind Má to cast a worried look at me, brow wrinkles and all, but I don't have any answers for her. Just a gut feeling that this day is not what we'd expected.

I shake my head at her, trying to convey my thoughts but failing, and turn to the scene in front of me.

Mr. Berg-Nilsen envelops Jeremy in a hug, his face crumpling as he bites his lip to hold back sobs. I can tell by Jeremy's face that he doesn't understand why. I don't even understand why.

"Where's Mom?" Jeremy asks, sipping from a goblet Sylvia offers him.

"She'll be here. She just had to step outside for a moment."

Mr. B. leads him onto the coffee table, and he stands there as his father joins our circle around him. Someone has painted a symbol on the tablecloth he stands on, but I don't know what it stands for. I've never seen it before. Several linked silver circles are all inside one big circle of words in another language.

Jeremy's eyes droop, and his father instructs him to lie down. When Mrs. B returns, hood raised and positioned behind Jeremy, he looks like he'll fall asleep any second. I'm not sure he even realizes his mom has returned.

Dr. Vanguard also raises her hood, and the rest of us copy her. She picks the book up and opens it, Sophie's hand still on her elbow. On her other side, Sophie's dad holds his wife's left elbow.

Only a few minutes ago, music was playing. Now, the silence envelops us. Not even Mrs. B sobs anymore. I can't make out her expression in the dim light and shadow of her hood.

No one speaks. We all stare at Dr. Vanguard as if waiting for her to start something.

"Mom?" Jeremy whispers.

Mrs. B is silent.

As Sophie's mom clears her throat, I narrow my eyes at her. Why is she touching the book? We're not allowed to touch the book. I've only ever seen it tucked safely behind its glass case, propped up on a stand.

And we're definitely not allowed to have our shoes on furniture. Why are they letting Jeremy wear his? Is it because it's his birthday?

"Great One," Dr. Vanguard begins, her eyes on the open book, "We gather here today in humility and supplication."

A breeze picks up and rustles my hair, and I shiver involuntarily, chilled even though I'm wearing long sleeves and a thick cloak. There are no windows open. Where is it coming from?

The rest of the adults have their eyes closed, their heads tilted slightly upward as their hair blows around their faces.

Sophie and I make eye contact again. At least I'm not the only one lost here.

"Hear us, oh Great One," Dr. Vanguard continues. "Let your divine and gracious benevolence fill our lives. In return, we offer up our youngest male. An innocent soul of ten years of age, ripe and ready to serve you. Jeremy Berg-Nilsen."

"Jeremy Berg-Nilsen," the adults repeat in unison.

Dr. Vanguard recites words from the book in a language I don't understand. The adults repeat each phrase as she finishes them. I look from Má to Ba, but neither seems to notice me. Their eyes are still closed.

"Má?" I say tentatively. Her bangs flutter on her forehead as she continues chanting.

She never ignores me. Why is she ignoring me? Maybe she didn't hear me.

"Má," I try again, a little louder.

Jeremy turns to me, tears forming in his eyes. "Ren? What's going on?"

Instead of words, a lump forms in my throat. No, I'm not going to cry. I'm angry. Adults are supposed to comfort kids. What is wrong with them? What is wrong with the Berg-Nilsens?

I wrench my hands free from Má and Ba's grips. It helps that they were *distracted.*

"*Ren, what are you doing?*" *they yell at me, but I ignore them.*

My focus is Jeremy. I reach for his outstretched hand, but the wind picks up, pushing me away from the table. The force is stronger than any wind I've ever known, and it swirls around Jeremy, blending with a sudden trail of thick, black smoke that blasts out of the book in Dr. Vanguard's hands. It's as if Jeremy is inside his own personal tornado. The adults continue, practically shouting now.

"*Má, stop.*" *The wind howls in my ears, and I'm not even sure if she's heard me. I try again. "Má, please. You're scaring him." I tug on Má's sleeve, but she brushes me off and continues to chant.*

Sophie's trying to get her mother's attention, but her attempts are just as useless.

Jeremy tries to prop himself up on his elbows but lays back down. He seems drained as if he needs to sleep for hours. The wind and smoke ruffle his clothes, tugging at his cloak.

"*Jeremy!*"

A hand wraps around his ankle, and his eyes bulge. A hand? No, not a hand. At least, not a human hand. It's a horrible ashen color. Boils dot the skin, and its bony, crooked fingers end in long, yellow claws.

My heart races. "Help him!"

Jeremy screams, and the sound pierces the gale of the tornado as tears stream down his face. A second hand identical to the first wraps around his other ankle. Sophie reaches for him, but her father tugs her back.

Jeremy and I lock eyes the same moment his feet leave the table. Jeremy's entire body wavers, losing its shape, and in a blur of smoke and color like an extinguished flame, follows the pair of hands into the open book.

What just happened? Where did he go?

The adults are silent as Dr. Vanguard closes the book with a snap.

The action breaks me from the unbidden memory, and I return to the present. The scent of incense lingers in my nostrils, but I'm no longer nine-years-old. And my name is not Ren here. It's Geraldine. Isn't it?

I wipe my wet cheeks and scan the room as if expecting a smoke monster to jump out at me from the shadows. But it's just me in this study. My eyes come to a screeching halt on a black and gray Maine Coon cat. I've never seen it before, but it's blinking up at me with indifferent green eyes, not paying much attention to my fiancé's lifeless body.

CHAPTER TWO
HERCULES

The bright lights of Hercules' arrival slowly faded, and soon, he forgot why they had even been there or that they were ever there at all. He licked his paw and ran it over his fur, grooming himself. His fur always tingled after the experience. It stuck up at odd angles, and he hurried to smooth it. It didn't help that his coat was on the thicker side.

The hay underneath him clung to his belly and the pads of his paws. Maybe he shouldn't be grooming himself in the stables. It was proving inefficient.

"Hoot," an owl called to him from the rafters, but Herc barely acknowledged the creature. If it had anything constructive for him, it could come down and face him. Anyway, what did he need to hear from an owl?

Squeezing out of the cracked door, Herc resumed his grooming under the clear, star-filled sky. The cool grass was softer than the hay, and he was glad for it. The nightlife in the forest beyond the stables chirped at him, but he paid them no mind. Like the owl, they offered him nothing but distraction.

He'd come for one thing only, and that was—

He twitched his whiskers, paw frozen in mid-air. What *had* he come here for?

His fur had returned to normal by the time Herc's ears pricked to attention at another noise. The sound of a human crying her eyes out drifted down from the house at the top of the hill.

Honestly, what was the thing with humans and crying? What was the point? A need for attention? Did the saltwater that fell from their eyes somehow clean them?

Curiosity got the better of him, and he found himself padding up the hill to an open window. With every step, the crying grew louder until it was clear whoever it was couldn't be far from the window.

Herc leaped onto the ledge and peered into the dimly lit room. He found the source of the racket immediately. Geraldine—

No, not Geraldine. Ren. That was her true name. Wasn't it?

Ren sat in the middle of the room, sprawled over a male human's body that stared unblinking into his eyes. Ren's tears fell on him freely and still, he never flinched. It didn't take much to figure out he was dead. Ren and William. A love story turned tragedy.

How had he forgotten Ren's name?

Hercules paused a moment to gather himself. He hated this place and its side effect of forgetfulness. *Think...* Ah, yes. He remembered how he'd arrived and what he needed to do. He clung to his newfound memories. He knew how disorienting this world could be, and he would not become a walking shell of his former self. He knew who he was out there, and in here. And right now, he needed to get to the weeping human. Maybe it would shut her up, and he could have a peaceful rest of the night. It was worth a try.

Herc slipped under the cracked window and jumped to the room's floor. Cautiously, he approached the woman, his tail straight out and slightly curled.

Ren's body faced Hercules, but she hadn't taken notice of him yet. Her sobs racked her body as the blood on the man stained her light pink dress and her shaking hands. The high frills of the shoulder cuffs almost poked into her eyes as she moved.

The melodrama almost made him turn tail and run, but he knew he couldn't. He needed to stay and urge her on to the end of her story. This was his fate. But did it have to be so slow going?

Finally, Ren looked up at him.

Hercules saw the change in her in the blink of an eye as awareness replaced her sorrow, and her tears stopped. A welcome switch. He'd grown tired of her crocodile tears. After months of this charade, she was awake.

He sat beside the dead human, staring into Ren's eyes and wishing he could communicate his disgust. If only cats could speak. The things he'd say.

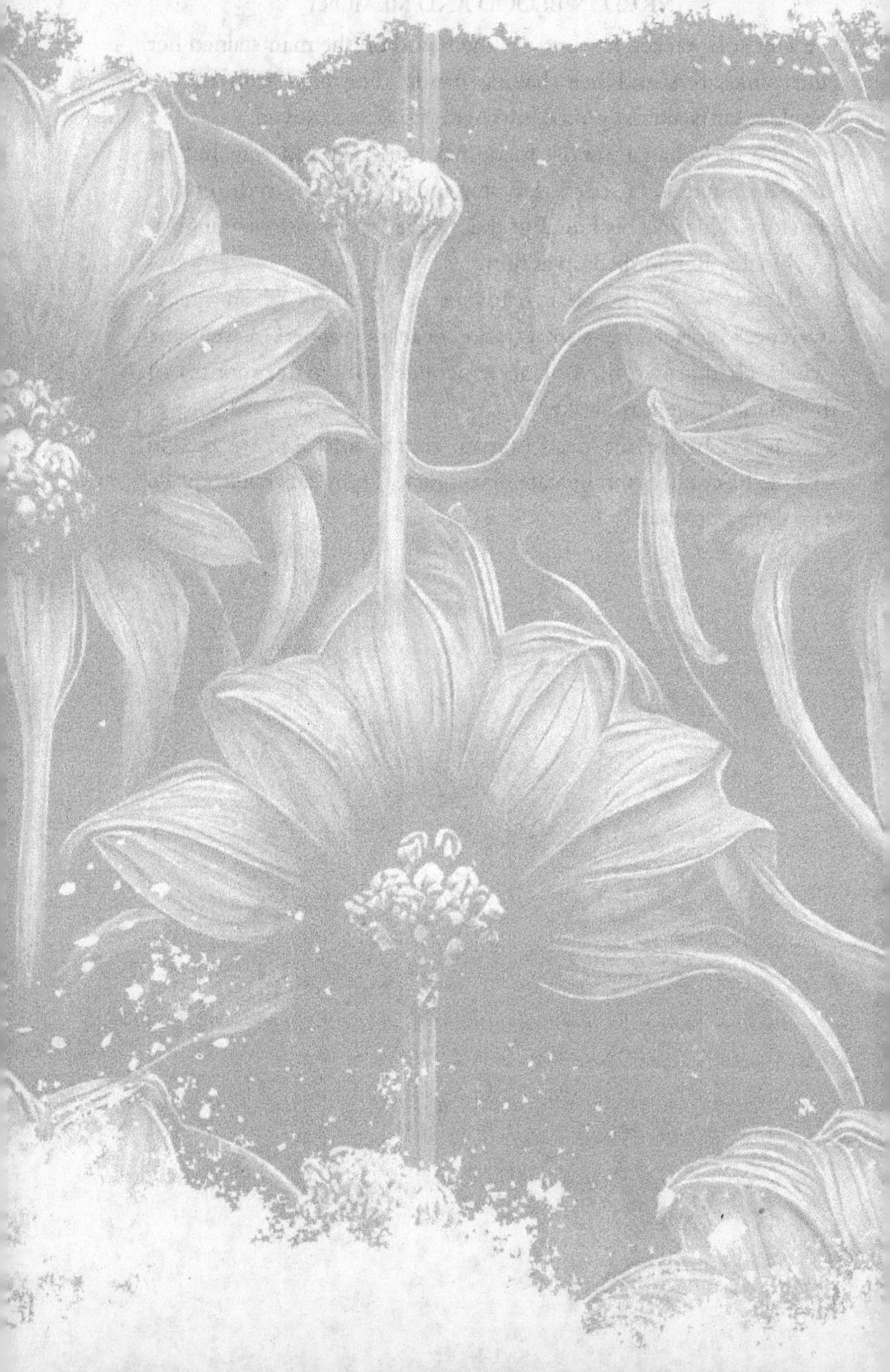

CHAPTER THREE
SOPHIE VANGUARD

The oddest feeling has come over me. I stare into my mug of hot cocoa, watching the powder dissolve into the steaming milk. It's like I've done this before in the same exact way in the same exact kitchen. Even though this house is a rental, and I never saw it before a few days ago.

I've always hated that feeling. It's like I'm jogging in place, and my life isn't going anywhere.

As I do my best to mentally shake off the déjà vu, I cup the hot mug around my hands and savor the warmth of the cocoa as it touches my lips and almost scalds my throat on the way down. Just a hair below burning. Perfect.

Oops. I forgot the marshmallows.

I place the mug back down on the granite kitchen island, licking my lips of the chocolate remnants, and turn to rummage in the cabinet behind me.

There they are.

A full, unopened bag of ooey-gooey deliciousness.

I tear into it with kitchen scissors, and seconds later I cover the surface of my cocoa with tiny marshmallows. I add a second layer just because. It seems like that kind of day.

In the living room, my copy of *The Count of Monte Cristo* beckons from where I left it on the overstuffed corduroy recliner. Villefort just locked Dantès up in the Château d'If, and I can't wait to see Dantès' next move.

The rental cabin's décor is exactly how I'd decorate my own home. "Cozy Maximalist," I think is the term. Books line every available space, a huge basket near the fireplace boasts several blankets, and string lights line the dark blue walls.

Settling back into my reading chair, I lift the book into my lap. My fingers skim across a piece of embossed fabric, and I turn the book over to inspect it. A location is printed there in raised red letters.

EVERLING INSTITUTE

Everling. I've heard that name before, haven't I?

My mind turns as I try to remember why the name is so familiar. It was on the tip of my tongue not one minute ago.

I shrug.

Oh, well. It's not important. I'm sure the name has always been there, and the name is familiar because I saw it there before.

The next morning, rays of sunshine filtering in through the window blinds wake me from a deep sleep. When I first arrived, I thought I'd miss the blackout curtains I have on my windows at home, but I haven't. The sun greeting me in the morning has actually been a pleasant way to wake up. The mattress is a bit too firm, but I'm slowly getting used to it.

When I stretch my hand out, it hits something on the pillow next to me. That's weird.

I blindly grab my glasses from the nightstand, put them on, and roll over, propping myself up on one elbow so I'm almost right on it.

INKED IN BLOOD AND MEMORY

When my eyes finally focus, I jump so far back I almost roll out of bed. I catch myself on the end table and crawl the rest of the way out of bed. The sheets are twisted around my legs, but I ignore them as the gears in my mind spin at top speed. My heart pounds.

This isn't happening. Did I actually see it, or is some part of me still dreaming?

Slowly, I poke my head above the mattress and force myself to check the pillow again, only to discover the opposite of what I'd hoped.

A blue passionflower lays there, which should be completely innocuous. Except I've seen the same type of flower randomly appear in various rooms around the house. Rooms that only I should have access to.

Passiflora caerulea. The flower's formal name will forever be burned in my brain since looking it up several days ago. Named by Roman Catholic priests and thought to symbolize the crucifixion. It's not a flower one usually sends to someone.

That flower wasn't there when I went to bed last night. I'm sure of it. Someone was here, towering over me while I slept. Close enough to touch me. Had he? Close enough to harm. To kill. I'm not alone here, and I don't think I ever was.

Lying next to the flower is a short note of bold calligraphy folded and propped up against the flower's stem.

We'll be together soon. I promise.

-Mason

And there it is. Proof that someone very real is doing this. Someone named Mason. I don't know any Masons, but apparently, he knows me. This is why I avoid going outside. Less chance of becoming a statistic. Of becoming a body stuffed inside a wall.

That's an image I do *not* want in my brain, but it's stuck there now. I've been so careful not to draw unwanted attention, haven't I? Apparently, not careful enough.

There goes my relaxing morning.

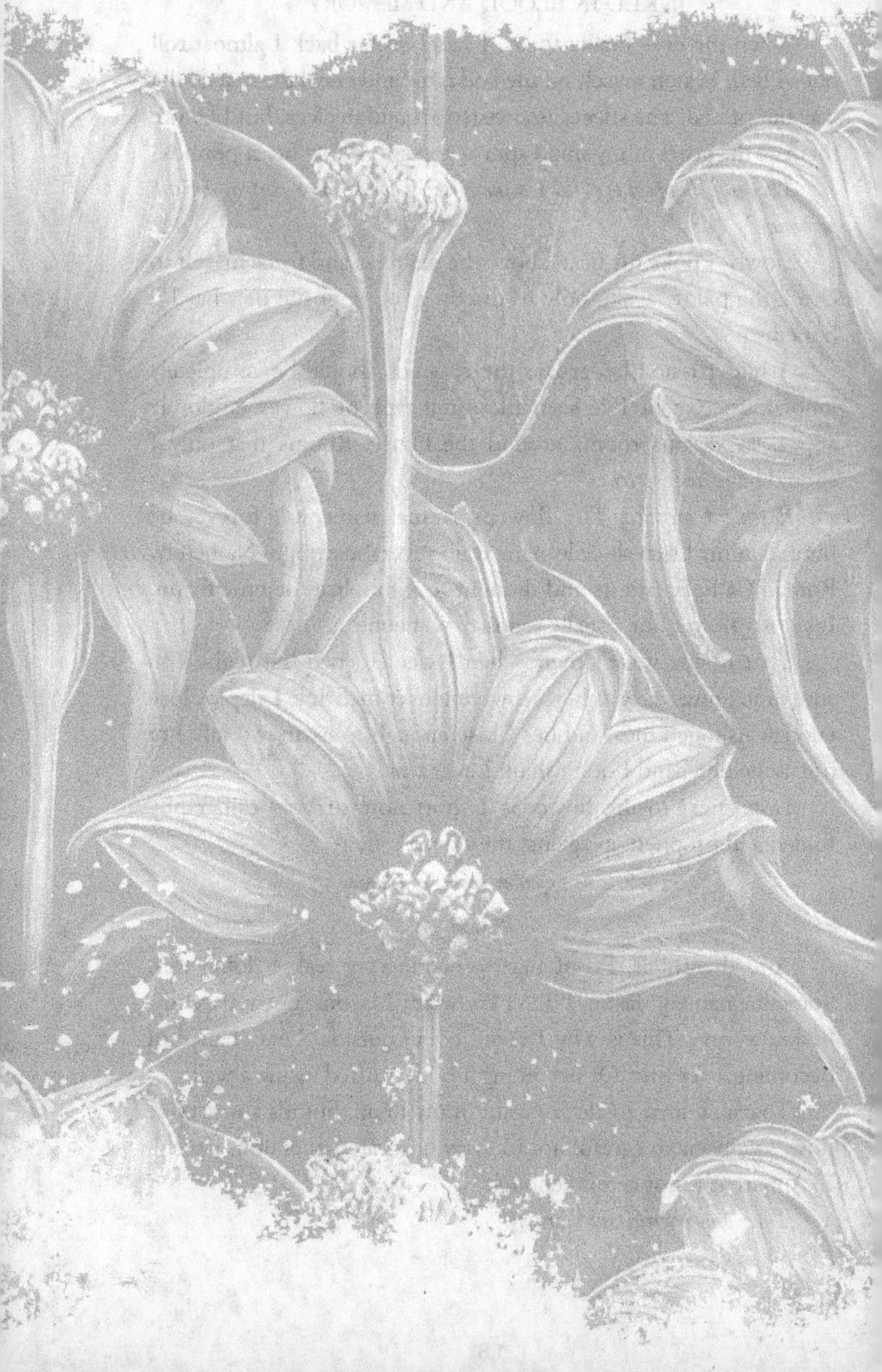

CHAPTER FOUR

JEREMY BERG-NILSEN
FOURTEEN YEARS AGO

I don't understand why it's so dark.

My first thought is someone has turned the lights out in the living room. I can't see anything, not even my own hand in front of my face.

And why is it so quiet? Not ten seconds ago, I could barely hear anything over the *whoosh*ing wind. But now, the air is still.

"Mom?" My voice echoes. Weird. It never has in this room before.

A sudden breeze rushes past me, and I shiver. It's freezing. And it's still *so quiet*.

Where is Mom and Dad? What about the others? Sophie and Ren?

"Hello?"

I shuffle my foot forward, thinking I must be close to the edge of the coffee table. The edge never comes. Confused, I bend down and run my hand around me, but all I feel is a cold, hard surface. I reach out further, almost lying flat, and still, the floor doesn't change. Did they lift me off of it and place me on the floor? No, I would at least feel the rug.

My eyes aren't adjusting. There are windows in the room that should be bringing in faint traces of moonlight, but not even that is visible.

My heart thuds in my chest. This isn't a power outage. I don't think I'm even in my house anymore. And I'm alone.

Everything is darkness. It doesn't even feel like I have a body. I don't understand.

A voice answers my thoughts, drifting to me from the void. *"Would you like to?"*

Adjusting to life in a demon's playground isn't a possibility. It didn't take me long to realize I could create things, shape the world around me. But keeping them the way you want is tricky to near impossible because my cellmate doesn't play nice.

Not long after arriving, I create a swing set identical to the one Sophie had—or *has*. I don't know which. It's hard to know how long I've been here.

I swing higher and higher. I've never been this high before, and I'm not scared like I usually am. My thoughts dart in and out faster than my swinging.

I wish I could apologize for whatever I did to deserve being sent here. If I could speak to Dad, say sorry for being a bad kid and promise to do better if he lets me out... How long am I going to be in timeout?

"You're not in timeout. They're not coming for you. They're never *coming for you."*

The words aren't my own, though they reflect my deepest fears. "Go away," I say, slowing my swinging a bit. *Someone will come for me. My mother. Sophie and Ren...*

Where are they now? How long has it been since I've seen

them?

"They're a part of this, too. They will never come for you. They think you're dead."

"You're lying!"

Hissss.

The left chain of the swing is slimy and *moving* like it's alive. I snatch my hand away at the same moment I notice the snake. It flicks its tongue at me, staring me down from less than a foot away.

"Ahh!"

My feet reach for the floor, but it's not there. Looking down, there's nothing but an endless black void. I cling to the remaining chain, feet kicking wildly. *Help.*

But there's no one here, and my arms are getting tired. And the snake is waiting to strike.

My hands slip on the chain because it's no longer a chain but a second snake. I lose my grip, my stomach dropping as I fall.

I scream, but the wind whips my voice away as I reach out for anything to break my fall. But there's nothing. Just me and the darkness. "Stop! Please!"

I close my eyes, preparing for impact, but it never comes. Instead, the wind halts, and a bright light invades the blackness behind my eyelids. I peek with one eye to find a white light in front of me. I'm not falling anymore. My feet are on solid ground.

Cautiously, I open my other eye and look around. The white light seeps out from a hole in the air. It hovers at eye level and is no bigger than a standard mirror. There are people inside it. "Hello?"

As my vision adjusts, I can make out blurred silhouettes, then a table, and then finally the full image. Sophie and Ren are sitting at the Lys' kitchen table. Their parents and a few other kids gather around them as my mother sets a cake down in front of Ren.

"Mom! Mom, it's Jeremy!"

But she doesn't hear me. None of them do. I can only watch as my parents sing to Ren, and she blows out a candle that says, "Happy 10th Birthday!"

It can't be May 8th already. It was just September. How is it May?

I reach out a hand. I don't know what I expect to do, but my hand hits a wall as if the scene really is inside a mirror. I hit it again and again with everything I have, but the image only ripples until, finally, it fades.

Tears spring to my eyes. "No, please! Bring them back! I'm here," I sob, but it's no use. I'm in the dark once again.

Time passes slower after that, with each month moving slower than the last. My one constant is a glimpse into Sophie's and Ren's lives. I start out wanting to spend every day looking in on them, but after a while, something changes. They never seem to be thinking about me. I never hear them say my name. It takes me far too long to realize they're moving on. They're not concerned with finding me, liberating me from this place. Why don't they care? I thought we were friends. It's like they've forgotten I ever existed. I want to shake them and make them remember, but I can't.

I don't get hungry here, but I conjure food anyway for something to do. It doesn't last long here. The demon rots it before I can take a bite.

And Sophie and Ren graduate high school. Their parents make sure they get into good colleges.

Meanwhile, I see only the worst of my mom's and dad's lives. Their divorce, my mother's imprisonment in The Everling Institute for Mental Health, the last time my father visits her.

It all plays out before me in real-time. These events are the only way I can tell time is passing at all. That and the markers of age as my mom withers away.

And every day, the demon asks me a question. And every day, my answer is the same. But already, I can feel myself considering another answer. How long can I stay strong?

CHAPTER FIVE
LY THI REN

Imagine my surprise when the grief for my dead fiancé simply evaporated. One second, I was in mourning for the life I could've had with this man, and the next, that fiancé became nothing more than part of a bad dream, and my queerness returned to me.

That's right. I'm a lesbian. How did I forget that?

I awoke from my dream a little over fourteen hours ago, but I didn't wake up in my bed. No, I awoke kneeling over William's body. One blink, I was completely oblivious to anything awry, and the next, I became entirely self-aware. And looking into the green eyes of that black and gray striped Maine Coon seems to have been the trigger. It ran off not a minute afterward, and I haven't seen it since.

Now, half a day later, I still haven't worked out what this world is. It looks like Earth; the dirt and grass underneath my and Adeline's picnic blanket smell like Earth. The estate down the hill with its stables is real enough.

And yet, I wonder.

Who could have trapped me in this idyllic and, admittedly, boring place? That is the feeling of dread I have. Like I'm trapped.

Am I dead? I have no memory of dying. But then again, I have no memory of my first day here either. Did someone use magic on me? I've heard stories of more and more people practicing, even thinking about trying it myself, but still. Why me?

Some movie I watched years ago had the character stuck in a snow globe. Is that what this is? Some version of a snow globe?

As if this dilemma isn't bad enough, another question races through my brain. It's one I've been asking ever since I woke but have been too afraid to ponder the answer.

A hand lightly touches my wrist and shakes me from my questions. "Geraldine, you look a fright. You should lie down, darling."

The voice comes from Adeline, a supposed friend of mine. I scrutinize her *Pride and Prejudice*-esque dress, which matches her parasol and gloves. It's all a nauseating yellow floral pattern.

Geraldine. My shrinking violet alter ego. I don't even *look* like a Geraldine. She's a part I'm forced to play in this world even now. I don't know who I can trust with my newfound knowledge.

I look harder at Adeline's features. Is there a hint of knowing behind those batting eyelashes and concerned expression? Or is she just as oblivious as I was less than a day ago? I can't be sure.

For now, I will play along with a smile. "I'm fine. Just worried about the Graysons' daughter, is all. And missing William," I add, plucking my "fiancé's" name out of my hazy memory. That way of thinking is like a dream, but one I can access if needed. Still there despite the fact that I'm now awake.

The first part of my statement to Adeline is true. Someone attacked Paulette Grayson while she was grooming her horse yesterday afternoon. She still hasn't woken up. Not long after, William turned up dead, and I had my epiphany straight after finding him. Why a cat would trigger my memory is anyone's guess. I'm still putting the pieces together.

And that weird-ass cat has to be a part of the bigger picture.

It crept into the room, sat right next to William's body, and stared at me with those soulless, dark green eyes. The markings on its front legs reminded me of a zebra, but I barely registered anything but those eyes. It seemed like it had wanted to tell me something. But I don't speak cat.

Adeline hums apologetically. "You poor dear. I'm worried for Paulette, too, but the inspector has things covered. Best to let him do his job whilst we stay out of trouble."

"I'm sure you're right," I say, forcing a meek smile. *I'll decide how much trouble I want. Thank you very much.*

"So, Geraldine—"

My name is Ren, I remind myself as I sip my gross Earl Grey tea. I won't forget again.

CHAPTER SIX
SOPHIE VANGUARD

January 14th:
I tried to leave today. Not leave exactly. More accurately, I tried to descend the porch steps to the thick blanket of snow. I figured if I could at least get that far, I could somehow get my legs working long enough to reach a neighboring house. The rental's landline hasn't worked for as long as I've been here, and my cell is dead. I can't seem to find my charger.

There were houses nearby, right? I couldn't remember.

It was all I could do to turn the knob. I swear I broke into a cold sweat as my hand wrapped around the doorknob. Blue spots dotted my vision as I swung the door open.

But they weren't dots. They were blue passionflowers, and they were really there. Sticking out of the snow like spots on a cartoon Dalmatian's fur. Hundreds of them just waiting for me to greet them.

Dozens of footprints surrounded the spontaneous and morbid garden. I could tell by analyzing one closest to the porch that the person who left it favored their right leg. If I could've mustered the courage to measure it and divide the length by .15, I would've figured out my stalker's height. Completely useless, but these are the things that race through my mind in times of stress.

Blood spatter pattern meanings, cyphers, the name of Emily Dickinson's beloved dog (Carlo). I know it all, and I think about them, among others, when

I'm scared, which, lately, is often.

I knew instantly he'd placed them there. Mason. Who else could it have been? Blue passionflowers are his calling card.

I don't know how long I have before he gets bolder and shows himself. He's already indirectly introduced himself. I'm running out of time.

My vision tunneled the same instant my mouth turned into a desert. I can't be out here in the open. I can't do this. This is too much. I need to get inside. Now.

I slammed the door, turned the three different locks, and collapsed against it, heart thudding like a hummingbird's. Tears welled in my eyes and blurred my sight, and I removed my glasses and wiped them from my eyes and cheeks. The glasses fell to the wood below, and I left them there. I focused on my breathing.

In. Out. In. Out.

My throat wasn't closing. I wasn't sweating or shaking uncontrollably. I was fine. This was nothing.

You're safe, Sophie. You're inside, and he's outside. Everything's fine.

It seemed to take hours, but finally, my heart rate slowed, and I was able to think straight.

Thinking back on it now, maybe I'm weaker than I thought. Maybe all there is for me is my semi-safe world of books and blue flowers.

Did I think I'd be able to start fresh after just a week? I can't. I'm too fragile for that. Too pathetic. There may not be any hope for me. Maybe Mason is all I deserve. Heck, he actually wants to be around me. I should count myself lucky.

I couldn't stop these thoughts, however twisted they might be.

I pressed my ear to the wood and listened for the crunch of snow-packing footsteps but found only the whirling blizzard outside. It wasn't the sound of a knock. And that was enough.

CHAPTER SEVEN
LY THI REN

It's not enough to be awake and self-aware in this hellscape. I want to be *free*, dammit. This world of corsets and endless tea parties is not me. It has *never* been me. And the fact that it ever placated me is sickening. My mind was altered without my consent. I feel violated.

How long have I been here? How much of my life has been lost as the real world continued without me?

Whoever did this to me will pay.

I have suspicions about suspects, but a part of me doesn't want to go there. Doesn't want to think that maybe whoever did this was right to. Maybe I deserve this. What I did to Jade…

I shake the thought of my friend's face from my mind. She's gone and definitely not coming back. Thanks to me.

Flashes of rollerblades and a roller derby track, my once-home, dart through my mind. There's no escape from the onslaught.

I have to focus on what I'm doing in the present, not what I've already done. There's no taking that back.

I clench my fists, using the pain from my fingernails to ground me. *Focus.*

I know what I have to do to earn my freedom. Truth be told,

a part of me has known longer than I care to admit.

Waking up next to my fiancé's corpse was the first clue. What followed only added to my theory. Events had proceeded faster after my awakening. As if that had been the catalyst of this story.

At my picnic date with Adeline, I'd looked into the sky for hints to support my theory and received one. There, amongst the white, puffy clouds and faded into the bright blue sky, were printed words. As if the sky were a book page. I couldn't make out full sentences in the haze, but I did find the only word that mattered. My name. My *real* name.

I'm in a book, but am I in *the* book? The one my parents worship? Have they done the unthinkable a second time? And if so, does that mean Jeremy is still alive?

I don't know for sure, but it doesn't matter. I know how to beat it. I'm a writer myself. I can write my way out of this prison by playing the role I was given. Geraldine Gibbons. 1800's debutante in search of her fiancé's murderer.

Everything about Geraldine lingers, mixed with Ren. It's enough to confuse the hell out of me, but it's an asset. I've managed to identify the murderer. The same person who'd attempted to kill Paulette Grayson.

Now, Adeline stumbles as she runs away from me down the hill to the Grayson horse stable. In her riding gear, she has the advantage. I'm still in my infuriatingly constricting corset, unwieldy dress, and heels.

I pause to kick off the shoes as Adeline ducks inside the building. My stockings slide on the cool grass as I take off down the hill after her, and I have to dig my toes in to prevent myself from falling. At the bottom of the slope, I stop at the door.

This is how I end this, I remind myself, wiping my clammy hands on my dress.

Gathering my courage, I follow Adeline inside.

Minutes later, a flash of light blinds me and accompanies a gust of wind that knocks me to my knees. The violence of the impact spurs the thought that my actions have incurred the wrath of some all-knowing deity. I'm preparing to face my judgment, my head feeling more and more like a balloon, when the light and wind ebb then stop completely.

I take a few seconds to gather myself, eyes closed, to prepare for whatever I'll find.

I peek.

I'm no longer in the stable. I'm in a library of some sort. On either side of me, bookshelves bear thick tomes. To my left stands a desk with a lit candelabra accompanied by a pedestal on either side.

When I push myself to my feet, I notice the hay-covered dirt of the stable has changed to a dark wood floor. The neighing of the horses has faded to a one-hit wonder of the eighties. I look up to see a speaker embedded in the ceiling.

Okay, I think it's safe to say I'm no longer in the era of corsets and women's oppression. I send a silent thank you to whoever may be listening.

I'm free.

Right?

It doesn't seem like I'm out of that prison. I don't feel any different than I did five seconds ago. The sticky patch of blood at my temple still exists, and my head throbs like it might explode at any second.

I force the last few minutes from my mind. I will not think about how I ended my imprisonment. Never again if I can help it.

In front of me, a book flips shut of its own accord. The cover thuds into place, and I see it. Confirmation of what I've been through in raised, swirling letters. I run my finger over my name, half expecting it to suck me back inside.

I knew it. Not a snow globe prison. A book. Pages bound in leather and glue. And not *the* book, either.

Adeline and Paulette. Even William and that demonic cat. They were just characters in a story. They were never real. Funny how I can still feel the wet blood on my hands.

Before it can sink in, the creak of a door brings me back to this world. I'm not free yet. Whoever trapped me in that book is coming.

But I'm at a dead end in this library, and my only way out is past my jailer.

I snatch up my book a millisecond before the man rounds the bend, and his eyes meet mine. I don't recognize him. He's a relatively tall man in a tweed jacket, probably in his early thirties. He has dirty blond hair with a mustache and goatee. Thin, brown spectacles frame his blue eyes.

One flicker of surprise—raised eyebrows—is all the emotion he shows. In the next instant, he breaks into a smirk.

"Welcome back," he says.

I eye him up and down. He's not much in terms of muscle, and I might be able to take him. But my head hurts like a mother. "Who are you?"

More eyebrow raising as he purses his lips. "You don't recognize me? I suppose that's a good sign. Just what I wanted, in fact. Splendid." He rocks forward on the balls of his feet, his hands clasped behind his back.

My eyes find a small penknife on the desk next to me. I snatch it up and hold it in front of me. "Stop with the cryptic answers. How long was I in that place?"

The man shrugs. "I haven't been keeping track of every single day, but roughly?" He bites his lip, looking to the ceiling. "About seven months."

"Seven months," I say dumbly. This bastard kept me prisoner for seven months of my life.

"*Seven months?*"

INKED IN BLOOD AND MEMORY

I could strangle the motherfucker right here.

"Why? Who are you?" A memory teases me, and I grab for it. "Wait. You were there at Everling. The doctor."

The man's face brightens. "Ah, you *do* remember!"

Dr. Lloyd was his name, right? But why would a doctor trap me in a book?

"I came into your office looking for Sophie…"

Dr. Lloyd's eyes dart to the desk to my left, and I follow his gaze. At first glance, it looks like an ordinary book, but the letters on the front cover shimmer just like mine did.

He's trapped someone else.

I take a step sideways toward the desk, keeping the penknife pointed at the man. The book's one-word title is clear to me now. An embossed name peeks out from under a handkerchief.

SOPHIE.

My heart drops. Has she been in there all this time? What are the chances we'd both be taken in the same way Jeremy was taken all those years ago? And by the same person after years of losing touch?

Hang on. That's not entirely true. There was that one day Sophie called me. It's slowly coming back to me. If the memory were a word, it would be on the tip of my tongue.

I brush my fingers along the name on the second book.

"You can't help her," Dr. Lloyd says. "There's a reason your name isn't on the cover, Ren. It's her story. Not yours."

If that's true, then why is the book flipping open? Why are its pages rustling as, one by one, they turn on their own and amber light spills from them?

My gaze flicks to Dr. Lloyd, whose eyes widen behind his glasses.

The universe sends signs. I've always believed that. If I'm not a part of Sophie's story, why is it calling me?

Before I can second guess my decision, I place my palm on the open pages, and an amber glow emanates from underneath my hand. Pins and needles prick my skin and travel up my arm, into my torso, and down my legs.

I take a deep breath. "I'm gonna regret this," I say over Dr. Lloyd's protests.

With one blink and a flash of light, I'm... still in the same room. Dr. Lloyd still stands in front of me, but he's now a transparent version of himself. He's looking around as if he can't see me.

The book with my name on it has fallen to the dark hardwood floor. When I reach for it, my hand passes right through it. The good doctor grabs it and places it back on its pedestal.

The penknife is still in my grasp, solid and real. I tuck it in my garter and wave my middle fingers in front of the man's face, but he doesn't react. I shrug and turn my back on him, locating a spiral staircase at the other end of the room. The music playing above me trickles down as if I'm under water. I can barely make out the words.

I slap my ears, but it does nothing. The sound is still muffled. "Weird." Okay, *that* sounds normal. "Hello, hello, hello," I test. All normal.

I descend the staircase to a lower level and get a wave of déjà vu. I've been here before. As I reach the bottom of the stairs and look out at the scene in front of me, I realize where I am. This is Jeremy Berg-Nilsen's old manor. And there in the center of the high-ceilinged room is the coffee table on top of which I'd last seen my friend.

The locked glass case behind it is empty. The book must be at the Vanguards' this time of year. I was taken in May—not long after my birthday—so it must be December.

December, I think, trying my best to quell my rising rage. *Seven fucking months.*

A boy sits by himself on the leather couch as the snow falls in sheets outside the windows behind him. He has his back to me, but he's playing with something on his lap and trying his best to whistle.

Jeremy.

No, this isn't Jeremy. After a few more steps, his face became clear to me. This boy can't be any older than five or six years old. He's just as see-through as the man upstairs. He's not in here with me.

A coldness grips my heart as my mother enters the room and sits next to the boy, who I now see holds a gold pocket watch. I'm beginning to understand what's happening, but I don't want to believe it.

She wouldn't, I think. *She said she never would again.*

Má smiles at the boy, and when she speaks, her words are muffled as if she's behind some barrier. "What do you have there, Carter?"

And there it is. Carter Vanguard. Sophie's brother was born on New Year's Day almost six years ago. His birthday must be coming up soon. How far into December are we?

I remember him now. His birth announcement had chilled me to the bone. A boy born to one of the most powerful families in the world. A world Carter is destined to be torn from.

CHAPTER EIGHT
SOPHIE VANGUARD

I'm on edge the rest of the day. Jumping at shadows or the random creaks of the house as the whirling wind outside continues to batter the exterior. I can't focus on reading, and my book of puzzles can't even hold my interest.

I struggle for an hour through a Sudoku labeled as medium difficulty—which should be child's play—before I finally give up the ghost. I flip the book closed and toss it onto the coffee table with a huff.

That's when I hear it. Just barely audible over the creaking shutters from the blizzard. A door swings open and hits the wall with a light *tap*.

Every nerve in my body stands at attention, and I prick up my ears. That came from the kitchen. Was it the back door or the hallway off the kitchen?

With a bit of wishful thinking, I creep to the latter. With every silent tiptoe, my heart picks up speed. Rounding the corner, shadows shroud the hall in front of me. The moonlight trickling in from the windows dimly lights the piece of kitchen I can see.

Something passes through it, and I freeze. My heart skips a beat. I'm running a hand along the wall in search of the light switch I know has to be here somewhere.

Where is it?

A sinking feeling overtakes me as I realize the switch is closer to the doorway than I thought. I take two more steps only to see a patch of darkness appear once more. Only this time, it doesn't dissipate. Out of the blackness, two yellow eyes fade into being and fix their gaze on me.

The shape hovers there for a moment, and I'm paralyzed with indecision. Do I walk the remaining three steps to flick on the light in that room, or do I run?

As I stand there, indecisive, it makes its own decision. It darts toward me, screeching inhumanly as its smoky body billows toward me like it's reaching for me.

The bathroom's right behind me, and in a few backward steps, I'm inside and slamming the door shut. My shaking hands fumble for the lock and turn it as whisps of black smoke seep through the crack. I stare at it as I retreat until the backs of my knees hit the bathtub. And then I fall into it and whip the glass door closed, practically ripping it off its track.

I can't see if the lock worked in keeping it out. The frosted glass of the shower door, combined with the darkness, makes it nearly impossible to see anything.

This can't be happening. This is not happening. You're having a nightmare, Sophie. Smoke creatures don't exist.

The entire house is silent. Not even the sounds of the high winds penetrate the cabin. My thumping heart is going to give away my location. I know it.

And then, all at once, muffled whispers breach the thin bathroom walls. Unintelligible mutterings that chill me to the bone. They're calling for me, but my name is the only word I can make out.

Sophie.

Sophie.

INKED IN BLOOD AND MEMORY

Sophie.

There's more than one of them out there. How many are there?

I clap my hands over my mouth to stifle my shuddering breaths, searching in vain for anything outside my tiny safe haven as the whispers grow louder.

The doorknob turns. I can't see it, but I hear something jiggling it from the outside.

So far, the lock's held up, but how long until those things are inside? How many are out there? What do they want?

They're pounding on the door now. The knob still jiggles, and I'm waiting for it to fall apart or for the thuds to knock the door down. It's just wood, after all. And who knows what those creatures are made of?

It's only a matter of time. They're going to get in.

This isn't possible.

Boom. Boom. Boom. Boom.

Sophie. Sophie. Sophie.

Each hit tears me out of my skin. Each hit, I realize it's the final straw for the door. And all I can do is push my hands tighter against my lips as my tears flow freely.

Why hadn't I grabbed a weapon? Though, I doubt it would've made a difference.

Just as suddenly as the whispers and thuds started, they stop without warning. I'm frozen in silence once more. I'm not sure how long I sit before the storm outside reaches me, a welcome replacement for the things on the other side of the door.

I can't seem to summon the courage to get to my feet. They must be coming back. They were so insistent, so determined to get inside. No, I won't move from this spot until the sun comes up.

I don't remember falling asleep in the cold tub. I don't even remember my eyes drifting closed. One minute, I'm staring at the frosted glass. The next instant, my eyes find the shadows in the corner of my bathroom ceiling.

I take a deep breath. *The shadows are just shadows.*

My knees crack as I stand, and my neck aches from who knows how long I was in that awkward angle. Every part of me listens for sounds outside the door, but I hear nothing. It takes all I have to slide the shower door open, a buried dread thinking someone will be standing there. No one.

The linoleum greets my bare feet, and a chill rushes up my spine. Closer to the corner, I can see that nothing is there, and I breathe a sigh of relief.

I dart out of the bathroom and up the stairs to my bedroom. Any second, that thing is going to drag me back to it. My feet pound the carpet, and I fall up the steps, practically clawing my way up.

Miraculously, I reach my room and slam the door shut, panting as I crawl into bed.

But sleep evades me.

Instead, I conjure demons in the blackness of the room, laying helpless and alone at the mouth of an abyss.

A gaping black hole beside the door. Creatures that are all too familiar to me and alien all the same. Hundreds of shades of black swirling in an endless void and widening by the second. And here I am, listening to their whispers that scrape at my brain one moment and are deafeningly silent the next.

I move to cover my ears, but I can't. My arms are stuck at my sides. My eyes peer around me but find nothing. I can see that much. Something rips into my leg, and I want to scream, but cotton fills my throat.

It's my own finger. I can move the middle finger of my right hand. I scratch my leg over and over and over. Until I draw blood. And still, I can't move.

My chest heaves as I hyperventilate.

Why can't I move? What is that sound? What are those things in the corners of my eyes?

As if answering my thoughts, the howls of the shadows start

up again. They cry in dozens of timbres. Screeching for me or for an end to their misery. Maybe both. Their pitches rise and meld together until they become one long, ringing noise. It fills every space of the room, every fiber of my soul.

My ears have to be bleeding. The sound is like pins in my ears. I can't take it anymore. *Please stop. Please. Please. Please. STOP.*

They stop.

My silent screams ring out in the silence, but it's just my voice now. The corners of the room fade to gray, illuminated by the dim moonlight as whatever was there a second ago disappears. The invisible bonds around my body dissipate, and I jump to a sitting position, retreating until my back hits the headboard of my bed.

I'm a scared little kid again, helpless against the monsters around me.

There's no one else here. It's just me. I'm alone. It's just me. There's nothing there.

I rock back and forth, clutching the cotton sheets in sweaty fists as I repeat the words. Drilling them into my head. As if I can somehow make myself forget the past... How long has it been? How did I get up to this room, and why can't I remember?

If I had any doubts before, I'm convinced now. I'm losing my mind.

CHAPTER NINE
LY THI REN
SIX YEARS AGO

Sophie cried the day her brother was born. Not out of happiness or celebration as every family member should. She felt what I felt. Fear. Dread. Despair. Anger.

Carter was a week past his due date by the time he finally arrived. I remember thinking that maybe some part of him knew what awaited him out here in the world. However stupid that sounds, it was like he knew before he was even born that his parents were pure evil.

New Year's Eve of our senior year in high school was like any other that came before. Every year, Sophie and I would dodge our parents' New Year's party by finding one to go to with kids our own age. Other townies from our private and privileged school.

Haglen Brook is a picturesque, upscale tourist town most visit on their way to or from Salem, Massachusetts. Our town's history is not as well-known as the witchy stop, but it is equally horrifying, in my opinion.

Founded in the early nineteenth century, the town got its name from the Haglen family, prominent colonists who undoubtedly murdered hundreds to steal the land. Sylvia Vanguard, Sophie's mother, took pride in the fact that she was a direct descendant of the Haglen bloodline. I'm surprised she didn't keep her maiden name so she could continue to bring her heritage up at every get-together. Who am I kidding? The name change hadn't stopped her from doing so yet.

Anyway, the legend my friends and I were taught was that Katherine Haglen, the eldest daughter, made a deal with the devil who resides in Wycanth Wood to help her family with the founding and solidify their place in the town's history and upper echelon of society for generations. The price was her firstborn son. Believing herself barren, Katherine made the deal without a second thought and received the book in return.

But nine years later, amidst a flourishing Haglen Brook, Katherine and her husband, Charles, welcomed a baby boy. Her husband had heard the rumors of Katherine's deal, but like most, he hadn't believed it to be truth. He saw his mistake when the demon came for their child on his fourth birthday.

Driven mad with grief, Katherine's husband killed her and threw himself off their roof.

But the Haglen line wasn't extinguished because before their tragic end, Katherine and Charles had a daughter, and she found her mother's book. One thing led to another, and the Haglen bloodline grew more and more powerful as the generations wore on. Until Sylvia Vanguard's grandfather passed the book on to her, and she expanded the family legacy by bringing in the Ly and Berg-Nilsen families. I'll say this for Sylvia: she's got an entrepreneurial spirit.

I've always wondered how Má and Ba chose Haglen Brook out of all the other towns in America. Were they drawn to it somehow, or were they fated to be roped into their unholy deal no matter what? Whatever the case, this was my life. But Sophie and I made our decision years ago. The Haglen bloodline and its extended legacy will end with us. The deal is over.

The year of Carter's birth, the New Year's Eve party was at the twins'—Dante and Marley. Their parents skied in Aspen every chance they got, oblivious to their children's escapades when they were away. Or maybe they didn't care. Maybe they even encouraged it.

The clock rolled to 7:52pm as I pulled my beat-up red secondhand convertible into Sophie's plan. Foxwood Grove was a fairly new cul-de-sac in Haglen Brook, each house complete with floor-to-ceiling glass and an indoor pool. The picture-perfect American dream.

My parents went for the American Colonial feel with sprawling acres and a horse stable. Not long after the Jeremy incident, Sophie and I were each presented with our own horse. As if that would ease the sting of realizing our parents were devil worshippers and our best friend was gone forever.

I pulled my car up to Sophie's driveway and found her standing on the curb in her favorite floral maxi dress that she'd had to hem to get it to fit her. It was out of season, but I was sure she had thick tights on underneath it. She'd thrown a jean jacket over it as if that would help keep away the winter chill.

"You're late," she said before I could turn the volume of my music down.

I spit the gum in my mouth back into its wrapper and twisted the dial as she got in, and the scent of her strawberry lotion accompanied her.

"Huh?"

"It's freezing," she said, turning the air vents to full blast. "You could've at least sprung for heated seats."

"You wouldn't be so cold if you actually wore winter-appropriate clothing, ya weirdo." I was proud of my used car, which I'd purchased with my own money from my normal summer job. Lifeguarding at the local public pool a town over.

Sophie sighed dramatically and reached into the backseat. Before I could ask what she was doing, she pulled a thick, checkered blanket into her lap. I recognized the pattern from her house, but I didn't know she'd put it in my car.

"Where did that come from?"

Sophie giggled. "I'm always prepared."

I shook my head as I made a U-turn and headed out of Foxwood Grove. "I don't know why I'm surprised."

Dante and Marley's party was in full swing by the time we pulled up the long driveway twenty minutes later. A few dozen kids milled about as an obnoxiously loud pop song played. Definitely not one of my favorites. Inside, Sophie pointed to the twins handing out drinks by the enormous fireplace, and I led the way.

Dante pulled off his Haglen Brook High hag mask—the football team's mascot—and flashed one of his famous smiles when he saw us while Marley refilled the ice. "Ren, Soph! Look at these outfits! Slayyyy." He grabbed an ice cube and held it to Sophie's umber skin, making a sizzling sound with his tongue. She shrieked and smacked it away, but I caught her smiling as Marley sighed and swiped the ice cube from the floor.

"Seriously?" she said with a flip of her afro, tossing the ice in with the rest. "We can't afford a lawsuit if anyone trips."

"Yes, we can," Dante said, winking at us.

We'd known Dante and Marley since kindergarten, and they hadn't changed a bit over the years. Dante was always joking, usually making a mess, while Marley, four minutes older than her brother, was left to clean up after him. Although half the time, she was in on his shenanigans.

Sophie's phone rang, and she pulled it out to answer. I hadn't heard it over the loud music, but she must've had it on vibrate, too. Her face clouded when she read the caller ID, which I couldn't make out from where I stood. But I could draw my own conclusions, and none of them were good.

"I have to take this," she said, not looking up from her phone.

Dante had already found someone else to flirt with, but Marley waved. "No problem."

I nodded to Marley and followed Sophie onto the patio, pulling my leather jacket tighter around me. I slid the door closed, muffling the awful mainstream music.

Kyra sat on the stoop by herself, smoking a joint. As Sophie tapped the answer button on her phone, Kyra offered me a hit with a silent arm extension. I declined, and she frowned and shrugged as if saying, "Suit yourself."

"Are you sure?" Sophie said, bringing my focus back to her.

The color had drained from her face, and she clutched the phone to her ear with both hands.

"What happened?" I mouthed, but she was looking past me and not at me.

A couple football players approached the patio, laughing loudly, but I motioned for them to wait a second. They shrugged, still beaming, and turned back to the party inside. Their world wasn't changing anytime soon, and they knew it. I wished I could say the same for Sophie and myself.

Sophie hung up her phone and slid to the cold cement, legs crossed. Her face was inscrutable as she set her phone on the ground with a shaking hand. She was seriously freaking me out.

Kyra flicked her joint into the yard and headed back inside as I joined Sophie on the ground. Ignoring my freezing legs, I took her hand in mine and squeezed it, knowing what she was going to say but praying she wouldn't say it.

Finally, she looked at me, and a tear spilled over her lashes. I moved to brush it away the same moment she said, "The baby's coming."

My heart dropped. Even though I'd been expecting it, it seemed some part of me had still been in denial. "No."

Sophie nodded with a thousand-yard stare out into the forest in front of us.

My mind raced a mile a minute. *The baby's coming. Carter. They named him Carter. Why even bother naming a sacrifice? Why 'Carter'? Where are they now? Is he already tucked into the Vanguards' arms? How many years will he get before the demon claims him?*

I forced my brain to a screeching halt. I could not lose it. Sophie was already there. She needed me. "What hospital? We should go." I jumped to my feet, brushing off the back of my jeans.

"My house," she said, not breaking her stare.

I took a couple deep breaths before kneeling back down on the cold patio and placing a hand on her shoulder. Her brown eyes reflected every one of my worries, and I almost lost myself in them.

Can't we stay here in this spot and pretend the other messed up parts of our families don't exist?

I knew it was impossible the second I thought it.

Instead of mentioning any of that, I said, "Sophie, Carter needs someone to look out for him. He needs his big sister."

I held out my hand, and she took it. "Let's go."

Four hours later, Sophie and I were the only ones still awake. We sat on the floor of her living room, our backs against the too-modern and uncomfortable black leather couch. Sophie leaned her head against my shoulder, wiping away silent tears.

"I hate that they made me hold him," she said through sniffles. "I hate that they made me look at him. It's *cruel*. They know he was only born for slaughter. And here they are, waving it in my face. And we're still as powerless as we were the night Jeremy—"

Images of that night returned to me. No matter how hard I tried to wipe it from my memory, they were always there in the back of my mind. Those gnarled claws grabbing Jeremy's ankles, Jeremy's wide eyes, the black smoke conjured by his supposed protectors. The loud, swirling wind.

Almost subconsciously, I got to my feet.

"What are you doing?" Sophie asked.

Good question.

A thought flitted through my brain in the midst of all the awful memories. It suddenly seemed like our only option. I crossed the room to the book that started it all. It sat unassumingly in its locked, reinforced glass case, facing us. If books could have expressions, I'm sure it would've been grinning like a cat that had caught the canary.

"I'm going to make a deal with a demon."

"What? Ren, you can't." Sophie grabbed my shoulder and forced me to face her.

The fear in her eyes almost pulled me up short, and I could've taken that moment to acknowledge my own trepidation, but I wouldn't. "Underestimating me, flower? It can't be *that* hard. All I have to do is steal the key, unlock the case, and follow the instructions inside."

Oversimplified? Sure. But those days, I tried to be a little more optimistic.

"You know that's not what I meant. You *can't*, Ren."

"Why not?"

Sophie moved her hands to enclose my left in them. "We said we'd never become our parents, making deals with demons for power. We promised each other."

We had. I remembered. But this was her *baby brother*. Not some selfish power trip. How could she not want to break that promise? Wasn't any risk worth it?

I let her pull me away from the case before crossing my arms in front of me. "You really don't want to use it?"

"I've thought about it," she said, eying the book warily as if it could move at any moment. "But you know it's never a fair deal. There's always a high price. Look at where it landed our parents."

I had to admit she had a point. I sighed. "Odds are the price for saving Carter could be our own firstborn."

Sophie looked up at me then, and I realized my phrasing mistake. "Not 'our' as in yours and mine together. That we would have. Obviously not. 'Our' as in yours *or* mine *separately*."

God, I was babbling. Only Sophie could do this to me.

She smiled and nodded, pink blossoming under her brown, freckled skin. "I know what you meant."

We collapsed on the loveseat. The only comfortable piece of furniture in the Vanguards' ultramodern white and black mansion. Sophie leaned her head on my shoulder again, and I touched her knee. The minutes ticked by on the large wall clock across the room.

How many does Carter have?

We wouldn't find out until his first birthday.

"They're never going to let him go, Ren," Sophie said. "Not until they sacrifice him."

CHAPTER TEN
JEREMY BERG-NILSEN
SIX YEARS AGO

Dad descends upon Mom the second she arrives home. "Why are you here?" It's not *her* home now. They've been estranged for years thanks to Dad committing Mom to Everling.

Mom opens her mouth to say something and then seems to think better of it. She closes her mouth before trying again. "Everling released me a few months ago. I've been trying to get my mind off of what today is. No luck yet, so I came here." When my dad stays silent, she continues. "It's been nine years since—" She cuts herself off as she follows my father into the kitchen, where dishes are piling up in the sink. "Nine years to the day. He would've been nineteen."

Ice rushes through my veins. She thinks I'm dead still. After all this time—*nine years*, it turns out—she believes I'm gone for good. I guess it doesn't matter what she believes.

I can't lie; the thought has crossed my mind that maybe I *am* dead, but I can't be. Otherwise, why would the demon still need me to say yes to him?

I'm not dead. I refuse to believe that.

But nine years in darkness. Nine years waiting for someone to save me, only to be disappointed every time. Nine years watching only the worst moments of my mother's life. I might as well be dead.

"I haven't forgotten," Dad mumbles, looking at the floor.

"I didn't say you had." Mom hesitates again, pursing her lips as if she may propose something to my father. I can tell there's something more she wants to say, but it's like she's afraid to. Is she afraid of Dad? When had that started? When he had her committed?

Is he hurting her?

I ball my hands into fists before forcing myself to focus on their conversation.

"I was at the Vanguards', reading the book," Mom says.

Dad tenses. "Caroline, we agreed to never open that book if we didn't have to."

"*I* had to!" Mom puffs out the words as if she'll burst if she holds them in any longer. "I had to know if what I felt was true."

"What do you mean?"

"A mother knows." Mom wipes her sunken eyes. "A mother knows if her baby is really gone, and I never felt like Jeremy was gone."

"Say the word, Caroline. Jeremy is *dead*." Dad crosses his arms.

Mom shakes her head emphatically. "He's not, Dan. Trust me. He's not. I've always known it, and this afternoon confirmed it."

"Because of something you read in the book?" Dad asks, his voice rising. "I've read that thing over and over, and so have you. There's nothing that says Jeremy could still be alive." Dad steps toward her. "You're sounding just like you did when I—"

I know what he was about to say. *"When I had you committed."*

Dad moves toward her, and I prepare for the worst.

I *swear* if he hurts her—

But he sighs, and his hands lightly caress her face, cupping it lovingly as he pleads, "Let him go, my love. *Please.* There's nothing we can do. We've lost so much already. We need to at least try to have a life. For Jeremy."

Something changes behind my mother's eyes then. It's as if she's come to some conclusion after hearing the words. Has she finally given up on me?

"You're right, of course," she says, patting his hands as they drop from her face. "I won't trouble you anymore. Goodbye, Dan."

"Caroline, wait—"

She's down the hall and out the door before he can say much else. I have to know what she's thinking.

The scene changes, and I find myself in my mother's house. It's smaller than the mansion I grew up in. A tasteful two-story in a small suburb just outside of Haglen Brook. I'm glad she at least got out of that town, even if it wasn't that far.

I follow Mom to her desk, where she scribbles into her journal. From my place over her shoulder, I read the words.

September 28th

I went to the Vanguards' today.

They were kind enough to let me read the book. I think they pity me. Let them. It will all be worth it once I bring Jeremy home.

I learned something new as I read from the book. Something that confirmed what I've always known. I tried to tell Dan, but he wouldn't listen. I saw in his eyes he was ready to send me back to Everling.

All these years, I hadn't believed Jeremy was dead. I never truly gave up hope. I only wish I'd made this decision nine years ago.

I'm sorry, Dan. Please forgive me.

She has a plan. She's coming to get me. I just have to hold out until it's time.

My life is not my own. My life consists of watching others affected by the book. They live life for me, occasionally offering me windows to their triumphs, their failures, their existential crises.

I am empty. Devoid of experiences. Of emotions. It is myself and the demon here, and I have held out for long enough. The emptiness has formed a pit in my stomach, and day by day, it has grown. Festering in its confusion and sadness.

My mother's "friends" left her to rot in Everling and forgot about her, washed their hands of her. I can relate. Now, we are each other's only hope for a normal life. We'll move far away from Haglen Brook. I cling to that hope, my only light in my perennial darkness.

One may wonder why I still fall for a demon's tricks, even now. I don't have an answer except for dumb hope or blind faith in my friends.

The two people standing in front of me are Sophie and Ren, as I knew them nine years ago. Still nine-years-old and in the clothes I'd last seen them in—their jeans and t-shirts under their kid-sized ceremonial purple cloaks.

Their smiles stretch so wide I think it's entirely possible for them to swallow me whole. And then, in a puff of black smoke, they disappear, and the billowing clouds blend into one. I know the sight all too well, but I'm not fast enough to dodge the oncoming force.

I'm shaken awake by my mother, still swatting at the onslaught of demon fog. We're in a room of the Vanguards' house. The book sits behind reinforced glass. And for the first time in nine years, I am on the other side of it.

How?

Mom weeps as she holds me tight, begging me to forgive her. She smells just like I remember—vanilla and marshmallow.

"How?" is all I can say. The word's been on a loop in my mind since I came to the realization that I'm out.

Mom pulls away to look me in the eyes. "Not here. It's not

safe. We need to go."

We're in the car before I realize we've left the house, and she tears down the driveway.

"How did you get me out?"

Mom wipes her eyes, her lip quivering. "I made a deal with the Great One. I knew you were still alive. I never gave up hope."

"Thank you," I say because I can't manage anything else at the moment.

We drive for hours before finally stopping at a rundown motel off the highway. I fall asleep shortly after arriving. Everything is happening in a blur. I just need to rest and let my mind catch up.

I feel like I've only just closed my eyes when a pounding on the door rouses me. I open my eyes to my mother opening the door.

Whoever it is pulls her out into the sunlight and slams the door. I run to it and fling it open in time to see her being pushed into a car.

"Mom!" I move to chase them, but my body hits an invisible barrier and knocks me to the ground. I jump up and try again, only to have the same result. I can't break through, no matter how hard I pound on it. It ripples like water and my vision blurs. It takes me a second to realize it's not my vision that's the problem. Everything in front of me is a blob of gray, just like—

Just like the scenes I looked in on from the demon's realm right before they became clear.

This can't be happening. I was out. I had to be. It was all so vivid. So solid.

A deep rumble emanates from my left. Like a growling, but it doesn't stay there. The sound travels around the room, and I turn with it as if I'll be able to see something. The entire room shakes, ceiling plaster falling to the floor, and I fall to my knees and crawl under a nearby table.

Chunks of the ceiling fall on top of it with *thunk*s. Framed generic motel art falls to the floor, their glass casings shattering. The ceiling fan crashes onto the bed in a flurry of dust as the wall sconces flicker out. And still, the debris keeps falling. The rumbling continues and grows until I can't hear anything else.

I place my hands over my ears, but it barely makes a difference. I don't know how long I'm there before the growls devolve into chuckles.

The chaos around me seems to have stopped, and I crawl out of my shelter and stand.

The ceiling is completely gone, but instead of the sky, there is nothing but a black void. It's confirmation of my worst fear.

It was a dream. A lie. I never left my prison. I'm still in the book.

With one blink, the rubble of the motel room, the motel itself disappears, leaving me with nothing but the endless abyss I've known for nine years.

But I don't have time to break down because the scenery in front of me changes. I'm looking at a version of my old house. It's the room we used to keep the book in when it was our turn to guard it.

The book is there now, but it's out and open on the coffee table. I can't see any faces except my mother's. Four pairs of legs surround her, all cloaked as they were all those years ago. I know what those cloaks are for, but I'm not really here. There's nothing I can do.

They've forced her to her knees, and a fifth cloaked figure enters.

This isn't happening. This isn't real.

"*Come now,*" says a disembodied voice. "*You know better than that.*"

Mom pleads with the new arrival, her tears flowing freely. "Please, you don't need to do this!"

Someone steps into my vision, but I can't see who. A knife descends, and flesh is cut, and when the figure moves, I see the horrible scene. Mom choking on her own blood, throat slit and draining quickly.

"No! Mom!"

I'm as powerless as ever, removed from what is happening.

I yell for the demon. "Help her!"

But it's not here with me anymore. The families have summoned the Great One to their side.

I can only wail as the demon rises from the book's pages and devours her.

"Delicious."

Something dies in me as I sob on the cold ground, unable to hold my mother's hand. Hours later, when I've cried all my tears, I call for the demon.

Somehow, they will pay for this.

The demon asks its daily question.

I answer yes.

The demon fills every part of me, his black smoke choking me as he pushes his way down my throat into my intestines. I'm stuck in place, unable to see anything but him, feel anything but him. There is nothing else. *I* am nothing else.

They will pay.

CHAPTER ELEVEN

LY THI REN
PRESENT DAY

Now on the other side of Carter, I can see the pocket watch's display clearly. It's nothing special, the same as every other watch I've seen.

"You remember what your dad said, right?" Má asks.

Carter nods and uses his fingers to illustrate what he's learned. "When the little hand is here," he says, pointing to the twelve, "and the big hand is here," he points to the space right next to the twelve, "it's time."

12:01am, New Year's Day. The exact minute of Carter's birth. The cold hand around my heart grips tighter.

Oh, hell no.

Má smiles, and I want to shake her and scream, "What's wrong with you?" But I know it would be useless even if I could touch her. She's learned nothing from her sins of the past.

"Very good," Má says. "The second time it says that tomorrow, it'll be time. But it'll go by fast. Not long now."

The watch reads 11:39pm.

No, not long at all. Barely over 24 hours.

Shit.

Dr. Vanguard enters the room, clapping her hands. She's one of those people who was never made for parenthood. Even when Sophie and I were young, she wasn't very warm. "Carter David Vanguard, isn't it past your bedtime? What are you doing out of bed?"

Yes, wouldn't want the boy to stay up past his bedtime on one of his last nights on Earth.

I've never been a fan of Dr. Vanguard. Regardless of the whole demon worship thing, she's never been the most approachable person. For as long as I can remember, she's worn a stern expression, her high black ponytail only adding to her strict demeanor.

"Sorry, Mom."

Carter places the pocket watch on the table, and the three exit the room. I take one last look at the watch and stop. It looks different than it had in Carter's hand. More solid.

On a hunch, I grab it, and it lifts easily into the air, leaving a second, more transparent version of it on the table. Two copies of the same object. The book's way of giving me a countdown? How thoughtful.

I snap the watch closed and stuff it into my cleavage, cursing how pocketless and dated my dress is. But that's the least of my problems.

There's not enough time. Less than twenty-five hours to play this book out to its final chapter, escape, and save Carter. What happened to Jeremy all those years ago is going to happen again if I fail. I need to find Sophie.

I'm outside the moment I think it. I almost fall over, disoriented from the sudden change of scenery.

INKED IN BLOOD AND MEMORY

Trippy.

A sharp gust of wind knocks into me and bites at my arms.

It's freezing.

In front of me is a tall, modernly designed house. Its inside is no doubt the polar opposite of the Victorian nightmare from which I emerged. With the thought of my previous surroundings, I check behind me.

What the hell?

Jeremy's house has disappeared, and a large expanse of tundra has taken its place. Nothing but snow and a starlit sky as far as I can see.

I force myself to remain calm. Breathe in and out. Focus on one problem at a time. First, Sophie. Then, we can worry about finding the house again. I hope her story's ending isn't as traumatic as—

I shake myself. I'm not going to think about that right now. Not the blood everywhere. Not the weight of the axe in my hand. It's not helpful.

The building I'm in front of rests on a hill above the front yard, allowing me to see nothing but snowy treetops swaying gently in the moonlight behind it.

A bout of dizziness hits me, and I fall to the wet concrete in a sitting position. The melting snow seeps into my dress, but I don't care. My fingers find the wound on my head and come away wet.

As my head practically splits down the middle, I weigh my options.

There's no telling what book I've stepped into. For all I know, there could be a chainsaw-wielding psychopath beyond that door. But do I have a choice? I need to start moving if I'm going to wake Sophie up in time to save her brother.

I stumble to my feet, taking a moment to catch my balance and trying not to think about my barely covered feet. *Why did I get rid of my shoes?* I creep around the side of the house, hoping to get a peek inside.

ALLISON IVY

There, in a downstairs window, seated in a wingback armchair, is Sophie. She looks the same as she did seven months ago. She tries to tuck a few strands of her tightly coiled ringlets of brown hair behind her ear. She's still wearing glasses, but they're darker and larger frames than I remember. They match her umber skin. She's focused on something in her lap. Is she reading? That's new. She's not a reader. Or at least, she wasn't years ago.

People change, Ren.

I make my way back to the front of the house and up the steps to the door. My feet wade through quicksand with every movement, but the chill in the air pushes me onward. Through the pain. Through the exhaustion. There's no other option.

The door looks normal enough. A plain wood facade painted black with a brass knob. No fancy accoutrements like a door camera or knocker. Just three locks and a deadbolt.

I take a deep breath. Raise my hand to knock. Then, stop.
Where do I even start?

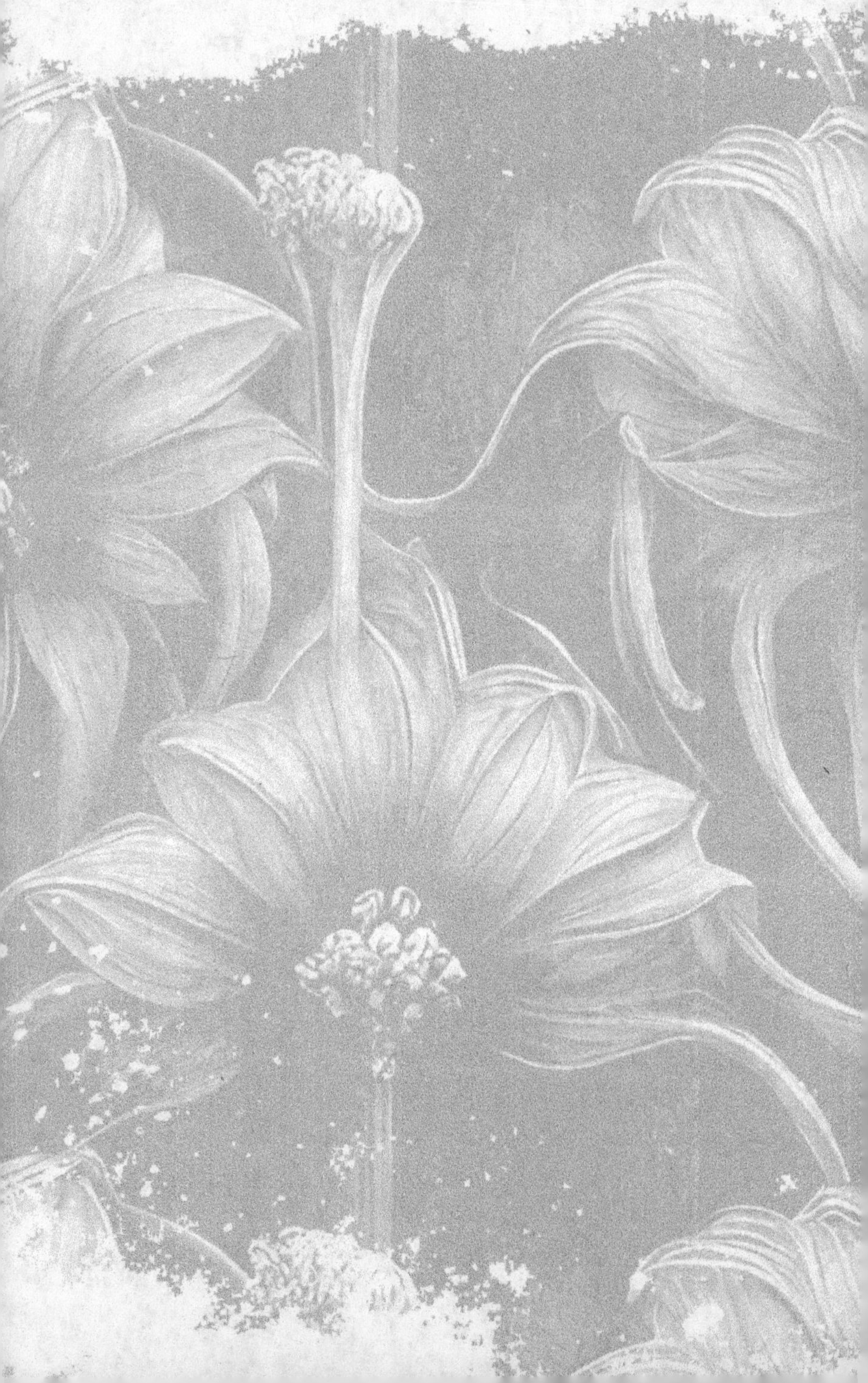

CHAPTER TWELVE
HERCULES

This isn't part of the plan, Hercules thought as he padded silently behind Ren in the old manor. *It's okay, though. Plans change all the time, don't they?*

Herc waited until Ren's feet touched the floor below before following her down the stairs, and he found her standing behind a young boy.

Ren turned around unexpectedly, and Hercules ducked behind a corner. The human stood there, staring down the hall, and he was certain she would retrace her steps and discover him. But no. She turned back around and focused on the other humans.

"Very good," the woman said, smiling. "The second time it says that tomorrow, it'll be time. But it'll go by fast. Not long now."

Herc listened to the boy and the woman's conversation, read the horror in Ren's face, the wonder in the boy's, and grew impatient.

The other human girl was around here somewhere, wasn't she? They needed to find her and get out of this place at once.

Hercules urged Ren to leave the room. Why was she moving so slowly? Hadn't she heard the same words he had? Human language hadn't escaped her, had it?

There's a small human's life on the line. Let's go! Stop playing with that timekeeper.

He considered revealing himself, but he didn't have to. Ren finally pocketed the device, and in the blink of an eye, they were both outside, staring at a house.

Herc seized the opportunity to dash into a nearby bush as Ren inspected her surroundings.

The snow bit into Herc's paws, and he shook them frequently, expecting Ren to enter the house in front of them. Apparently, that was asking too much of her because it seemed she'd rather spy on the human inside instead of warm herself by a fire.

Too long, forever it seemed, she dallied in the cold, then came to her senses and knocked on the door. Is this how slow she'd be this entire ordeal? Did she want to waste time?

Knock. Knock. Knock.

"Hello?" Ren said. "Is there anyone in there? I could really use some help."

That's an understatement.

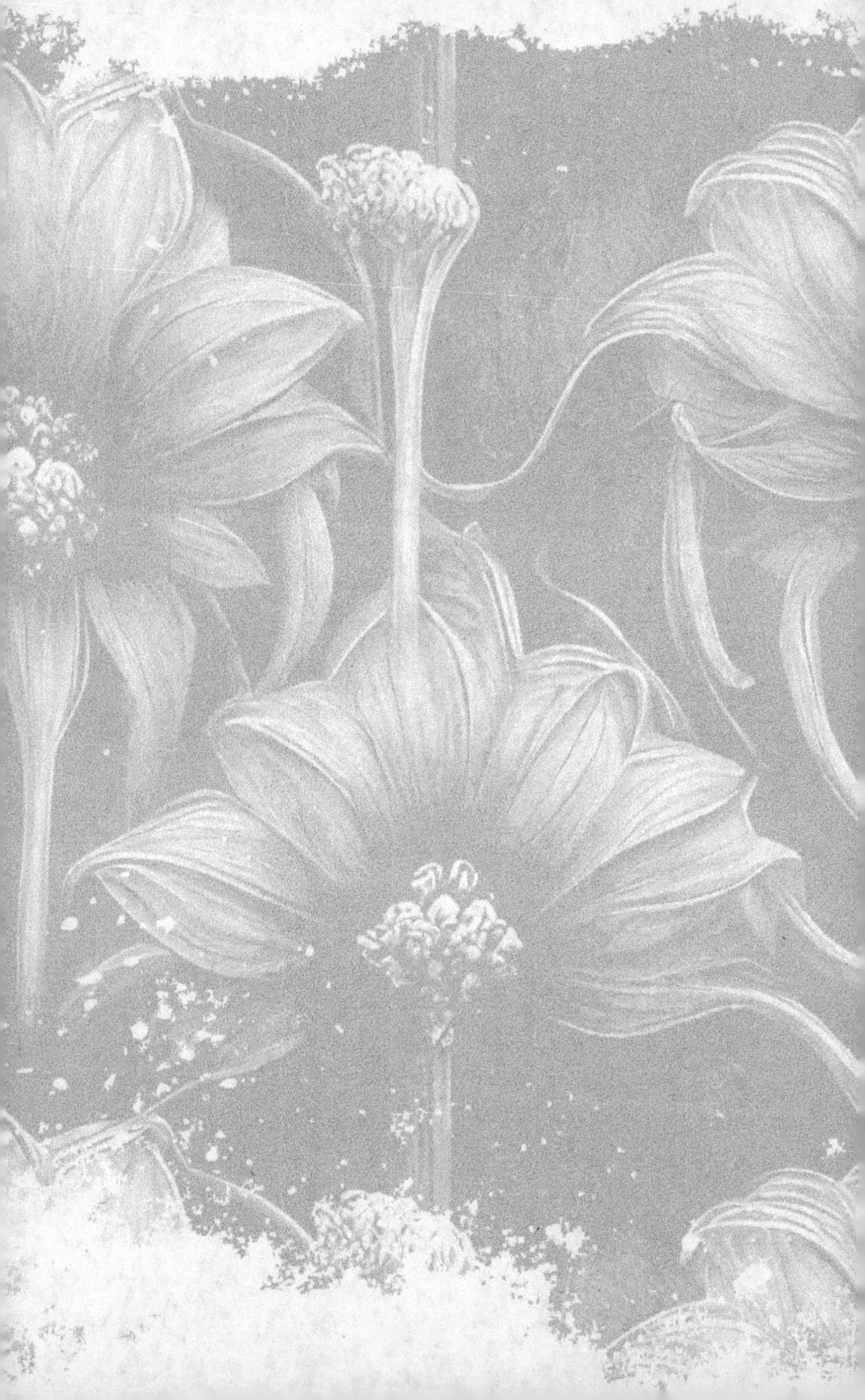

CHAPTER THIRTEEN
SOPHIE VANGUARD

There's someone on the front porch. I know before their knuckles touch the door because the floorboards of the porch creak from a sudden weight. It must be him. It's always him. The man who won't leave me alone. The man who leaves the blue flowers everywhere I look and whispers my name in the middle of the night.

Mason.

There are certain names that are forever tainted by horrible experiences, and I know "Mason" will have lasting terrible connotations for me.

I reach to turn off the light, then stop. What good will that do? Whoever's out there has undoubtedly already seen it. At the most, it'll just scare me more because I'll be in darkness. I leave it on, letting the heat from the bulb warm the skin on the back of my hand and holding my breath as I listen for the slightest creak.

Knock. Knock. Knock.

I practically jump out of my skin. My heart hammers dangerously loud. Can he hear it? More importantly, why is he knocking?

My hands fumble with the blinds behind me as I try to close them soundlessly. They clatter against the glass before I grab them and hold them still. Not subtle at all.

Every inch of me is hyperaware.

"Hello?" a feminine voice calls from behind the wood.

Not the type of voice I'd expected, but why not? I've never seen their face. And the whispers that haunt my nights may, in fact, be the same voice.

"Is there anyone in there?" the stranger calls. "I could really use some help."

If I wasn't petrified, I'd roll my eyes. Was that the best they could do? Using the oldest trick from the stalker's handbook. Next, they'd say their dog's missing, and they need help finding him.

I wrap my cardigan around myself and cross my arms as if that's enough protection. I should be headed straight for the knife block. Instead, I say, "Who are you?"

"Sophie?"

I'm not sure how it's possible, but every part of me tenses even more. Somehow, I find the courage to repeat my question. "Who are you? How do you know my name?"

A thought flashes through my mind and propels me from the armchair to the door. The locks. What if I hadn't locked them? It's never happened before, but what if I somehow forgot?

Relief floods me when I see the locks. Crisis averted. They're all engaged.

"It's Ren," the person outside says. "I've known you my whole life. Just like you've known me."

"Ren." Not "Mason."

After another check of the locks, I move to the peephole and look through it. Someone with short black hair stands on the other side. Their forehead and nose seem to be bleeding, but for all I know, it could be corn syrup. That was what movies used for blood, right? Where had I heard that? And what is with those clothes? Is it some sort of Civil War reenactment costume? Whatever it is, it's not suitable for this weather.

INKED IN BLOOD AND MEMORY

I've never seen this person before in my life.

"What kind of sick pickup line is that?" I ask as I try to get a look at their hands. I can't tell if they have anything in them. "I don't know you. I've never seen you before, and I would very much appreciate it if you'd leave now."

I pray I sound more resilient than I feel. *Please go away.* I will it with all of my being.

"Ren" places a hand on their temple and stumbles but catches herself before she falls.

I squint my eyes at her through the tiny peephole as if it'll help me decipher if it's an act.

I can't tell.

Ren sighs. "Listen, I'm freezing my tits off out here. Think we could maybe have this conversation inside? Maybe over some Irish coffee?"

Meow.

Ren shrieks abruptly and launches into a string of curses. From my limited view, I can make out a fluffy gray-striped tail flicking the air from behind the visual of the back of Ren's head.

"Damn cat. Why are you here again? You're not real. SHOO."

"You have a cat?"

Why did I ask that? It shouldn't matter if she has a cat. I am *not* opening the door.

"Wait," Ren says, flipping around to peer through the peephole. A brown eye fills the small space. Even though there's a barrier between us, and I know they can't get to me, I jump.

"Can you see him?" Ren asks.

I nod, then realize I'm not visible. "Just the tail, can't make anything else out from in here. Why?"

"He's from the other book. I don't know how he's here, too." Ren winces. If it's not from pain, it's pretty convincing. "Any chance we can talk about this inside?"

My heart thuds. "Stop asking me that. Go back to wherever you came from and leave me alone. And take your cat with you. It's too cold to be putting him through that."

Meow.

None of this makes sense. Not Ren's words, not their sudden appearance, and least of all, the cat. But I'm not letting them in.

CHAPTER FOURTEEN
LY THI REN
11:48PM

I'm getting nowhere. I sigh and throw my head back, and then I instantly regret it as my head spins.

Shit.

I squeeze my eyes tight and take a couple deep breaths. It does nothing for the pain in my head, but maybe I can calm some of the dizziness.

"You know, when a beautiful, bleeding woman shows up at your door, it's common courtesy to let her in or help her or something," I say to the closed door, leaning my forehead on the cool wood. "A bandage would be nice," I add, my mind returning to my bleeding temple, which now has its own pulse.

"Go away," Sophie says, voice wavering. "Your cat can come in, but not you."

She's scared. Of *me*, of all people. And she's trusting this stupid cat instead? That pair of whiskers is the *least* trustworthy option. This place has its claws deep in her mind. It's going to be incredibly tricky waking her up. And I'm running out of time.

"Not an option," I reply. "We need to get going."

"I'm not going anywhere, especially with a crazy person."

"Crazy person?" I say under my breath. "Look, I know I look like a trainwreck, and nothing makes sense, but you need to listen to me. You're in a library."

The throbbing in my head increases, and I wince, sliding down to my knees. Can a head implode? Is that a thing?

Over my shoulder, the cat stares at me with mocking green eyes, and I glare at it.

"This isn't a library. This is my rental. At least for the week, which means it's currently my property, and I'd like you off of it, please and thank you."

Every ounce of strength I had a minute ago is now nowhere to be found. My eyelids are closing of their own accord, and I can't seem to remember a good enough reason to keep them open.

"That's not what I mean," I say, but I'm not even sure it's loud enough for Sophie to hear.

"And stop with the flowers," Sophie's muffled voice continues. "It's not romantic. It's creepy."

Flowers?

I turn my back to the door and slide to the porch floor. My legs are jelly, my vision stars. Something touches my leg, and my adrenaline spikes, sending my heart off at top speed. But it's just the devil cat pawing at me.

I can't muster the anger to yell at him anymore. "What are you doing here?" I mumble.

Of course, the one cat I don't like followed me into this world. That's the way my life works. I attract the opposite of what I want. I'm a shit magnet.

Death seems to follow me everywhere. Adeline and William, and before that, Jade. I'd almost forgotten about her until this moment. I'm not sure how. I don't deserve the peace of forgetting.

I brush the cat's paw away as my eyes flutter closed once more. If I could rest them for a few minutes…

CHAPTER FIFTEEN
SOPHIE VANGUARD

It's gone silent out there, but it's too much for me to hope that Ren has left. She could be picking the lock.

I creep back to the door, pushing my ear against the wood, but there are no sounds of an impending break-in. Only the raging blizzard.

"H-Hello? Are you still there?"

I peer through the peephole once more, only to find it empty. *Did I lock the back door?* Panic grips my heart as I fly to the kitchen to check. Yes. Those three locks are still turned as well, and the deadbolt is in place.

When was the last time I talked with another human being? It had to have been a week ago, but I can't remember the exact instance. The storm outside is a convenient way for me to keep my introvert battery charged. These days, crowds of people, even at the grocery store, exhaust me at the least and induce a full-blown anxiety attack at the most.

I pull a knife free from the block on the kitchen counter and return to the front door. I clutch the table in the foyer with my free hand as I stare at the wooden barrier in front of me.

This is not how I wished to spend my evening. I just wanted a quiet night of reading and sipping tea in front of the fireplace.

I stop myself.

Isn't that what I've always done? Sit and read and wait for something to change? If this stranger is in as bad a shape as she seems, she could be bleeding out and succumbing to hypothermia. What if she's telling the truth? What if she really needs my help?

But how does she know my name? She seems to spout nothing but nonsense.

I bite my lip, caught in indecision, then place my ear to the door once again. Still nothing but the whistling wind.

An image of a blue-skinned woman and a cat huddled for warmth invade my brain.

I roll my shoulders as my hand hovers close to the doorknob. I've made my decision. If this is how I go out, so be it. I'm not okay with leaving someone out there to freeze to death. I will never be that person.

I open the door.

The girl's been asleep on my couch for the past fourteen hours. In that time, I managed to drag her to the couch of my reading room and heave her unconscious body onto it. I had to push her part of the way up with my back, and once she was barely up, I huffed and slid to the floor, already sweating. I hadn't realized just how out of shape I was. And that period dress hadn't helped anything. Where had she come from? The Civil War reenactment theory is looking more probable by the second. She doesn't even have shoes, just stockings soaked from the snow.

After wrapping the girl's feet in a wool blanket and covering the rest of her body with a second, I bound the girl's right wrist to the coffee table using a third blanket, knotting it twice. Her legs were next. That's when I realized I hadn't bound her left hand. I could tie her other hand to the coffee table as well—a somewhat awkward position for anyone, let alone a possibly concussed person. Option two involved an extension cord around her wrist, which also wrapped around the side table behind her head.

In the end, option two won out, though I'm not too sure how much more comfortable it could be. Her arm now rests on a pillow above her head.

In the past fourteen hours, I've also had the chance to go over every possible scenario. The first of which involved the girl faking unconsciousness so I'd let my guard down. I'd pushed that theory aside after the clock ticked its way toward hour two. Exactly one hour after first dragging her in, I placed a can of tuna and a bowl of water on the floor for Hercules—the name divulged by his collar. He seemed grateful, rubbing against my leg and hooking his tail around my knee.

By hour three, I'd worked up the courage to dab the blood under the stranger's nose away and clean the nasty cut on her forehead, sure she'd wake up and grab my hand. She didn't. I found a change of clothes for her—joggers with an elastic waist and ties since she's thinner than I am—and a t-shirt. I've placed them on the coffee table, along with socks and a pair of sneakers on the floor under them.

After the immediate necessary tasks were done, I settled back into my armchair and allowed myself to take in her features. She'd said we knew each other, but I don't remember her. Her heart-shaped face is striking, dark brows perfectly plucked and full lips. The kind of beautiful that I can't decide if I'm jealous of her or want to be with her. Those soft-looking lips on mine—

Stop.

Hour four: I made myself a grilled cheese and tomato soup.

Hour nine: I did a few half-hearted crunches.

Hour fourteen: I'm reading *The Count of Monte Cristo* and trying to keep from dozing off when she bolts up with a scream. Or, rather, *tries* to bolt up. Her bindings stop her before she can move too much, and she looks down at them.

"What the hell?" she says, almost to herself.

One of my hands moves to the steak knife I'd tucked by my side while the other sets the book down on the coffee table.

The girl quirks an eyebrow at me. "An extension cord? Really?"

I shrug, hoping it looks nonchalant and not as twitchy and nervous as I feel. "It was all I had."

"I'm guessing you don't get a lot of visitors." She tugs her arm from behind her head and scoots into a sitting position, pulling the coffee table with her.

My ineptitude is so obvious it practically slaps me in the face. Hercules jumps into my lap and purrs as I stroke his back. Ren narrows her eyes.

"Don't worry. Hercules is fine. All warmed up."

"Hercules?"

"Your cat. I saw his collar—"

"He's not my cat."

"Oh." I expect the girl to elaborate, but she doesn't.

Her body goes rigid. "How long was I out?"

"About fourteen hours or so," I say.

The girl's face blanches. "Please tell me you're kidding."

I shake my head.

The girl balls her shaking hands into fists. I prepare to bring my knife out, expecting the girl to lash out. Instead, she shakes her hands out and takes a few deep breaths.

"Okay," she says finally, not looking at me. "Not ideal, but okay. I have time."

"Time for what?" *To murder me? Chop me into pieces and hide me in the floor?*

"What did you say your name was?"

"Ren," the girl says with a nod, meeting my gaze once more.

I check behind me for a bird, and she chuckles. "That's my name. Ly Thi Ren. She/her pronouns. And you're Sophie. Remember your last name yet?"

"Why would I forget my last name?" I take comfort in the firmness of the knife's handle. This girl isn't making sense.

89

INKED IN BLOOD AND MEMORY

Ren bites her lip and looks around. "This is a pretty nice place you've got here. How long have you lived here?"

Why are you dodging my questions? But I let it slide for the moment. "Like I said, it's a rental."

Ren nods, almost to herself. "Right. Just you? No family? Friends?"

I squint my eyes at Ren as she coughs into her arm.

"Why so many questions?" I ask. "And what's with the Jane Austen getup?"

"I lost a bet. Speaking of which, is there a way for me to get out of them?"

"And let you out of those ties? I don't think so."

"Oh, so you want to undress me yourself then?" she says, wiggling her eyebrows.

I hope I'm not blushing, but her smirk confirms my fear.

When I don't respond, she sighs. "Fine. Can I at least get some water? My mouth's kind of dry."

How stupid does she think I am? But that was the one thing I hadn't considered.

Reluctantly, I place Hercules on the floor and leave the room, keeping my ears open for any sounds of escape.

I'm back in under twenty seconds, and Ren's already furiously flipping through my journal as she balances it on her knees. Her left arm is free of the extension cord, while her right arm is still wrapped in the blanket.

"Excuse me!" I yell, plucking the book from Ren's lap. "What makes you think you can just go through a person's private thoughts?"

Ren sets to work on freeing her arm. I eye my knife's hiding spot.

"Hate to break it to you, girly—"

"Sophie." I grit my teeth.

Ren works one of the knots in the blanket free and continues on to the second. "—but that journal's not as private as you think. And it's not as scintillating either."

"I don't write in it to be 'scintillating,' I write for myself. I know I don't lead an exciting life, but—"

"Not what I meant. Have you noticed it repeats the same seven days over and over?" she asks as she breaks free of the final knot.

I take a step back. "What do you mean?"

"I'm betting the guy who put you here made sure you'd never think to look back at your past entries. See for yourself."

"The guy who put me here?" I turn to a page close to the beginning of the nearly filled notebook, which is dated *January 14th. That can't be right. Today's January 14th. I haven't been here for a full year. I only rented this place for a week.*

I continue reading, keeping one eye on Ren. She's still perched on the couch, but she's staring at a gold pocket watch that reads 1:55.

...I tried to leave today...

...Sticking out of the snow like spots on a cartoon Dalmatian's fur...

... Maybe I'm weaker than I thought. Maybe all there is for me is my semi-safe world of books and blue flowers... It wasn't the sound of a knock ..."

Why is my entry from today at the beginning of this journal? I know I turned to a page close to the back.

Ren is now right in front of me, and I jump back. I'd lost myself in the conundrum and failed to watch her. She seems to sense my anxiety and gingerly flips the pages following the 14th. I glimpse the dates as they go by. *January 8th, January 9th, January 10th, January 11th, January 12th, January 13th, January 14th, January 8th—*

What?

I grab Ren's wrist and pull the book back so I can read the next January 14th entry. The same journal entry, word-for-word, is written once more. And after that, the same days repeat. On and on, the journal entries continue their cycle, never altering in content. Never extending past January 14th. It's my handwriting throughout. I'm sure of that. The same phrases rush by, filling my eyes before they begin to blur behind my glasses.

How is this possible? What is going on?

Finally, I slam the notebook shut and throw it onto the couch.

INKED IN BLOOD AND MEMORY

"I don't understand." I hug myself to hide my shaking hands, but my lips tremble.

Ren removes her stockings and pulls on the joggers underneath her dress. "You've been caught in a loop of the same seven days for what looks like months, judging by the size of that journal."

"It's a trick. You switched it or something."

"Come on, tiny. You're smarter than that. You have to be with all these books around." Ren gestures to the bookcases and then tries to loosen her corset strings but can't quite reach them. She motions to me, silently asking for help.

I oblige, fumbling my way as best I can, focusing on my hands instead of my thoughts, until she's able to pull the corset off and let her skirt drop to the ground. She's topless in only the joggers, but she doesn't seem to mind. I almost roll my eyes as she moves to the T-shirt I have waiting on the coffee table for her. Oh, to be as comfortable with my rolls as she is with her hourglass and bump-less figure.

I drop onto the armchair, not ready to sit next to the journal quite yet. My fingers curl tightly around the cushion underneath me. "Did you drug me? Hex me? I've heard of people being hexed before. And from what I can tell, it's not a pleasant experience."

When Ren speaks again, now fully-clothed and sliding into her sneakers, it's quiet but firm. "You are stuck in a book."

I swallow the lump in my throat. "A book about a boring recluse? Who would buy that?"

Ren laces her shoes and nods, seemingly deep in thought. "It *is* weird that your catalyst never showed."

My fingers run the length of the cushion. I can't seem to sit still at the moment. "My 'catalyst'?"

"You know, the thing in a story that pushes the character to begin their journey," Ren says.

"I know what a catalyst is, but I'm a *person*, not a character. And this is real life."

Ren rolls her eyes and runs a hand down her face. "Right.

Listen, do you have anything I could eat? Fourteen hours on your back leaves you pretty starving. Also, a bathroom?"

I point to a door next to the kitchen, and Ren throws two thumbs up and heads there.

"I'll make you something to eat," I call after her.

But I don't head into the kitchen. I'm not letting her sneak up behind me. Instead, I wait for her outside the bathroom door.

As I lean against the wall, I try to come up with a reason my journal repeats the same entries. Other than my prevailing theory—I'm losing my mind—I come up empty.

Last night's sighting, the whispers, the blue passionflowers I have no explanation for...

"*You're stuck in a book*," Ren had said.

Assuming that impossible concept is true, who would want to trap me in a book? I'm—

I freeze. I know my name, how old I am, and how I like my tea, but the rest of my life is a blank page. My life before this house is not available to me. I grasp for any sort of information but come up empty. How is that possible?

My heart jumps into my throat as Ren exits the bathroom.

CHAPTER SIXTEEN

JEREMY BERG-NILSEN
SIX YEARS AGO

My mother shakes me as I come-to on a hard surface. "Jeremy, is that you? Are you okay?"

I blink up at familiar rafters, the pungent smell of incense assaulting me. Slowly, I sit up to see what I already know. We're in the Vanguards' living room. Again. And there's the book in its secure enclosure. Though, this time, the door is ajar, and the tome is splayed open.

How?

No, this is a trick. It's got to be a trick. This has happened before. Mom weeps as she holds me tight. "I'm so sorry, Jeremy. We never should've made that deal all those years ago. Can you ever forgive me?"

It's all too real, but it felt real before. *Stop it, demon! I don't want to go through this again! I can't see her die again.*

"How many years?" I murmur, breathing in her marshmallow scent in spite of myself.

Mom holds me tighter, if that's even possible. "It's been a little over nine."

Nine years. I knew that, of course. I blink stupidly. "How did you...?"

Wait. I've experienced this before. I know how she'll respond before she does. *"Not here. It's not safe. We need to go."*

Mom pulls away to look me in the eyes. "Not here. It's not safe. We need to go."

My stomach drops. She's not here, and I'm not out. I don't know why I followed her out of the house and to her car outside the gate. I shouldn't be playing along with the demon. But I can't help it. I miss my mom. I'll miss her after this hallucination is over.

I catch sight of myself in the rearview mirror. At least, I assume that's what I look like now. But the eyes aren't mine. They're a glowing amber. Eyes I know all too well.

"Pull yourself together. This is real."

The voice reverberates in my skull, something the demon's never done before. New tricks for his jaded audience.

As I watch, my eyes return to a normal human shade, and I tune back into what Mom is saying. She keeps looking over at me, and if this was reality, I'd be afraid she was going to drive us off the road.

"I still can't believe you're here," she says. "You look so different, but then again, it's been nine years."

"You look as beautiful as ever," I reply. I can't insult this version of Mom, no matter how hard I try.

I'll give you this, demon. The illusion is a lot more detailed this time around.

To my surprise, we don't drive to a motel this time. Around fifteen minutes later, we reach Mom's house on a quiet suburban street. It's the kind of neighborhood I wished I'd grown up in. Quaint but demon-free. Though, what did I know? The neighbors could be into black magic. Every neighborhood could be full of it now.

I recognize Mom's house from looking in on her over the years, but it's more vibrant this time. More present somehow.

Inside, her sweet-smelling perfume permeates the air. She

keeps it warm in here, but it's the kind of warm I've missed. Cozy.

Mom hangs her jacket on a coat rack by the door and throws her keys on a table. She crosses to the couch and pats the space next to her. As I sit, she asks, "Can I get you anything to drink? Or eat?"

"I'm fine."

It's quiet here except for the ticking of a cuckoo clock. Somehow, that's what does it.

I break, the words tumbling out of my mouth in stutters. "Why didn't you come for me sooner?" I sob.

"Oh, sweetheart." Mom hugs me, and I hold her tight. This is different than before. She's really here. This isn't a lie. I'm here with her. I'm *out*.

"That's what I've been trying to tell you. Besides, how else would you be able to get your revenge?"

Revenge on everyone but her. She was never a part of it.

"Of course, dear Jeremy."

She's *alive*. Her death was a trick to get me to say yes. I should be outraged, but I don't care. I'll happily be possessed 'til the end of time if it means Mom can live.

"Your father had me committed. I've been in and out of the Everling Institute for years. Everything I would say came off as insane to whoever heard me."

"Except Dad. He could've listened to you. He knew about the deal. I hate him."

"No, Jeremy. It's not his fault. He had every reason to believe you were gone for good. I even started to believe it."

"What stopped you from giving up?"

She bites her lip. "Blind hope mostly. Mother's intuition, maybe."

"Thank you," I say as she grabs my hand and squeezes.

"I never should've gone along with the sacrifice."

My stomach drops. "What?"

"I told Dan we shouldn't go through with it, but he pushed, and he said it was the only way. That we didn't have a choice."

"You were there when they..." My throat closes.

Mom squeezes my hand. "Please understand. The second we did it, I regretted it."

I can't breathe. I stand as if that will help. Of course, it doesn't. "I called out to you. You knew I was scared, and you did *nothing*?"

I see red. My own mother was there on that terrible night. She chose for this to happen, thinking I would die. And here she sits, doe-eyed and wanting me to forgive her. Dad was bad enough, but this...

"Jeremy—"

"Stop."

My vision cuts out. I shake my head, and it's back. I'm still here with Mom. Nothing has changed. But why do I feel like I'm going to be sick? It's more than a feeling of being betrayed.

"Jeremy? Are you okay?"

I hold my head as I swoon, overcome with a bout of dizziness. "I'm fine. I—"

Everything goes dark.

I awake slowly as if I've just had a midday nap. I'm rubbing my fingers together, feeling something coating them. Like honey, a sort of viscous feeling. Or glue. I'm standing, not laying as I should be. Was I sleepwalking? And something heavy is in my left hand.

I bring both of my hands up to my face as my eyes slowly regain their focus.

Blood. And a knife dripping with the stuff. I drop the weapon with a *clatter*.

"*Excellent*," says the demon.

I don't want to look down, but I have to. I have to know.

My eyes find her right away. My mother. I was just talking with her on the couch, but now she's sprawled on her living room floor. Dead. Her throat bears a ragged and deep cut. Her outstretched palm has been carved with a symbol that's familiar, but I can't place it.

I sway, vision failing for a moment. This can't be real. This is another trick.

But I'm not waking up.

I was angry with her, but I would never—

I fall to my knees, sobbing. "Mom! Please don't leave me. Please, I'm sorry!" I hold her in my lap. She's still warm.

It's just like the demon's vision, but I'm alone. The others are nowhere to be found. Were they here earlier? Do they know what I've done? What I've done...

My hands stained red with blood. *My* hand that slashed her—

Images flood my mind of the last few minutes. A group of figures in purple cloaks in my mother's living room. How many are there? Five? Seven? The scene isn't clear, and it's like I have double vision.

And Mom falls to the floor. Just like before.

"What have you done?"

"I did nothing but honor a deal."

"Who killed her?"

"I'll tell you when you calm down."

I need air. I can't be here.

I flee the house, running down poorly lit alleys and back streets until I reach Wycanth Wood. I don't stop until I'm miles into the overgrowth, closer to my childhood home.

None of this makes sense. She was never part of the deal. I didn't want her to die. I didn't want to kill her. Why is she dead?

My legs give out, and my lungs are bursting. And even then, I want to continue running. I want to exhaust myself to the point of no return. I want to find the nearest cliff and jump.

Her blood still coats my hands. Dry and cakey now, but still there. If only I'd kept the knife. A fast exit.

"Why?" I yell desperately into the night sky.

"Do you want to know a secret?"

I don't have a choice because the demon continues. *"Your*

mother made a deal with me to save you on the night another firstborn son was born. In return, she gave herself to me."

"No."

The demon laughs, deep and rasping. *"You should've stayed where you were. Thanks to you, your mother died in vain. And those closest to you delivered her to me."*

"Fuck you!" I choke out before taking off again. I know these woods. I grew up in them. Even though it's been years, I know there's a steep cliff nearby.

"Stop that," the demon tries, but I'm not listening. The blood pumps in my ears, I'm gasping for breath, but still, I run. On and on until I'm yards away from the edge. Just a little further—

"I said stop it now!" My legs cease abruptly, my heart pounding and chest heaving. I try to will my legs to move. Even a toe. But it's like I'm paralyzed. I can't even speak.

Give me back my body.

"Not while you're suicidal," the demon's voice says, using my mouth and vocal cords. "That won't do at all. I quite enjoy this body. After all, it would be a shame to waste it after it took me nine years to procure."

I strain to move anything. One measly muscle. But it's no use. The demon has full control of my body, and he's putting me back under. *Who killed her?*

Five Years Later

"Five years?!"

The demon—or Edmond, as he's chosen to call himself now—has finally allowed me some form of consciousness. I'm a voice in the back of his head—*my* head—as he uses my legs to pace at the front gate of my old house. My twenty-four-year-old legs, as it turns out.

"It's not quite September," he says with my mouth. "You're

INKED IN BLOOD AND MEMORY

still twenty-three."

I scoff. *"My mistake."*

"I had to bide my time until the deal could be completed. If I break my end— Well, it could turn out very bad for me."

"You didn't have to steal five years of my life!" I yell. *"That was never part of the deal!"*

"Yes, it was. Be grateful it wasn't longer. I haven't fed in a while, and it's become harder to keep you at bay. You agreed to allow me to be the instrument of your revenge no matter the cost."

An instrument of my revenge. The demon says it as if I have control over him, wielding him like a sword. But as usual, it's a lie. Smoke and mirrors to keep me complacent.

"Stop whining. You should know better than anyone how deals are carried out. Not in fairness and rainbows, but with blood and viscera."

He's right, of course. Still, I grit my teeth. Or try to, but I can't even do that. I'm digging into my anger because if I don't, I'll come undone. If I dwell on the night I—*someone* killed my mother—

I can't. That night might've been five years ago, but it's still fresh in my mind, like it happened yesterday.

Edmond stops pacing and smooths out his suit while I try to take a deep breath. *"You want to tell me why it's five years later?"*

"Carter Vanguard turns six soon, but we have a problem. Two actually. And those problems' names are Sophie Vanguard and Ly Thi Ren."

"Wait a second. Who's Carter Vanguard?"

"Oh, that's right. I've been keeping you in the dark about him. Don't want your human conscience screwing things up for me. This sacrifice must happen."

"Carter's Sophie's brother?"

"Yes."

"Why would that be a problem for me? If he's sacrificed, she suffers."

And if she was really there the night my mother died, she deserves every bit of pain coming to her.

The old Berg-Nilsen estate, situated on the edge of Lake Asota, is slipping into the water, bound to be lost to erosion at any minute. Its dozens of windows are boarded up, and a recent fire has taken out part of the east wing.

Edmond swings the cat and mouse doorknocker and hits an eviction notice. The door opens to his fresh smirk. The man standing inside has seen better days. His gray shoulder-length hair is patchy and knotted, and his clothes bear holes where moths had a feast. I recognize him immediately.

"Hello, Dan," Edmond says with my voice.

Dan Berg-Nilsen's polite—if fatigued—face drops as soon as he sees me. Though Edmond disguised my face with a blond mustache and goatee and placed glasses over my eyes, my dad can tell something was wrong.

Nine years of anger have led me to this moment. Nine years of waiting to see this look on his face. Almost fourteen years, if I'm truly honest with myself. Ever since my tenth birthday. Over half of my life was spent in an endless abyss, and here I am. Finally out.

It's not as if it was easy. But it was worth it.

What is the expression he wears? Surprise? Fear? Resignation? Anticipation of death? Surely, he knew I was coming for him. Ever since he let them kill my mother. But I won't make it that easy for him.

"Can I help you?" Dad asks.

"I'm Edmond. Jeremy sent me."

Dad's practically shaking. "Jeremy is dead. Is this a joke?"

Edmond pushes the door open further and walks over the threshold as Dad stumbles backward, nearly falling to the ground.

"Oh, he's very much alive, Dan. And he's looking for payback."

The once great Berg-Nilsen residence is crumbling inside as well. The hardwood floor is scratched, and cobwebs hang on the chandelier. It's dark. Electric company cut the power?

"No thanks to you, that's for sure," Edmond continues. "I'd ask if you missed him, but the answer's obvious."

"Even if we'd found out he was still alive, there was no way we could've gotten to him."

Edmond inspects his fingernails—*my* fingernails—as Dad quivers. "Come on, Dan. You know that's not true. Jeremy's mother got him out all on her own." Edmond creeps closer, and I relish the effect his appearance has on him. A part of me wonders if he'll stroke out before we get what we need. "Tell me, why'd you have her committed when you could've easily slit her throat?"

What little spark remains in my father's eyes ignites then. His mouth turns down as his eyes narrow. "How dare you? I loved Caroline with everything I had. I would never—"

"You left her alone in that hellhole of an institute! Don't tell me you cared one bit for her!" Edmond yells, reading my thoughts. His nails dig into my legs through my pant pockets. He's holding back until we get what we came for.

"Why are you here?" Dan practically whimpers. "To kill me?"

"You're going to make a phone call for me. In return, I may let you live."

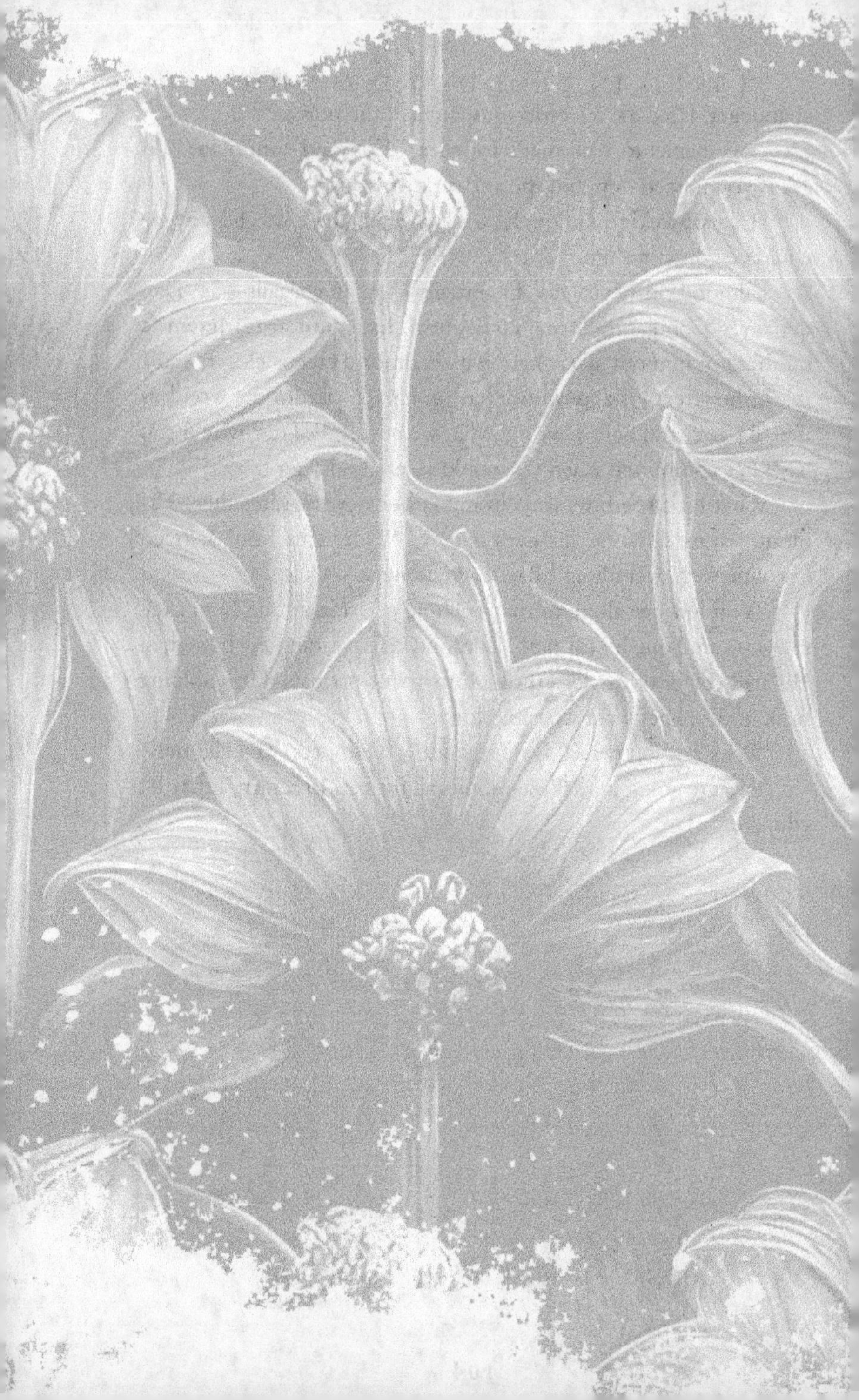

CHAPTER SEVENTEEN
SOPHIE VANGUARD

Ren takes one look at my face and drags me into the kitchen, where she directs me to a stool at the island. I sit, and she leans over the other side of it, arms extended. "What is it?"

My mind is spinning. In my effort to focus on remembering, I can't remember *anything*. Why can't I remember? What's happened to me? Is Sophie even my real name?

"I can't remember anything about myself. My memories, they're all gone," I say, placing my forehead in my hands. I massage my temples as if that will somehow jog a flashback. No luck. I'm getting a headache.

Ren nods as if it's the most normal thing in the world. "I get it. It happened to me just before I remembered my own past. This is a good thing."

My voice raises several octaves. "How is this a good thing?"

Ren turns to the cabinets behind her and opens a couple until she seems to find what she's looking for. Bread and peanut butter. Then, she searches for something else, and I assume it's a knife.

"Here," I say, gesturing to the drawer in the island on her side. Whatever gets her to complete her self-appointed mission and spit out an explanation faster.

Ren pulls the drawer open and extracts a knife. "Ace."

She smiles at me, and I guess I should be scared that a stranger is in my kitchen, holding a knife, but I'm not. It's odd. Something about her is so familiar to me. Maybe I really *did* know her. I pull myself out of my thoughts to say, "Well?"

Ren raises an eyebrow as she spreads the peanut butter on her bread. "Right. The panic about your memory loss is a good thing because this is the first step to waking up, to becoming the Sophie I know out there."

Hercules jumps onto the island and sniffs Ren's plate, and she brushes him away. He swishes his tail, glancing up at her. If Ren notices, she ignores him, instead smushing her sandwich together and moving to the fridge.

My response comes out of my mouth automatically. "I don't kn—"

"You don't know me. Blah, blah, blah. To that, I say, how do you know who you know?" Ren takes out a jar of pickle spears and fishes one out. Then another. Then another. She arranges all three on the outer rim of the plate, locking her sandwich in pickle prison.

She's right, of course, but I'm too distracted by her choice of lunch. "Gross."

"What? It's *your* jar of pickles. Don't tell me you have a jar of pickles for no reason. You like pickles, I remember."

I ignore that comment for the time being. "Not three at a time. And with a peanut butter sandwich? That's unholy."

Ren rolls her eyes and crunches down on one, maintaining eye contact with me as she does it. I look away, but only partially because of the weird feeling I get when I look at Ren. I glance behind me because it's a habit I have in this cabin. It's like I'm never truly alone here. I feel someone else watching me at all times.

When I turn back to Ren, she's still watching me. She waves her second pickle spear in the air as she speaks. "It'll come back. I promise."

INKED IN BLOOD AND MEMORY

It takes me a second to realize she's talking about my memories and not the shadow thing I saw. I hope she's right because right now, it's like I'm out at sea on an untethered lifeboat searching for land.

Ren locks eyes with Hercules, then. He hasn't stopped watching her even as he grooms himself.

"What are you looking at?" Ren asks him, a bit of pickle still lodged in her teeth.

Hercules makes a small noise in the back of his throat but doesn't break eye contact with her.

"You don't like cats?" I click my tongue at Herc, and he pads over to me and ducks his head into my awaiting hand.

"No, I like cats. This dude's—" Ren waves the remains of her second spear as if searching for the word. "–off," she finishes, placing the bite in her mouth. She leaves her third pickle and moves on to her sandwich, taking a huge bite. She's barely swallowed before taking another bite.

How long has it been since she last ate? Or does she always eat like this? Cramming food inside her body as if someone may take it at any moment.

"I think he needs to get used to you. That's all."

Herc rubs against my arm and purrs as I scratch his head, green eyes closing slightly.

"He sure got used to *you* quickly, shorty." Ren stuffs the last gigantic bite of sandwich into her mouth, her cheeks puffing out.

"*Sophie*," I correct her. "Where did he come from if he's not your cat? He showed up with you."

"He's from the other book. I don't know how he's here, too," Ren had said.

When Ren finally finishes chewing, she shrugs. "He followed me in from the outside."

"That's what I said."

Herc lays between us, stretching the entire width of the island with his tail extended.

"No. I mean, the cat followed me in from the outside *world.*

The *real* world. He was in the other world, too."

'*Other world?*' I'm still having trouble digesting her words, but I can't ignore that something is wrong here.

Before I can respond, Ren drops her plate in the sink with a *clang*. Hercules raises his hackles, but she doesn't notice. She's checking the plain gold pocket watch she's tugged from her joggers. "Right. We'd better get going before—"

The kitchen light above our heads flickers out the same moment the storm outside dies. It's eerily quiet as the hairs on my arms stand on end. Herc's ears flick forward as the tip of his black and gray striped tail twitches.

"Has this happened before?" Ren asks.

I shake my head. "Not that I can remember."

It's the shadow come back to take me. It's going to finish what it started.

I strain my ears as I try to listen for the whispers. So far, it's silent. I almost hit the ceiling when a crash sounds from above our heads. The noise is followed by a more familiar one.

Footsteps.

I know all too well who those belong to.

Ren's eyes are cast to the ceiling as she whispers, "Is someone else in the house?"

I stand, my legs mostly jelly. "There's always someone else in the house."

One more creaking footstep, and I'm flying through the swinging door separating the kitchen from the living room. It practically slams into Ren, but she catches it and follows me out. No one's on the stairs. Yet.

Ren touches my arm, and I spin to face her, feeling like my eyes can't focus on anything. She's taken a knife from the block, and I eye it as she tucks it into her pocket. "I don't like the sound of that. Explain," Ren says.

Another creak followed by the top step whining in protest as weight is lowered onto it. I've never realized how messed up what I've said sounds until this moment.

"It's him," I manage, my eyes glued to the stairs. If I didn't know better, I'd say the man would soon round the bend and stand no more than ten feet away from me. But I do know better. I continue, "He never comes downstairs, but I know he's up there. Watching me."

"Who?"

Another groan of floorboards, and my heart thuds unbearably fast. I can see his polished Italian designer shoe. Why can I see his shoe? I've never seen his shoe before. "Mason," I say at the same time a voice says, "Sophie?"

My legs buckle, and I'm sitting in the armchair again. "He's not supposed to do that. He never comes down this far." Every fiber of my being is listening for that voice. The voice I've never heard rise above a whisper. There's a baritone quality in it that somehow makes it all the more unsettling. I'd much rather he had a nasally voice, something meek and timid.

"Your catalyst," Ren says like that means something. I'm not a character. I'm a *person*.

"I can hear you, lovely Sophie," the voice says as the European shoes descend another step.

Why aren't we running? We should be running, right? "Stop talking about catalysts. This isn't a book. This is real life!" I practically shriek.

"Okay, so tell me something, *Chiquitita*. How long have you been stuck in this house? How long has that blizzard been going on for? Do you even remember a time when it *wasn't* winter? *Think*."

Of course, I remember the other seasons. Fall was just—

I open my mouth to speak and close it again.

I don't remember driving up to this house. I don't remember filling the kitchen fridge. And that journal—

My eyes slide to the book that still rests on the couch. I can't explain its contents, but that doesn't mean I'm words on a page.

"And why the hell haven't you called the cops on this dude?" Ren continues. "You're just living with a psycho?"

I have to admit she has a point. Why had it never occurred to me to call for help? I decide to go along with Ren's ramblings for the moment. "Any idea what kind of book we might be in?"

I still don't believe I'm in a book, my every move recorded, but I can no longer deny that my life is not what I thought it was one hour ago. Repeating journal entries, unexplainable circumstances, a cat with a mysterious origin.

Ren smiles, her eyes sparkling. She's not paralyzed with dread. She's excited.

This girl is a lunatic.

CHAPTER EIGHTEEN

LY THI REN
2:21PM

My face hurts from how wide I'm grinning. "Only the best genre there is," I whisper, grabbing one of Sophie's shoulders. "This is a horror novel. Isn't this ace?"

Sophie tenses under my palm and frowns. It's a look I know well and usually reserved for the disapproving of my ideas. "If by 'ace' you mean 'terrifying,' then yes. Definitely," she says.

"*Come here, beautiful Sophie,*" the man on the stairs croons.

My heart races not from fear but from adrenaline. "Trust me. I write horror for TV. This is going to be easy."

The fourteen hours I've lost to get to Carter aren't even a setback. It's only 2:21pm, and I've already found Sophie. Plenty of time to wake her up and guide her out of the book before midnight.

I can make out the creep's knees down to his feet now. His long, thin legs wear neatly ironed dress pants. And I recognize his shoes as the latest in Italian fashion.

The clothes are far from the combat boots and denim I

expected from a guy living in an attic, but it doesn't matter. Evil can be fashionable. Sophie and I know that better than anyone.

From behind his legs, two large, white dogs appear and barrel down the stairs. However fluffy and cuddly they seem at first glance, one look into their faces tells me the opposite. Their mouths contort in hideous snarls as their fangs drip saliva onto the wood. These dogs aren't on their way for snuggles.

My smile falls, and Sophie shrieks.

"Dogs? Really?" I say. "How does that make any sense?"

How has this guy been feeding them or exercising them up in that cramped space? Has this book lost the plot already?

Sophie grabs my hand and tugs. "Who cares? Just run!"

And we do. Out of the library and into the kitchen, Sophie throws open the back door, and Hercules hops down from the island and shoots out. Sophie pulls me with her. All the while, the beasts snap at our heels.

At the last second, I catch sight of a couple jackets on a nearby coat rack and pull them with me. The rack collapses as I slam the door in the slobbering dogs' faces.

CHAPTER NINETEEN

EDMOND SINCLAIR
SEVEN MONTHS AGO

Edmond arrived at the Vanguard estate as the midday sun hit its peak. Driving a car had been a new and exciting experience, but he wished he'd run into a pedestrian. That would have upped the excitement. Ah, well. Next time.

Tossing the keys to the Audi on the seat and slamming the door, he approached the Vanguard estate.

Tucked into a gap in the woods, the house and its dark trimming seemed to grin at him. Or at least, that's what Edmond imagined as he stared up at it. As if it were saying, "Ah, there you are. I've been expecting you."

Edmond adjusted his cufflinks and pinstripe tie. At the very last second, he plastered on a pleasant expression.

He considered swinging the locked door open with his hand or perhaps bursting it off its hinges, really making an entrance, but he restrained himself. He chose the boring route. A knock.

Once.

Twice.

What was that phrase about opportunity?

Dr. Roger Vanguard—a prominent neurosurgeon and part-time bodybuilder by the looks of him—opened the massive steel door, scrutiny falling over his brow before realization dawned. "Mr. Sinclair, I presume," he said, sticking out a beefy hand and pulling it even tauter over his wide frame.

Edmond flashed what he thought was a winning smile— but had been told had the tendency to come off wolfish—and shook Roger's hand. It disappeared in the man's mitt. "Edmond, please. Roger, is it?" He took pleasure in Roger's perplexed hesitation at the informal address.

"Yes—" Roger paused. "Sorry, it's just— You seem a bit young for someone with a resume as extensive as yours."

Edmond rearranged his watch, drawing Roger's attention. His mouth twitched up in amusement. A nice watch, an expensive suit, and confidence. Just as Edmond had anticipated, Roger's brows lifted in admiration. "I don't think you'd be surprised to know how often I hear that."

Roger opened the door wider and stood aside. "Yes, well, please. Come in."

As the two men settled in the parlor, Sylvia Vanguard joined them. "Roger, where are your manners? Our guest needs tea if we're going to talk business."

A polite guest may have waved off the suggestion. Edmond did not wave off the suggestion, and Roger left to prepare the tea.

Sylvia took her husband's chair, adjusting her long, form-fitting skirt as she crossed her ankles, hands folded neatly in her lap. "Mr. Sinclair—"

"Edmond."

Sylvia's piercing, heterochromatic eyes bore into him, and had he been a different person, he imagined it would have a withering effect on him. Factor in the high cheekbones, vampiric skin tone, slick, black hair pulled taut into a bun, and dark eye shadow, and the complete look was intense, to say the least. "Very well," she continued. "Edmond, you come highly recommended by a friend of ours—Daniel Berg-Nilsen. He tells us you have a solution to our wayward daughter problem."

"Sophie, yes? I've heard all about her."

"Then, you've heard how difficult she can be. How... exhausting."

"Well, kids will be kids, as they say. I have access to a powerful magic that has aided me countless times. The Berg-Nilsens were my first clients years ago."

"How fascinating. Do you mind if I ask what you did for them?"

"Yes," Edmond said simply, folding one leg over the other and adjusting his blazer.

Sylvia straightened. "I don't mean to sound like I'm prying. It's just that the matter is delicate. We would need a guarantee that this magic of yours wouldn't do any irreparable harm."

Roger returned with a tray of three teacups, sugar, cream, and a teapot full of liquid. The spread even included biscuits and jam. *They're pulling out all the stops, aren't they?* The items almost looked miniature in Roger's hands.

"I must say, I find what you do fascinating, Edmond," Roger said, pouring his guest a cup of tea. "Sylvia and I tried our hand at it on numerous occasions but had no luck." He set the cup in front of Edmond and continued on to Sylvia's.

Edmond wagered Roger rarely used the complimentary tone his voice currently held.

He must be desperate.

Whereas Sylvia played everything close to the vest. But Edmond had always been good at reading people. The tight smile, the way she clasped her hands. She was just as desperate.

"What I do isn't luck, Roger," Edmond said, clearing his throat. And as I always say, 'Those who can't do, make deals with demons.'"

His hosts laughed, and Edmond grinned that predator's grin.

"I suppose you have us there," Roger said, settling into his chair.

"But I understand your concern, Sylvia. Perhaps a demonstration?"

With an exchanged glance at each other, the Vanguards nodded, and Edmond began his work. With a flurry of hand movements and muttered words, the air around the three picked up, ruffling their hair and swaying the chandelier above them. The pages appeared out of thin air, one at a time, slow at first, and then faster and faster until, finally, a cover wrapped itself around them. In a final flash of warm light and whoosh of air, the book settled into Edmond's hands, and the air stilled.

He placed it on the table and sat back, raising a hand lazily as Sylvia recovered from the show first and reached for the book. "I wouldn't. It's imperative the only one who opens it is your intended target. Is there anyone else in the house?"

"Just our au pair and our son," Roger said.

"Perfect," he said with a beam. "Call the au pair here for me."

Roger cleared his throat. "Eve? Could you join us down here, sweetheart?"

A young blonde woman in a colorful knee-length skirt and pastel crop top appeared seconds later. "I just got Carter down for his nap. What did you need, Dr. Vanguard?"

"This is Edmond Sinclair, a friend of ours," Roger said, gesturing to Edmond. "We wanted you to meet him. He has a task for you."

"A task?" Eve tilted her head; her earrings—bright purple frogs—wobbled with the movement.

"More of a simple favor, really. All you need to do is open that book and read the first page for me." Edmond waved his hand toward the book on the table.

Clearly confused but not wanting to disappoint her employers,

INKED IN BLOOD AND MEMORY

Eve complied. Her eyes—heavily lined with eyeliner—narrowed at the first page. "There are no wor—"

She disappeared in a flutter of pages and golden light.

Edmond caught the book as it fell and handed it to Roger. He waited as they read, knowing what they'd see. Eve trapped but clueless. Her routine laid out for all to see, never altering and never causing her harm. As long as she remained oblivious, which she would. For as long as he chose.

"This is her?"

"Do I have your attention?"

"And this is a safe magic?"

Edmond spread his hands, palms up. "But of course. Anyone you wish can be contained in these pages, and no harm will come to them. It's my guarantee."

The doorbell rang.

"That'll be the Lys," Sylvia said, rising. "You can do this to anyone?"

"Of course."

"The Lys have a daughter as well—Ren. I'm sure they'll want to hire you for her. Money is no object."

Edmond grinned wide, his white canines flashing. "It shall be done."

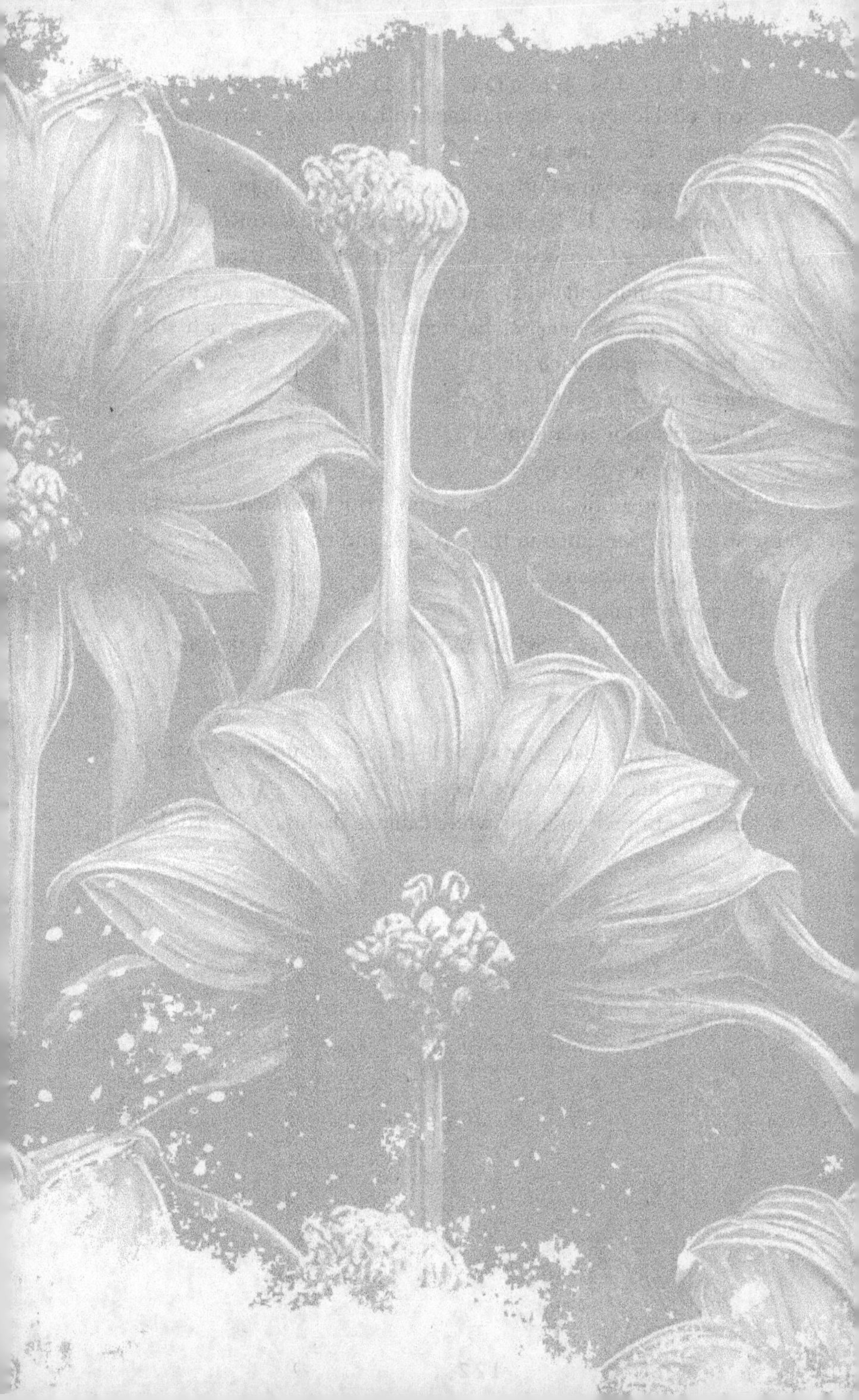

CHAPTER TWENTY

SOPHIE VANGUARD

Outside, the freezing wind whips my hair into my eyes, and I claw it away. My skin constricts at the sudden change in temperature. At our feet, Hercules meows incessantly, shaking out one paw after another but never freeing himself of the snow.

"Out of the fire and into the biting cold," Ren says with a sigh, handing me a coat.

It's a reversible trench coat that's currently faux fur inside. I scoop Hercules out of the snow and into my arms. As he clings to my chest, bones rattling and mewing miserably, I envelop him in the coat and tie the belt tight.

Ren's only option is a measly jean jacket, and I want to suggest trading, but I can't manage the words, and she and Herc aren't exactly fast friends. My throat tightens as I look around me, arms crossed against the cold and to keep Herc in place.

So much space. And from every direction. Who knows what's out there beyond the whirling snow? Is there anything at all? Which outcome am I more afraid of?

My vision blurs, blackness at the edges threatening to invade at any moment.

Which way did we even come from? I can't make out my house anymore. Everything is darkness and snow and cold. The moonlight is barely a trickle from behind a patch of clouds.

With no other option, I lean on Ren, and she places a hand on my back as I focus on taking in air and exhaling. Hercules' claws sink further into my skin as I move. I try to focus on that.

"You're having a panic attack," she says.

I scoff. "No shit, Sherlock. An agoraphobe outside for the first time in who knows how long? It would be a miracle if I *didn't* have one."

"You're agoraphobic?"

She says she knows me, but she doesn't know this? My tongue can't form the words. I'm too focused on breathing.

Ren continues. "Riddle me this, gorgeous. How did you travel there then without having an attack? If the house is a rental? Why would you leave wherever you were before?"

"I—" That was an extremely good point. How *had* I traveled here? I can't remember. And even the attempt at a thought process is dizzying. "I don't—"

With her free hand, Ren tugs her jacket tighter around herself. "Shut up."

"*You* shut up," I reply halfheartedly. It's not my best comeback, but I'm in no state for witty repartee.

"No, I mean, you shouldn't talk," Ren says. "It'll make it worse. Just breathe and take it one step at a time."

"*You're* the one asking me questions," I grumble.

Ren laughs. "My bad. I guess *I'll* shut up."

I nod. Or at least I think I do. My focus is on moving my feet, but each step is like wading through glue.

Can I lie down and let the snow cover me? Is that an option? Hypothermia is not the worst way to go. Hallucinations will kick in, making me feel warm. Some people start to remove their clothes. Eventually, I'll fall asleep.

The facts trickle in of their own accord like water out of a faucet. Except I can't turn it off.

INKED IN BLOOD AND MEMORY

After a moment of slow trudging through deep snow, Ren speaks up again. "You know it's all in your head, right? You're not even agoraphobic out there. You're not that adventurous, but you've never been afraid of open spaces."

Rather than scolding her for continuing the chatter, her words spur a question. "How do you know me?"

Still no sign of shelter. Why is there so much space? Where are the buildings? The residences? Won't we run into someone else? There are so many questions, but one stands out among the others: Why am I like this? It's just the outdoors. I'm away from the man in my attic, so I should be happy. Instead, I'm fighting the urge to curl up in the fetal position.

I shift Hercules a bit, checking on him with a quick glance. He looks as miserable as I feel. He stares up at me with big green eyes.

A wave of frustration washes over me. I'm completely helpless and hopeless. I can't even handle a few minutes of fresh air. Granted, it's frigid fresh air, but still.

Ren sighs. "We've known each other our whole lives. Even had a small fight in high school before losing touch in our college years. Except for that one day—" She cuts herself off. "You don't remember yet, but you will."

One wolf howls in the distance and is closely followed by more. My stomach clenches. Herc gazes up at me, a faint mew stuck in his throat. I scratch his head.

Ren reaches into her pocket, but she doesn't remove the knife yet. "If we're not wolf bait first." She spins in a circle, searching the area. "Can you tell which way that came from?"

I shake my head and then realize she's not looking at me. "No," I whisper as the wolves howl again. I still can't tell. Maybe on the left? I wish this wind would stop for one second.

"Pick."

"What?"

"Pick a direction," Ren says, turning to me.

"Why do *I* have to pick a direction? *You* pick

a direction."

Everywhere I turn is darkness and whirling snow. The wolves could be anywhere. They could jump out of the abyss at any moment. Now, I *do* have something to fear out here. *Breathe, Sophie. Just keep breathing.* I turn all my focus onto my lungs as I inhale and exhale the biting air.

Ren sighs. "Fine. Right," she says, shooting off into the darkness.

"Ren!" I follow stupidly, falling over myself in the deep snow. I feel like a baby deer whose mother just left her to fend for herself.

I manage to keep an eye on Ren's jacket as we run, Herc bouncing awkwardly against me. The howling continues, this time closer and definitely at our backs. Have they caught our scent? We're running against the wind, so I'm guessing yes.

I turn to look, but I can't make anything out. I spin around at the same time I collide with Ren. We fall to the ground, Herc yowling all the way.

The snow envelops my legs and seeps into my waist, seeking out my remaining warmth and extinguishing it.

Ren and I dust ourselves off as best we can, and she points below us. We're on a hill looking down at a log cabin off in the distance. Smoke trails out of the cabin's chimney, and I almost whimper at the sight.

Warmth. Not only that but an enclosed space. No more whipping wind, hungry wolves, and vast tundra.

My teeth chatter as I move toward the cabin, but Ren stops me with a hand on my shoulder. When I turn to her, she nods to a spot a few hundred yards to the right of the cabin. And there they are. The pack of wolves we've been hearing. If my eyes are to be trusted, we seem to be closer to the cabin than they are. But these are *wolves*. Skilled hunters in the snow.

We may make it to the cabin if luck is on our side.

If.

"I say we make a run for it," Ren says, eyes still on the wolves.

"Are you *insane*?" I reposition Hercules and fight my chattering teeth.

Ren turns to me, hunching in her measly jean jacket. "What choice do we have? This is where the book's leading us."

This again.

"The book," I scoff. "You're wrong. You're insane. You're... some other adjective that I can't think of right now because I can't think straight."

Ren's gaze snaps to mine as she forces her voice to a whisper. "You're so stubborn. You've always been like this. Ever since we were kids."

And just like that, it's as if she's flipped a switch in my brain. The illusion of who I am is shattered as snippets of memory come to me unbidden. I live in an apartment somewhere it never snows. I don't live in that house. I wouldn't even *vacation* in the snow. The New England winters I endured growing up were enough to last me a lifetime. I hate the cold. This is not my life.

These days I've spent reading and sipping tea— How many days? How many pages in a redundant journal? They were nothing but a holding pattern. I don't read much fiction. That's always been Ren's thing. When I have to brush up on facts, I pick up a nonfiction book.

My name is Sophie Vanguard, and I'm estranged from my family except for my little brother. *Carter.* My baby brother's sixth birthday is approaching, and here I am, struggling to survive open spaces. What month is it? It was May the last time I checked. Is it already December?

"I remember," I mumble, but Ren doesn't hear me. She's back to staring at the wolves.

"We need to move before they see us. Now," Ren says as she takes off down the hill, snow kicking up with every footfall.

I follow her as best I can, feeling like a toddler learning how to run. It doesn't help that Herc is clinging to me for dear life, digging his claws into my skin through my top. He bounces uncomfortably as I fumble through the deep snow.

On top of it all, memories return to me, flashing through my mind as I try to place where each belongs in the timeline of my life. Jeremy, Ren, and I as kids, inseparable in all of our adventures. We called ourselves "The Haglen Brook Bandits." The unspeakable truth of our inheritances. Jeremy's forced sacrifice. Ren and I as teenagers, jaded and fed up with our families. The day my parents told me they were bringing a baby boy into our world. My vow to protect Carter with everything I have. My estrangement from Ren after our high school graduation. Learning a few spells to protect Carter when it came time. My days at the Everling Institute and why I was stuck there—

It all floods in. Jigsaw pieces clicking into place.

Finally, we reach the bottom of the hill, but we're not safe yet. The cabin is still a good hundred yards away.

I turn back to the wolves at the same time they spot us. The biggest of them with the lightest coat lets out a howl and takes off, leading the pack straight to us.

That's when Hercules freaks out and decides my coat is no longer a safe place. He claws up my chest, tearing into my flesh as he makes his way to my shoulder and jumps to the ground.

"Herc! Come on!" I yell, slapping my knees in desperation.

But Hercules has other ideas. He shoots off in the other direction. I move to follow, but Ren stops me. "Forget the stupid cat. We gotta go!"

She tugs me forward, fingers bruising my arm. My lungs burn as I suck in the icy air, and my legs scream with the effort I'm putting them through. They're protesting the sudden workout after months of inactivity.

We're fifty yards away from shelter, and the wolves are closing in. The leader communicates orders to the others. The pack spreads out.

That's when the door swings open, and a crossbow peeks out. I can't see the person holding it, but they fire at the closest, missing the animal by an inch. The lead dog swerves and comes to a stop, and the pack follows suit.

Ren makes it inside the cabin, and I follow her as the wolves let out one last chorus of growls behind me. As we stand in the doorway with our savior, the largest wolf turns its back and leads the pack away and into the unrelenting blizzard.

Ren and I back up as the man swings the door closed, locks it, and leans the crossbow against the wall. He's taller than either of us by a good six inches.

My glasses fog in the sudden warmth of the cabin, and I have to take them off and clean them on my coat. Ren pulls me back as the man crosses to the table and sits.

When I put my freshly cleaned glasses back on, I see the man for the first time. His graying, unbrushed hair falls to his shoulders as his brown eyes stare at us impassively. They're eyes that have seen too much, sunken and bagged. Something about him seems familiar, but I can't place him.

He nods to the chairs at the table, and Ren and I sit, me on the very edge of the seat and Ren backward, her hands draped over the back of the chair. Her hair sticks out at all angles from the storm. I smooth my own out, and I'm sure my kinky curls look ten times worse.

The cabin is small with an open floor plan. The living room flows into the dining room, which spills into the kitchen. Behind the man's head, a wolf's head hangs on the wall. A fire crackles in the fireplace next to the table. It's closest to where I sit, and I bask in its glorious warmth.

Ren speaks first. "Thanks for that. You saved us. We would've been wolf food."

The man squints at her then, forehead wrinkling as he does. "You're Ren." He turns to me and nods. "Sophie. Been a long time."

I freeze. So we *have* met before. "You know us?" That voice is so familiar. I realize who he is a second before Ren speaks again.

"Oh my God. Mr. Berg-Nilsen, is that really you?" she says.

Of course. Mr. Berg-Nilsen. Jeremy's dad. I see it now. I remember his stern brow for everyone except his wife. He only ever looked at her with love. I always thought he had a limited supply of patience and compassion and used it all up on her. The kids and other adults only received scrutiny from him. Especially Jeremy.

"I thought you were dead," Ren continues, tilting her chair up on two legs. "Or at least a hermit."

That was the story, wasn't it? That Dan Berg-Nilsen had retreated deep inside his empty manor after years of spiraling caused by his wife's suicide. A weirdly tragic end for people who sold their souls to a demon.

Mr. Berg-Nilsen straightens his posture and smiles a smile that doesn't reach his eyes. The only thing that flickers there is the light from the roaring fire. "I *am* dead."

Ren and I exchange a look as Mr. Berg-Nilsen jumps to his feet. "Let me get you girls a drink. And those look like they need to be cleaned." He points to my neck and ducks into the tiny kitchen before we can ask him anything else.

I'd forgotten about the scratches, but now that he's mentioned them, the pain reaches me. I try to ignore it. "How is he here?" I ask Ren, who shakes her head.

"Wait, you remember him? Does that mean—?" Ren leans over the back of the chair. Hope in her eyes.

I nod. "I remember everything."

Ren exhales a sigh of relief and tucks her short, black hair behind both of her ears. "Thank God. It's good to have you back, bug."

I forgot how much I missed Ren's random nicknames for me. The seven months apart feel like nothing and an incomprehensibly long time all at once. It's so good to see her again. My joy is accompanied by a pang of guilt. After all, it's my fault she's in this mess, isn't it? She was out, and I'd pulled her back in.

Mr. Berg-Nilsen sets a teapot and three cups in the center of the table. He takes a cloth and a bottle of hydrogen peroxide out of his pocket and hands them to me. Then, he removes a flask from the inner pocket of his coat and pours some of the liquid into his cup before offering it to us with a silent gesture. Ren and I both decline, and he sits down, finishing the flask in a few gulps.

"You can call me Dan, girls," he says, wiping his mouth of excess liquid. "You're both adults now, and we're all in the same boat, it seems."

I unscrew the cap of the peroxide and douse the cloth. "Mr.—Dan, you said before that you're dead. Why do you think that?"

I can't be dead. I have to save Carter. He's counting on me. Or he would be if he knew how much danger he's in.

Dan quirks an eyebrow. "It's obvious, isn't it? This is hell."

For one terrible millisecond, I think he knows something we don't. That all three of us died and ended up here, in a sort of purgatory. *No*, I remind myself, *that can't be right. Unless that weird orange light killed me.* Dr. Lloyd and that book of his. That must be where I am.

"Or it might as well be," Dan continues, and I relax slightly. "It's where I belong after sending my son to that demon. What we did to Jeremy—" He shakes his head. "This is our punishment."

I brace myself as I bring the cloth to my skin; I wince at the sting but stay silent.

Ren leans forward in her chair, her hands wrapping around her teacup. "'*Our?*' Sophie and I didn't do this to him. We trusted you, and we tried to stop you, but we were just kids. And now, it's about to happen to Sophie's little brother, too."

Dan's eyes snap to Ren and then to me. "Carter's six?"

"Almost," I say. It's too terrible to think about. Not five minutes ago, I didn't remember I even had a brother. Now, his face has returned to me, and I have an overwhelming need to get back to him and protect him.

Ren checks her watch. "In less than ten hours."

My stomach drops. That's not enough time. How are we supposed to leave this place?

Dan is silent as he finishes his tea and opens his flask once more, apparently forgetting he'd emptied it. "You can't let them sacrifice that boy."

"You act like we're sitting back and watching it happen," Ren says, her voice rising as she throws her hands in the air. "We're doing all we can to get back there, but we could use your help."

Dan chuckles humorlessly as he sits back in his chair. It creaks with the movement. "You don't need me weighing you down. I'm the reason any of this happened. Your parents and I. We did this."

"That's why you need to help us fix your mistake," I say after finishing my tea. The warmth of the drink has restored me, and the sting in my cheeks has dissipated. "We can get out of here and save Carter together."

"You think it's that simple? He won't let you go now that he has you," Dan says before downing the last of his drink.

"'He?' You mean the guy with the library? He didn't seem so tough," Ren says.

"I don't know anything about a guy with a library, but you must be talking about Edmond. Tall, fancy suit, blond mustache and goatee, glasses."

Ren and I exchange a look. That sounded like Dr. Lloyd. Or the man who called himself Dr. Lloyd.

"He trapped me here," Dan continues. "Said it was a message from Jeremy."

Ren sits back in her chair, and I think she's going to fall off it, but she doesn't. "What do you mean? Isn't Jeremy dead?"

"I'm not so sure anymore. Maybe he's been alive all this time, letting the Great One influence him." With that, Dan rises, taking his cup to the sink.

I swallow hard. Is Jeremy really alive? And if so, what has the demon done to him? Is he really so different from the friend I knew?

Jeremy, the demon, Dr. Lloyd, our parents. No wonder Dan's given up. The odds seem insurmountable. What chance do we have against all of them?

"So, you're just going to hide in this cabin and rot?" Ren asks, rising from her chair. When Dan doesn't answer, she hurls her glass at the wall in front of him. It shatters, pieces falling into the sink, but Dan doesn't turn around, so she speaks to his back. "You said it yourself. *You're* the reason Jeremy was sacrificed, Dan. This is on *you*. And now, you won't even help us?"

"I deserve to be here, not out there," Dan says, finally turning around. "I do hope you save the boy, though."

Ren's about to respond, and by the look on her face, it won't be pleasant. I cut off the sentence before it even begins. "There's something I'm confused about. How are you awake?"

Dan furrows his unkempt brow so I clarify. "Ren and I have been under some sort of memory spell where we didn't know who we were. Did you have to go through that?"

Dan clears his throat and shakes his head. "I wasn't so lucky. Jeremy wants me fully cognizant of who I am and what I've done."

I'm still not sure Jeremy's behind this, but I stay silent.

Something scrapes the back door, and my heart leaps. *Hercules.* That must be him. That poor cat. Why'd he run off in the first place?

"*Sophie.*"

"What?" I ask Ren.

She looks bewildered. "I didn't say anything."

I narrow my eyes at her as the voice returns. "*Sophie. Lovely Sophie.*"

The hair on the back of my neck stands up.

Ren and Dan both look to the back door, and I realize I hadn't imagined the voice. The scraping at the door wasn't Hercules.

"No." I stumble out of my chair and backward to the front door as the other two look around. "He's found me." The room spins.

"Who?" Dan asks the same second the back door swings open and slams against the wall. A cloaked figure appears, curved blade in hand. His face is shrouded in billowing shadow as he steps into the cabin.

My chest heaves as I stare at the man. He's followed me here. He's never going to stop following me. My eyes lock on the knife in his hand, and I wonder if he intends to use it on me after he kills Dan and Ren. I can't move. I can't do anything.

"You two, out the door. Now!" Dan yells.

My stalker, Mason, brings his knife up, ready to slice into Dan, but Dan grabs his wrist and slams the newcomer against the kitchen island. Ren moves to help, but Dan throws up a hand. "Go!"

The cloaked Mason punches Dan in the gut with his free hand in succession until his grip on his attacker's wrist slips, and the hand with the knife descends, connecting with his shoulder. Dan cries out.

Mason removes the knife, and Dan gets in a punch. The knife falls to the floor, and the attacker wraps his hands around Dan's throat.

Ren hasn't listened to Dan's instructions. She's crept to the other side of the island and taken the cast iron skillet off the stove. While Dan struggles for control of the knife, Ren swings the skillet at the stranger's head. It hits his skull with a *crack*, and Mason relinquishes Dan and crumples to the floor.

Dan gasps for air, one hand on his throat and the other on one of his knees as he stands over my unconscious stalker. He nods a thanks to Ren, who sets the skillet down.

"Let's get out of here," she says, joining Dan on the other side of the island.

Clutching his shoulder with one hand, Dan reaches down to remove Mason's hood. Every inch of me is on high alert. I'm finally going to see the face of the man who's been terrorizing me all these months. But Dan never gets the chance.

Mason brings the knife up and into Dan's stomach. Then out and back in. The motion is quick and precise. A blink and you'll miss it moment. But the damage is done.

"No," I gasp.

Mason turns to me then. Even though I can't see his face, I know his eyes have found mine. A shiver runs up my spine, but I still can't move. He pulls the knife out of Dan, and his victim falls.

Ren dodges Mason's arms and urges me out the door with a nudge. Her touch breaks the spell of fear I'm under, and I fling the door open and run out into the night. I'll take wolves any day if it

INKED IN BLOOD AND MEMORY
means avoiding that man. Ren follows close behind.

All I can think as I run is I could've helped them, and maybe Dan would still be alive. But all I could do was watch.

CHAPTER TWENTY-ONE

SOPHIE VANGUARD
SEVEN MONTHS AGO

For as long as I can remember, I've been a watcher. I watched my parents sacrifice Jeremy. I watched their greed and power grow and did nothing. I stopped Ren from making her own deal on the night Carter was born. Even now, I watch people walk the courtyard outside from my second-story window.

I've never been a woman of action until recently.

With Carter's sixth birthday fast approaching, I don't have the luxury of standing by anymore. But the second I lifted a finger to do something, I ended up here. The Everling Institute for Mental Health.

"Why won't you listen to me?"
"They're going to hurt my brother!"
"They probably put a spell on me to get me out of the way!"

I said a lot of things my first week here. But I learned fast. Nothing you say here matters. You could be screaming the sanest sentiments, and they'd fall on deaf ears. No matter that magic is a real thing for a lot of people. At Everling, only one truth matters—those committed need professional help. And anything they may say doesn't matter.

After that first week, I fell silent. There's no point in shouting into a void. That's a good way to lose your voice, to become numb and raw.

I have to admit I'm not the most mentally capable person these days.

It started about a month ago.

Black spots in my peripheral vision, shapes that disappeared when I looked at them head-on. There one second and gone the next. I wrote them off as a form of stress or maybe floaters brought out by the bright sunlight. Normal human things for a normal human. Wishful thinking.

That was before the whispers began.

They came individually at first. Short, clipped, unintelligible sentences seemingly right at my ear, but when I turned, there would be nothing there. Even tormenting me at the movie theatre. Thankfully, the only other person in the room had been in the very back row. But it was enough for me to know that something was very wrong.

After that, they ramped up, with multiple voices jockeying for my attention, even surfacing out of nowhere so I dropped the eggs I'd just bought. Sometimes shrieking, sometimes a growl, but always upsetting.

The occurrences became so frequent I barely left my apartment. I'd get my groceries delivered, cut off all contact with friends, and rarely even opened a window. Wouldn't want the neighbors to hear me screaming at nothing.

Almost three weeks passed this way, but one event would have to break my cycle. A family picnic.

An unavoidable consequence if I wanted to be in Carter's life. Ren hadn't shown up, but I hadn't expected her to. Except for

Carter's first birthday party, she hadn't returned to Haglen Brook since graduation. I envied her freedom.

That day at the park, I made sure to do all of Carter's favorite things, which for a five-year-old was a lot of slides and monkey bars and teaching him all the strange children's rhymes we all learn in our childhood about stabbing knives in your back and Miss Mary Mack with her silver buttons.

They came for me on the swings.

As I bet Carter I could swing higher than him, the shapes appeared. More than I'd ever seen before. But this time, turning toward them did nothing. They remained, spots of darkness in the bright grass, as tall as a human but varying in height.

I dug my heels into the sand, jolting me to a stop. Carter took no notice and continued to swing, and part of me was glad. But a bigger part of me was terrified. He couldn't see them. I really was imagining them. The shapes' whispers weren't whispers. They came out of nowhere and started at one volume—full-blown screams. Not words, just ear-bleeding wails.

The families found me curled in a ball in the sand, hands firmly over my ears, and rocking back and forth. Praying the sand would cover me. Anything to escape the noise.

So maybe I do belong at Everling. But I can't stay here. Carter needs me, and I'll be damned if I leave him to the wolves.

My one last hope is Ren. Definitely not the cops. What would I even say to them?

Ren's shock had been evident when I used my only call of the day on her. But was it a good shock or a bad one? I couldn't tell.

"*I need your help.*"

"*Sophie? Where are you calling from? I almost didn't pick up. I don't recognize the number.*"

I grit my teeth. "*I'm at Everling.*"

She'd inhaled sharply. "Why the hell are you there?"

"It's complicated, but I need you, Ren." My hands had tightened on the phone and its cord. "I know we haven't spoken in years, and it's probably my fault. Whatever I did, I'm sorry, but I don't have anyone else to turn to. I just really need you to—"

"Whoa, pumpkin."

I'd almost smiled in spite of myself. Her nicknames always made me feel special. And hearing one after so long, it was as if no time had passed. As if nothing had changed.

"Slow down," Ren continued. "I'm coming to get you. Give me ten hours."

"Sophie."

Ren's voice pulls me out of my memory. She's here. And it only took her eight hours. She looks as effortlessly fashionable as ever in red leather pants and a black lace top, her short black hair in perfect curls.

I'm suddenly *very* conscious of my nappy brown hair and patient uniform. I know my eyes have black circles under them.

But she's *here*. She really came. She hasn't abandoned me.

My smile stretches wide, and I leap to my feet. When she sweeps me into a hug, my heart's so full I might explode.

Too soon, the hug ends, and we stand looking at each other in the middle of the rec room. I know I'm smiling like an idiot, but I can't seem to stop.

Ren speaks first. "It's good to see you, sugarbunch."

I'm blushing now. Because, of course, I am. Why is she here again?

Right. Dire circumstances. Pull it together, Sophie. She doesn't even like you like that, but that's not the point. I can't be thinking about this right now. *Focus.*

"I'm sorry for calling you," I say as we sit down opposite each other on the vinyl couch and armchair set. "I didn't see any other option. Carter has less than a year left, and I need to get to him. I've taught myself a few spells to help protect him, but they're useless to me here. They keep this place locked down tighter than Fort Knox." The words tumble out like I have no control over them. Seeing Ren here after all this time and after where we left things, I'm not sure where we stand. But she's here, so that's a good sign, right? She must still care a little, right?

Ren touches my knee, and I force myself to stop rambling. "Whoa, sweet pea," she says. "Slow down."

She strokes my knee with her thumb before removing her hand, and I'm left dwelling on the warmth of her palm.

"I can't believe your parents put you in here," she says after clearing her throat. She looks around at the other patients. A couple plays chess in a corner across the room while some work on a puzzle and even more play a card game. A couple orderlies stroll around the room. It's all so normal, I can almost forget most of us are here against our will.

I shrug. "It's not so bad. We have movie nights and Taco Tuesdays. Even some vegan options."

"Fancy." Ren quirks an eyebrow. "But we need to get you out of—"

She breaks off abruptly at the sight of an orderly, and we fall silent until he's gone.

Yes, getting out of here is a definite need, but I've had way too much time to think while I've been in here. I don't know how Ren and I turned out like we did, relatively unscathed by our parents' journeys past the point of no return. They've lost themselves in their love of power. It makes me wonder...

"Ren, do you think we'll ever become—" I stop myself, choking on the words as a lump forms in my throat.

"We could *never* be like them. *You* could never do what they've done. You're too good."

She can't know that for sure, of course, but her confidence is comforting. "So are you."

Ren looks away. She has something on her mind, but before I

can ask her what it is, she's moved on. "Our parents are blind to who they really are," she says. "The Vanguard Family Foundation is a prime example of that. Everyone thinks they're so great for helping the less fortunate, but really, they're only in it for the power grab and tax breaks. They're in so deep, they're walking around blindfolded, and that's no way to live."

Ren inclines her head as if saying, "Heads up," and I turn to see Dr. Ramirez approaching. She has a warm smile, the kind I have a hard time believing could be anything but genuine. I've had practice figuring out the difference.

"Ms. Vanguard, your family therapist is here to see you," Dr. Ramirez says.

"Family therapist?"

"Dr. Lloyd."

Who?

I exchanged a look with Ren before following Dr. Ramirez.

"No worries. I'll be here checking out the upcoming attractions," Ren says, pointing to the bulletin board.

The noise of the rec room fades as we make our way down the hall. I've never heard my parents even mention a Dr. Lloyd, but maybe they can act as a proxy for them. Maybe they've apprised the doctor and want to discuss my release. Maybe they're remorseful about throwing me in this place.

Maybe I need to stop daydreaming and help Ren break me out of here.

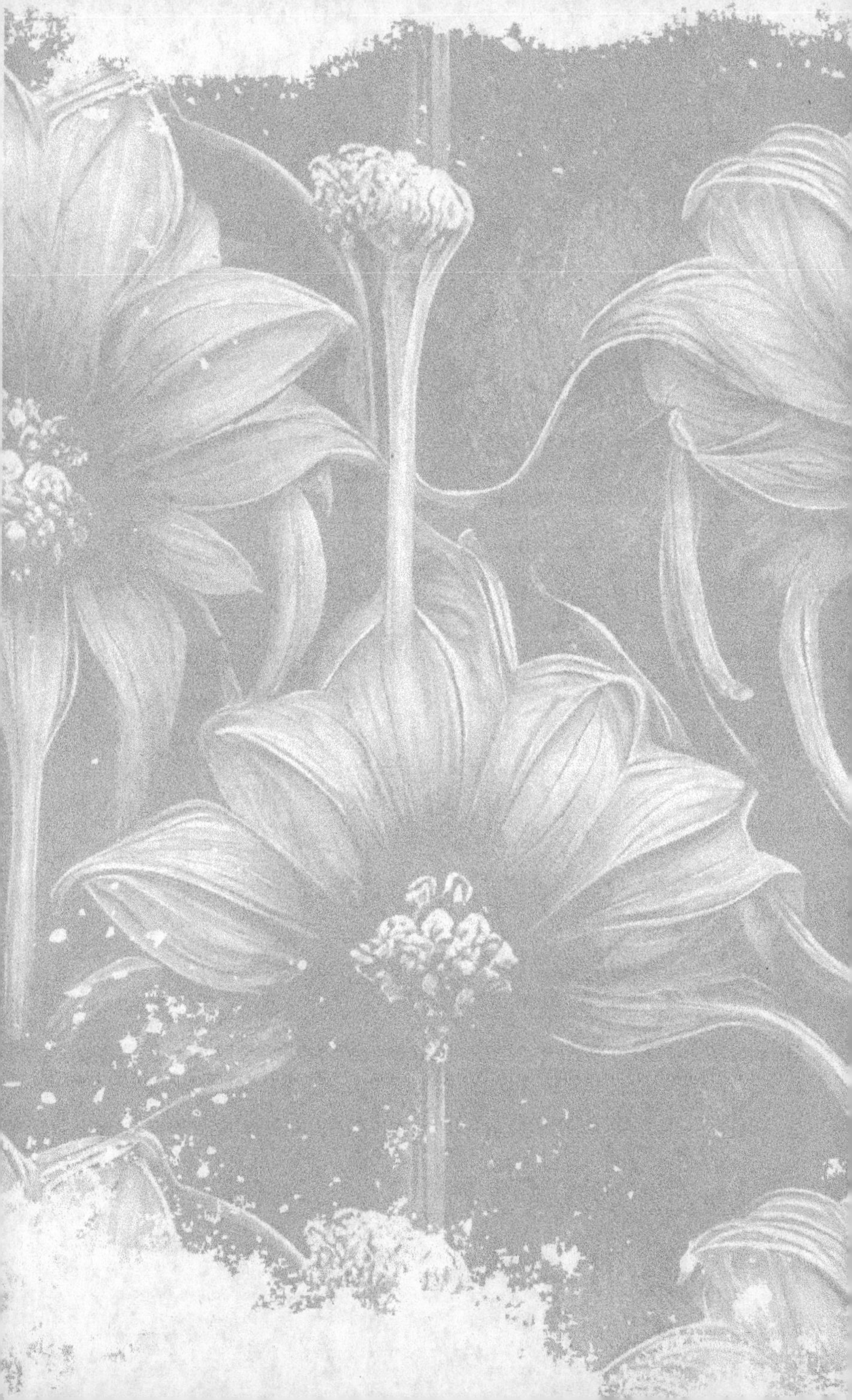

CHAPTER TWENTY-TWO

EDMOND SINCLAIR
SEVEN MONTHS AGO

I'll be damned, Edmond thought, pulling up to The Everling Institute for Mental Health. The first of the two addresses he'd plugged into his car's GPS hadn't mentioned the name of his destination.

Turning off the ignition and checking his appearance in the rearview mirror, he chuckled to himself.

This would be fun.

Thanks to the Vanguards, posing as Sophie's therapist had been easy enough. Not ten minutes later, Edmond found himself behind closed doors with his mark.

The good Dr. Ramirez, chief of staff at the institute, had been gracious enough to lend her office to the two. "Anything to help Sophie's recovery," she'd said.

Now, Edmond smiled across his temporary desk. The book he'd created for Jeremy's father lay between them. Not even a title on the cover for that bastard. There was no harm in Sophie seeing it first. It was unassuming, just another book. It could've been a book on psychology for all she knew.

Edmond thought about having Sophie lay on the chaise in the corner of the office to enact a cliché doctor-patient therapy session, but he restrained himself. Best to limit his time here and move on. He adjusted his thin brown glasses and stroked his dirty blond mustache and goatee. A disguise he'd created to appear older and more distinguished.

Sophie slumped in the chair across from him. She'd freed her socked feet from their slippers and now hugged her knees to her chest. The gray of her clothes paled her usual tan skin as if leaching the golden tone from it.

She's so weak. Like a tiny mouse.

The ease of this job almost took the fun out of it. Almost.

"Thank you for joining me, Sophie," he said. "My name is Dr. Lloyd. Your parents sent me to help you."

Sophie tensed immediately, gathering the cotton fabric of her pants in her hands. "What do you mean 'help' me?"

He knew what she must be thinking. Electroshock therapy and various other unpleasant treatments. Maybe he could try them out before— No, no time. Too many variables. Besides, he had another job after her.

"You've been seeing things, yes? Things you can't explain." He scooped up a pen and clicked it.

Sophie hesitated, then nodded. "I know it doesn't make sense. I know they're not really there."

"They scanned you for hexes when you were admitted, yes?"

Sophie nodded again.

Edmond put the pen down and sat back in his chair. "I believe you, Sophie. I think the answers to all your problems lay in here." He tapped the book. "Do you see what this cover says?"

Sophie leaned toward the desk for a better view, her feet slipping off the chair and to the ground as she craned her neck. Just what Edmond needed.

INKED IN BLOOD AND MEMORY

"I don't see any words—"

Edmond's smile widened as she flipped the book open, and its pages ruffled, spilling out brilliant amber light.

"What's happening?"

Sophie tried to move back, but the book held her in its grasp. It was too late. The light from the book spilled over the edge of the desk, encircling her ankles and dancing up her legs until it had a firm grasp on her torso.

Edmond loved this part. He relished the look that came over people's faces when they knew there was no escape. The terror that masked their features when they had no clue what awaited them. Sophie was no different. When she looked at him, it was clear she knew she was caught.

As if Sophie were made of air, the light began to take her with it, receding into the pages of the book. She screamed in desperation, trying to hold onto the chair, but there was no use fighting.

She lost her grip, and in a flash of wind and light, Sophie vanished with a strangled yell.

Edmond closed the book with a chuckle. His hair settled back onto his forehead, no longer disturbed by the wind. The cover now bore Sophie's name.

"Sophie?" a voice called as the door swung open to reveal a girl with short dark hair.

"Who are you?"

"Ren, and you are?"

What a coincidence. His second target stumbling in right after his first.

What is she doing here? She's supposed to be at the second address.

Edmond hated complications. No matter. He could improvise. It was his specialty. And for this one, a little something extra. A little twist to her tale. Her self-righteous bearing rubbed him the wrong way. Nonetheless, he flashed a smile. "I'm Dr. Lloyd. How can I help you?"

Let's see how self-righteous she is after this.

"What did you do to Sophie?" Ren asked, closing the door behind her.

"Who?" He stalled, his mind conjuring as he spoke and the free hand behind his back working overtime to remedy his lack of the element of surprise. But Ren had no magic. She was no match for him.

Despite her homecourt advantage, Edmond's talent would prevail. He was sure of it. He'd put her in the same prison as Sophie, but their parents had asked they be kept apart. Less likely to cause trouble that way. Edmond would oblige, but really, where was the fun in that?

Ren narrowed her eyes at him. "I heard her in here with you. What did you do to her?"

There. Done.

Edmond smiled; his new creation clutched behind his back.

"What are you hiding?" As Ren lunged at him, he made his move, whipping the new book from behind him and opening it the same instant she reached him. Instead of colliding with him, she dove headfirst into the pages.

Edmond snapped the book closed and placed it with the first on the table in front of him. He stroked both titles, beaming with pride, then strode out of Everling with the two tomes in his hands.

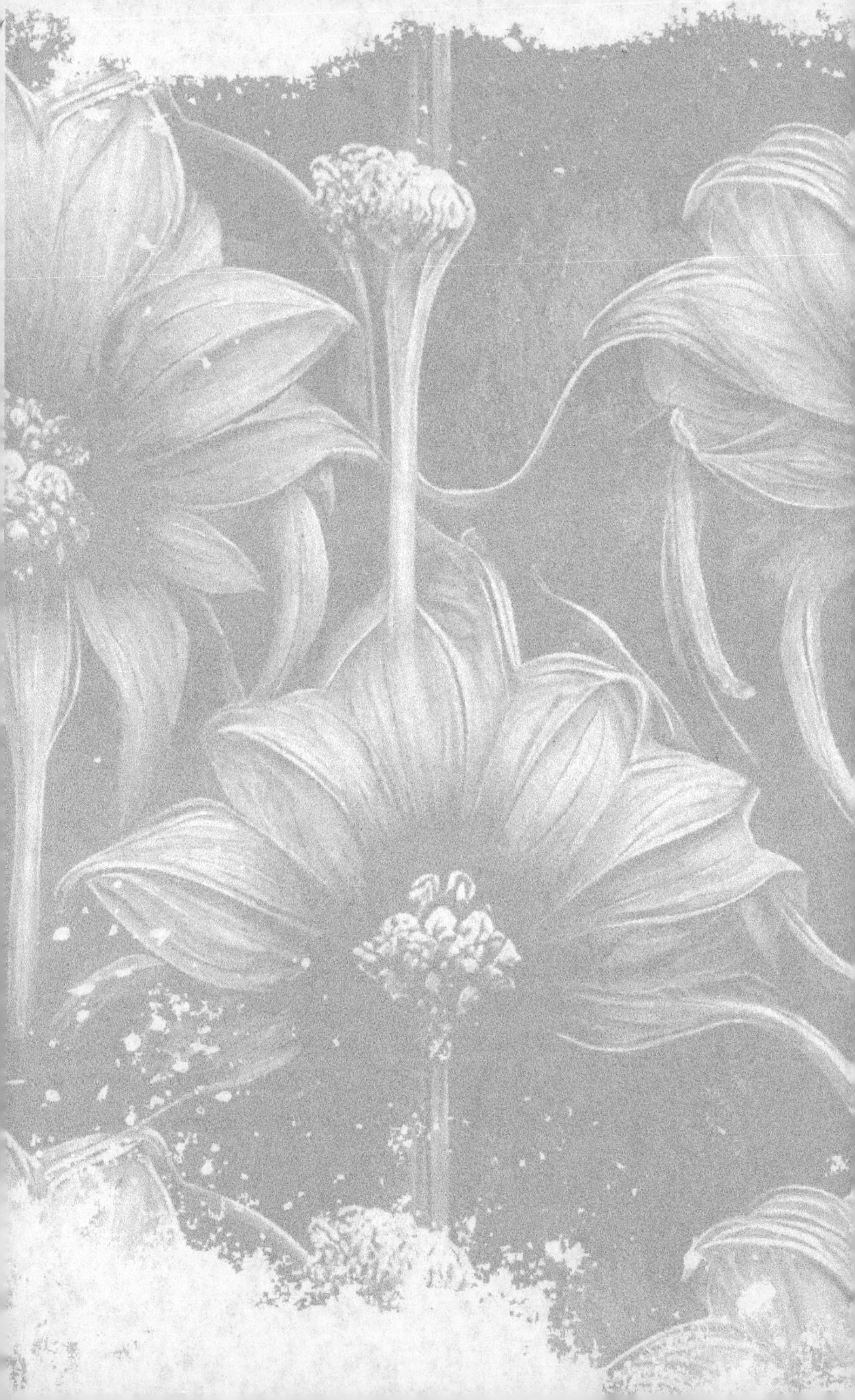

CHAPTER TWENTY-THREE

LY THI REN
2:53PM

We've stumbled into calmer and warmer weather, but Sophie is far from calm. Her breaths come fast as she clings to a particularly thick tree trunk. She's bent over and trembling.

I can't blame her. That was yet another close call with her stalker. And death is never easy. Especially violent death.

I rub circles on her back as she focuses on her breathing. I'm glad I have her to focus on. Otherwise, Dan's death may have gotten to me as well, bringing up things I don't want to think about. Like knives sinking into warm flesh, hot blood dripping down skin—

I shake myself, forcing my ears to tune into Sophie's words.

"He's dead," Sophie says. "Mr. Berg-Nilsen is dead, and I just stood there. I just watched." She chokes back a sob and sniffs.

I try to speak, but Sophie cuts me off, shaking my hand from her back. "I froze up like I always do. What kind of person does that make me?"

"You were scared. It happens."

She rounds on me, and I see the disgust in her eyes behind the tears. Disgust at herself. Shame. She's really torturing herself over this? I'm glad she *didn't* do anything. If she had and something had happened to her— I shake away the thought. I can't go there. Not ever.

"I was petrified, but that's no excuse," she says, shrugging out of her thick coat and letting it drop. "What use am I if I can't even fight for my own life?"

"You're being too hard on yourself."

Sophie scoffs and takes off, striding angrily through rows of...tombstones? We're in a cemetery, dried leaves crunching under our feet. Trees with dying leaves border the cemetery, some changing color as if it's suddenly autumn. It's a welcome change from a snowstorm and wolves, so I try not to question it. If Sophie notices, she doesn't show it. She continues walking as I try to see an end to the plots. I can't. They seem to go on forever. How many people are buried here? Well, I guess not *people*. *Characters*. Words on a page.

"Do you remember what you said to me at Everling?" she asks over her shoulder. "Right before Dr. Lloyd—or I guess that was Jeremy's friend—called me into his office?"

I don't. "Remind me?"

"You said walking around sheltered and blindfolded was no way to live. That sooner or later, you had to face reality. Well, here I am, Ren. I'm facing reality."

"It's been a while, but I'm pretty sure you're paraphrasing, and I wasn't talking about you. I was talking about our parents."

"Doesn't matter. It's still true. I've been sheltered my entire life and blindfolded to who I really am. But the blindfold is off now. I see what I am. Useless."

"Whoa," I say. Sophie turns to walk forward, but I grab her shoulder and swing her back around. "You are *not* useless."

She opens her mouth to speak when a twig snaps and leaves rustle from behind the mausoleum we've reached. We freeze, and my hand goes to the knife in my pocket.

I don't get a chance to pull it out before the thing dashes around the structure.

"Hercules!" Sophie yells as the cat trots up to her and nudges against her leg.

"I'm so glad you're okay," she says, scooping him into her arms. He nuzzles into her neck and purrs.

I wave a hand at the animal. "Look. You found the demon cat. See? Not useless."

She shoots me a look as she massages Herc's ears, then lowers him to the grass. We continue walking in silence, following Herc, who periodically looks back at us as if making sure we're coming.

After a bit, Sophie points to my head wound. "Who beat you up? You never told me."

Speaking of blindfolds.

To reveal that would be to remove my own, and I'm not entirely ready for that to happen. She's changing the subject, but I let it go for now.

"That is a very long story," I say, removing my jean jacket and draping it over my arm. "Seven months long if I was told the truth about our length of stay."

"*Seven months.*" Sophie shakes her head. "I guess it would have to be that long if Carter's birthday is here already. Seven months wasted when I could've taken him and been putting as much distance as possible between me and him and our parents."

I sigh. "We'll get him back, Soph."

Hercules has stopped leading us. He sits on a mound of fresh earth, striped tail curled around his paws as he blinks up at me.

"What?"

The word barely leaves my lips before the dirt moves beside Herc, and he runs to Sophie.

"Squirt, look there," I say, pointing.

"Still doing that thing with the nicknames, I see." She stops short as the dirt moves once more and shares a look with me.

I can't help it. A pang of excitement hits me.

"What do you think?" I ask. "Zombies? Vampires?"

"Zombies and vampires aren't real." She crosses her arms in front of her. "And why are you smiling?"

I throw my arms out to gesture around us. "Newsflash, buttercup: none of this is real. It's Jeremy and his friend's playground."

Sophie rolls her eyes. "If Jeremy's even alive. Dan might not be a trustworthy source."

A gray finger edges its way to the surface, then another. Soon, a whole hand reaches skyward, and on cue, a crack of thunder and lightning sounds overhead. Sophie flinches.

"It's alive!" I yell as the first drops of rain splash down.

Another hand breaks through the grave, and whoever—or *whatever* is underneath pushes down as if trying to crawl out.

Okay, yes, this is exciting, but I'm not stupid. It's also dangerous.

I drop my jacket, pull my knife free from my pocket, and elbow Sophie in the ribs. "Time to go."

We begin making our way further through the cemetery, following Hercules, but that isn't the only grave moving. Everywhere I look, the earth quakes. Freshly dug dirt and overgrown plots alike. We have a ways to go before we're free of the cemetery, but I finally see the iron gates.

"There!" I break into a jog, and Sophie follows.

"Got another weapon? A weapon would be extremely comforting right now. Maybe that blade in your hand?" Sophie asks as she eyes the weapon's gold hilt.

I roll my left pant leg up to my thigh, uncovering my garter with the penknife.

Sophie's eyes widen. "You had that there the whole time?"

I remove it and hold it out to her, letting my pant leg fall back into place.

She scoffs. "A penknife?"

"You really think I'd give you *my* knife? Best case scenario, you lose it in a zombie's chest cavity. This baby's too pretty for such a fate."

INKED IN BLOOD AND MEMORY

"It's *my knife*! You got it from my fake cabin. Ergo, *mine*."

I scrunch up my nose in fake disgust. "Wow, Vanguard. I never knew you were so *possessive*. Besides, the penknife's so cute!" I wiggle it in the air before she swipes it. "You're welcome."

Sophie rolls her eyes. "You still have trust issues."

"Nope. I just trust myself way more."

Movement to my right catches my attention. "Hold that thought."

I leap over a tombstone, rolling into a somersault to reach our first monster—male-presenting in jeans and a graphic tee. Its right arm hangs by disintegrating sinews, but the rest of him is in good shape for a corpse. Even his eyes, which are piercing blue, are actually kind of nice. A bit of a letdown, really. I was hoping for more gore.

"Hey, gorgeous."

It snarls in response and reaches for me, but thankfully, it's slow-moving. "Not on our first date." I dodge and lodge my knife into its ear canal, and it crumples. "Can you believe that guy? Nothing but hands."

Sophie watches with wide eyes. "So, is this who you are now? A badass warrior? 'Cause you were never a weapons girl. I even had to beg you to go to kickboxing classes with me."

I shrug, wiping my blade on the grass. "I'm still not. It's weird. I can switch between who I am in this world and who I am out there."

"And who are you out there? Have you changed a lot since college?"

Let's see. Roller derby, a growing belief I'm not worth a damn, blended in with a dash of "I think I'm headed straight to hell." Does that count as change?

"Such a personal question. You gotta buy me dinner first." I wink and embed my blade into the zombie's forehead over my shoulder. I don't even look at it as it thuds to the ground. That's who I am in here. A take-no-prisoners zombie-killing machine. It's empowering.

Staying here and forgetting the outside world does have its

perks, but it's not an option. I can't let Carter follow Jeremy's path. I won't.

A high-pitched snarl sounds from behind me, and I spin to find Hercules leaping into the face of a zombie I hadn't clocked. He scratches at the corpse's eyes.

"Thanks, hellspawn," I say, eying Hercules warily. I don't like not being in the know. Especially about this cat. I mean, it took on a full-fledged zombie and barely ruffled its fur. I'd hate to be on the receiving end of the furball's fury.

With a final yowl, Hercules jumps from the corpse, and I finish it off before rounding on another diving for the cat.

Hercules runs off into the trees.

"You're welcome," I call after him.

"Ren," Sophie yells, pointing.

Three more bodies have risen. I stop short at the sight of the middle zombie. What is that body doing here? That body is six feet under in the outside world. She can't be here.

Jade.

As in life, Jade's incredibly long platinum hair is tied in a ponytail. She's still wearing the uniform I'd last seen her in—knee and elbow pads, too. A sick part of me laughs, thinking she'd actually be on her rollerblades. She's not. Instead, she's wearing tennis shoes. Much more sensible for a cemetery.

I make quick work of the other two corpses flanking her. I don't recognize their faces, and it's easy to put them down. A knife to each of the brains. Clean and over with.

But Jade's still standing there, moving slower than I've ever seen her before. Her green eyes are glazed and unfocused. She doesn't recognize me. *She can't recognize me*, I remind myself. *It's not her.*

"Ren?" Sophie's voice pulls me out of my memories.

I tamp everything inside me down. I can't feel this now. Maybe not ever.

She's not real. She's not real.

I aim for her forehead like the other zombies. At the last

second, her dead eyes draw me in, and the knife goes through her cornea instead. Her body goes slack. She's dead weight on my knife. But I'm still staring into her eyes, knowing they won't ever light up again. I've seen them look like this before, and that image shoots through my mind.

I shake myself and pull the knife out, one hand on her shoulder for leverage. I guide her body to the ground, and of course, Sophie notices the care I take.

She steps forward and places a hand on my shoulder. "Who was she?" she asks.

I swipe my knife on the grass once more to clean it, refusing to meet her eyes. "Doesn't matter much now, does it?"

Sophie still watches me closely. "I saw the way you looked at her. You knew her, didn't you?"

"Just drop it, okay?" I hate that my voice is rising. I hate that I don't know why Jade is here. Or *how*. Most of all, I hate the past she brought with her. This is supposed to be Sophie's story. Not mine. Why are *my* ghosts haunting me?

I sigh as we continue along the path and force myself to be gentler. It's not Sophie's fault, so why am I snapping at her? "I'm sorry, flower. I don't want to talk about it right now."

Sophie looks around her, and I wonder if she's looking for Hercules or more zombies. Possibly both. "Then, tell me *something*," she says. "Like why we stopped talking to each other the summer before college. What was that about anyway? You never explained it to me."

I squeeze my eyes shut, tilting my head upward and shaking it. "It was so stupid. I don't even want to tell you."

"Oh, now you *have* to tell me," Sophie says through her laughter.

I sigh. "Do you remember Zach Barrett?"

"Zach, as in your ex-boyfriend, Zach?"

"Yeah."

"Yes, I remember him. Why?"

"He dated me for three months before I found out he was only dating me to get closer to you."

Sophie hits me playfully. "He was not."

"It's the truth."

Sophie opens her mouth to reply only to be interrupted by a zombie scrabbling for her ankle. I prepare to put it down as Sophie shrieks. Before I can, she flicks open the penknife I gave her and drives it through the corpse's glazed eye with a sick *squish*. Pus oozes from the eye, but the body isn't dead. The penknife didn't reach its brain.

"You have to—"

With a *pop* and a grunt of effort, Sophie removes the knife and plunges it into the zombie's rotting ear and out again. The zombie drops to the ground, still halfway in its grave.

I turn my mouth down and nod appreciatively as she flings brain matter off the flimsy knife.

"Eww, so gross!" she says, shaking as if her skin is crawling. It's pretty cute.

"There's hope for you yet, Fun-Size," I say as she catches up to me, and we continue our walk.

"So that was all that was? Jealousy brought on by Zach's betrayal?"

I shake my head. "Only partly. The other part was me distancing myself from our shared family values. I didn't want anything to do with that world anymore, and stopping contact with you seemed like the only thing to do."

She's not mentioning the last time we saw each other. Before Everling, I mean. Do I want her to? I'm not sure.

"Is that still how you feel?"

I take my time answering. Around the time we graduated, I thought it was the only option. A clean break from my past. But to be honest, I've missed Sophie. Growing up, she was my only confidante, especially after the Jeremy incident. If anything, we became even closer after that. She was the only part that made high school bearable. Cutting her out of my life felt like amputating a limb.

Sophie's waiting patiently for an answer, and I finally say, "It was one of the biggest regrets of my life."

She stares at me as if waiting for me to laugh it off. Make a joke of it. I don't. Instead, I say, "So, what about you? Where were you before Everling?"

Sophie's staring down at the corpse she just put down. "Doesn't matter much now, does it?"

I shrug. "Humor me?" I check around us for straggling zombies but only see a couple in the distance.

"I fell in with a group of investigators. You know, the kind who look at cold cases and see if they can solve them? This girl I knew from college, Mindy, was a part of the team and remembered that I'd helped her with something our senior year." Ren looks at me to elaborate, but I shake my head. "Long story. Anyway, Mindy knew her team needed to consider the supernatural in their cases, so she brought me in."

"How did they take that?"

"They were as skeptical as you can get, but since then, they've seen some things."

"Like what?"

Sophie doesn't respond, and when I turn to her, she's facing away from me, toward the tree line. The brain matter still drips from her tiny knife.

"Sophie?" I call at the same time someone else does. I know that voice.

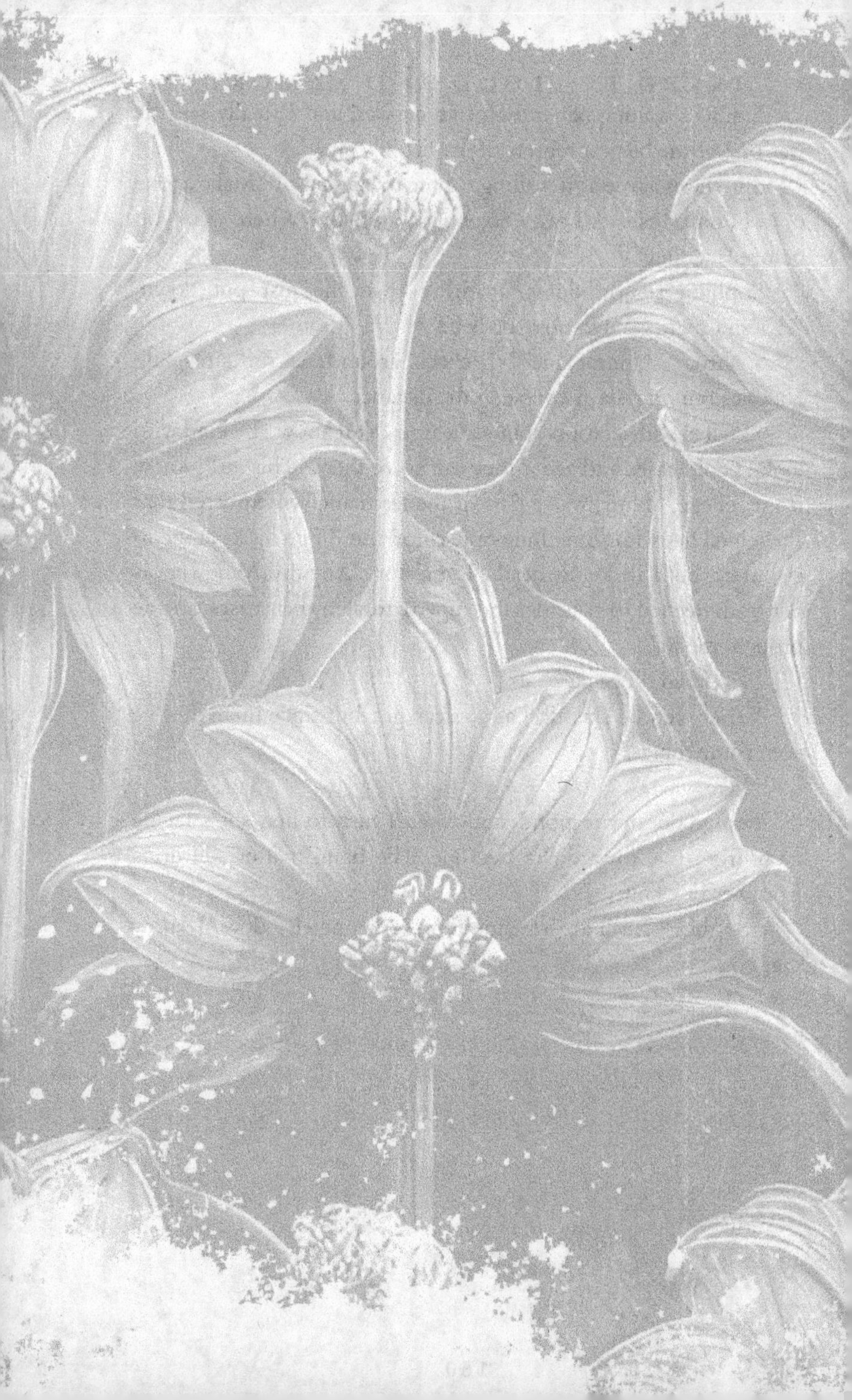

CHAPTER TWENTY-FOUR
SOPHIE VANGUARD
FIVE YEARS AGO

I don't see the point. You throw birthday parties for people you care about. People you love. Not for people you're raising to sacrifice. Although, who knows? Maybe "The Great One" will be generous and let Carter live for longer than Jeremy had. Maybe he'll even be able to go to college.

The first birthday in a sacrifice's life is the most important. It's the day the families crowd around the book and wait for the demon to announce how many years he'll let the sacrifice live before taking him. In true Vanguard fashion, we've dressed it up as a New Year's Eve masquerade party for the locals. If only they knew the real purpose.

I take my exit off of the turnpike and switch the radio off. My mind is noisy enough. I don't need the latest true crime episode crowding my thoughts.

What if it's tonight? What if, after the party, the demon decides to take Carter right then and there?

The thought sends a chill up my spine that travels down my arms and into my hands, shaking the steering wheel. Before it can get any worse, I pull over and put my flashers on. I rest my forehead on the wheel, forcing myself to take deep breaths until my racing heart slows.

I can't do this. I can't lose it yet.

Don't worry until it actually happens, a voice in my head whispers.

Easier said than done.

I pass at least a dozen cars parked on the sides of my parents' long driveway before the sight of Ren's red convertible halfway down pulls me up short. I didn't think she'd be here. She'd gone to college three thousand miles away from here to get away from all of this.

Why is she back?

The illogical side of me wants to believe she's here for me, but I push away the notion. She probably left something behind and came to pick it up. I haven't heard from her since she left for school four months ago.

By the time I find a parking spot, my anxiety has hit its peak, and I have to sit there for a minute to steady myself. I check the clock before switching off the car. It reads 10:09pm.

Less than three hours.

The New Year's party started at seven, but I refuse to be around my parents for longer than I have to. As soon as the clock hits 12:02am—a minute after Carter's birth and directly after the demon's announcement—I'm gone.

Inside, various Haglen Brook royalty mingle, most holding champagne flutes. I spot the mayor and her wife deep in conversation with my dad, who waves when he sees me. I smile and nod and walk the other way. The mayor's family is just like ours, or they aspire to be. There have been rumors of their tendency for the black arts ever since I was in elementary school. I'm sure Dad is giving them pointers on brokering their own deal, and I want no part of that.

INKED IN BLOOD AND MEMORY

As it turns out, going left brings me straight to my mom, who holds Carter. "Mother."

Her ostentatious blue mask is slightly askew, like Carter has been playing with it. She's matching it with a deep blue sequined dress that ends in a fishtail. Her long black hair is up in its usual high ponytail. I shake off my surprise at seeing Carter in my mother's arms and not with an au pair. Of course, she's holding him around everyone. Have to keep up appearances.

"Sophie, I'm so glad you're here," Mom says, exasperated. "Viola's taking a break." Ah, scratch that. Not keeping up appearances tonight. "You can take Carter. He's getting fussy." She hands him to me and immediately falls into conversation with one of the catering staff.

"Good to see you, too," I mutter, holding Carter against my hip. "Hey, bud. Remember me? Your absentee older sister?"

Carter babbles, but he's smiling. I'll take the small victory.

"You two have the same nose," someone says over my shoulder.

I freeze. I'd know that voice anywhere.

Sure enough, Ren leans against the doorway to the dining room, arms crossed. Her short black hair is slicked back, and she wears a mask that reminds me of a swan. Her eyeshadow underneath is winged and smoky, and her short white dress somehow goes perfectly with her black knee-high combat boots. She looks breathtaking.

And here's me with a simple sleeveless, high-neck emerald dress with a slit up the side of one leg. I couldn't find a great mask, so I went even simpler—plain black felt that I hold up on a stick. Glasses and masks do not go together. I have most of my box braids down with some tied behind my head.

"Hey, I saw your car out front," I say. "You drove all the way here?"

"No, I left my car here when I went to college. I flew in and picked up my car at my parents'."

"Oh." That makes a lot more sense. I shuffle my feet. The black stilettos with straps halfway up my calves were a bad choice. They're already pinching my toes. "Are they here?"

"Yeah, I think they're upstairs with Dan and Caroline."

I nod, and Carter waves to Ren, who smiles.

"So, how've you been?" we say at exactly the same time. We smile. Not awkward at all.

What's wrong with me?

It didn't used to be like this. It used to be as easy as breathing. Less than one year apart, and here we are.

Thankfully, Carter is the center of attention. Countless people stop me to chat and say hi to my little brother, some wishing him a happy birthday and me a happy new year. By the time I look back up, Ren has disappeared. Her absence is simultaneously a relief and a reason for panic. Part of me wants to talk to her and figure out what's going on. Maybe she wants to leave all of Haglen Brook behind, myself included. I honestly wouldn't blame her, but I want to hear it from her.

I find her an hour later by the punch bowl.

"Why do rich people like masquerades so much?" Ren says, sipping from her glass. "The Holloways had one last Halloween, and the Coopers two years before that."

"Remember the Knight wedding?"

Ren and I love a good themed wedding—even a masquerade wedding if done well—but the Knight masquerade wedding was something to remember. And for all the wrong reasons. Neon bridesmaid dresses with matching groomsmen ties and everyone wearing masks wouldn't have been too bad, but mix it with heavy drinking and a lake? Half the wedding party was soaked before the ceremony even began.

Ren bursts into giggles. "I forgot about that! Wow, that was forever ago."

I smile, choking back my own laughter. "A lifetime." I wait a beat, stealing a glance at her and chewing my lip. "Can we talk?"

Ren's eyes sparkle at the question. Or maybe that's just my

wishful thinking. She nods and downs the rest of her drink while I spot Carter's current au pair, Viola, coming out of the bathroom.

She flashes me a radiant smile. Viola has the brightest teeth I've ever seen, and all are perfectly straight. Her black curls rest at shoulder length as usual, and today, she's chosen a purple shade for her lips. "Sophie, it's so good to see you! How are you, darling?" She embraces me, and I'm caught up in her lavender perfume.

Though Viola is a good two decades older than me, she's always treated me as an equal. We bonded on her very first day ten months ago when I caught her reading one of those Whodunnit books—the kind with dozens of short stories that let you figure out the answers to the mysteries yourself.

As we separate, Carter reaches for Viola and squeals. "Guess he misses you already," I say, passing him to her. "I'm hanging in there. How are you doing surrounded by Vanguards 24/7? Oh, and how's Elizabeth?"

Viola rolls her eyes, but she's smiling. "Do not get me started on that child. Lizzie's being Lizzie. Driving her mother up a wall."

"Uh-oh. New boyfriend?"

"New boyfriend with a *motorcycle*, and she's added *four* new piercings since you last saw her. I swear my mother's laughing in her grave. She always used to say I'd end up having a daughter just as spirited as I was. Turns out she's worse."

I chuckle. "Sounds like all is right in the world. Tell her I said hi, okay?"

"Of course."

Ren catches my eye and gestures with her head to the door leading to the rooftop before pushing it open with her back and disappearing.

"Take care of yourself, Vi," I say with a hand on her back. I kiss Carter on the top of his head. "See you in a little bit, baby bro."

The rooftop garden is a relic from the days my grandfather was alive. He passed when I was in kindergarten, and the only thing I really remember about him is his love for this space. Neither of my parents is much for the outdoors, but they have the gardener keep it alive in his memory.

Had he lived longer, I don't think my grandfather and I would've gotten along. From what my mom says about him, she seems to be a chip off the ol' block. Despite who he was in life, I couldn't help but agree with his taste in hideaways. I'd always find myself retreating here when I needed to be alone, the frequency of visits increasing as I grew older and more jaded about the Vanguard legacy.

The garden itself uses the only level portion of the roof available—a tiny twelve-by-twelve area. The rest of the roof curves and slopes or comes to points in sharp spires. In the center of the garden, Ren sits at a worn picnic table, a joint in her hand. Plants line the perimeter, many towering over us or climbing up the walls. The only light besides the moon comes from a few string lights I installed myself during my freshman year of high school.

I take a deep breath of the rosemary-scented air—now tinged with weed—before sitting next to Ren on top of the table. The wood is freezing, and I stuff my hands between my legs to spare them a bit of discomfort. Already, I'm shaking. Though that may be from the nerves. I'm acutely aware of how close my leg is to Ren's. I could easily touch hers with mine, but I don't.

I'm not sure how we got here or where we stand now that we're both so far away from each other. Everything has changed.

"That's a great dress," Ren says.

I look down. "Really? Thanks. Yours is pretty. I like the feathers on the skirt."

"Thanks. It's reused from Halloween. Don't tell anyone." She smooths her gelled hair.

"I won't. So... Berkley, huh? How is it?" I want to cringe. *Why does my voice sound so stiff?*

Ren blows out a big breath, sending a white puff into the air along with the smoke. She coughs. "So different. In a good way, though. There's so much creative energy everywhere you go. Oh, I'm writing a musical."

She passes me the joint, and I hit it and cough more than she did. It's been a while since I've smoked. My eyes water as I raise an eyebrow. "Yeah?"

She nods and takes another puff but manages to stifle her cough this time as she passes it back. "Not an original. It's an adaptation of *The Grudge* and one of my friends—Audrey—is writing the music. We should be able to get the drama club to perform it without worrying about copyright issues. We're not going to charge anything for tickets."

"That's so great! I'd love to come see it when it's ready."

Ren smiles. "I'd like that."

We sit in near silence as we try to discern what song is currently playing downstairs. Blink 182 comes to mind, but I'm sure my mother wouldn't have them on her playlist.

Ren touches my hand, and electricity shoots through me. "Sophie—"

"Yeah?" I say too eagerly.

Her hand leaves mine as she takes the joint back.

I laugh awkwardly. "Oh, right. Sorry."

"How's everything with you?"

"Good!" *Wow. My voice is way too high. Tone it down, Sophie.* "I'm good," I say at a lower decibel. "Not incredibly sure what I want to do with my life, but…"

"You have time," Ren says, waving a hand. "It's only freshman year. No one knows what they want to do."

"*You* do," I point out. "You're writing a *musical*. And you'll get some fancy writing gig after college. I know it."

Ren offers me the last puff, but I decline. She finishes it and stamps it out, then says, "I'm a freak of nature. We've already established this."

I giggle and bump my shoulder into hers. "You're definitely one of a kind."

Ren scratches at an imperfection in the wood between us. Something has shifted in the last minute. I'm not sure what comes over me, but I place a hand over hers. "I've missed you."

She crinkles her nose. "I've missed you, too, *heo*."

I scoff. I haven't heard that nickname since we were in middle school when I would eat every piece of chocolate I saw. I had a pretty much constant sugar high. "I thought we retired that one! I am *not* a pig."

I move to take my hand back, but she holds it in both of hers. "You're the cutest pig, love," Ren says with a laugh. Even though I've always been heavier than her, she's never commented on my weight. And her nickname isn't really about it, either.

My cheeks feel like they're on fire. Without warning, Ren kisses one of them. It's a light peck, but it surprises me. The only other time she kissed my cheek was the night Carter was born.

Now, she doesn't completely pull back. Her fingers tighten around my hand. My breath catches. She still smells like cinnamon. I've missed that scent.

"Ren, what—"

She moves closer once more, our noses practically touching.

She pulls away. "Sophie, I wanted to tell you…"

"Yes?" My heartbeat is in my ears. I close my eyes. The four months we were apart means nothing. They've never happened, as far as I'm concerned.

Light reaches my closed eyelids, and I open them to see Ren has pulled away to her original position.

"I need to go."

"What?" I snap pin straight. *Did she just say she needs to go? What did I do? Is it my breath?*

Ren jumps off the table and backs away as she speaks. "I just remembered I left Audrey alone with our foster dog, and I forgot to grab her medicine. She's allergic to dog fur and—"

I know a desperate excuse when I hear one—I'm the *queen* of dodging social events—and this takes the cake. "And you have to go right this second?"

INKED IN BLOOD AND MEMORY

Another step back. "I promised I'd have it there for her when she got home, and we have this good thing going, and I don't wanna jeopardize it—"

Oh, so Audrey and Ren are a thing? Then, why did she— I stop myself from that train of thought. It's only making me angry. "I get it. You don't have to elaborate."

Her face falls. "That's not what I—"

"Save it, Ren. It's almost midnight anyway. I need to find everyone and see how many years Carter will get to live. Enjoy the fireworks on your way off the grounds." My voice cracks at the last word. *Dammit. I was doing so well.*

I let the door to the garden slam behind me and hurry down the stairs before I completely lose it.

Back inside, I shut myself in one of the bathrooms away from the party, avoiding everyone until it's five minutes to midnight. I emerge not a second earlier and slowly make my way downstairs.

My mom descends on me the second my feet hit the bottom of the stairs. "Sophie, there you are. We've been looking everywhere for you." She drags me into one of the backrooms where the Berg-Nilsens and Lys are already gathered around the book on its pedestal. Candles line the wall behind it, the only lights in the room. They all wear their purple cloaks, hoods up so their faces are in shadow.

I look around for Ren, counting the people here, but she's nowhere to be found. *I'm so stupid. Why did I have to make it weird? And to storm off in a huff like I'm still in high school? Real mature, Sophie.*

My father places Mom's cloak around her and moves to help me into mine, but I wave him off.

"Cloaks are traditional, Sophie," he says.

I give in. It's not worth it. I pull the cloak tight, running my fingers over the velvet.

"Have you seen Ren?" Lien asks. She holds Carter, who has his own mini cloak.

My cheeks heat at the mere thought of our conversation on the roof. "Not since earlier."

Outside the door comes a muffled "3, 2, 1…Happy New Year!"

"It's time," Mom says, approaching the book and launching into a string of archaic words. "Oh Great One, we call on you this night of our humble sacrifice's birth. Please share with us your guidance. How old will your next sacrifice be at the time of his taking?"

I'm grinding my teeth, but I can't help it.

With a *whoosh* of impossible wind, all the candles are snuffed out. The room has no windows, and there isn't a draft. The next sound in the silent room is of pages turning.

I flick the light on. To hell with traditional candles. I need to see how many years I have.

The book has turned to page six. Red ink encircles the number.

The floor drops out from underneath me. Jeremy was only ten when he was sacrificed. And now, Carter won't even reach that age. My vision blurs with tears as Mom thanks the "Great One." It sickens me.

The walls are closing in on me. I can't breathe. I rip my cloak off and let it fall along with my stupid mask, backing away until my back hits the door. I fumble with the doorknob and finally fling the door open.

Someone stands there, but they're a blob, thanks to my tears. They turn before I can wipe my eyes, and when I do, I recognize Ren's back. "Ren?"

She rounds the corner to the foyer, and I take off after her. "Ren, wait!"

But she's too fast, and a couple partygoers stop me to wish me a happy new year. By the time I reach the driveway, it's too late. Ren's in her car and speeding off into the night, leaving me shivering in the winter air.

INKED IN BLOOD AND MEMORY

Deep in the east wing of my parents' manor, the chalk circle is drawn, and the candles are lit. I kneel in front of the book, which is open on the floor. Everyone has left, and the house is eerily quiet. My parents think I've left, but I snuck back inside while they were distracted. Throughout the past year, this idea has slowly taken shape.

I read the ancient-sounding words from the book before finishing with: "I beseech you, oh Great One, to hear my words. Fill this room with your magnificent presence." The words pain me, but I'd rather not be flayed alive tonight. That won't help Carter.

"You *'beseech'* me?" a voice booms. "That's a great word. Though I get the sense you don't truly mean the rest." In a burst of fog black as coal, the Great One springs from the pages. At first, he's a towering, formless cloud with glowing yellow eyes. But as I watch, he slowly gathers himself and meets the ground, an ever-moving humanoid storm cloud not much taller than myself. "Do us both a favor and drop the act, Sophie Vanguard. Otherwise, you insult my intelligence."

I eye the chalk circle. He's contained and standing on the book's pages, unable to cross the border for now.

I clear my throat and drop the humility in my voice. "I want to know if there's a way to save my brother."

The demon's clouds pulse with yellow veins, the smoke of his body darkening. "The deal has already been struck. A beloved soul in exchange for endless riches and power. Your parents want to enter politics. Do you really want to mess things up for them? For all three families? Then, Jeremy's death would be in vain, no?"

So Jeremy *is* dead. Somehow, hearing that out loud breaks open a fresh wound. I push my grief down. I have a deal to broker. "I'm not here to renege on a past deal; I'm here to offer an alternative soul."

The demon's embers for eyes burn brighter as if intrigued by the idea. "'An alternative soul'? I may consider sparing Carter Vanguard if the price is the only other soul that matters to you."

I was fully prepared for this, and I won't hesitate. I'll give myself over to the demon so Carter can have the hope of a normal life someday—after he gets out from the crushing Vanguard responsibilities. I've left a letter to Ren in my mailbox that will go out tomorrow morning. In it, I ask her to tell Carter the full truth unclouded by the three families' perspectives.

But the name the demon says is not my own. "Bring me the soul of Ly Thi Ren."

My stomach drops. That is not what I'd been expecting. "No, not Ren. You can have my soul. Please. Just spare Carter."

The "Great One" *tut-tuts* and wags a smoky finger at me. "That would be too easy. You know deals have to have some *heft*. Some heavy sacrifice. A splash of tears. Otherwise, where's the fun?"

I may not be on the best of terms with Ren, but I would never sacrifice her.

"My answer is no," I say with a gulp.

Does this make me a terrible sister? What other chance does Carter have?

It's as if the demon can read my mind. He sucks his teeth. "Choosing a friend over your own flesh and blood, Sophie? Shame, shame."

My hands shake. "You have your answer, Great One."

The demon straightens, his wispy hands clasped behind his back. "The deal still stands if you change your mind."

"I won't," I say.

"Everyone says that at first. You won't be any different, Sophie—"

The demon dissipates as I snap the book closed and cut him off, leaving my name to echo around the room.

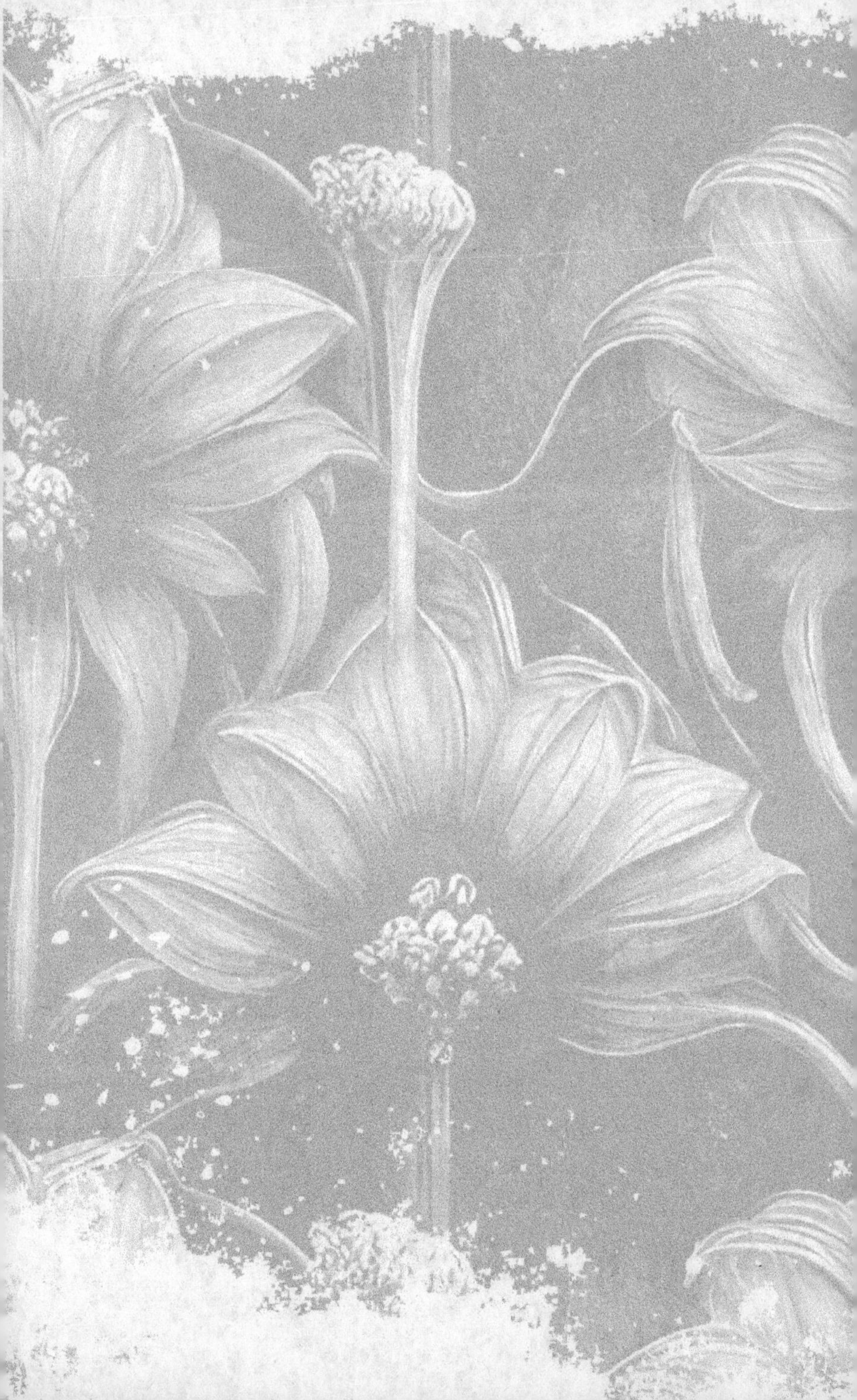

CHAPTER TWENTY-FIVE

SOPHIE VANGUARD

The trees are whispering my name. As soon as I think it, I almost laugh at myself. Trees don't speak. It has to be *him*. That whisper on the wind. Dan's murderer. My attic squatter. Mason.

"*Sophie,*" he repeats, his voice dancing on the breeze.

"Was that—?" Ren asks, and part of me is relieved she can hear the voice, too.

I haven't completely lost it yet. I squeeze the penknife tight. "He's found me."

Without another word, I take off in the other direction, through the gravestones on the right and away from the path.

"Sophie, wait!" Ren calls.

I can't stop. If I stop, I'll freeze up again. And someone will get hurt. *Ren* may get hurt.

"*Sophie...*"

His voice is everywhere. It's invading my thoughts. No matter how fast I run, I can't escape him. I crash through trees and underbrush, ignoring the pain as they tear at my flesh.

I have to keep going. Lead him away from Ren. I know she'll

be killed just as mercilessly as Dan if she's found with me. Mason's after *me*. Not anyone else.

Something tugs me down, and my first thought is a hand is encircling my ankle. I fall hard and kick out to free myself, but it's only a bush. I can't stop. I have to keep going.

"*Sophie.*"

"No!" I get to my feet, but a hand grabs at my arm. I try to shake them off, but they hold on.

"Sophie."

It takes me a second to realize the voice isn't a man's. It's Ren. She holds my shoulders firmly so I can't free myself no matter how hard I try. "Let me go! He's coming! He can't find you!"

She grips me tighter. "I'm not going anywhere."

Slowly, my breathing evens out, and my eyes dart around the trees while I listen for anything that isn't normal woodsy sounds.

Ren touches my cheek, forcing my eyes to hers. "Hey, I'm right here. Just focus on me. Listen to my voice. You're safe."

"*Sophie.*"

I look in every direction, sweating and panting, and there, right in front of us, is my house in its perpetual blizzard. There's an apparent—if invisible—line where the fallen leaves of autumn stop and the fallen snow begins.

The dirt path through the forest ends abruptly at my front step. This is the house we left behind hours ago. The house with *him* inside. Do I dare go inside again?

"*Sophie.*" That rasp snaps me out of my daze and into motion. It came from behind us. I'm sure of it. I practically drag Ren up the steps of the house and through the door, slamming it behind us.

"Isn't this your house?" Ren says. "How are we back here? We can't've gone in a circle. I'm an excellent navigator."

"Sophie, let me in!" Mason screams desperately, pounding on the door.

I jump and yelp.

He pounds so hard and incessantly on the door it whines against the hinges, bowing cartoonishly. The penknife slips from my sweaty palm, and I snatch it up a split second after it hits the floor.

"That door's not going to stop him," I whisper, shaking uncontrollably now. Dan's lifeless eyes glistening in the firelight flash through my mind. I'm next.

I'm next, and all I can do is wait. I fly to the living room, and Ren follows me.

The pounding grows louder, and I swear it moves out on both sides until the sound surrounds us. Every wall in the room shakes with the impact. Paintings and other various wall décor waver before crashing down in sprays of glass. Books fall from their shelves, landing with *thud*s at our feet.

All I can think is this is my fault. We're going to die, and it's my fault Ren is here. I asked her to help me save Carter all those months ago. She was safely away from all this in California, and I pulled her back in. I'm ashamed of myself. I was too weak to save myself from Everling, and I'm too weak now.

Ren grabs my arm. "Go to the back."

"What are you going to do?" I ask.

Ren shoves me hard. "Just go to the back and out the door. I'll meet you in the yard."

I hesitate a second longer before heading for the kitchen, taking one final look at Ren as she faces the door.

If anyone can handle herself against an obsessed stalker, it's Ren.

I've seen her handle a cemetery full of *zombies*. This would be nothing for her. I'm out the door as a *crash* reaches me from the foyer.

The back door doesn't lead me to the porch. I'm in a long hallway, the same style as my house. The hardwood floor stretches out in front of me, and two white doors wait at the end of it.

As soon as the door closes behind me, all noise ceases. It's as if I've just entered one of those soundproof booths where people record audio. There's no evidence of the chaos I've escaped. No Ren. No threatening, faceless man. Just my footsteps and heartbeat to keep me company.

What am I doing?

I can't leave Ren back there with Mason. I have to go back. I try to turn the knob, but it doesn't move. My heart skips, and I try it again, even putting a foot against the wood as if that will make a difference. But the door may as well be made from solid steel because it's not budging.

"Ren!"

I pound and pound, but it's no use. I'm locked out and no help to Ren. I rest my forehead against the door. Yet again, I was a coward. I shouldn't be surprised at this point.

With nowhere else to go, I turn around and move toward the doors.

As I walk, I drag my hands along the sides of the midnight blue walls. The hall is narrow enough for me to be able to brush my fingertips along both sides as I walk down the middle. The corridor seems normal enough, but it's never been here before. I'm on edge with every step. It's too quiet. And not the kind of quiet I usually relish. The kind that's comfortable, a welcome companion while I pore over a cold case. This kind feels dangerous. Like I'm not alone.

What have I just walked into?

A part of me wants to break out in a sprint until I reach the doors, but what's behind them? I've got a 50/50 chance of choosing wrong, and maybe the consequence of that is losing my life.

I hope Ren's okay.

The door behind me creaks open and shut, and before I can turn to look, Ren is in front of me. I breathe a sigh of relief, one hand on my racing heart. "I'm so glad to see you."

She's not dead. Not hurt, as far as I can see. As gorgeous as ever, eyes wide with adrenaline and cheeks flushed.

She beams at me. A rare but comforting sight. "Did I scare

you?"

"A little," I admit. "What happened back there? Are you alright?"

Ren doesn't reply. Instead, she gazes intently at me.

"What is it?" I try to read her but come up empty. Is something wrong? Is there something on my face? Is she mad at me for leaving her? She'd told me to leave her. Maybe I should've tried harder to help her. It was Dan all over again. I hadn't even thought about fighting until I was behind a locked door.

Shame washes over me.

"Sophie," Ren says calmly as she continues to stare at me.

"Yes?"

Her eyes scan my entire body, and I'm suddenly self-conscious. I've never liked people looking at me, and now is no different. It doesn't matter if I've known Ren my entire life. She's never looked at me like this before.

I pull at my hair and adjust my glasses as I wait for her to say something. Why do I care what Ren thinks? I never have before. What is she doing anyway? She's not angry. I can see that now. If anything, she looks curious. Shouldn't we be escaping?

Ren moves toward me, and I back up until I'm against the wall. Her signature scent of cinnamon is absent. In its place is a smoky aroma like the aftermath of a summer bonfire. Strange, but not unpleasant.

Why am I thinking about the way she smells? She's eccentric and infuriating, and there's no way she's even attracted to me like—

Ren pins one of my wrists against the wall under her hand, then the other. The sensation of her fingers on my skin sends a thrill up my spine.

Okay, I'm in trouble. This is not what I would ever expect from Ren, but the way she's looking at me—like she's starving and I'm exactly what she needs—stirs something inside me. A rush of butterflies I didn't know she could trigger in me fly from my stomach to my throat.

Ren's eyes sparkle deviously as the light above the door we

came from flickers out, shrouding half of Ren's face in shadow. And still, she stares at me. Heat hits my cheeks.

"Quit messing around, Ren," I whisper, clearing my throat.

Without warning, Ren licks my neck in one long and swift movement and my heart races. Okay, weird. But why did I actually find that kind of hot? There's that tingle again. Every inch of my body is aware of every one of Ren's movements as she drinks in the sight of me.

"I can't help myself," Ren rasps as the light above us goes out. "I never knew how tasty you are."

Four or five more lights remain on to my right. This isn't the place for this. Whatever *this* is. We should be putting as much distance between us and my stalker as possible. I open my mouth to say so when Ren says, "I want more."

She grins even wider and tightens her grip on both of my wrists.

I wince. "Ow. Ren, that hurts."

"Does it, Sophie?" Ren asks as she squeezes harder, her nails digging into my skin.

Since when does she call me by my actual name? And she's suddenly interested in jumping me in the middle of all this craziness. She's smiling like an animal. Like a wolf in sheep's clothing. The answer is right there, and I feel like an idiot for not seeing it sooner. This isn't Ren. It can't be.

My blood runs cold. But then, who is this? *What* is this?

"You're good enough to eat." Ren digs her nails in deeper, and I can't take it anymore.

"Stop!" I yell at the same moment the rest of the lights go out with an electric *buzz*, and her touch disappears. She's nowhere to be found. Only her scent lingers. I will my vision to adjust to the sudden darkness. I'm too vulnerable.

I feel around frantically for a light switch but come up empty. I hug the wall, grounding myself in its solidity. The only sound is my thudding heart and panicked breaths. I fight the urge to become a whimpering puddle and somehow stay upright.

INKED IN BLOOD AND MEMORY

If that wasn't Ren, then what was it? And where is the real Ren? She could be in trouble or already dead by Mason's knife. And here I am, struggling to stay on my feet.

A waft of putrid air slaps me in the face, and I clap my hands to my nose, coughing. I can't escape the smell. It's a fetid, sickly-sweet scent like rotting meat.

There's something else underneath my panicked thoughts and gagging. A light tapping as if something is dropping. No. *Dripping*. Like it's raining outside, and there's a leak in the roof.

Drip...

Drip. Drip...

Whatever it is, it's right in front of me.

I gather all my courage and reach out a hand before I can talk myself out of it. Something wet falls onto it, and I snatch my hand back, rubbing my fingers together. It's thicker than water. And warm.

The light above the two doors clicks on, illuminating the hallway, and I take the opportunity to inspect what's on my skin.

Blood.

I stagger back with a gasp and flick it away, rubbing it on the wall behind me. Anything to get the stuff *off* of me. But what did it come from? *Who* did it come from? Against everything inside me screaming not to, I look up—

—and regret it immediately.

It's Ren. The *real* Ren. I wouldn't be able to recognize her if it weren't for her clothes—the clothes I gave her. She's pinned to the ceiling, skin hanging in pieces as her blood drips to the floor in rivers now. Her mouth is contorted at an awkward angle. Something has broken her neck, and her arms reach out for me, stiff and twisted like the roots of a tree. Her eyes are empty sockets, the blackest color I've ever seen.

I sink to the floor, unable to take my eyes off of her even as tears cloud my vision. What happened to her? What is wearing her face and speaking in her voice?

The lights blink again before coming back on. When they do,

Ren's body is gone.

The Ren thing now stands at the beginning of the hall, but she doesn't move toward me. She's just standing there, unblinking, holding a box with a red bow on top.

"What do you want?"

Not-Ren moves in stiff, stop-motion movements as she lays the box in front of her, removes the lid, and returns to her original position. From where I sit and in the dim light of the hallway, I can't see what's inside the box.

Slowly, I get to my feet, reminding myself that I can't trust anything. For all I know, Ren could still be alive somewhere. I cling to that hope as a sort of lifeline. Much needed in this corridor, which I'm beginning to see is something's lair. A spider web for me, the fly.

A gray, humanoid arm shoots out of the blackness of the box and lays a hand on the hardwood below. Then a second. Followed by pointed and bony shoulders. As the creature rises, its head cracks one way then the other. And this thing is Ren, too, but not. Her gray skin sags as if decomposing as she rises and takes a cracking step out of the case.

Schlick.

The flesh on half of her face sloughs to the ground, exposing the red muscle tissue underneath, one eye bulging.

She takes a stiff step forward, hands cracking and stretching as she peels the rest of her face off and lets it fall.

And she's tearing at the rest of her skin, growling like a dog shaking its favorite toy, working fast and shedding it from the neck down until she's a pulpy mess of blood and veins and muscular tissue. Her flesh accumulates in a pile next to her.

And through it all, I stand paralyzed, entranced in horror at the whole show. Some part of me wants to be sick, but I can't even be that. I have to keep my eyes on these things.

Not-Ren unleashes an unholy scream, and the second one joins in, stretching their jaws inhumanly. My paralysis breaks.

I tear down the corridor toward the two doors, but it's like I'm not moving as fast as I could. All the while, the Ren creatures *thump thump thump* down the hall after me. But the doors aren't getting any closer.

Thump. Thump. Thump.

And the hall is growing narrower until I'm moving sideways, inching my way through the increasingly small space, desperate to put as much distance between me and the things chasing me as possible.

THUMP. THUMP. THUMP.

Finally, I reach the end and look back to see the creatures not far behind.

I choose the door on the left at the last second, bursting through and slamming it behind me, the monsters' shrieks echoing in my ears.

CHAPTER TWENTY-SIX

LY THI REN
3:32PM

Once Sophie's out the door, the creep makes himself known, breaking through the front door. He's not much taller than I am, and he wears a simple white shirt with dark pants. His dark eyes peek out from under thick eyebrows, and his unkempt black hair hangs in greasy strings. The combination of those features with his milky skin makes me think he's some sort of vampire wannabe. Knowing where this book tends to lead, I wouldn't be surprised if he *was* a vampire. If I had to guess his age, I'd say mid-thirties at the most. Assuming he's only human, he's not much in terms of muscle. Basically skin and bones.

This should be easy.

I remove my knife from my pocket as Mason takes another step forward.

As he scans the room, his face falls. "Where's Sophie?"

"You won't be seeing her again."

He narrows his eyes. "I very much doubt that. You know nothing of our love."

I scoff. "*Love?* Give it up, dude. You're *obsessed* with her."

The man cracks his knuckles.

"No bodyguards this time?" I ask, eyes flicking behind the man to double-check.

He clasps his hands behind his back. "I won't need them."

Big mistake, bro.

I swing first, and he moves back, but not quick enough. A shallow cut appears on his stomach. I smirk and swing again and again. Each time, my blade connects with skin, but they're not deep enough to have much impact. I'd have to swing hundreds more times before making much difference, and by then, I'd wear myself out.

On the next swing, he grabs my wrist and punches me. Pain shoots through me. I knee him between the legs and elbow his nose. While he's incapacitated, I seize the opportunity to stab him in the heart.

It slides in like butter. My mind flashes back to all of the bodies I've dropped with my own hands, and I almost regret my choice.

He's not real, I remind myself. *He's just like William, Paulette, and Adeline.*

Still, everything about this is very lifelike. VR on a radical level. Note to self: never sign up for a slasher VR.

"Guess you should've rethought the bodyguards," I say as he chokes on his own blood. His shirt is more red than white now.

But he doesn't fall to the ground. His eyes don't even glaze over. Because he's not dying.

This *was* too easy.

Confusion trumps fear for the time being as I stare at him with narrowed eyes.

He smiles. And laughs. Even as his blood spurts past his lips. As he wraps his left hand around the hilt of the blade and pulls. And when it's free of his body, he cackles, blood still dripping down his chin.

"What the hell?" I whisper, taking two steps back. Maybe this guy *is* supernatural. I mean, besides the fictional character thing. Still, I don't see any fangs on him. Another zombie?

INKED IN BLOOD AND MEMORY

Mason's grin widens, and he drops the knife. It's his turn.

I move for the knife, but he tackles me, and my back hits the stone floor. I'm dazed as he places his legs on either side of my torso and kneels over me, grabbing my wrists. He grips both firmly in one of his own hands. "Tell me where Sophie is, and I just might let you live."

I feel around with my foot until my heel finds the knife, but I can't kick it my way until I have a hand free. The creep grabs the weapon with his free hand before I can make my move and places it on my throat.

"Have it your way," he says, still grinning, bringing the blade closer to my skin.

It pinches into me as I headbutt him.

I grab the weapon from his loosened grip and push him off me, briefly wondering how much brain damage I'll have after this book ends. A matter for another day. I wipe the knife clean on the back of Mason's pants and tuck it back inside my joggers. It's no use to me, and I'd rather have it out of play than used against me. We get to our feet at the same moment.

I go to kick him, but he catches my foot and backhands me. He actually *backhands* me. Like I'm not even worth a punch. I lose my balance and tip backward. But I'm falling longer than I expected. Instead of hitting the hardwood floor, I pass through an open door and into brightness.

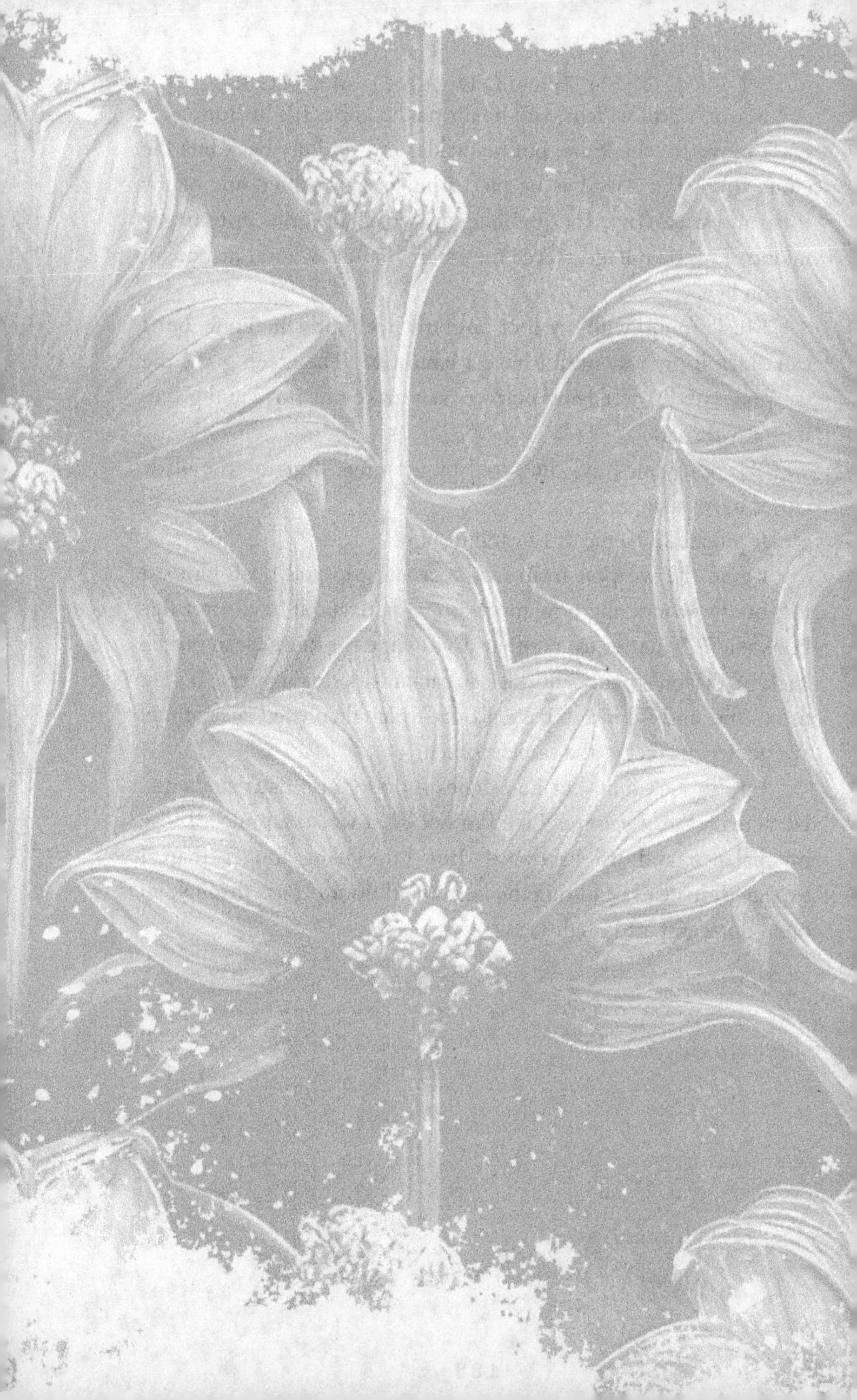

CHAPTER TWENTY-SEVEN

SOPHIE VANGUARD

My feet sink into something soft. Something squishy. Whatever it is, it makes a sucking sound as it molds around me and pulls. My momentum, combined with the abrupt stop, causes me to lose my balance, and I fall backward into the substance, my feet sticking where they landed. Some of it splashes onto my glasses. I don't need to glance down to confirm my fear, and though my first instinct is to panic, I take a deep breath.

I'm trapped in wet quicksand on the shore of what looks like a marsh. Dense, tall trees surround me on all sides. Above and around me, birds chirp and squawk. I thank whoever's listening that it's not dry quicksand I'm dealing with, which can swallow you whole.

Okay, what do I know about getting out of wet quicksand? The gears in my mind whir at lightning speed as I pull out the random quicksand facts I once heard.

Number one: Don't panic, and don't shift your weight any more than you have to. Check. Number two: Find a branch or bar, anything long and solid, to place under your hips to leverage your lower body out of the sand. I'll be out of here in no time. Hopefully.

Scanning the immediate area for anything I can use, I find a long stick within reach of my left hand as a ripple catches my eye from the swamp in front of me. I freeze. A second tiny ripple moves toward me, a fraction closer than the last. Something is moving under the surface of the water. Something big. My first thought is it's an alligator, and I have to work to tamp down my fear again.

I reach for the stick and barely touch it with my middle finger. Painfully slowly, I inch it toward me as I keep one eye on the now still water. Finally, it's close enough for me to grab, and I do, placing it under my hips.

I push as hard as I can until my feet unstick and rocket to the surface. But I've lost my shoes. I'm now floating with my legs and bare feet in the open air when the ripple returns and shoots forward. I grab at the roots around the pit, dragging myself awkwardly until I reach a small ledge of earth. My legs clear the pit, and my feet touch dry grass as the thing in the water reaches me.

It rises without warning, standing on two...feet? I can't tell what it has below the surface of the murky water. The thick mud runs off of it in globs, and yellow eyes blink out from its mud-caked face. Below the mud, dark green scales peek out. The creature hisses, parting its razor-sharp rows of teeth.

Where is Ren? If she's still alive, she'll be too late. I'll be in this thing's stomach in no time. No one's coming to save me. And here I am, hanging practically upside-down with a swamp creature.

I clutch the stick in my right hand, still partially submerged in the quicksand. The creature dives for me, mouth open, and I bring the stick up as it clamps down on it. As it rears back with another hiss and flings my only weapon away, I hoist myself the rest of the way out of the quicksand. When I'm on my feet once more, the creature lunges for me a second time. I dodge its webbed hands and dash along the swamp bank. The creature dives back under the water, swimming faster than I can run, and is blocking my path to the trees in no time. That's when I see its lower half.

INKED IN BLOOD AND MEMORY

Although its markings are covered in mud, I can tell that it, in fact, does not have feet but a tail. It bounces there, the end of it creating ripples in the murky water, staring me down and baring its teeth.

It's the hallway all over again. I'm terrified and completely clueless.

If I die here, Carter is doomed. Ren may be doomed, too. I'll be nothing but words on a page. A life extinguished. Inked in blood and memory to be shelved and forgotten.

That will not be me.

I weigh my options as I frantically pat my pockets for anything that can help me. My hand finds an object in one of them, and I realize I never gave the penknife back to Ren. I try not to think about the corpse gunk that's undoubtedly still all over it and flick the blade out.

Before I can talk myself out of it, I rush the swamp monster, shrieking a battle cry as I do. It holds its ground, using its nictitating membrane as it stares at me. It lashes out with its tail, sweeping my legs out from under me, and I fall backward into the marsh as I cling to the tiny knife with all my might.

It's my one lifeline as my head sinks below the brackish water, which is more like slime. I claw my way back to the surface as it clings to every part of my body, coating my face and threatening to creep into my nose and settle in my lungs.

I'm all too aware that the swamp creature can tug me down and drown me at any point, but it hasn't yet. I've gone from one spiderweb to another, and each time, I've been at the bottom of the food chain. A plaything.

All of this flashes through my mind as adrenaline fills my body, and I break through the thick coating of the swamp and breathe in the glorious oxygen. Miraculously, my glasses have remained on my face, but they're so dirty I can't see a thing. I tug them off and stuff them into the front pocket of my jeans.

I kick forward, hoping I can get a grip on the shore before the creature—

A webbed hand wraps around my ankle.

Any other day, I'd shake it off and chalk it up to seaweed, but this isn't seaweed. The hand has the same slimy feel, but as I kick out with my leg, it tightens and pulls me under. I barely have time to hold my breath before the slime engulfs my head once more.

Despite having no desire to open my eyes in the stagnant goo, I do.

To a pair of yellow eyes staring at me no more than a yard away from my own. My eyesight without my glasses is not great, but it's enough to see the ridge above its eyes lower as if it's daring me to make a move or angry that I even tried to escape. Maybe both.

The gills on its neck twitch as I stare it down. Some old knowledge of animals comes to me, then, and I panic because I'm doing the exact opposite of what I've heard. I'm looking directly into a predatory species' eyes.

Before I can avert my gaze, it lets out a piercing shriek of fury, once again baring its teeth and startling me backward. It slashes its webbed hands at me, and something sticks into my left forearm. Pain shoots up my arm as though a hundred bees have stung me at once. I cry out, releasing a precious gasp of air in a stream of bubbles.

At the same moment, something stops my retreat, pressing at my back, and I realize it's the thing's tail. It's coiling around me, embracing me tighter and tighter.

The creature detaches its palm from my arm, leaving something stuck inside my skin. I don't have time to worry about my arm. I need to worry about my life first.

I'm still submerged and running out of air, but I have my minuscule lifeline clutched in a death grip. I don't give the monster the chance to squeeze any harder. I strike out with the knife, sinking it in and out again and again as the fish thing shrieks at me. It retracts its tail, hisses once more, and swims off into the depths below.

My chest constricts as my heart and lungs scream for air, and I claw for the surface. When I reach it, I don't hesitate to find the shore. I am incredibly out of shape, and my legs and lungs beg for rest, but I keep going, pulling myself out of the marsh painstakingly slowly. A huge part of me still expects to be dragged down again, but the creature doesn't return. Finally out, I collapse in shock at what I've just faced. Am I actually still alive? Who'd have guessed that?

A chuckle bubbles to the surface as I stare at the treetops swaying in the slight breeze. Blurry without my glasses, but beautiful all the same. I'm still alive.

"Sophie!" A distant Ren, the *real* Ren, calls out from somewhere on my right. I haven't heard that tone in her voice before. It's like she's desperate or scared. And Ren scared? I can't compute it, and honestly? It scares me even more than swamp monsters. But I'm armed with a penknife and adrenaline, and right now, I feel pretty damn invincible.

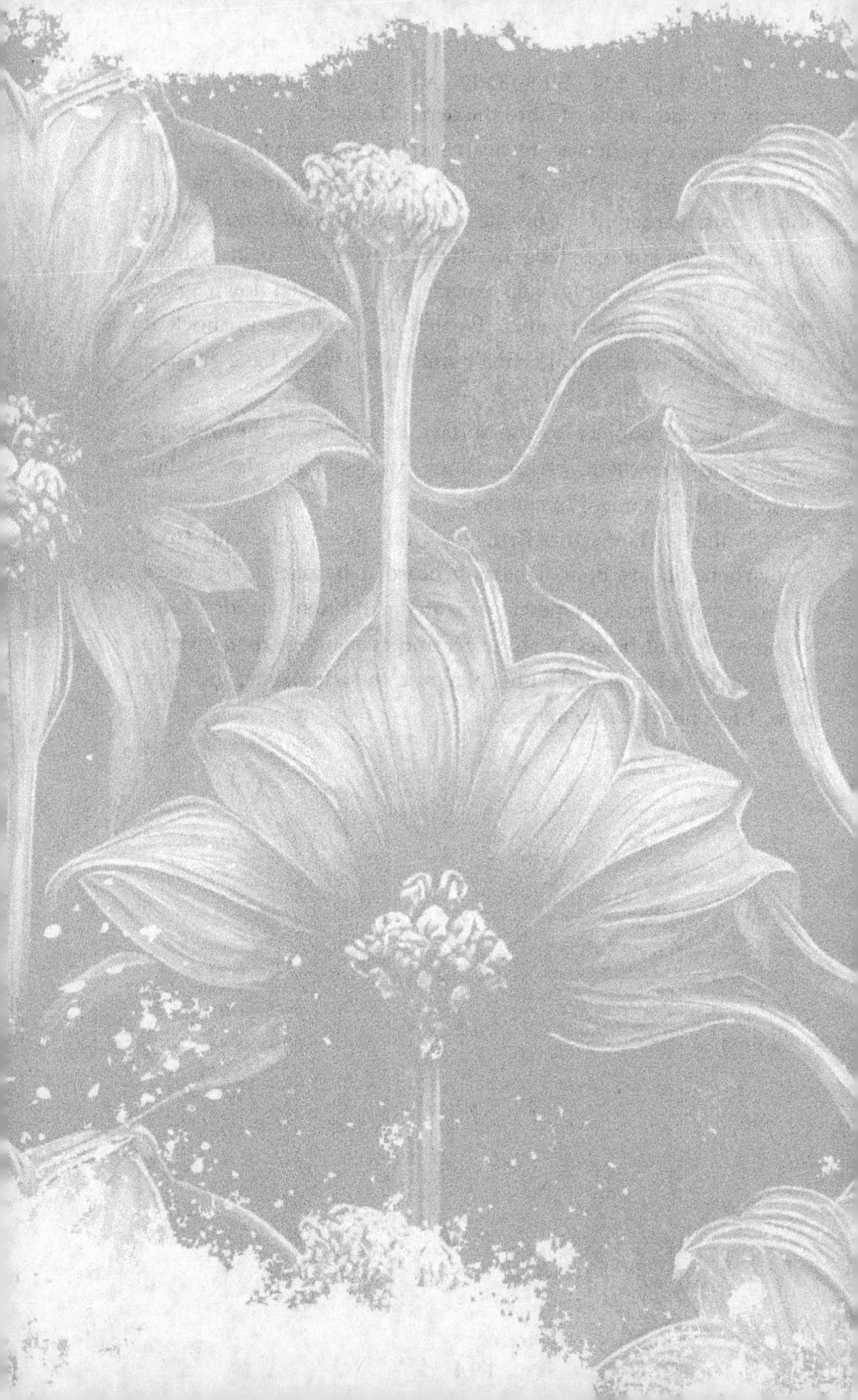

CHAPTER TWENTY-EIGHT

LY THI REN
3:37PM

The cabin door spits me out into a park, not the woods. I land hard on my stomach on the ground below, the wind knocked out of me. I'd had the good sense to protect my face from the fall, but my knees throb with the impact. I take a second to get my bearings as I wonder why I'm not freezing. My hands clutch—

Is this grass? Wasn't it snowing? Am I back in the cemetery?

Cautiously, I get to my feet and look around. Across a great stretch of bright green lawn, families dine in pavilions, and children play on a playground. Sophie is nowhere in sight. I spin in a circle only to find Sophie's rental is also gone. A cloudless blue sky hangs above. The sun—or this version of it—beats down on the park.

Okay, now it's summer?

Behind me, people mill about a town square. There's even a clock tower. A portable speaker on a nearby picnic blanket blasts a cheery Chicago song. Trumpets blare as the song reaches its chorus. Kids laugh, and some run with sparklers. It's smiles all around. A picture-perfect afternoon.

Except five minutes ago, this park wasn't here, and the weather was much colder. Somehow, I miss the wolves.

Something's wrong here. It's too happy.

"Sophie?" I call, but no one answers.

I approach a woman in a sundress serving lemonade. Her blonde hair is pulled tight in a bun on top of her head, and purple frogs dangle from her ears.

"You look a bit shaky, dear," she says with a smile. "Would you like some lemonade?"

What's the phrase? "Don't drink the Kool-Aid?"

Despite the frequent misuse of the phrase, it still runs through my mind.

I don't think taking drinks from random fictional people is a smart thing to do at the moment. At least, not until I know what I'm dealing with. What devious intentions lie behind that smile?

"No, thank you," I say with a polite smile. "What are you celebrating?"

I scan the lawn while she's chattering about her child's birthday, searching for anything odd.

There. A kid's teddy bear swivels its head at me. It's big, the same size as the boy, and its black eyes stare me down menacingly.

Oh, hell no.

I'm not about to be a part of some *Child's Play* reenactment. Although a part of me is thrilled at the concept, logical Ren can't help but butt in. I have a strong suspicion Sophie is rubbing off on me.

I march over to the kid's blanket and snatch the toy away from him. "Come here, Chucky."

I shake it a bunch and finally throw it on the ground, where I stomp and jump on its oversized head. It's only then I notice the kid and the family staring at me with horrified expressions. The kid's eyes well with tears, and shame rushes through me. Did I really just beat up a kid's toy and make that kid cry? Granted, it's a fake kid's toy and a fake kid.

I open my mouth to apologize, but the boy is pointing behind me. At the woods at the edge of the park. At the start of the tree line lays a checkered blanket with a basket in the center. Teddy bears of varying sizes and fur colors skip around it.

You don't see that every day.

I should be running in the opposite direction, but the scene draws me in. I walk closer, not able to help myself, to get a better look at what is inside the basket. Body parts. But not just any body parts. They're stuffed animal limbs and heads, the stuffing and eyes popping out at odd angles.

"This is so splatterpunk," I mutter, smiling to myself in spite of the strangeness. This is more like it. Gore and terror at the expense of no one. Just random stuffed teddies.

That's when the bears stop and turn to me simultaneously. Their glass eyes stare through me. I brush off goosebumps as more stuffed bears crop up behind them. They peek out from behind tree trunks and from under bushes, all looking at me. When I think they've all made their entrances, another one appears. And another.

And then they begin to move. Slowly at first and then faster and faster until they're almost at the picnic blanket. Too many for me to stomp by myself.

"Yeah, no thanks," I say, putting my hands up and backing away slowly.

When the forest bears reach their comrades, they become a toddling stampede of teddy bears, of growls and furrowed brows.

I turn and haul ass.

"Run! They're coming!" I scream.

The oblivious partygoers finally catch on when they see me pass them, but they're too slow. They weren't expecting teddy bear madness. The teddies overtake the families spread out on the blankets, who elicit bloodcurdling screams into the sky. The bear I stomped tackles the kid, but his parents are just as preoccupied with their own bears.

I force my eyes away and focus on the town square. There's

nothing I can do for them, and they're not real anyway. I'll duck into a building and out of view of this freak show. Almost at the pavement...

Bam!

Pain vibrates through my body as I run right into an invisible barrier and bounce right off of it. The force sends me flying backward, not far from a group of bears. The one I beat up narrows his fluffy eyebrows at me.

"Oh, absolutely aces," I groan.

I get to my feet only to be pulled down when a teddy with an intestine necklace rushes my leg and punctures flesh.

I cry out. Those teeth are not felt or plastic. They're real. And sharp.

I kick it off me, but more bears are on me immediately. Their claws rip at my clothes and flesh as their growls and gnashing teeth fill my ears. They pin my arms to the ground, and several more grab my legs. The bears dig into my stomach, and my vision darkens. My strength leaves me. No part of my body is safe. I feel every agonizing second, every movement of the bears. I'm going to die.

This isn't right. I've come all this way, and for what? To be killed in a random chapter of a book? What was the point of all this?

I can't... I don't... I can't string words together... The pain... Please make it stop...

I'm sorry, Sophie.

My eyes close on a bear intent on gouging my eyes.

And then I'm back on the lawn and staring at the pavilions and playground. No teddy bears, no guts, no screams of terror. The same Chicago song plays from a speaker nearby. The very same line. Like the last few minutes never happened.

I clutch at my stomach and find no tears in clothing or flesh. I'm alive.

Tears spring to my eyes, but I choke back my sobs. I can't afford to break down when I have no clue what's happening. For all I know, the bears may still be waiting for me.

I brush myself off and walk over to the woman I talked to last time. The party hostess with the purple frog earrings.

"You look a bit shaky, dear. Would you like some lemonade?" she asks, smiling at me as she pours the lemonade into a red plastic cup.

I'm back where I started. Everything has reset, including the skipping bears. And I have nowhere to run to, thanks to the invisible fence.

"Shit."

This is going to be harder than I thought.

"You look a bit shaky, dear. Would you like some lemonade?"

It's the fifth time she's asked me that. The third time, I threw the drink in her face, and the fourth, I pushed her into the path of the bears to save myself. Both instances got me nowhere. If anything, they only made me feel bad for a fictional person.

I'm not sure how many loops I've had where I didn't approach Lemonade Lady (or Eve, as I found out on loop number three). No matter how I start the loop, the outcome is always the same. Ripped to shreds by rabid teddy bears. The barrier never drops and seems to encircle the entire park.

And the pocket watch never resets. The hands tick on incessantly. I've wasted a good three hours in this park.

Is Sophie going through this, too, somewhere else? Or is she experiencing something worse? I hope not. I hope she's safe, but something tells me she's anything but. I've had some time to think about my confrontation with her stalker, and I think I've finally cracked it.

My futile attack reminded me of how I'd escaped my own prison. Nothing worked until I made a move. It was my book. My battle to fight.

I was an idiot to think I could make much of a difference.

I can't hurt stalker-boy. Only Sophie can. This is *her* book, after all. Not mine. She has to fight her way through it. It's the only outcome the book will accept. And that includes taking on her stalker.

I take my red cup full of lemonade to a nearby table and watch as the teddy bears launch into their gory attack. They rip the picnickers to pieces as I sip my refreshing beverage.

Eve is downed by a white blur of fur speckled with blood. She takes the lemonade bowl with her, and it splashes the white bear, which only angers it more. It tears into poor Eve's neck, enjoying her tendons as if they're a delicacy.

I wince and look away.

Some of the toys give chase as they wield freshly amputated limbs, and two are actually playing catch with a severed head. And there's Hercules ripping the white teddy on Eve away from her and shredding it with his claws.

As I watch, he bats a pocket-sized teddy like it's a ball of yarn. It's the first time I've seen him in a loop.

How the hell did he get here?

The bears have noticed me once more. I didn't want to admit it the first several loops, but I need help.

"Sophie!" I yell desperately into the sky as I drop my head to the wood in front of me. "Help," I add in a pitiful whisper.

I wait for the stampede of stuffed bears to reach me and reset the loop. Peeking out with one eye, head on the table, I see their tiny bodies wobble closer, and I'm about to close my eyes when they stop suddenly and fix their gaze on something in the town square behind me.

That's new.

I raise my head to look behind me, and there's Sophie. She's barreling across the town square, yanking a golf club free of its bag when she reaches the park. Her muddy clothes stick to her body, her hair caked and wild. She looks absolutely feral. Even her glasses are splotchy.

My heart leaps at the sight of her. I was worried about her, and

INKED IN BLOOD AND MEMORY

the sight of her now sends an unexpected smile to my face.

Sophie swings her new weapon at the fluffy terrors as she nears my picnic table.

She's a muddy wrecking ball with glasses. A force of nature as she knocks the bears aside with her golf club, issuing her battle cry as she goes. Stuffing flies all around her, but she doesn't pause. Not until she reaches me.

"You called?" she says, out of breath. Her eyes dance with adrenaline.

I shake my head at her. I'm in awe. She's come a long way from the scared girl in a snowed-in house, and she's never looked more beautiful.

"My hero."

Sophie turns to me, her expression clearly searching for the sarcasm in my voice. She won't find any because I'm serious.

Her search complete, she smiles wide. "I've never been anyone's hero before."

A lump on her left arm catches my eye, and I gently pull it toward me to get a closer look. Something is lodged in it, but I can't make it out. "You're hurt."

Sophie yelps at my touch and pulls away. "I'm fine," she tells my worried expression. Her eyes drift behind me and I turn to see what's caught her attention. Hercules is swatting at more bears.

I turn back to her in time to see a bear with fairy wings flying right at Sophie's head.

"Watch out!" I pull her to the grass in the nick of time, and the bear zooms past us, colliding with a tree.

We slide under the picnic table and take in the chaos around us. Teddies of every size and color run rampant. We won't be safe here for long. They find me wherever I am. Climbing trees doesn't even work.

My hand finds Sophie's, and I thread my fingers through hers. "Ready to run?"

Sophie nods, and we crawl out of our shelter. The summer wind catches pieces of cotton innards and scatters them about. It's the second blizzard we've run through together. This is quickly becoming a habit of ours. We run through the flurry of feral stuffed animals until a team of four bears connected at the hips blocks our way. They stand there, growling, with all the confidence of fully grown grizzly bears. Somehow, I don't think making ourselves look bigger will work.

Sophie swings the golf club at them, but they're faster than the average teddy. The leftmost bear catches the club and pulls, tugging it out of her grip.

Sophie sends me a message with one look. It's a look that says, "Let's get out of here," and we break apart, running around opposite sides of the bears. We join hands when we're clear of them and continue our sprint.

We're circling back to the edge of the park, and before I can tell Sophie she won't be able to exit, we breach the barrier as if it was never there. But so do the bears.

Our feet pound the pavement as we pass normal-looking buildings. We turn a corner and see the tiny brick alcove at the same time. She ducks into it, pulling me with her. The few bears who have followed us run past our hideout, their growls disappearing as they tear down the street.

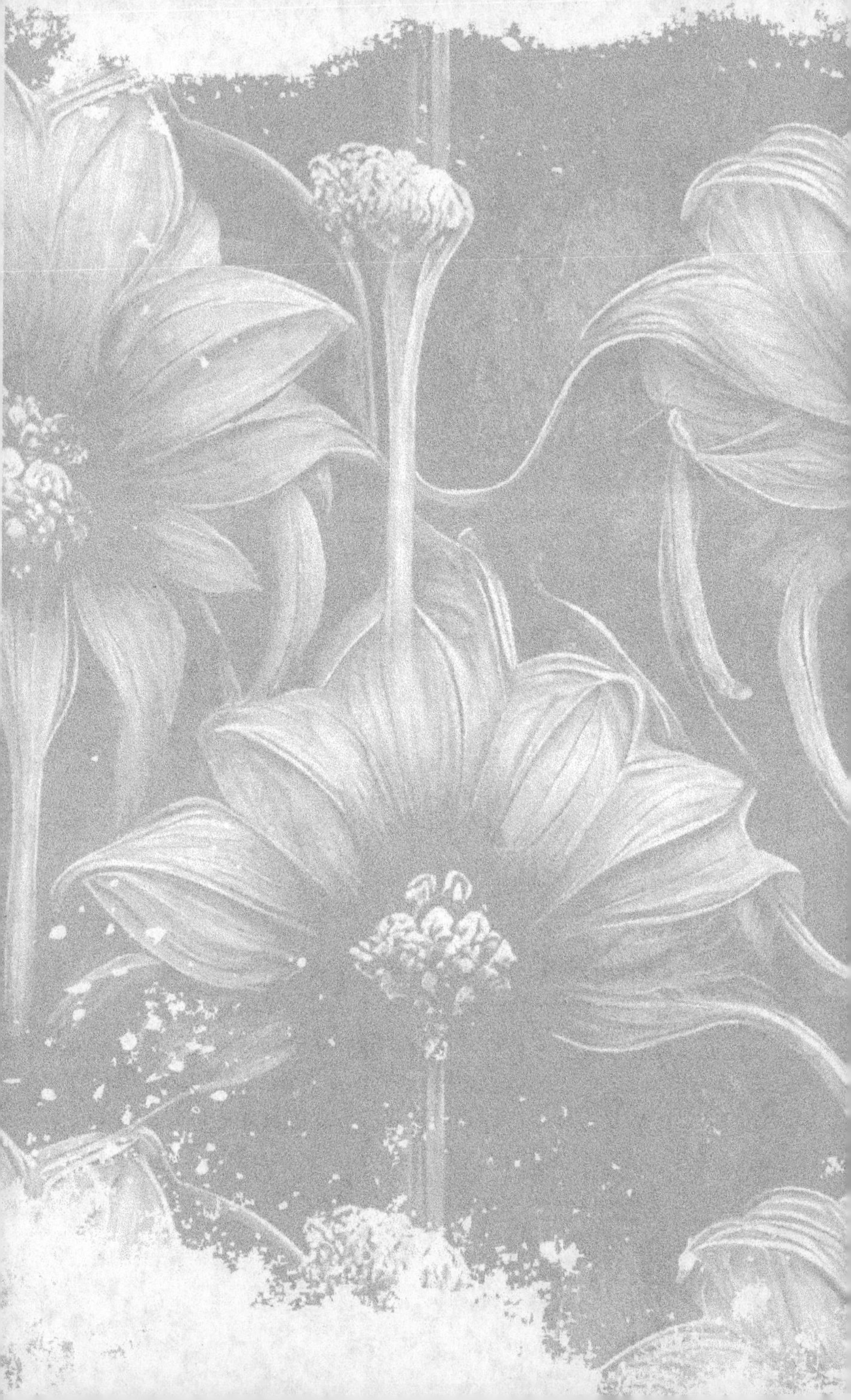

CHAPTER TWENTY-NINE
HERCULES

The humans were in trouble yet again. Well, at least one of them. Not the one he'd been expecting, either. Ren seemed more than capable of killing stuffed animals and breaking a time loop.

Unless...

There was something else to it. Outside forces conspiring against her. To ensure she couldn't break out of the endless picnic. Not on her own, anyway. That must be it. He'd done it again. One step ahead of the humans as usual.

Hercules arrived on the scene not two minutes before Sophie. It was a massacre. Teddy bears ripping each other apart and turning on humans. The scent of blood tinged the air. Pure chaos.

A miniature bear toddled over to him, and he pounced, batting it from paw to paw as if it were a ball of yarn.

Before he knew it, Sophie had found them and pulled Ren toward the park's exit.

A gurgling ahead of him drew his curiosity, and he found the woman almost instantaneously. Her neck bled profusely as a white teddy bear drenched in blood tore into her.

Rage filled Hercules until it spilled out of him in a frenzy. He ripped the bear off of the woman and unleashed on it. Seams ripped, stuffing flew, and still, Hercules clawed. Until rage blinded him, and he'd forgotten his reason for it.

Only when it no longer resembled a bear did he stop and pad back to the woman.

He was too late. There was no saving her, which he found he wanted to do. Curious.

Her blood had slowed since finding her. It wouldn't be long now.

He'd seen her before when he was a different person. A tiny wave of guilt washed over him as he looked down at her.

He waited for her to draw her last breath, watching her eyes glaze over, then followed Sophie and Ren. He turned left, away from where he'd seen them fleeing the stuffed monstrosities, and disappeared down an alleyway.

With a blink, he summoned another exit, and a rift of amber light opened in front of him. He strolled right through, exiting the book. He'd gotten the hang of it since the first few times. Now, it came naturally to him.

Hercules stood up on his newly returned two legs and slicked his blond hair back. Running his opposable thumbs over his clothes (he'd never take them for granted again after this ordeal), Jeremy adjusted his suit jacket and strode away from the book behind him.

CHAPTER THIRTY

SOPHIE VANGUARD

I'm panting heavily when we finally reach the alcove, which is barely big enough to allow three feet in between the both of us.

Did that just happen? Did I just take on a dozen crazed and bloodthirsty teddy bears with a golf club? I never had the knack for golf, but maybe I should look into some batting cages. *Look at that, Dad. I'm not entirely uncoordinated.* And I have to admit: the soft thuds of their tiny, evil bodies had been extremely satisfying. Therapeutic even.

I'm a mixture of pride, shock, fear, and adrenaline by the time I can finally rest. I lay my head back on the rough wall and work on bringing my breathing back to normal. One corner of Ren's mouth curves up in amusement, and annoyance flashes through me and pushes out every other emotion.

She's laughing at me. I know I'm out of shape and a muddy mess on top of that, but does she have to rub it in?

"What?" I ask, an edge to my voice as I toss my long brown hair out of my face and adjust my glasses. And now, Ren's shaking her head and chuckling. Actually *chuckling*.

The nerve of this girl.

I just saved her life. She called out for *me*, and I came to her rescue. And she's laughing at *me*?

I'm wavering between walking away and demanding Ren tells me what's so funny when she plucks a piece of stuffing from my hair, flicks it away, and says, "They should name a hurricane after you."

That...was not what I was expecting to come out of her mouth. A snippy remark paired with a "tiny" seemed a more appropriate response for her. What she'd actually shown was...respect? Awe? Pride? No one has ever looked at me the way she is now. Like I've impressed her.

I've impressed myself, if I'm being completely honest. I've never been the one to come to someone's rescue. Not since third grade, anyway. And there was nothing incredible about saying a couple sentences to some bullies.

I've always been the damsel in distress, so to actually succeed at something like this? This is huge for me. I'm not the girl withering away in Everling, waiting for a hero. I'm not completely helpless. What a revelation.

The look in Ren's eyes sparks a memory in me. I can't help but flash to the not-Ren creature and the way she made me feel when I still thought she was Ren. The way she'd taken my wrists in her hands and pinned them to the wall as her hot breath hit my neck. In that hallway, I'd wanted that eccentric horror lover despite her inability to use my name and general lack of humility. Not to mention our past baggage, which I still don't fully comprehend.

And now, she's looking at me in the exact same way, making my heart skip a beat.

Before the gears of my mind can turn anymore, Ren takes two giant steps toward me and scoops me into her arms. An instant later, Ren's lips find mine, and my heart leaps.

Her hands are entangled in my hair, pressed against the nape of my neck, and I'm too stunned to move. This girl who doesn't trust me to slay zombies without cutting myself but also saved me from my tiny world is now kissing me. The girl I've known since before preschool somehow wants *me*.

Her lips are incredibly soft, and my insecurities rise to the surface despite my best efforts to keep them at bay. I'm pretty sure my lips are cracked, and I'm so out of my element. Kissing my best friend is not something I'd anticipated when I woke up today. The cinnamon scent that seems to follow her everywhere curls around me. It's intoxicating.

Ren breaks away and seems to sense my shock. She bites her lip, drawing my eyes to the spot, and suddenly, I need her like I need oxygen. She's backed up a foot since breaking the kiss, and I pull her back in, deepening the kiss as she presses into me, and I back her into the wall. We're crashing together and riding the waves at the same time, closer than ever to each other and still too far away. I want to show her today wasn't a fluke. That I'm always going to be there for her, that I'm sorry we didn't talk in college. And I want to tell her all of it wordlessly. I want to communicate over twenty years of our friendship and what she means to me. I want her and nothing but her.

A *boom* in the distance jolts me back into our current situation as if waking from a deep sleep. We lock eyes, lingering there, until Ren recovers first and peeks around one of the alcove's corners to inspect the alley. "I think they've gone."

But my eyes are focused on her neck and the way her black hair grazes her shoulders. I sweep her hair away from her skin and kiss it. Ren issues a small gasp as she turns back to me, and I smile and taste her again, biting down gently.

"You came for me," Ren whispers, eyes half-closed.

I bring my lips to meet hers at the same moment my hands slip into her back pockets. "I had to repay the favor," I say between kisses. I think I could kiss her forever.

Pain flashes through my wounded arm as it scrapes the brick, and I pull away, wincing. Twisting it to inspect it more, it seems worse than before. And now that my adrenaline is ebbing, the pain rises. In the park, it seemed like nothing, like a small burn, irritating but manageable.

Now, the wound itches and throbs. Are those veins? Greenish-black lines stretch out from the gash, and something's *moving* under my skin. I don't like that feeling at all. I *hate* bugs, and right now, it feels like an entire colony of ants is inside me.

"Sophie?"

All at once, the pain shoots up my arm and infects the other parts of my body. It's everywhere.

I scream.

And fall into blackness.

CHAPTER THIRTY-ONE
SOPHIE VANGUARD

I awaken slumped over Ren's back. Her shoulder blades dig into my clavicle as she works on something I can't see.

I hiss in pain when my wrist reminds me it's not a happy camper. Ren falls forward in the same instant but catches herself. I straighten as best I can, fighting bouts of dizziness and nausea. Through my cold sweat, I realize she's broken into the building below the clock tower.

"Look who decided to wake up. Could've warned me before fainting like that, girly."

I give her the evil eye as she guides me to a lumpy couch, where I practically fall onto it. I really don't want to look at my arm. I look anyway and almost pass out again as a wave of fire washes over me.

The gash in my forearm has sprouted countless abscesses that wiggle slightly with every movement of my body. Like Jello. I gag. There *is* something under my skin. I want it out. Now.

"We need to chop it off."

My head snaps up, but Ren's smiling, a mischievous twinkle in her eye. "Not funny," I mumble.

She shrugs before kneeling beside me to get a closer look,

gently turning my arm. "They look like—" She stops herself, looking up at me.

"What?" I ask a little too sharply. I have to move my legs. I have to sit up. I have to be anywhere but here. I kick out, swinging my legs to the floor. I groan and rock back and forth. It's like the worst period cramps I've ever experienced all concentrated in my forearm.

Click.

My eyes go wide. "Why did you just open your knife?"

"Shhh."

I wriggle on the couch but don't really have anywhere to go. The room isn't much larger than my old living room, and who knows if the bears are still out there?

"Why haven't you told me what they look like? What aren't you telling me?" I'm hyperventilating, imagining losing my arm.

Ren puts both hands in the air and casts the knife aside when she notices she's still holding it. It spins away on a low table. "Hey, listen. I'm not going to do anything until I explain, but we may not have much time."

A squelching emits from the boil close to my elbow. I hadn't imagined it. Something is *definitely* moving there. As I think it, the boil *pops*, sending a shudder through my bones.

Something slaps my leg on the couch, and I jump a mile away from it. Ren scrambles back on her palms as the thing writhes on the couch. The thing that just *came out of my body*.

It grows as it tosses and turns, screeching, limbs slapping the side of the couch. Its dark green skin reminds me of a slug, but it has arms to accompany its tail. I don't want to believe my eyes as it stops flailing and screams in Ren's face, a mini copy of the swamp thing.

It lunges for Ren's face, but she's already snatched up her knife. In a flash, she slashes it and nails it to the ground. She barely hesitates as she yanks her knife free and runs to me. Two more of my wounds hatch as she reaches me, falling to the ground. Ren stamps them out before they can come after her.

INKED IN BLOOD AND MEMORY

The swamp monster laid eggs inside my arm. *The swamp monster laid eggs inside my arm. How many are in my arm?*

"They're eggs," I state the obvious.

"Congratulations, you're a mommy. I always knew you were." She winks.

"Shut up, Ren. They're eggs. They're eggs. Holy— Aggghh."

They're squirming inside my skin. It seems like dozens of them. It can't be dozens of them. Can it? I can't do dozens. *Please don't be dozens.*

"How many are there?"

I feel like slamming my arm into a wall until I'm numb. This is skin crawling on a whole new level.

Ren's voice is even. "I don't know, but you gotta trust me, gorgeous."

Her knife is dangerously close to my flesh. And she's moving it closer still.

"I need you to stay still. Can you do that?"

Everything in me wants to run far away, but there's no escaping what's inside my body. Maybe she should just cut the whole arm off. Anything to be free of this pain.

Finally, I nod. "Just do it. Whatever you're going to do, do it. I trust you."

"Stay still," she repeats, tightening her free hand around my wrist.

And proceeds to stab my arm several times in quick succession, holding my arm tight with her free hand. I feel like a baked potato, the fluid and blood escaping from me like steam. It takes everything inside of me to stay motionless. I bite my lip, whimpering. Every jab is torture, and after each one, she flicks a tiny body to the ground.

The blows stop as my knees give out, and I drop to the floor. Ren slashes a curtain to shreds and joins me on the ground, wrapping the makeshift gauze around my arm. The wriggling has ended, and with it, some of the pain.

But are they really all out? Are there more in there?

"That was like whack-a-mole. What's my prize?" Ren says, tying off the bandage.

We're surrounded by at least ten swamp baby corpses. They lay in puddles of various fluids. I promptly turn away before I gag again. Those things were *inside* me. My whole body shakes. Even as Ren embraces me, the tremors remain. "You're sure they're all out?"

She nods against my shoulder before pulling back to make eye contact. "I'm sure."

I don't know why I look over Ren's shoulder to the white wall close to the door, but I do. And freeze. Every hair on my body stands on end.

Ren senses the shift immediately. "What's wrong? Is it your arm? Did you feel something?" Her hand grazes my cheek, but I hardly feel it. The wall has completely invaded my thoughts. I rise and move toward it until I can touch the flyers on the bulletin board hanging there. These flyers shouldn't be here. They have no business being here.

Ren's voice reaches me through the flurry of my thoughts. "Why are there flyers for Everling groups here?"

Why, indeed? There's a simple answer to this. Maybe not the happiest reason, but certainly the most likely. There's a bulletin board here because I'm not trapped in a book world created by a sorcerer. I'm trapped in my mind back at the Everling Institute. Of course, I am. These flyers and brochures with smiling, happy people and breathing exercises. I saw them every day in the rec room at the hospital. I've practically memorized every paper here.

"I'm still there. I never left," I finally say, almost to myself, still dazed. *I am such an idiot.*

"What do you mean? Still where?" Ren says from her place on my left.

"The hospital. This board. These flyers. All of them. I saw them every day. I'm still there, and I've finally lost it." I rip the closest one off, and its tack goes flying. I don't stop there. I pull as many as I can see in my now blurred sight. Tears flow rapidly, heating my cheeks and forming a lump in my throat. Through it all, Ren tries to calm me down and get me to stop, but I don't stop until they're all crumpled or shredded at my feet. I don't stop until I've ripped that stupid bulletin board off the wall and thrown it on the ground. Never mind the throbbing in my arm. It doesn't matter.

I rip my glasses from my face, stuff them into my pocket, and wipe furiously at my eyes with my sleeves, which are still stiff with mud. "You're probably not even real," I say to Ren, who blinks at me.

My words snap her out of her voyeurism, and she comes to my side, placing her hands on my shoulders as I slide to the cold floor once more. I'm waiting for the sharp pinch of a needle in one of my arms. I should've felt it by now. The orderlies are really slacking today.

"Sophie, hey," Ren says, trying to get me to meet her eyes. "Sophie, look at me."

I blink back even more tears. Here I was actually working though some of my issues when I find out none of it is real. Not my escape in the hall, not my skills in the swamp or the park, not even Ren. Maybe this is a new form of therapy. Put your subject inside a magical hallucination and let them work it out. If that's it, I've got news: it's not working.

"How could you be real?" I continue. "You're too perfect. You're my lifelong friend who's also a self-reliant monster fighter, drop-dead gorgeous, sarcastic, and intelligent. It's like my mind created you as a coping mechanism. A form of therapy. We've been estranged for years, and suddenly you're back?"

Ren scoffs. "Well, I am extremely flattered, and you're right to think I'm so perfect." She kneels in front of me, moving her hands to my knees as I sniffle. "But I'm not a monster fighter out there, remember? Believe it or not, I'm probably even more fearful than you."

The way Ren dodged my question in the cemetery about who beat her up returns to my mind. She'd been afraid to answer it. Will she ever answer it?

Ren ducks her head, and I wonder how long it's been since she's opened up to someone. If she's even here. "And you called me. Remember? I know we've had a couple bumps, but— I think this book is influencing who we are slightly," she continues. "It explains why your agoraphobia disappeared after you woke up to reality. And why you're still doubting yourself. These things will disappear when we get out of this place. I guarantee it."

I shake my head. I've doubted myself longer than I've been in here. And anyway, this can't be real. Any of it. It's too fantastical. And considering my history... "I've always doubted myself, and this wouldn't be the first time I imagined something."

When Ren casts me a questioning look, I plow on. "I've seen things before. Shadows following me or going after people around me. My family had me committed to Everling who knows how long ago. The shadows didn't make any sense, and no matter the prescription my therapist put me on, they never went away."

"Do you see them now?" Ren asks.

I look around just in case, then shake my head. "No. Whatever the doctors here have me on is working."

Ren squeezes my knees. "You're not in the hospital, chipmunk. I promise you."

I laugh humorlessly. "Of course, you would say that. You're a figment to help me through my trauma. We haven't spoken in years."

"Stop it. Listen to me. I'm really here. I remember those posters, too, when I came for you. Just before that guy trapped us in here. Remember? Our parents put us here so we wouldn't get to Carter in time. They're messing with us. Dr. Lloyd—if that's even his name—is probably laughing at all this pain he's causing, but he's flesh and blood, and he can pay for what he's done to us. But we can't make him pay if we stay here and give up. What reality would you rather believe in, Sophie? One with me by your side and a plan of action, or the one you've made up where I'm a hallucination, and you have no hope at all of ever getting out of here? Where Carter's lost forever?"

INKED IN BLOOD AND MEMORY

I sniffle again as I peer up into Ren's eyes. I turn over everything she's said, thinking as she does. This prison could be influencing our personalities. And let's face it, when has my imagination ever been so vivid? Shadow people, sure, but briefcase monsters and rabid teddy bears?

But I need at least one answer once and for all. "If you're really here, tell me your side of what happened on Carter's first birthday. Why did you disappear again?"

Ren looks down at her lap, where she picks at her nails. She's not going to answer me.

"Forget it. You don't have to—"

"I must've talked myself out of going ten times," she says slowly, as if choosing her words carefully. Maybe they're painful to her and hard to reminisce about, like so many of our shared memories. "Family gatherings have never been my thing. Or yours, I guess. It's why I moved to California. To escape Haglen Brook. To be something other than the daughter of Đài and Lien Ly, the great realtor team, and all that came with that life. If anyone can understand the pressure of a family legacy, it's you, Soph."

I swallow hard. She's right, but where is she going with this? "Ren, what are you saying?"

"For every time I talked myself out of going to that stupid New Year's party, your face made me reconsider. The way I shut you out after high school... It didn't sit right with me. I wanted to see you. To explain, among other things."

I send her a questioning look.

"I went to that party for you, Soph. No one else." My eyes widen, but she continues. "I made up some excuse when we talked on the roof because I was a coward."

"Ly Thi Ren was a coward? I don't believe it."

"It's the truth. Seeing you amplified everything inside me, and it was too much. I don't open up to people, and even though I had in the past with you, that night I—" She runs a hand down her face. "I'd planned on telling you how I felt, but then I chickened out and mentioned Audrey for some reason—"

"Does that mean you *weren't* dating Audrey?"

She abandons her nail picking. "No, we never dated."

"Because you said you two 'had a good thing' and I thought..."

Ren nods and grabs my uninjured arm. "I know what you thought, and I let you think it because it was easier than letting you in."

I'm thrown. Utterly speechless. Of all the things she could've confessed, a declaration of love—even I can read between the lines—is the last thing I'd considered.

"Please say something."

I shake myself. "Right, sorry. I had no idea. I always thought I'd done something wrong or said something to drive you away. For months, I tried to pick apart that night and came up empty."

Ren frowns. "I'm so sorry, Sophie. I never meant for you to blame yourself."

I let the truth of that night sink in, listen to the old building creak around us.

"You have every right to be mad," she continues.

I squeeze her hand. "I understand. I just wish you would've told me."

Hypocrite. I still haven't told her about what happened after she left and I summoned the demon.

"Did you—What would you have said?" Ren asks.

I've never seen her like this. She's usually so sure of herself, but now she looks like a fish out of water. I pull her toward me. Our lips meet and move in sync. I deepen the kiss, and my tongue meets hers until I break away to rest my forehead on hers. "For starters, I would've done that." She releases a breathy laugh, and I continue. "And I would've told you the truth. That I've been waiting for you since before I knew what real love is."

We giggle. We've known each other for ages, and yet, this is uncharted territory. It's about time.

Ren clears her throat before getting to her feet, dusting off her pants, and holding out a hand. I grab it, and she pulls me up. "Have I convinced you I'm real yet?"

INKED IN BLOOD AND MEMORY

"What reality would you rather believe in, Sophie?" This one. Most definitely, this one. I nod, taking her hand. "You've convinced me." I kiss Ren's nose. "Thank you."

Ren bops me lightly on the chin. "Don't mention it." She looks down at my bare feet. "Where'd your shoes go?"

"I lost them in the swamp."

"Swamp? You gotta get me caught up."

"I will. I promise."

"First, take these."

She begins to remove her shoes, but I stop her. "No, Ren. I'm fine.

But Ren won't take no for an answer, and two minutes later, she stands in socks while I wear the shoes I gave her earlier. She peeks through the blinds on a nearby window and gestures for me to join her. "Think that's our next stop?"

I pull my glasses out and return them to my face before following her hand. I can see why she would think it's our next destination. On a hill in the distance, a manor towers, generating its own night and fog. There's even a full moon with a patch of clouds. It's a gothic horror setting, if there ever was one.

I sigh. "Please don't be vampires."

"Ooh, I hope it's vampires." Ren's practically vibrating with giddiness.

"That would be ace."

Ren swats my shoulder. "Now you're getting it! Even got the lingo down!"

"That was sarcasm."

CHAPTER THIRTY-TWO

LY THI REN
6:58PM

On the way here, Sophie told me about her adventure with her swamp monster, and I am insanely jealous. Though, I don't know how I would've dealt with the whole armful of eggs thing. Granted, I got some badass cannibal teddies, but still. "Swamp monsters?" I gasp. "That's ace, Soph. Seriously. And you took them on by *yourself*?"

Sophie tucks a stray curl behind her ear and ducks her head. "It was just the one. I beat it back until I could escape. Once I got out of the quicksand, I just wanted to find you."

"Quicksand!" I turn to stare at her, eyes wide. "Okay, now you're just showing off."

"I haven't even told you about the two yous yet." She giggles and adjusts her glasses.

I smile, enjoying the sound as our feet touch down on the long cobblestone driveway. The iron gates tower over us, open as a monster's mouth. Like someone's expecting us. The archway above reads: BERG-NILSEN.

The driveway's bordering lights extend into the fog, and the manor's spires peek out in the distance.

I hold my hand out to Sophie. "Ready?"

She takes a deep breath as she places her hand in mine. "Ready."

The worst part about the long walk in partial blindness? The silence.

You'd think crickets would be singing, an occasional owl would hoot, or a wolf would howl at the moon. Even a chittering bat. Nope.

It's dead silent.

We're in a vacuum.

Only the *crunch* as our feet hit dead leaves dropped by the trees on either side of the path. I'd never admit it out loud, but I'm glad to have Sophie squeezing my hand. Without her, I think I'd lose my way or turn back.

I can't see anything ahead of me. Any kind of creature could be out there, waiting to strike. We could be walking straight into danger and never know it. I rest my free hand on my knife, just in case.

Our pace gradually increases as if both of us are expecting something to jump out of the fog and attack us.

I consider telling her what I'd figured out while I was trapped in the time loop, but chicken out at the last second. I have to tell her soon. I know that. But it's easier said than done. Fighting Mason had been tougher than I thought it would be, but Sophie is meant to take him down. I know it. I'll hold Mason down for her if I have to.

And I haven't even covered Jade.

Seeing her in the cemetery brought up a lot of things I thought I'd sufficiently tamped down. And stabbing her through the eye like that? I almost shiver just thinking about it.

INKED IN BLOOD AND MEMORY

I'm keeping so much from Sophie, but I'm not brave enough to broach any of it at the moment. I'm using all my energy to deal with the fog.

"You got any plans once all this is over and Carter's saved?" I ask instead, mainly to fill the silence. My voice is surprisingly even. I'm glad.

Sophie shakes her head. "You sound so confident."

"You're not?" I ask, looking over at her. She's picking at her nails with her free hand, pushing her thumbnail under the other fingernails as she stares off into the distance. I squeeze her hand and gently shake it to bring her back.

"The odds are against us in every way," Sophie says.

"Except for one. You love Carter more than our parents love their empire. And besides, it's you and me. We've gotten this far together. We can do anything."

Sophie smiles. "You know what I can't figure out?"

"What's that?"

"Where is Jeremy through all this? I mean, if he's really still alive and behind everything, when did he have time to meet someone like Dr. Lloyd? And we're not in the book our families had since before we were born. We're in something else. So how did that happen?"

"Do you think there are two more demons?" I ask, a pang of fear striking me. One demon is bad enough, but *three*? Talk about terrible odds.

"Maybe."

I grimace. "Wouldn't that be ace?"

"Or he made his own deal."

I hadn't thought of that, but it would make sense. "A deal always has consequences."

"So does magic."

At the end of the driveway, the fog parts as if welcoming us. I stare slack-jawed at the building before us. Ivy vines have overtaken most of the brick, and gargoyles flank the staircase, their claws extended and mouths open wide. It's not the same castle we saw from a distance. The manor must be the same as the one we visited on our play dates with Jeremy, but it seems a lot more menacing than before. It's as if the jig is up, and the house has nothing to hide now. No more pretending.

We're here.

Sophie's glancing bemusedly at me, and when I realize, I close my mouth. "It's my emo teen gothic wet dream," I say as we ascend the steps.

"Is this really the Berg-Nilsen manor? I don't remember it being so big."

"Me neither."

At the top of the stairs, two doors twice our size greet us. On the dark wood is a doorknocker depicting a cat with a mouse hanging by its tail in its jaws.

"Bit on the nose, isn't it?" I say mainly to ease my nerves.

When we push open the enormous doors and step inside, it's as if nothing has changed. I fight the urge to gasp and fail. The foyer is breathtaking. The dark green paint on the walls pairs well with the original wood accents. Two grand staircases on both sides of the room each end with a hallway that branches into two wings. A vintage crystal chandelier hangs above us. It must be as tall as me. Between the two sets of stairs, a hallway stretches and opens into a back room. We head there first.

It's a small music room lined with books on either side. In the far righthand corner sits a baby grand piano. Accordion glass doors stand shrouded in floor-length black curtains, and I brush them aside and peer out into the backyard. My breath fogs the glass as I do, and I rub it with my sleeve to clear it. Instead of the lake I remember from childhood, rows of green peek out of the fog. "Really? A hedge maze? Could it be any more *Shining* here?"

Sophie freezes in her place at the center of the room and raises

INKED IN BLOOD AND MEMORY

a hand. "Shh."

I tilt my head, trying to hear what caught her attention. There. Emanating from the floor above this one. "Are those—?"

Sophie nods. "Voices."

The manor's not empty, but I expected this. We're cutting it dangerously close to Carter's birth minute. Of course, the others are here.

Sophie picks up a lit candelabra, and I follow her up the grand staircase, unsheathing my knife.

As we near the top of the stairs, bits of conversation drift out from the largest room on this level. Straight ahead, the double doors to a sitting room stand ajar, and two well-dressed adults sit on a couch. Má and Ba. It would be a normal scene, except for the transparency of their bodies—like ghosts.

Even closer to the source, the voices are still muffled, like I'm listening from underwater. I'll never get used to it.

"What's wrong with them?" Sophie asks.

"They're not really here."

Sophie has seen something else in the room, and she bolts to it. A couple steps later, I see what caught her attention. Carter is also here. He's in a high-back armchair, swinging his legs and listening to my parents the way only a little kid can get away with—impatiently.

"I've never had a party before," Carter says as Sophie reaches him and I enter the room. Not true, but I guess he wouldn't remember his climactic first birthday party. "You said today's special?"

Ba nods. "That's right, Carter. And so are *you*."

I fight to quell a surge of rage at the familiar words and fail. That's what everyone told Jeremy all those years ago. How "special" he was. What a crock.

Knowing I can't actually affect them, I pick up an overstuffed throw pillow and throw it at Ba, who's sitting nearer to me. It goes right through him and settles inside the outline of Ma's body.

With a blink, the pillow is back in its original position as if it never moved. Because it didn't. Not in the real world.

Carter smiles at the idea of his special day, but then his smile fades. "Will Sophie come?"

Sophie places a hand on Carter's arm, but it passes right through to the chair. "I'm right here, buddy."

"We don't know, honey," Má says.

My anger reaches a crescendo, and I get in her face. "Tell him the truth, Má. Tell him how you don't want him to have another party after tonight. How his sister is the only one in his family looking out for him. How the grownups have failed him and have done nothing but fail him his entire life."

Sophie stands and grabs my hand. "Ren."

"I'm sorry, babes. I'm just—"

"I know how you feel," she says, squeezing my hand.

Of course, she does. Carter's *her* brother.

"We're right here, but we might as well be a thousand miles away. Time check?" she asks, and I oblige.

"7:07."

Má adjusts Carter's headphones so they cover his ears, and he directs his attention to the tablet.

Má drops the patronizing tone in her voice and turns to Ba. "Are you sure about this?"

"You know we have to," Ba says as he weaves his hand into Má's and squeezes. "Don't worry. Ren isn't going to make it."

"Thanks for the vote of confidence, Ba."

"Why isn't Sophie here now?" Carter has pushed his headphones off again. "I miss her."

CHAPTER THIRTY-THREE

LY THI REN
7:10PM

Not long after Carter asked his question, I pulled Sophie out of the room and back down the stairs. In the foyer, she tries to ascend them again, but I stop her.

"What are you doing? Carter needs me," she says.

I hold her arms firmly. "Yes, love. He does need you. But staying up there and letting the clock run out isn't helping him."

Sophie stops struggling then, and I drop my hands, shaking them out. "Geez, squirt. You're tiny, but that was still a workout."

"What's your plan?" she says, fidgeting with the bandage on her arm.

I hesitate, and she misinterprets my silence.

"You do have a plan, right?" Sophie asks, biting her lip. "How did you get out of your own book?"

I'm saved by the front door opening behind us. Two men I've never seen before enter arm in arm and smile at us. No, not *at* us. *Through* us.

A hand plunges through my chest and shakes their outstretched hands.

Sophie squeaks and covers her mouth.

"Tony, Michael, thank you both for coming," the person attached to it says.

I don't feel the impact, and the hand is the same shade of transparency as my parents and Carter. The moment the hand retracts, I back up to where Sophie stands and see him.

The man greeting the two can't be older than thirty, and he wears a tweed jacket. He stands at an imposing height with blond hair, a mustache, a goatee, and brown spectacles. The same man who'd met me on my escape out of my book. "Dr. Lloyd."

Sophie turns to me. "What is he getting out of all this?"

"I'm guessing we're about to find out."

Dr. Lloyd ushers the two men into a room to the left of the foyer, and we follow. We pass through the dining room and into a room with three-story-high ceilings. At the very back, an atrium boasts dozens of overgrown plants spilling onto the tiles. Before that, around twenty people occupy three rows of foldout seats, all facing a podium at the front of the room which is raised slightly on a platform. Like Má, Ba, and Carter upstairs, they are equally ghostly.

Once the men have found seats, Dr. Lloyd moves to the front, addressing the crowd. It takes me a second to train my ears to make the words out. We're still on the wrong side of the conversation.

"As I was saying, I'm talking about your very own muses," the creep says with a smile. "More than that. They create the story for you. No more writer's block."

Sophie looks as focused on listening as I am. "What's he talking about?" she whispers.

I can't take my eyes off the stack of books on the table next to him. My stomach lurches. Dr. Lloyd may be pathetic, but he can still do a lot of damage. "Us."

"Esteemed guests, I know what you're thinking. You're thinking I can't possibly have accomplished something this grandiose. A book that writes itself? Who in their right mind would believe that? But I have proof of the success of this experiment in these pages." He flips the book open to a random page and begins to read. *"Maybe I'm weaker than I thought. Maybe all there is for me is my semi-safe world of books and blue flowers."*

Sophie gasps, and I turn to see her face has drained of color. I know she's fighting the urge to run and hide. It's one thing to know you're in a book, but to hear your innermost feelings laid bare on paper—

He's done the same to me. Forced me into a role I never asked for with Paulette, William, and Adeline.

I ball my fists as a woman in cat-eye spectacles in the third row stands. "What does that prove? You could've written that yourself."

At the podium, Dr. Lloyd finds a page later in the book and smiles.

I run a hand through his smug face as Sophie leans against an archway.

"I can't wait to hear this," I say.

Dr. Lloyd reads from one of the last pages. *"What does that prove? You could've written that yourself."*

He hands the book to the woman responsible for the words, and I peek over her shoulder. There the words are. Like magic, because it is. The blank page on the right fills up even as I stare at it. "Son of a—"

"But how?" the woman says as she hands the book back to the man.

He places the book in the hands of the person beside the woman and stuffs his hands in his pockets. "Ren and Sophie are with us. Right on time, too. They're due for a climax."

The audience passes the book around, whispering to each other and looking everywhere as if to catch a glimpse of a ghost. It's like we're celebrities without the perks.

He addresses the crowd once again. "Let me bring you into the loop, my friends. Sophie Vanguard and Ly Thi Ren are my test subjects. Together, they have braved obstacles that are only possible in the world of literature, becoming new people with different personalities. And when the story's done? They'll be returned to our world. No harm done." Dr. Lloyd takes the book back, and I know why he does. Wouldn't want anyone to know the truth.

I narrow my eyes. *'No harm done?'* Tell that to Sophie's arm. Or to the stalker very much trying to kill us. Or to Dan Berg-Nilsen.

"Hello, girls. I trust it's been an experience," Dr. Lloyd says, clasping his arms behind his back. "You see, you've been a part of my experiment. Can therapy come out of a good book? I expect you've had quite the experience, and I can't wait to ask you about it."

I scoff. "Like we'd help you. 'Quite the experience.' Can you believe this guy?" I ask Sophie, who has regained some color and seems to be as angry as I am. "Don't forget to mention you're working with a demon and a group of devil worshippers, *doctor*."

Dr. Lloyd continues almost gleefully, unaware of my commentary. He's not looking at the book but around the room. "Right about now is when a bomb is dropped in a story. A twist or 'OMG' moment, if you will." He sits at the edge of the raised platform and kicks out his feet, looking very much like a petulant child. "How's this for one, Sophie? The reason Ren doesn't want to tell you how she completed her own story? It's a juicy one. Care to come clean, Ren?"

CHAPTER THIRTY-FOUR

SOPHIE VANGUARD

I shake my head and blink back angry tears. What gives Dr. Lloyd the right to profit off our torment? To play God like this? Has he no shame? I push down my fury for the time being, turning to Ren.

"Is he telling the truth?" I ask, my voice incredibly calm considering the shakiness of my thoughts. "Is there a reason you haven't told me how you escaped?"

Ren sighs, her eyes on the carpet. "I haven't told you because the second I do, you're never going to look at me the same way again. And that would *kill me*, Soph."

I take a deep breath and grab her hand, leading her to two empty chairs in the back row. We sit in silence for a few moments until I can't take it anymore.

"I've been keeping something from you, too, if it helps."

Ren looks up from her lap, eyes shining. "What do you mean?"

There's still time to backtrack. Still time to eat my words and pretend like I never said anything. My hand is still tucked inside hers, and I focus on that as I force myself to continue.

"Before all this, before you came to get me at Everling, I did something I'm not proud of. I was committed for seeing and hearing things. You know that. But what I left out was that I'd let my darkest thoughts consume me in my weeks there. I didn't have proof, but I convinced myself that the things I'd been seeing were conjured by my parents. The timing seemed too perfect. What better way to get me out of the way for the sacrifice than to convince me I'd lost my mind?"

"It does make sense."

"Exactly. Anyway, I got to thinking about what I'd say to my parents if I ever saw them again. What I'd do to them. Stupid, awful scenarios I conjured in my head. I just wanted to confront them and—"

"—kill them?"

A part of me is surprised she made that leap on her own. But Ren always has intuited things, especially about me. Those thoughts seem so long ago now. Another lifetime almost.

"Not for real. It was just my imagination. You know, playing out stories in my mind." I pull at my neck, remembering my headspace from those days. It was not a pretty sight. Sometimes, I'd purposely act up just to be sedated and drift off into thoughtless oblivion for a few hours. My version of survival. "Ren, they were nothing but intrusive thoughts. We all have them. It doesn't make you a bad person. I'm not a murderer."

"I am."

"What?" I must have heard her wrong. Had she even spoken at all?

Ren squeezes my hand and then pulls it out of my grip, hugging herself instead. "You're the kindest person I know, Sophie. Of course, you didn't mean those things, but I'm different than you. I might be more like our parents than I realized."

My mouth runs dry. "You're scaring me." *It's still Ren. She could never be like our parents.*

Ren bites her lip and pushes both sides of her hair behind her ears. After adjusting her position, I see the moment she decides to confess everything. The worry in her eyes is palpable as she looks over at me. It makes me want to stop her before she says anything else, but I hold back.

"The book Dr. Lloyd put me in was a murder mystery set in some discount Jane Austen world," she says.

I nod, remembering the dress she'd had on when she'd first arrived at my cabin. Frilly and restrictive and not at all a dress she'd pick out for herself. Her tastes were more simplistic, more elegant. Like the black floor-length semi-sheer dress she'd worn to our homecoming dance senior year.

"One of the characters in there—Paulette—was attacked by the killer, and my fiancé, William, was killed," Ren continues.

She was engaged? *Not real, Sophie.*

"When I found his body, I woke up and remembered everything. I think that demon cat had something to do with it because he was there. I didn't want to believe what I remembered. After a while, I had to believe it. It was the only way I would ever get out."

"I don't understand. Believe what?"

Ren's face almost crumples. She barely contains her sobs as her lips waver. A few tears escape, and she swallows hard and wipes them away before continuing. "The person Dr. Lloyd made me play in that book was the murderer. *I* had killed William. *I* had attacked Paulette. And—"

I don't know what my face is telling her, but Ren takes one look at it and jumps up, pacing the aisle of chairs. Ren rarely cries, and to see her like this breaks my heart.

"To get out, I came to the only possible conclusion in my mind," she says.

The full picture of Ren as she'd appeared on my doorstep comes back to me. Not just her period dress but the blood spatters and head wound, too. I reach my own conclusion.

"You had to keep killing." I swallow hard, mouth completely cottony now.

Ren faces away from me when she stops pacing. "I chased my best friend, Adeline, into the stables and finished it. She fought me, which, of course, she did. Who wouldn't? And I—"

She breaks down, falling to her knees and still not facing me. For a moment, I watch her back as she tries to calm herself. She'd been through all that before even knocking on my front door?

Maybe it's twisted to instantly forgive her, to acknowledge and push away what she's told me instead of holding it against her. But it comes naturally to me. She's still Ren. And to tell me all of that and hold nothing back, to be that brave, makes me love her even more.

I join her on the floor and gently peel her hands away from her face. Her eyes and nose are red, and a couple of eyelashes stick to the skin underneath her left eye. I gently brush them away.

"You must think I'm a terrible person," Ren says between sobs.

I shake my head and push her hair back. "Ren, you were trapped in that mindset for seven months. You weren't yourself, and those people weren't real. None of it was real. I can't imagine what you had to go through, but you're out now. You won't have to do anything like that ever again."

She sniffs. "How do you know I won't want to?"

"Have you wanted to since you left that world?"

"No."

"Right, because that wasn't you," I say, catching her chin gently before she can break eye contact. "That was who Dr. Lloyd wrote you to be. You did what you had to do to survive. That doesn't make you our parents."

"How can you be so understanding about this?" Ren asks.

"You're forgetting that I'm another victim of Dr. Lloyd's. I know how the line can blur between who you are and who you're written to be."

Dr. Lloyd has finished answering questions from the audience. As Ren collects herself, I throw a nearby candelabra at him, ready to do whatever it takes to wipe that smugness off his face. But it just passes through him and drops to the ground harmlessly. A blink later, it repositions itself on the table.

I help Ren to her feet as Mom and Dad walk in. I freeze. "Why are they here?" It's a stupid question. They're here to sacrifice my little brother, of course. Their immediate appearance is still a surprise for me. I have to stop myself from adjusting my clothes like I'm still seeking approval from them.

"They look pissed," Ren says, sniffling. She's stopped crying, and I'm glad to see it.

I ball my hands into fists as they sit in the row across from me, and I analyze their faces. My mother has always been inscrutable in her expressions and now is no different. Her hair is pulled tight, her jaw and cheekbones as sharp as ever, and her dark lips pursed. My father, however, wears his anger for everyone to see, and he stares daggers at the boy on the raised platform.

Dr. Lloyd spots the two of them and clears his throat. "Esteemed guests, thank you for coming. I will schedule future consultations in a few moments, but these consultations will be booked soon, so it's best to grab them while you can. In the meantime, please enjoy the party. Happy New Year!"

As the audience gathers their belongings, and the first person walks up to him, Dr. Lloyd excuses himself and approaches Mother and Father, who rise to meet him.

"Dr. and Dr. Vanguard," he says, shaking their hands. "It's good to see you."

Not one to beat around the bush, Father says, "Drop the pleasantries, Edmond. Why did you call us down here? We should be preparing for later. It's been seven months, and *now* there's a problem?"

"Is she close to escaping?" my mother adds, a hand over her heart. "It's too soon. We're still five hours out."

It's what I was expecting, but the confirmation is still a gut punch. Seven months. *Seven months* of obliviousness, of days that could've been spent with Carter. Seven months of crippling paranoia and fear and waiting for my life to resume. For what? Maintaining their lifestyle? I reign my rage in enough to listen to the rest of the conversation. I follow "Edmond" as he ushers my parents into the music room.

"Where the hell is Dan?" my father asks. "You said he'd be here for the sacrifice."

When we reach the doorway, Edmond—or Dr. Lloyd or whoever—has dropped his disguise. He looks to be in his twenties, like Ren and me. Dr. Lloyd's shaggy hair, goatee, and glasses are gone, and Edmond sports a cropped, dirty-blond look. He has one of those faces that seems to be permanently pulled into a smirk. The expression on his now smooth face only adds to the obnoxiousness of his posture—too straight and bordering on awkward.

"He will be," he says. "We still have a few hours. Besides, we have a bigger issue."

"And what's that?" Mom asks, practically pinning Edmond where he stands with her icy glare.

Edmond gulps and flips the book—*our* book—open, turning pages while explaining how close I am to completing my "journey." "Hours, in fact."

My mother yanks the book out of Edmond's hands, who tries to grab it back. My father blocks his way, and he's much more formidable than the scrawny man.

Mother turns to the last page of text, which is still filling. "Oh, my God. Roger, she's here with us now."

"That's what I've been trying to say. She's close."

Father hushes him and joins Mother. "Sophie?" she calls. "We're so sorry, honey. But it had to be done. You were scaring us. Threatening the families. Our way of life. You'll understand one day."

"So, I try to save my brother, and you throw me into a horror novel with life-and-death situations?"

My parents, or *Sylvia and Roger*, read my words on the page as I say them.

"What does she mean?" Father says, rounding on Edmond. "You lied about the kind of book you put her in?" He pulls Edmond up by his shirt, and he squirms. A worm on a hook.

"No! You have to believe me, Dr. Vanguard. I didn't think Ren would go in there after your daughter. They were meant to be kept apart. She's to blame for all of this."

"*Ren's* in there with her?" Mother asks. "I thought she was supposed to be in a separate book?"

"She *was*, but she completed her story and escaped. She was out, but she chose to go in there after your daughter. I tried to stop her, but—"

"That doesn't explain why Sophie is being chased by monsters," Father says.

"Yes, it does. Ren's a writer for a horror TV show. Her imagination is sabotaging Sophie's world."

My heart drops.

Ren takes a step back, glancing at me, her eyes wide.

"Ren, did you—"

"Get her to stop," Mother says. "Can't you get her out of there?"

Father tightens his grip on Edmond's shirt. "Why weren't we notified about this sooner? Why didn't you stop Ren? Why is this even possible?"

Edmond puts his hands up. "I thought I had it handled. I put her in an impossible situation, a time loop, but Sophie stepped in."

Mother gestures to Father, and he steps aside so she can get in Edmond's face. "Fix it, now. Get rid of her."

My stomach drops. *Get rid of her?* That doesn't sound good. Ren is family. They've said as much on countless occasions.

Edmond swallows hard as he attempts to straighten his tweed suit. "It will be done, Mrs. Vanguard."

"*Doctor*," Mother says through gritted teeth.

"*Dr.* Vanguard, my apologies," Edmond says, wincing.

The three of them leave the room, and I spin to face Ren, who's dropped onto the piano bench. My question falls away when

I see her face. She's as shocked as I am.

"I didn't know, Sophie. I had no idea I was doing all this. I'm not *trying* to. I don't understand."

I know when Ren is keeping things from me, and this is not one of them. I soften my expression and grab her hand. "I think I do. It's your subconscious feeding this world. Dr. Lloyd—or *Edmond*— must've built that aspect into it when he realized what an uninspired writer he is." I offer a small smile and a squeeze of her hand. "Besides, I was stalked before you even got here."

"But the swamp monsters? The quicksand? Everything else? That was me."

"Hey, none of this is your fault. I saw things before you came for me."

"You did?"

I nod, remembering the shadow creature and the whispers. "You saved me."

"Not yet," she says as I join her on the bench.

I take a deep breath. "Tell me you have a plan to get out of here. I'm so done with this place, Ren."

"That's where your stalker comes in," she begins, dropping my hand and joining both of hers in a triangle and pointing them at me. "It looks like you're our only hope for getting out of this book. You need to kill him."

I am motionless, not sure if I've heard her right. But she's waiting for a response. I rise slowly from the bench, and Ren copies me, watching me closely. I can't think. I can't speak. I'm numb. Everything about that idea is *wrong*.

"I realized it when you were passed out," she continues. "I stabbed the guy in the heart, and he acted like it was a papercut. I couldn't make any impact on him, and it hit me. I'm not the main character in this story. *You* are."

I don't know how to respond to that sentence. I can barely hear her over the pounding of my heart. *I'm* our only hope? And it involves the same man who killed Dan and has terrorized me for months? I refuse to look at Ren as I storm past her onto the back patio that faces the hedge maze.

"Ace, Ren," she mutters as she stands by the piano. "Fantastic way to break the news."

I drop to the cement steps, breathing in the cool fog wafting out from the hedges. The maze's entrance is a black hole, and the more I stare at it, the more unsettled I feel.

Confront Mason? That's an idiotic, half-baked plan. And she doesn't even know it'll work. She's just guessing.

A pair of dirty socks appears at my side. Ren has followed me out, but she doesn't sit yet.

I speak only to break the uneasy silence and to get my mind off the hedges, my breath visible in the night air. "You're insane. You are certifiably, undoubtedly, off your rocker if you think I'd actually face that monster again."

"I get it. You're less than thrilled." Ren bends to place a hand on my shoulder, but I stand before she can and spin to face her.

"No, you *don't* get it, Ren," I say, pausing to stiffen my lip. My legs are wobbling of their own accord, and I hate them. I descend the rest of the steps and pace part of the hedge. "Ever since I got stuck here, I've felt someone watching me. Every minute of every day, it's like I was trapped behind the glass of his personal zoo. Like my purpose was to dance for him, to serve as his sick entertainment. Dr. Lloyd's bad enough, but this...*thing*." My voice cracks, and I pause to swallow the growing lump in my throat. "I can't stare into the eyes of a creature like him. I don't think I'd ever recover."

Ren descends the steps but doesn't try to touch me again. "He's not even real, Soph. He's just another creation of Edmond's."

I stop pacing. "The *trauma* is real. Why can't you understand that? You don't know the fear I experienced on a daily basis that I know I'll feel for a long time, maybe even the rest of my life. You don't know."

I even feel it right now, is what I don't say. I eye the hedge maze entrance once more. I know the feeling of being watched all too well. Ren hasn't picked up on it yet. *He's here, isn't he?*

"You're right," Ren says. "I can't imagine the way you lived for those seven months. But I do know that this book is designed to keep you in it. You specifically. So, it makes perfect sense that the thing keeping you here is your worst fear. Just like with me, my fear was becoming our parents—a killer. If you aren't involved in taking him down, the climax will never happen, and this story we're in will never end."

I wrap my arms around myself. "You can't put that on me."

"I wish I didn't have to, but if you don't, we'll be trapped in here forever, and Carter will be sacrificed. He'll suffer the same fate as Jeremy, but he may not be able to get out like him. And your parents don't seem to like me that much. So we may have less time than we think."

She's right, of course. My parents can be intimidating, but more than that, they can be murderous. What will they do while Ren's parents are preoccupied with Carter?

Is something moving closer to the entrance of the maze? I speak without looking at Ren. I'm unable to tear my eyes away from the hedges. "It's not so bad in here. It was actually pretty cozy back at my house."

Ren scoffs. "With a creep watching you every minute? Sounds real cozy."

I don't reply because I'm not fully listening anymore. I'm squinting my eyes at a movement nearby. A pair of red eyes peer out of the darkness, and a puff of hot air drifts into view. Something scrapes the stones in the same space. Not Mason. It can't be the shadow thing that came with the whispers. That had yellow eyes.

"Sophie? What are you looking at?"

"We need to get back inside," I whisper. At the same time, something steps out of the maze and into the moonlight.

The beast is on all fours—two hind cloven feet and two clawed front hands. It paws at the stones with one back leg.

Goosebumps rise on my arms as my legs become glued to the

spot.

"What the hell is that?" Ren whispers, even though I'm sure she knows. We both had an obsession with Greek mythology as kids.

With a huff, the creature rises to stand on two legs so that it is as tall as the hedges around it. Its nostrils flare as it towers over us, muscles rippling, silhouetted by moonlight.

"My parents' backup plan, I'm guessing," I say.

The minotaur shakes its head like a dog and rolls its shoulders.

With a final scrape of its hoof on the patio stones, it roars and lunges at Ren, darting forward on all fours.

The beast isn't interested in me at all.

The minotaur ignores me, grabs a fistful of Ren's hair, and drags her into the hedges.

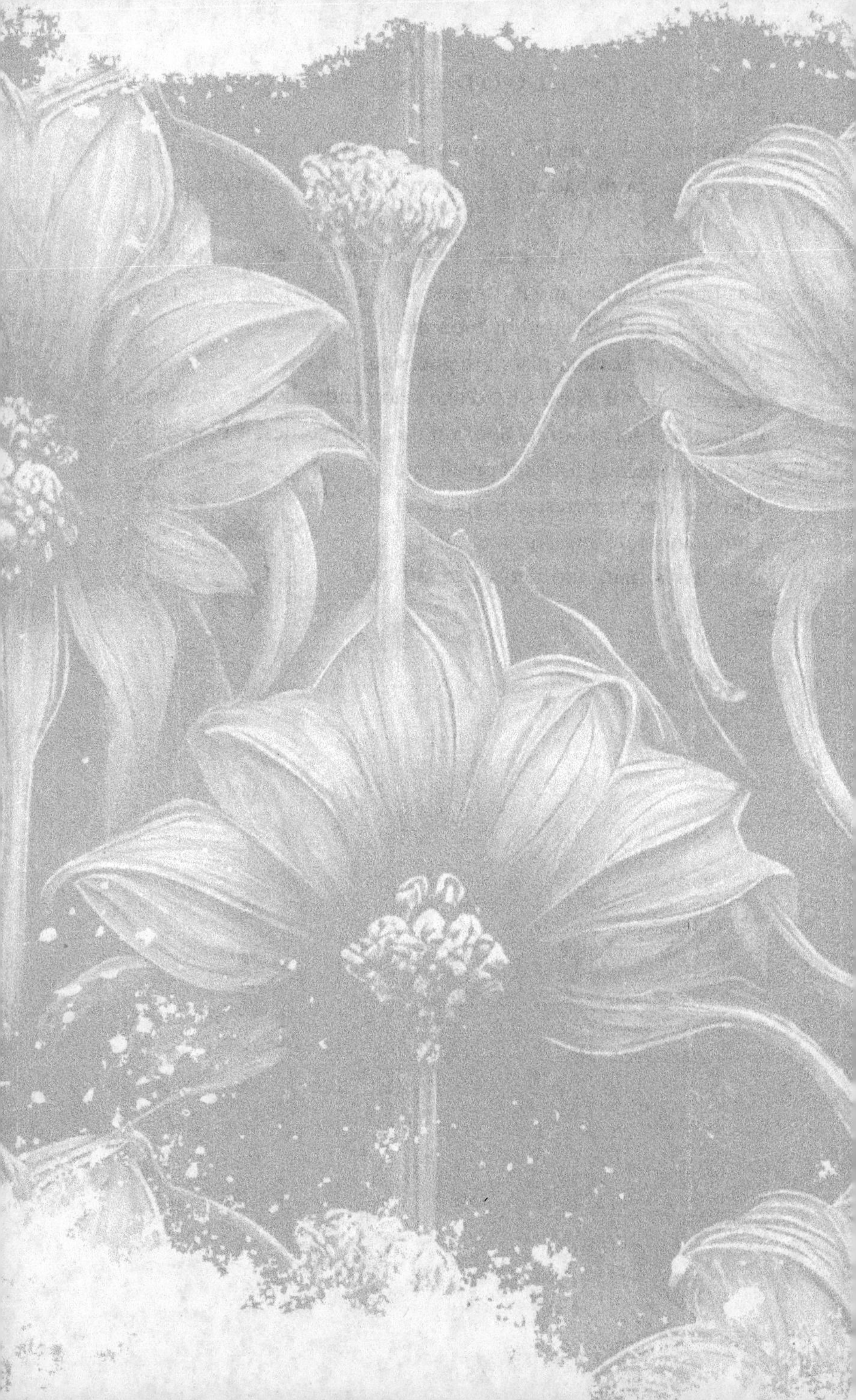

CHAPTER THIRTY-FIVE

LY THI REN
7:43PM

I lose sight of Sophie almost immediately as the minotaur drags me into the hedge maze. My scalp screams where the creature's claws dig in. I scrabble in vain at the stones underneath me and then at the hedges. The branches scrape at every inch of my exposed skin as green leaves flash by.

I dig my nails into the minotaur's hand...paw? But there's no escaping its grip.

It's scaling hedges one-handed, dragging me behind all the way. Feeling each bump, I can barely think straight. The minotaur drops onto a back patio area overlooking a cliff, and I land awkwardly on my back and elbows. That final drop shakes an idea loose.

My knife is within reach in my pocket. I unsheathe it and bury it in the minotaur's forearm, which releases me immediately and unleashes a bellowing roar of pain. I scrabble to my feet and take off in the direction I think will bring me to the exit. Whatever gets me farthest from the monster now chasing me.

The minotaur is on me in no time at all. With a roar, it knocks me to the ground, and I spin to face it as it pounces, pinning my arms under its paws and roaring in my face, spewing steam and spit from its yellow fangs.

Is this how I die? Torn apart by a minotaur in a hedge maze in a book prison? At least it's not a boring death.

The minotaur rears up to sink its teeth into my neck, and I prepare for the worst.

"Hey!" Sophie calls out from behind me.

The minotaur whips to face her with a growl as Sophie flings her penknife at the beast. It sails as if in slow motion.

Spinning.

Spinning.

And thudding hilt-first against the minotaur's pelt, where it slides harmlessly down its dark fur and falls to the pavement.

Damn. I thought she'd had it.

Sophie groans in frustration, but she's given me all I need. I bring my knees up to stop the monster's descent to my neck. My strength is no match for a full-grown minotaur, but it's enough to stall. At the same time, I search for the knife on the ground with my left hand. The minotaur gnashes its teeth at me, dripping saliva onto my face in sticky globs. My legs burn with the effort of keeping it away. They're about to buckle.

I smile in spite of it all. My fingers have found the flimsy penknife, my only hope. I bring it up to meet the minotaur's eye with a *squish*, and it wails as it retreats.

I rise, knees cracking, as Sophie comes to my side. "Are you okay?"

I'm too exhausted to speak at the moment, so I nod, dropping my hands to my knees.

But the minotaur isn't done. It's coming back for more. It flings the knife away, and it skids across the pavement.

"Incoming," I say. Drudging up as much energy as I can, I duck at the last minute and push against the minotaur's legs with all my might. Sophie understands and follows my lead, and the minotaur's momentum sends it tumbling over the railing of the cliff. But not before it gets in a lucky slash.

INKED IN BLOOD AND MEMORY

I cry out as blood seeps from my side.

"Ren!" Sophie yells.

"I'm fine," I say, but Sophie hadn't yelled out of concern for me. She'd been calling for help.

The same claw that drew blood from me hooks onto Sophie's shirt and pulls her over the side. They both fall.

"No!"

I grab Sophie's arm, straining with the sudden weight and the pain in my side.

I'm not strong enough.

I'm losing my grip, and Sophie's blinking up at me with eyes full of fear. Just when I think I'm going to lose her, the minotaur's claw tears clean through Sophie's shirt, and it falls. It lets out a final roar, which fades as it drops into the foggy void. And it's silent once more.

"I got you," I manage, arms aching.

It's agonizingly slow, but we work together until Sophie is back over the railing, and we collapse in a heap, panting.

I clutch my side, wincing. "Our parents are truly evil."

We make our way back to the manor in tense silence, detouring to the outer border of the hedges to shorten our route. It's the way Sophie caught up to the minotaur. Now, she hugs herself the whole way back, and I can practically see the gears of her mind working. Somehow, I'd rather face another minotaur than continue our previous conversation.

A twinge of pain shoots through my side when I step down harder than I'd meant to. I've bound the gash on my side with Sophie's undershirt, but I'm pretty sure it's going to need at least a few stitches. It's my own fault. My imagination conjured up that monster. Maybe this wound is karma.

ALLISON IVY

When we're inside the manor with the doors closed once again, I open my mouth to return to our previous topic of conversation.

That's when Edmond walks in, our book open in his hands. He shuts the doors behind him and sits on the chaise in the corner. "This is so weird," he mutters.

Sophie and I exchange a look. *What is he up to?*

"Sophie? Ren? I know you're there." He looks around the room, but it's like looking for ghosts. He won't find us. "Listen, Bandits, I don't have a lot of time. It's me, Ruby and Sapphire."

A chill runs down my spine.

"Did he just say—"

"Our codenames." Only Jeremy knew them from our games of Haglen Brook Bandits, where we'd pretend to be infamous bank robbers. Dan Berg-Nilsen was right. Jeremy's alive and free. I want to be happy for my friend, but a question nags at me. Why would he be helping our parents—the ones who sacrificed him?

I should've seen my ex-friend under that disguise earlier. "Jeremy."

Jeremy reads my thoughts from the book. "You guys are good. I'm impressed."

I grit my teeth. "Save it. Why are you working with them?"

"I'm not. I—"

The doors fly open, and Roger Vanguard ushers Jeremy into another room. My friend hurriedly closes the book.

"Unbelievable," Sophie mumbles, throwing her hands up.

Laughter bubbles out of me, and Sophie shoots me a look. "Sorry, it's just— I can't believe the person who's trapped us in here is some lanky boy from New England."

She snorts in spite of herself.

It *is* pretty ridiculous. Who would've thought the three of us would end up here? And why? What did we ever do to him?

Who knows how many people this boy has trapped in

nightmares for his sick power complex? How many have died because of it?

"Maybe he's been alive all this time, letting the Great One influence him." Dan Berg-Nilsen's words run through my mind, but even staring at this new Jeremy, I still can't get the old one out of my head.

A part of me wants to follow Jeremy and Roger, but we're running out of time. I know what needs to be done. I just need to convince Sophie of it.

I turn to her, hoping she'll hear me out. "About what I said earlier, I know facing Mason again is the last thing you want to do, but that's what makes it so perfect," I say.

When Sophie doesn't immediately jump down my throat, I plow on. "I couldn't fight that creep when we ran into him before, but you can."

"How am I supposed to fight him if *you* can't? I'm nothing special." Sophie's voice has lost its previous edge, but her words make me step back.

"'Nothing special?'" I say. "Buttercup, there's no doubt in my mind you can do this."

Judging by her expression, Sophie isn't convinced. As my hands move to her cheek, she closes her eyes. A tear drops, and I wipe it away with my thumb.

"I'm not like you," Sophie says. "I'm not some badass, take-no-prisoners kind of girl. I never have been. I can't do this, Ren."

A smile plays on my lips, which doesn't go unnoticed by Sophie when she finally looks back at me.

"Why are you smiling?" she asks, biting her lip.

"You don't think you're strong?"

Sophie looks down. "I know I'm not, so don't lie to me."

I laugh. "You are so infuriatingly oblivious."

"Thanks. You really know how to make a girl feel better." She smirks.

"The girl who stood against psychopathic teddy bears, who just took down a minotaur, who refused to be agoraphobia's bitch, now says she's not a badass." I throw my hands in the air. "Make it make sense."

"Ren, I can't. Please don't make me." Sophie's shoulders heave with effort as she tries to breathe. I run a hand over her back, hoping to quell the oncoming panic attack before it gets worse. "There has to be another way."

"Soph. Hey, look at me."

After a few concentrated breaths, she finally meets my eyes.

I push Sophie's hair behind both her ears, cupping her face with my hands. "You won't be alone in this," I whisper. "I'll be right beside you for all of it. I promise. Just like with those zombies in the cemetery, just like now with the Minotaur."

Sophie seems lost in thought before she speaks again. Her eyes search my face for something. "You could've left me in here. We'd lost touch on the outside. Nobody would've known, and you wouldn't have had to deal with all this. With me."

I drop my hands from her face and gesture around us. "And pass up all this horror and suspense? Never."

"Thank you," Sophie says so low that I barely hear her.

When I shrug, Sophie grabs my hand, and electricity shoots up my arm. "No, seriously. Thank you for coming in after me. You didn't have to."

We're so close, I can smell her strawberry lotion, and I realize just how painfully cute her freckles are. They run under her glasses, across her nose and both cheeks like a real-life Instagram filter.

I brush my lips against her ear, and she shivers. "I'm so glad I did," I say.

Sophie's lips meet mine, soft as pillows, an instant later. And it's the alleyway all over again. I can't resist. I nip them, and she giggles. I smile. I want to make her giggle again.

I kiss her harder, backing her up into a nearby armchair, and she sinks into it as I climb onto her. My knees sink into the cracks where the cushion meets the chair, but I don't care. I twist her hair in my hands, tilting her head up and moving my lips to those delicious freckles.

I never thought we'd be here, but now that we are, it feels right.

INKED IN BLOOD AND MEMORY

Sophie pulls me down, bucking up to meet my hips. I lower myself, and she gasps. I grip her long brown curls with one hand as I run my fingernails down her back and up with the other. She is everywhere and not close enough and s*weet sassafras*.

She's sucking on my ear.

We move as one, hips moving together, our hands moving lower and lower.

It's what we've been moving toward all these years, and I hadn't even known it. This is where I belong. With her. It's where I should've been so long ago before we lost touch. It's right in so many ways; I can't believe I didn't see it before.

Her fingers slip into my pants.

Yes.

My hands work of their own accord, pulling her in for a long, deep kiss as desire floods through me.

The muffled clink of glasses and peals of laughter from the other room reach my ears and bring me out of my daze. Sophie blinks at her surroundings as if she'd forgotten where she was. I know the feeling.

We got carried away, but this isn't the time or place for this. Later.

It takes everything in me to kiss her forehead and stand, smoothing the creases of my shirt with my hands, then offer one to Sophie.

Her cheeks are flushed, but something in her eyes has changed. They sparkle in the dim light of the room. When she takes my outstretched hand, I put my finger on what it is.

Determination.

As my knees wobble, I wonder briefly if Sophie has given her nerves to me or if I'm shaky from what just happened.

"Don't leave me," she says, her voice steady.

My heart flutters. I squeeze her hand and clasp my other hand over the two. "Wouldn't dream of it."

Just like before, the house appears instantly. We step through one doorway and find ourselves at the steps to Sophie's front porch. There's no wind this time, just an eerie quiet. The calm before the storm.

Sophie's house looms over us as if it's playing a game of chicken, expecting us to flinch first. The only light on inside seeps through the bottom of the front door.

Am I right in thinking she's the key? I mean, she has to be, right? What other ending is there? I tamp down any doubt I have. It's not helpful, and Sophie needs me to function at one hundred percent. We don't have time for any other options.

Too soon, Sophie's turning the doorknob, and we're stepping into the house. The heat inside presses down on me, a shocking contradiction to the biting cold outside.

I'd expected to see Sophie's stalker—Mason— standing in front of us, ready to pounce, but the foyer's empty. Nothing but the entry table with its familiar floral centerpiece of gardenias and peonies. Straight ahead, past the short corridor to the kitchen, a light flickers, making shadows dance on the walls.

Sophie and I exchange a look, and I hope with all my heart that I don't look as nervous as I feel. I need to be strong for Sophie. Her face is still set in that determined expression, but I can't tell if it's an act.

"Ready?" I ask quietly.

She closes her eyes for a moment, then nods.

Slowly, we make our way toward the kitchen, the creak of the floor our only companion at first. The sound of a piano joins in and grows louder with each step we take. I stop at a closet, grab the first pair of shoes I see—black combat boots—and slide them over my damp socks.

When we enter the kitchen, a piano is nowhere in sight. Instead, a record player spins away on the counter.

INKED IN BLOOD AND MEMORY

Mason waits for us at the head of the table, standing stiffly with both hands on the chair in front of him. He's taller than I remember, dressed in an all-black suit and tie this time. His black hair is slicked back with so much hair gel I wonder if he's used an entire tube. His beady eyes flick to Sophie, then me, then back to Sophie. Every hair on my arms stands on end.

A bouquet of at least two dozen blue passionflowers sits in the center of the kitchen table. On either side of the centerpiece is a lit candelabra, and the table is set for two. One setting is at the head, and one is to the left of it.

Sophie stills. Whether at the sight of the flowers, or the man, or both, I'm not sure. I touch her hand to bring her out of her panic. I don't miss the glare the man gives me before refocusing on Sophie.

He pulls out a chair, the legs scraping against the hardwood floor a little too loudly. "I've been waiting for you, Sophie."

CHAPTER THIRTY-SIX

SOPHIE VANGUARD

The first thing I see when we enter the kitchen is the bouquet of blue flowers right in the middle of the table. Those flowers have haunted my nightmares, and the horror rushes back the second I see them on the table. Every instance I found a flower where it shouldn't be races through my mind. On the windowsill. On my pillow that morning. And then in the hundreds right outside my door only days ago. Or hours ago? I'm losing track. How many times had I opened my door to them?

Everything inside of me screams to flee, to deal with this monster another day. Another *year* even. I can see myself curling back up in my cottage, watching the snow whirl on the wind as the months pass. But the feel of Ren's hand on mine brings me back to the present.

My future is not the only one at stake. Carter is depending on his big sister to save him, or he would be if he knew he was in danger. Ren is depending on me to get us out of this prison. She *believes* in me. God knows why, but she does.

I can do this.

Mason grips the back of a chair with one hand as the other

dangles by his side. Empty, as far as I can tell. "I must say, I didn't expect you'd bring a friend. It will be awfully difficult to get to know one another with a third wheel, don't you think, Sophie?"

My spine tingles at his pronunciation of my name. He whispers it and almost draws it out as if he relishes every syllable.

I fight to keep my voice level and swallow the growing lump in my throat. "If you want me to stay here with you, she stays, too."

He balls his fist and clenches the chair tighter as a vein pulses in his neck, and I know he's decided not to compromise one bit of his fantasy. He'll lunge at us, an unleashed animal. I can see it in his eyes.

But the moment passes. His hands relax, and his face softens into a smile.

"Whatever makes you happy, my dear." He gestures to the chair in front of him, undoubtedly expecting me to sit there.

I cross to the chair at the opposite end of the table, amazed my legs haven't buckled yet.

Instead of taking the hint, he moves to the seat on my right, across from Ren. The two stare each other down.

I glance at her, gathering my strength and forcing my voice to stay level. "This is quite the setup, Mason."

Mason smiles in what he probably thinks is a charming way, but it makes my skin crawl. "I knew you'd like it, my dear."

Why am I playing this game with him? I should just take up a steak knife and stab him through the heart. Ren wouldn't even hesitate.

But despite my violent thoughts, I can't bring myself to move. Even if this pathetic excuse for a man is a figment of this pretend world, I don't think I'm capable of stabbing him. I'm not as bold or brave as Ren.

Stop it.

I force myself to conjure Ren's earlier words. *"The girl who stood against psychopathic teddy bears, who just took down a minotaur, who refused to be agoraphobia's bitch, now says she's not a badass."*

I've done all that and more. And some of it by myself. So this should be nothing. The music switches to a different piece.

"I love this composition, don't you? Brahms's 'Clarinet Quintet in B Minor.' Listen to that string composition. Just beautiful." He sighs audibly, his eyes closed.

I glance at Ren, but just as our eyes meet, Mason springs to his feet, his hands outstretched.

"Come. Let's dance," he says.

Panic flashes through me as I stare at his palms. I can barely look at him, and now I have to *touch* him?

If Mason notices my repulsion, he ignores it, grabbing my hands and yanking me to my feet. His left hand meets my waist, and I want to gag. His clammy, spindly fingers wrap tightly around my left hand as he whisks me into a waltz.

I haven't waltzed in years—not since Carter's first birthday—but the muscle memory is there, and I hold my own. *Forward with my left foot, to the side with my right...*

Mason's hot breath wafts in my ear as he speaks. "I don't mean to be condemnatory, but your acquaintance is not worthy of your company."

His words stun me, and I'm unable to school my expression before he notices. *To the side with my left...*

He rushes to explain. "She's perfectly fine if you're in need of a sounding board, but if you're looking for stimulating conversation—"

My eyes wander to Ren until he grips my chin firmly in his hand. His brows narrow, and for one sickening second, I think he's going to kiss me. Mercifully, he doesn't.

"Anyway, that doesn't matter anymore," he says instead. "You have me, now. I can discuss the significance of the yellow wallpaper in Charlotte Perkins Gillman's tale or how elegantly Ezra Pound crafts modernist poetry."

Right. I'm supposed to be a bookworm in this world. The knowledge is there if I look for it, but it's not me. This man—if you could even call him that—doesn't know anything about me other than my first name.

Backward with my right...

"So can Ren," I blurt, catching Ren moving from her seat from the corner of my eye.

Maybe she's rethinking my guts. Taking things into her own hands. I wouldn't blame her. What am I doing anyway?

I bite my lip as Mason's eyes snap back to mine.

"She was an English major. Now, she specializes in horror, but her education covered all the classics. She's not as dull as you make her out to be. She's quite fascinating, actually."

I'm babbling like a moron. I don't even care about discussing literature. Mason has no idea who I really am outside this book persona. But I can't say any of this. I'm more than likely on the verge of angering a madman.

Reign it in, Sophie.

I soften my features and channel my mother. "But she does have her limitations."

Mason raises a thick brow. "Oh?"

"Yes. Throughout our time together, I've found myself trying to keep the conversation flowing. It's been exhausting."

Not true. In fact, it's just the opposite, but Ren's raising a candelabra above Mason's head, and I need to keep him looking at me.

Mason tsks. "You poor thing. I see I arrived just in time."

Ren's weapon crashes down on Mason's skull with a horrible *thonk* that sends him spinning away from me.

"What happened to 'You can do this. There's no doubt in my mind?'"

Ren shrugs. "Still no doubt, I'd just like to get out of this book before Jeremy dies of old age, and I can't kill him myself."

She holds a hand out for mine, but when I reach to take it, she slaps a knife into my palm. Her trusty kitchen knife I wasn't good enough to use in the cemetery. I would feel honored if I wasn't terrified.

"Finish it."

I know Ren's right. This cretin is nothing but words on a page,

INKED IN BLOOD AND MEMORY

but still— "I can't." My breath quickens.

"He's not real, Sophie."

Ren's hit only pushed Mason a few feet, and now he's glaring at her with barely contained rage. A wild animal let out of its cage. I almost drop the knife when he lunges without warning at Ren.

The two fall, and Ren hits her back at an awkward angle on the table's corner before slamming into the hardwood floor. Her head takes most of the impact, and she lays motionless as Mason wraps his hands around her neck and squeezes.

The sight breaks me out of my paralysis, and I dart forward, plunging the knife into Mason's left side. It sinks right in.

I actually stabbed someone.

In my shock, I release the handle, and the weapon stays there in Mason's side. Of course, it does. What did I expect it to do? Fall out of him?

He screams and falls off of Ren, but he doesn't stay down. Almost inhumanly fast, he pulls the knife from his side with a squelching sound and holds it up as if examining it. His blood drips from the blade and onto his knuckles. From behind it, he stares me down. "Sophie, why would you hurt me?"

Genuine confusion clouds his eyes. He's deluded enough to have that lack of awareness.

My legs almost fail me as Mason steps over the now broken candelabra and toward me, the knife still in his hand. For every step he takes forward, I back up. My eyes flash to Ren, and I will her to wake up with everything inside me, but she doesn't.

I'm on my own.

"Why are you backing away? I'm not going to bite." He flashes a smile full of bright white teeth and moves to grab my arm.

I yelp and dodge him, running for the door. The hallway stretches impossibly long before me as Mason's footsteps pound after me. He's too fast, and he catches me almost immediately, spinning me to face him.

My lower back rests against the small table in the foyer as Mason's deep blue eyes glisten. He strokes my cheek with the hand still holding the knife, and his hot, rancid breath drifts into my eyes. The tip of the blade is too close for comfort. His other hand digs into my good arm. I'm sure I'll have a bruise there.

I'm feeling around for anything to use as a weapon as he leaves a trail of his blood on my cheek. My skin crawls at the warmth of the liquid, but my hand wraps around something, and my heart soars. The vase of flowers. In one motion, I bring it crashing into the side of Mason's cheek. Water and flowers fly everywhere as the remaining part of the vase falls out of my hand and shatters into a thousand pieces on the floor. I move for the kitchen, but Mason yanks me back.

Small cuts mar his cheek, and his black hair hangs in wet strings as he snarls, eyes ablaze. "I'm not one to resort to violence, but I must say, you bring it out of me."

He whips the blade through the air, and I block it with my hurt forearm. The pain spots my vision, and I scream louder than I ever have. It sinks in deep, right past my bandages, and I swear, I can feel it hit bone.

Maybe Mason's surprised at my shriek because he releases the knife, leaving it embedded in my flesh.

"You made me, Sophie! Look what you've done!" He grabs the back of his neck with both hands, mussing his hair. He's still bleeding from his side, still not standing upright. None of his wounds have healed.

Ren is right. I'm our ticket out of here. I can hurt him.

His words wake me in a way. I've had enough of the victim-blaming, the whining, the obsessive stalking. It's grown old, and I'm ready to be rid of him. To start my life out of his shadow and take Carter far away from the people calling themselves our "family."

I'm through being the victim. I'm taking control of my story.

I ignore the flash of pain as best I can, pull the knife out of my arm, and slash the air in front of Mason. One way, then the other. He dodges both, all the while gazing at me like a lost puppy. Like he can't understand why I'm attacking him instead of apologizing.

INKED IN BLOOD AND MEMORY

The tables have turned, and I am the predator. He brings a hand up and knocks the knife from my grip, and it clatters to the ground and spins away down the hall.

I tuck my wounded arm under me and dive, landing hard on the ground and reaching out with my good arm, but I don't fall far enough. The knife is still a few feet away, and Mason grabs at my legs. I scrabble forward, gaining a few inches. I'm out from under him now, and I bring my foot up hard against his face. Twice. His nose cracks open and gushes like a red river. Mason grabs at his face, freeing me from his grip.

My hand encircles the handle of the blade, and I don't think about what's next. I just act, arcing it back and up, thrusting it straight through the soft spot under Mason's chin.

His eyes widen, his face a mess of blood, unleashing a gargling moan, and I can see the knife peeking back at me from behind his teeth a second before his eyes roll back, and he collapses in a heap.

I'm never getting that image out of my mind.

I sit in silence, wondering if I'm going to be sick, trying to register the fact that I just *killed* someone for what feels like hours before Ren groans from the kitchen. The spell is broken, and I rush to her side and kneel by her head.

"Did you get him?" she asks, wincing. I help her sit up enough to cradle her head in my lap.

I laugh with relief. "Yeah, I got him."

"Ace," Ren whispers, "That's my girl."

My arm throbs, but it's a battle scar. I'm lucky it wasn't worse.

A beam of amber light begins from under the crack in the back door, and a rush of wind bursts through, slamming it against the wall. Beyond it, the light is all I see.

"What is that?" I ask as it increases in intensity, streaming in through the windows onto our faces.

Ren and I cover our eyes. "You did it, Soph!" Ren yells as the scene around us changes. The walls and roof of my prison collapse in a *whoosh* of inked pages around our feet as the light grows brighter until I can't escape it. There is only the light and the weight of Ren's head in my lap.

And then the former is gone, and I'm blinking the stars away and taking in our new surroundings. The darker wood floor and towering bookshelves greet us. I rise, helping Ren to her feet slowly.

"Look familiar?" I brace myself for her answer.

She grins. "We're out."

The book we've just escaped from thuds closed, and three words on the cover stare up at me.

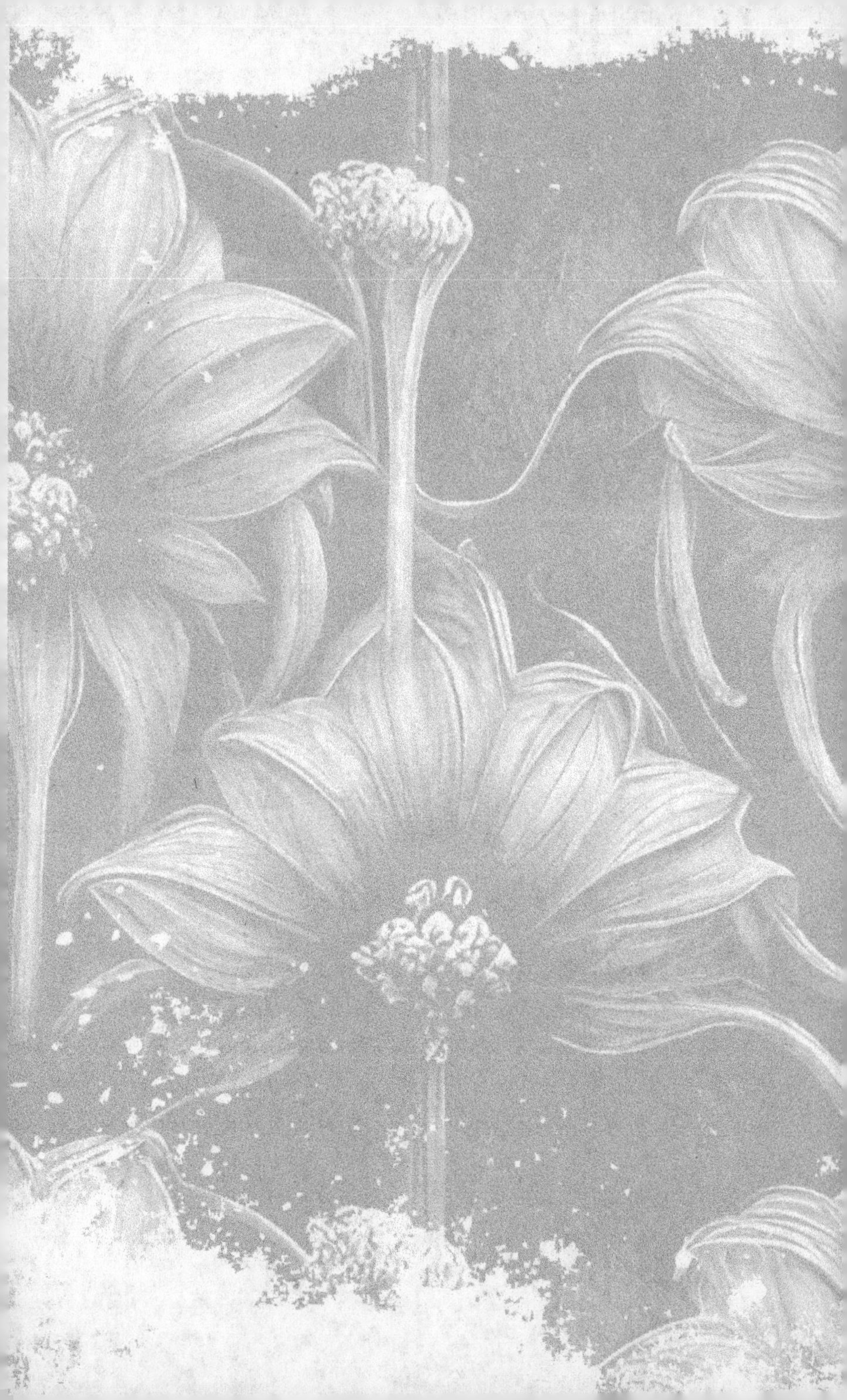

CHAPTER THIRTY-SEVEN

LY THI REN
9:24PM

After the blinding light subsides and I'm on my feet, it becomes clear that we're not alone.

"Sophie!"

Carter runs into Sophie's arms, barely giving me time to get out of the way.

"Carter," she says, eyes wide in disbelief. "It's so good to see you."

Carter pulls back, a frown on his face. "Where have you been? I missed you."

I hold back a laugh. He's more articulate than other toddlers. Not exactly what I'd been anticipating.

"It's my special day, and you're late," he continues, placing his hands on his hips.

Sophie lightly touches his hand. "I know, buddy. I'm sorry. I tried to be here sooner."

Carter's eyes drift to Ren. "Who are you?"

Why am I nervous in front of a six-year-old? I smile, but it feels weird. Am I doing it right?

"This is Ren, my..." Sophie blushes and looks at me. "Girlfriend?"

I like the sound of that. I smile and nod as Carter sticks his hand out. I shake it. "It's very nice to see you again, Carter. You know we met when you were a little baby."

He scowls. "I'm not a baby anymore."

I chuckle and gently cuff him on the chin. "No, you're not."

"Carter, there you are." Roger Vanguard stops short, expression frozen in reprimand as he sees Sophie and me. "My God, you really did it."

"Surprised?" I ask.

Sophie's seemingly unable to form words at the sight of her traitorous father.

Sylvia enters next, but she's schooled her features into their usual stern, disapproving look. There's a flash of something in her eyes, but it's gone before I can place it.

"Edmond," or Jeremy, arrives last, a smug grin on his face. Not what I'd expect to see from a failed jailer. But then again, I don't know him that well. No matter how much I once thought I did.

Roger grabs Sophie. "Get off her!" He wrestles with her until her wrists are confined in his hands behind her back. Jeremy skips to me and forces my hands back with something that feels like wind but must be magic.

"I don't think you're in a position to make demands, Ren," he says.

"Good to see you, too, Dad," Sophie says finally.

I narrow my eyes at Jeremy. "What do you get out of this? It's more than a payday for you."

"All I want is for this sacrifice to go as planned. It's certainly well on its way, thanks to you. The deaths you've caused have been wonderful appetizers," he says with a twisted smile, throwing something on the ground.

"What is this from?"

I'm blinking at the image, not believing my eyes. It's William, but the ID says Eric Wilson. His familiar face stares up at me under dyed purple bangs.

"Oh, come on! You know. It's the person you sacrificed in the name of the Ly, Vanguard, Berg-Nilsen empire."

"No."

"I guess the apple doesn't fall far from the tree, huh? He's dead, but hey. You can always visit him in limbo." He holds up the book.

Jeremy throws Adeline's ID to the ground. Her blonde hair is the same as I remember. The eyes that were full of mischievous gossip in our book.

Everything inside me shatters. But their names weren't on the cover. They couldn't have been real, right?

My hand hovers over my mouth. This can't be true. I didn't kill two women.

Jeremy throws one last ID, and there's Lemonade Lady, Eve, which really had been her name. Eve Öztürk. I pull it off the pile. *No.*

"Oh, yes. Her. The nanny. She was alive when you met her, by the way. Can't say you left her that way."

"You're lying!"

I kneel down to see them better and wish I could gather them, but my hands aren't budging from behind my back.

"Ren," Sophie calls, and I look over to see her nod to the book we were in. The cover reads *Eve, Sophie, Ren.*

Looking back on the first time I saw the cover, I remember the cloth that had covered part of it. I hadn't seen Eve's name underneath it, but it's clear now.

Jeremy giggles. "Uh-oh. Looks like it's the truth."

William's and Adeline's names are missing. Does that mean they weren't real?

I glare at him.

"They were as real as you or me once upon a time." Jeremy scoops up the three rectangles—some of the only things left of them—and tucks them into my front pocket, smirking.

Sophie struggles against her father's hold but can't break free. The guy's a tank. "How could you do this?" she asks.

"We had to ensure you two didn't get in the way of the Great One's feast," Sylvia Vanguard says. She crosses her arms and shifts her weight to her other stilettoed foot. *Feast.* That's how she speaks of her six-year-old son.

"Don't act all dainty on me, now, Ren. We're cut from the same cloth."

He's not a sorcerer, not a god like he thinks he is. He's just a pathetic excuse of a man. Just a boy with cheap magic tricks. When I speak, my voice is even, icy. "Fuck you."

Jeremy snaps his fingers and points at me. "There she is, folks. Ly Thi Ren, perpetrator of the roller derby incident."

My stomach drops. Of course, he knows about that. It still hits me like whiplash. Every time I think I'm free of that memory, something or someone reminds me of it.

"That was an *accident*," I hiss.

Jeremy frowns, then shrugs. "Maybe so, but all that death you leave in your wake? All that gore and carnage? That was inspired work. Just pure artistry."

"I didn't know they were real. I would've never—" I will *not* cry in front of this bastard.

"But some part of you must've known it was possible. A 50/50 chance, really. And all from your imagination. I mean, teddy bears." He shakes his head, smiling wide.

The white bear tearing into ~~Lemonade Lady~~ Eve's neck flashes into my brain like lightning. Her shrill screams as she went down. Again and again and again. How many times was it? How many deaths did she have to endure because of me?

And William and Adeline...

"We can go back in. The books are still here—"

"Sorry, no go. Books aren't time machines. Once the story is played out, you can't change it. But you can read about it." He taps the book.

My hands shake, and I try to steady them by balling them into fists. My nails cut into my sweaty palms. Somehow, I keep my voice steady. "Why the hell are you doing this to us?"

INKED IN BLOOD AND MEMORY

Jeremy's smile could chill the devil. "All in good time."

The Vanguards escort us from the room.

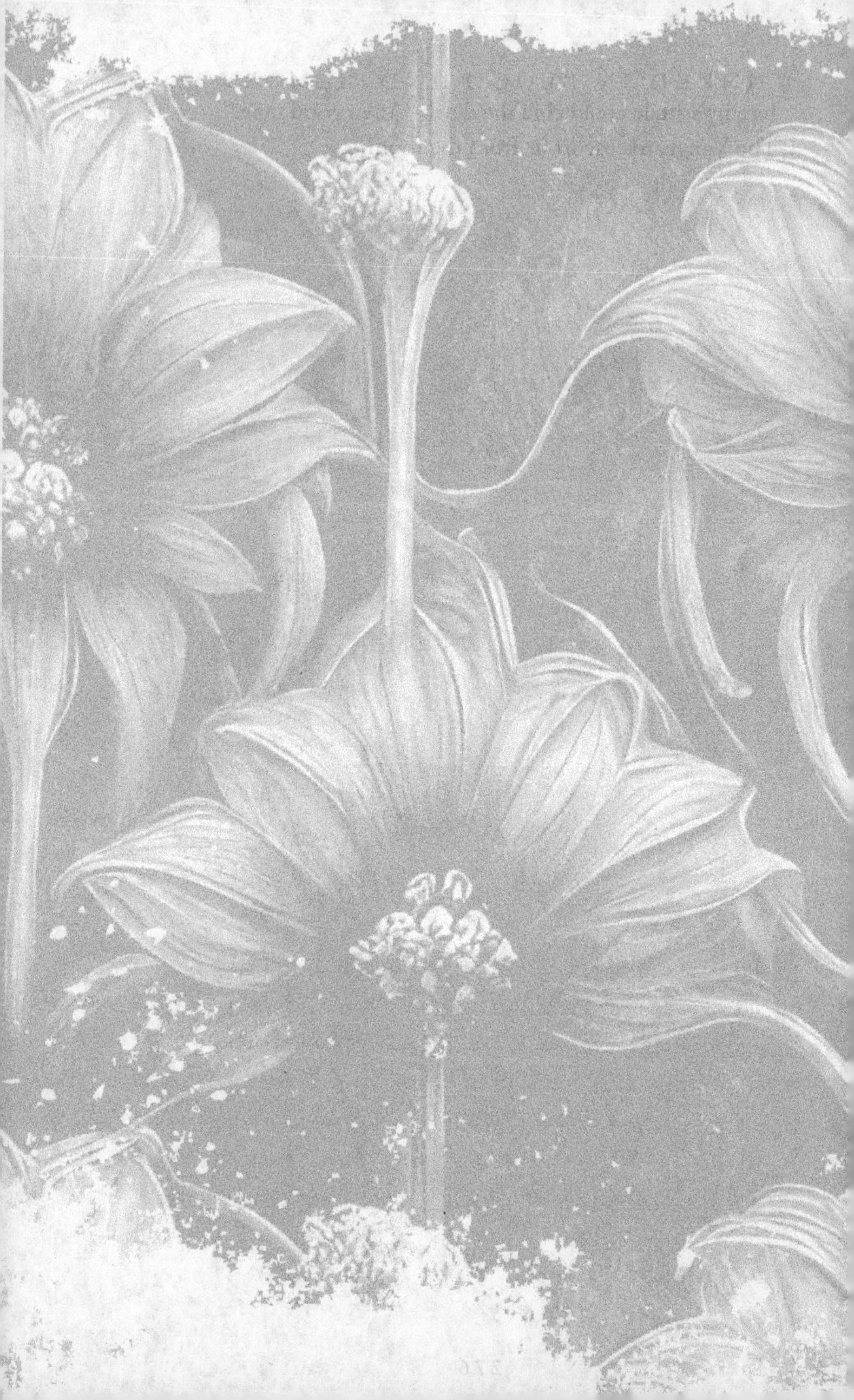

CHAPTER THIRTY-EIGHT

~~LEMONADE LADY~~
EVE
SIX HOURS AGO

This isn't my story. I know everyone likes to think of themselves as the main character of their life, and even before all this, I was the same. Yes, I finally remember a world before this too-bright and cheery birthday party.

And I think it's thanks to the girl in front of me. Ren. I saw her fall out of the sky as if something had dropped her in mid-air. No matter how much I looked, I couldn't find anything different about the sky above us.

My days consisted of serving lemonade and chatting with those who came up to me. I was on autopilot for—I don't know how long. It's never night here; there's no way to measure time. All I knew was my son was having a birthday party, but I don't have a son. And teddy bears have minds of their own in this place. Though, they'd never been homicidal until recently.

That was before I died. Before I was reborn on this very spot, all my memories returned to me. To my knowledge, I've never died before that, and maybe Ren caused it. But I'm grateful to her. I'm awake now. My life at this perpetual birthday party before her arrival was nothing more than a dream. Or maybe I have died, and this is purgatory. Either way, I need to say something to Ren.

I open my mouth to thank her, but that's not what comes out of my mouth. "You look a bit shaky, dear. Would you like some lemonade?" *I say instead, ladling the liquid into a cup.*

Why did I say that? That's not what I meant to say. I've already said that.

I will my hands to stop. They don't even waver.

I'm screaming inside my mind. I'm not like them! I'm awake! I'm like you! Surely, *she can see the terror in my eyes? The tightness in my smile? The slight edge creeping into my voice?*

"Shit," Ren mutters.

My heart soars. She's figured it out!

But no. Her eyes have already slid past me, and she has no clue I'm in the same situation as she is.

I'm in trouble.

I've died nine times today. Each time, I think it'll be the last. Each time, I wonder if I'll wake up with control of my body. Each time, I'm wrong on both hypotheses.

"You look a bit shaky, dear. Would you like some lemonade?" *It's the fifth time I've asked her that.*

Ren takes a red cup from the stack and extends it to me. "Why the hell not?"

When I'm done filling her cup, I watch her walk to a picnic table and drop onto the bench. The teddy bears have noticed her and have started their stampede, but she barely acknowledges them.

No, you can't give up now.

The partygoers around me fall victim to the plushies as they always do, and there is the white bear who's always focused on me no matter the loop. Like he has a grudge against me.

In one of the loops, Ren saved me a second before she herself was tackled by the monsters. It was the only loop I didn't die.

INKED IN BLOOD AND MEMORY

Now, I urge Ren to get to her feet, to keep going. Even as the bear with blood spattering its white fur takes me down for the tenth time. I bring the lemonade bowl with me, and liquid showers the bear. It lets out a ferocious snarl, mostly pink now from its bath, and tears into my neck.

I never get used to the pain. If I'm lucky, I pass out before it gets too unbearable. This is not one of those times. I'm awake for all of it. The bear's teeth gnash in my ears, and I search for Ren, but she's gone.

Someone has pulled her to her feet, and they flee the oncoming stuffed animals, past the park, past the sidewalk with the invisible barrier keeping Ren here.

Yes! They've done it!

Shadows tease the corners of my sight.

Though I can't affect my smile outwardly, inwardly, I beam wider than my face shows. I'm happy for them. They're strong, and they have each other. They'll get through this. I know it.

Their cat approaches me, his hooked tail in the air. He sits beside my head, so close I can't see his face above his furry chest. I want to pet him. I wish I could pet him. I've always wanted a cat but never got around to adopting one.

This is how it was always supposed to happen. I know that now.

I roll my head to the other side of the park and see the girls' two pairs of feet retreating into the distance. It's the last thing I see before the darkness at the edges of my vision takes over. The cat meows. The stereo sings. Then silence. Then oblivion. This is not my story.

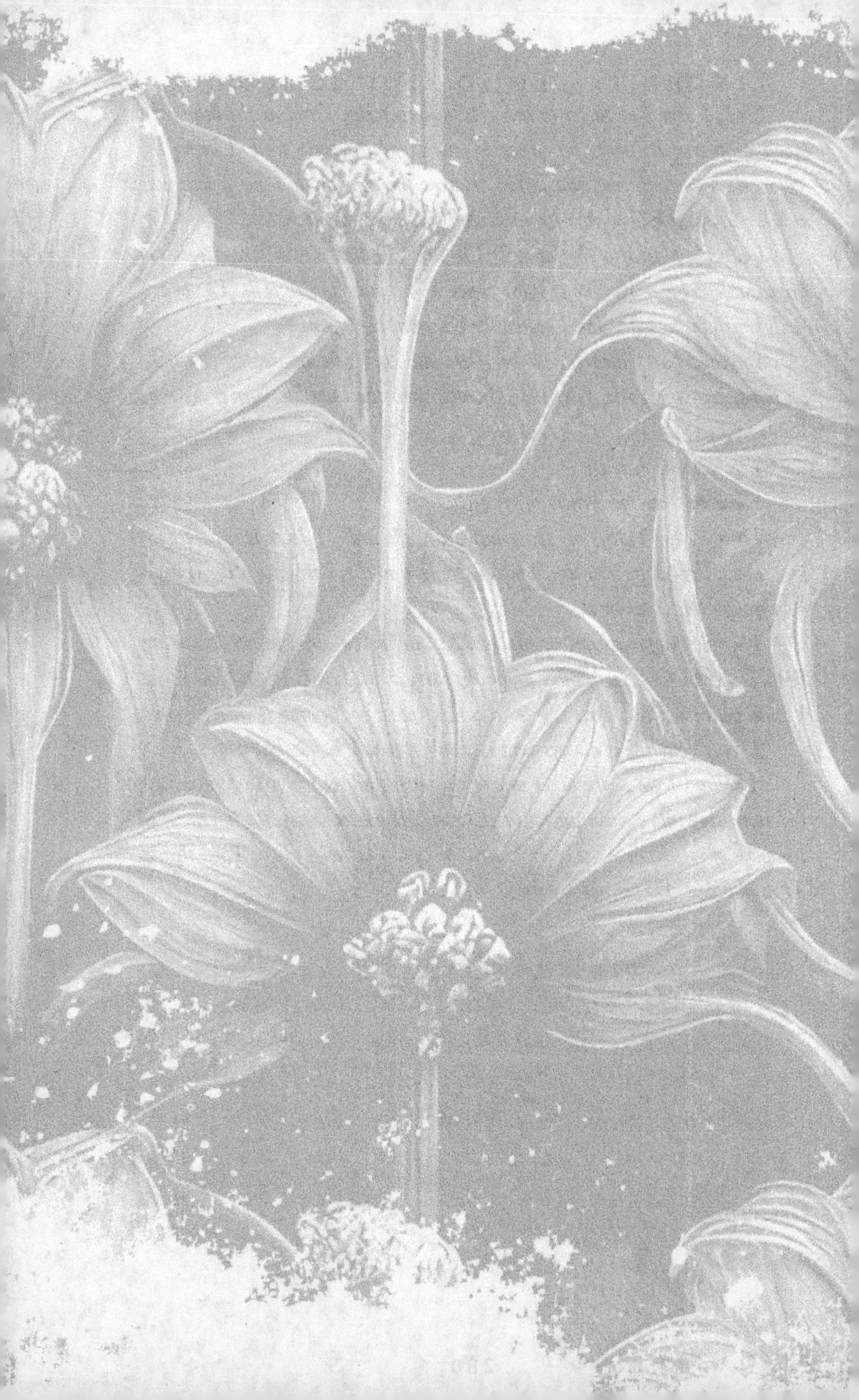

CHAPTER THIRTY-NINE
LY THI REN
11:22PM

Dammit!

I slam the book closed and throw it against the door. It lands straight up, cover facing out as if taunting me with Eve's name. *This is one of the women who died because of you. You could've saved her if you weren't such a self-involved ass.*

We're trapped in a room in the basement of the Berg-Nilsen mansion, our legs bound together with duct tape. There were two sets of chains attached to the wall on either side of the room. Just enough for Sophie and myself. Our wrists are enclosed tightly in our iron bracelets, metal scraping at our skin and rubbing it raw.

How could I not have known that Eve had been crying out for help all that time? And that one loop in the park I'd thrown her in the path of—

"All that gore and carnage...pure artistry." Jeremy's words ring in my mind.

I thrust my fists into my eyes as if I can stamp away the memory. I'm such an idiot. How self-centered must I be to think I was the only one apart from Sophie who had a life away from the book?

When I take my hands away and open my eyes again, Sophie's watching me from across the room. She hasn't read what I have, what Eve experienced because of me, but she does the math. I must be an open book.

"He wasn't lying, was he?" she asks.

I shake my head. "She was conscious through all of it. Every time she died—" Were William and Adeline awake like that, too? Unable to say anything and screaming inside their minds for help? "All three of them were trapped, and I did *nothing*."

"You couldn't have known."

"It should've at least crossed my mind! The possibility that there were others. But it didn't. They're dead now because of—"

"Jeremy. Because of Jeremy. Not you."

I can't reckon the old, kind Jeremy I knew years ago with this sadistic version of my friend. My brain refuses to acknowledge them as the same person. Is there any part of the old him left? There has to be, right?

I pull the three identification cards out of my pocket. Or, at least, I *try* to. But the only one there is Eve's. I feel around for the other two, even checking my other pockets and scanning the floor around me, but they're gone.

"What is it?"

"William's and Adeline's IDs are gone."

"Do you think that means they were tricks?"

"We can hope."

"I remember Eve," Sophie says. "She replaced Viola when she retired. She was kind to my brother. I'm sure she had no idea what my parents did in their spare time."

"Not the way to make me feel better."

"Sorry." She grimaces.

We fall silent. It's not long before I can't take it anymore. "Can we talk about these chains?" I ask, hoping desperately to change the subject. "Why did the Berg-Nilsens—? Ohhh." I'm taking in the rest of the room and the various mechanisms and putting the pieces together.

Sophie tilts her head. "What?"

"Well, I guess it's too late to be grossed out about sitting on the floor," I say as I hold back a laugh.

"Why?" Sophie still hasn't connected the dots. Her naïveté is endearing at times like these.

I point to the piece of furniture by the door. I say "furniture," but it's not much more than a couple poles with a few loops of fabric. "That, girly, is a sex swing." I wiggle my eyebrows.

Sophie's eyes widen behind her glasses, and I lose it. In spite of it all, I'm laughing my head off. We've come all this way to be chained up in Jeremy's parents' old sex dungeon.

Sophie squeals. "Ewww!"

"You're such a prude," I say between fits of laughter.

"Not about that. It's Jeremy's mom and dad. That's so gross," Sophie says, but she's laughing now, too.

When we finally compose ourselves, my sides hurt, and my head pounds. I wipe away my tears and try to catch my breath as we fall back into silence.

Sophie breaks it first. "Ren, what did Jeremy mean by 'the roller derby incident'?" Her voice is gentle, but I still wince.

Yet another occasion I'd failed to save someone and possibly caused their death. It's not a moment in my life I like to think back on, but it will stay with me for the rest of my days. However long that turns out to be. Jade, Dan, Eve, possibly William and Adeline... Who's next?

I swallow the lump in my throat, brush my hair behind my ears, and take a deep breath. "A couple years ago, I joined this roller derby league on a whim. I sucked," I say, forcing a laugh. It comes out weird and cracked. "My teammates were encouraging, always there with pointers on how to fall and the importance of cross-training."

"I didn't know you were into roller derby, but knowing you, it makes sense." Sophie adjusts her posture.

"This was right after we lost touch," I say, forcing a smile at

Sophie's comment. "I'd just moved to California, and I wanted to make some friends who had no idea what kind of screwed-up family I'd come from. A fresh start."

"I get that," Sophie says.

Of all people, she's the one person who could ever understand. She'd done the same, after all. "Yeah, well, I was on the team a few months as a blocker and getting pretty decent on skates," I continue. "During a game, I got distracted and collided with another member of my team. Her name was Jade. Instead of falling in one of the ways she'd shown me, she fell on her back, completely exposed to the oncoming pack."

I close my eyes and rest my head back on the wall. The events play out in my mind as I speak, but I have to get everything out. I've never spoken about this to anyone before. "Some fell over her while others were able to stop safely. I remember this hush came over the entire building once the refs blew their whistles, and the music stopped. I stood back as they and Jade's friends checked her out. It didn't take long to realize Jade was dead."

I pause, caught up in the past, staring at the brick wall above Sophie's head instead of her. I don't even look at her when she asks, "How did she die?"

"We didn't know exactly what happened until the medical examiner released the official report. Her heart stopped. Simple as that."

I remember the shock that rippled through our team upon hearing the news. Jade was perfectly healthy. We knew of no preexisting conditions, and she rarely ate anything that could be considered bad for her. None of it made any sense. It still doesn't make sense to me.

"Ren, that wasn't your fault," Sophie says. "Sometimes, things like that happen. No one knows why."

"Maybe," I concede. "But Jade's still dead. Just like Eve. Just like Dan. And I can't help but wonder if Jade would still be alive if I hadn't joined the team? Why is death all around me, you know? Is it because of our parents that we're fated to bring death everywhere we go, and if that's the case, how do we live with that?"

I'm saying "we" as if Sophie has her own guilty conscience over a mysterious death. She doesn't correct me, and I'm grateful. She's silent for a while, no doubt formulating the right things to say as she always does.

"If that's true, we live with it the only way we can. By knowing it wasn't our idea to make a deal with a demon. The blame belongs to our parents. Not us."

She's right, of course, but a part of me is stuck in the middle of that vicious cycle of guilt where I'm thinking back on all my past mistakes. And somewhere in the mix, Jeremy is there again, mocking me. *"All that death you leave in your wake...inspired work."*

CHAPTER FORTY
EDMOND SINCLAIR/
JEREMY BERG-NILSEN

Edmond inspected his fingernails, listening to the time tick away on his desk clock. They weren't his fingernails minutes ago, but that was irrelevant. It felt late. The manor had fallen silent as if anticipating the main event. But no. It wasn't completely silent. There were footsteps in the hall, a quiet "Shh."

Edmond smirked and exited his study, following the light noise of someone trying their best to stay unnoticed until he reached the foyer. Lien and Đài Ly stood with Carter by the front door, speaking to him in hushed tones. Đài's hand hovered above the doorknob to freedom as he held Carter with the other.

Edmond crossed his arms and cleared his throat, and the Lys jumped simultaneously. Edmond stifled a laugh, eyes narrowing on his prey, relishing the moment before he could descend upon them. "What are you two doing?"

"We're going on a trip," Carter said, apparently oblivious to the shift in energy of the room.

"Is that so?" Edmond said. "And why would you go and do something like that?"

Đài placed Carter on the ground, the fear in his eyes a delicious treat. He even gulped. "Go play, Carter."

"But—"

"Listen to Uncle Đài, Carter. We'll see you in a moment." Lien gently pushed the boy, who looked uncertainly at the Lys. They nodded to him, and he left.

Edmond clicked his tongue. "Bad form lying to a child. Don't you think?"

"Edmond—"

Edmond raised his hand, then gestured for them to follow him to the study. He turned his back on them, knowing they had no other choice. The silence enveloped them as the door to the office closed. The two schemers didn't break the quiet. Smart.

Edmond crossed his arms, leaning back on his desk. "What to do with you now?" he asked, almost to himself. He caught sight of himself in the reflection of a brandy glass on the bar cart. That's all it took for him to lose his grip on his body.

I've lost time again. Every time I come to after being away, it's like I'm waking from a deep sleep without the rest. No, it's more like I've used all my strength to claw my way to the surface of my consciousness. It's become easier to do as the demon grows weaker. I'm rewarded with a puzzle—gaps in my day. This time is no different. I'm exhausted.

"What are you going to do to us?" Lien Ly whimpers, gazing up at me with wide eyes. Đài sits, just as terrified, next to her.

"Why would I do anything to you?"

They think you're someone else. Him.

Before either of the Lys can answer, I raise a hand. "Leave me."

They don't have to be told twice. They jump out of their seats and exit in the span of three seconds. I'm lying if I can't say that feeling of power, of being in control and being the one to be feared, isn't tempting.

INKED IN BLOOD AND MEMORY

I wish I could remember what happens each time Edmond takes over, but no matter how hard I try, I'm never able to.

I remove my jacket and straighten my tie just as someone knocks on the door to my study. "Come in."

Carter peeks his head in, and I soften my expression and voice. "Hey, little man. What's up?"

After taking a couple steps inside the room, Carter hesitates, shuffling his feet and looking down. He still clutches the pocket watch, and I glimpse the time: 11:29. My heart skips a beat. *Is it really that late?*

"Why were you mad at Aunt Lien and Uncle Đài? Because they wanted to take me somewhere before the special day?"

Understanding dawns. I could kick myself for shooing the Lys away.

"No, I'm not mad." I close the door and bend down to Carter's level. "You nervous about later?"

"Yeah," he mumbles.

"That's completely normal, but I'm going to let you in on a little secret. That is, if you promise to keep it between you and me."

Carter nods, finally meeting my eyes. "I promise."

I look around the room as if checking for listening ears, but of course, no one is there. "I had my own special day when I was a kid. In this very house."

Carter's eyes widen. "You did? What happened? Was it scary? Did it hurt? No one will tell me anything." He picks at his cloak, still the same purple as years ago.

I gulp down the lump in my throat, the rising tide of anger inside me. I lie. "Not scary at all, and as a bonus, I got a bit of magic." I wiggle my fingers, and amber light glows from them. The only good thing about being around a demon for so long—after a while, you start to learn the tricks of the trade. A fact I've kept hidden from the supposed Great One.

"How'd you do that?"

"I'll teach you tomorrow. But right now, you better get ready. It's almost time."

ALLISON IVY

I send Carter away even though everything inside me is screaming to take him far away from here. I can't do that. Not yet. I have unfinished business. People to repay.

CHAPTER FORTY-ONE

LY THI REN
11:36PM

Sophie breaks the silence a couple minutes later. "What time is it now?"

"11:36," I say, but not because I'm checking the pocket watch for the hundredth time today. No, that disappeared when we escaped the book, and I'm betting Carter still has its real-world counterpart in his pocket. Luckily, there's a clock on the wall above Sophie's head. Ticking away as if it's just another day. Like it's mocking us.

It's been an incredibly long day, and everything in me is screaming to close my eyes. But I know the second I do, I'll fall asleep, and who knows when I'll wake up. Exhaustion coupled with head trauma (how many times have I been hit on the head today?) isn't the greatest feeling. Thoughts of wounds draw me to Sophie's arm, which now sports clean gauze thanks to Roger Vanguard. He even stitched my side up. How kind. "How's your arm?"

"Better. I'll take a stab wound over swamp monster eggs any day."

I nod. "Amen."

"And your side?"

"Bearable," I reply.

"It's really over," Sophie says, her voice cracking on the last syllable. She places a hand over her mouth as she sobs.

It breaks my heart to see her so hopeless. It reminds me of the night Carter was born. I wish I could hug her, but our chains keep us firmly apart on opposite sides of the room. I do the only thing I can—offer words of reassurance. "Hey, Sophie. Look at me. Even if they send Carter away, we'll find him. I promise you. If Jeremy found a way out, Carter can, too."

"It took Jeremy years, Ren. And look at him now. He's a monster. If Carter comes back like him—"

"He won't because we're not going to let that happen. Trust me, Sophie. We'll take on the demon himself if we have to."

I don't know what our parents' plan is for us, but it can't be good. Maybe even worse than the book prisons. Why didn't I learn magic when I had the chance?

That reminds me.

"Didn't you say you know a couple spells? They might come in handy right now."

Sophie removes her glasses and covers her face with her hands. "I've tried already. They must be using something to dampen magic like they did at Everling. I'm powerless." She sniffs. "They're going to lock us up and throw away the key. Probably in separate books again. Wipe our memories of all of this."

"I won't let them," I say firmly. "And even if they do, I'll find you. I'll be your catalyst again and again if that's what it takes."

Sophie leans her head back against the old brick wall, her tears falling silently. "Was that really Jeremy? I can hardly believe it. He's changed so much."

"Did someone say 'Jeremy'?" The door swings open, and there he is. In a dark pinstripe suit with a matching vest and purple tie on top of a black shirt. "My ears are burning." He flashes a devilish grin.

"Speak of the devil," I mutter.

Jeremy places a hand over his heart. "You're too kind, my love."

Sophie wipes her tears away and replaces her glasses as he leans on the sex swing's chain and asks, "How are my little muses?"

I sweep my bound legs to knock him over, but he dodges them easily, laughing.

"I'm not your fucking muse," I say through gritted teeth. "And neither is she."

"Whoa! Is that how you talk to your friends?" Jeremy moves to sit and then seems to think better of it, pulling a face as if a haunting image has passed through his mind. And now it's running through mine.

"Friends? Is that what we are?" Sophie asks, glaring at him.

"Why not? Bygones and all that." He flits his hand.

My hands tighten on my chains. "*This* is how you treat your friends? After what you said up there?"

I can't decipher Jeremy's expression, but it's gone in a split second as if it never existed.

"Besides, I don't think I can be friends with someone who can kill and laugh about it," I continue.

"Kill? Who did I kill?" He crosses the room to the wall opposite the door so he's in between both of us, leaning his back against it. He seems genuinely confused, squinting his eyes as if we've presented him with a puzzle, a Rubik's cube he needs time to decipher. He raises a finger to his lips.

I stare blankly at him until understanding dawns in his expression. His eyebrows lift. "Oh, you mean Eve?"

I nod. "For starters." I'm using all my strength to keep it together and not yell obscenities at him.

"That wasn't my idea," Jeremy says, running a hand through his blond hair. "That was all your parents. They didn't like the idea of you two being patients zero—so to speak—when it came to the magic. They didn't know I'd already tested it on my dear old dad. I had to convince them I knew what I was doing, so they offered Carter's au pair. I didn't think Eve would be in any danger."

I scoff. "How are we supposed to believe that?"

Jeremy shrugs. "Believe what you want, but I never meant for her to die. There were things I couldn't predict. This form of magic is still pretty new. There are a lot of variables we— I didn't account for when I put all of you in there. And as you heard earlier, your parents had no way to predict Eve's fate either."

His words trigger something in me. What had he said earlier? Something about my imagination sabotaging the book? My guilt hits its peak. No, this wasn't Jeremy's fault. And as much as I want to blame it on my parents as well, it wasn't theirs either. It's one hundred percent my own. My love of horror did this. Eve and Dan are both dead because of *me*. William and Adeline— No one else is to blame. It was all me.

Jeremy could be lying now for all I know, but my gut says he isn't. Looking into his eyes and hearing the words he isn't saying, I see the truth. He's being honest with us. At least about Eve.

"You locked us away for *months*, you erased our memories, and you expect us to all be *friends* again?" Sophie asks. "Your mother would be ashamed of you. I wish she hadn't taken her own life so she could see you now."

Jeremy stands up straight, eyes flashing. "That's not funny."

Something has changed in the room. An intensity has entered the air. Jeremy squares his shoulders, staring Sophie down.

"I wasn't trying to be."

Jeremy's on her in an instant, pulling her to her feet and slamming her into the brick behind her. She gasps.

I jump to my feet, tugging futilely on my chains. "Leave her alone, or I swear you'll wish you were dead."

"Big talk coming from the girl chained to a wall," Jeremy says, one hand still holding Sophie's shoulder against the wall. She squirms against his grip, but there's nowhere for her to go. He turns back to her.

"What happened to you, Jeremy? You could've done anything you wanted with your life, but instead, you chose to work for *them*?" I say, gesturing to the door.

INKED IN BLOOD AND MEMORY

"I wanted you to suffer!" He turns back to Sophie. "Sounds like you deserved it. Here you are defending a bunch of killers to the face of the victim's son," Jeremy laughs mirthlessly. "Real classy, Soph. You can't put my mother's death on me. For all I know, you two were in on it with them. Were you in the room? Were you the one who slit her throat?"

His mother? What did any of this have to do with Caroline Berg-Nilsen?

"What are you talking about? Your mom died by her own hand," Sophie says. "No one was 'in on it.' It was a suicide."

Jeremy slams his palm on the brick beside her face, and she flinches. My hands tighten on my bonds. I'm waiting for a reason to unleash on him.

"Stop lying!" he yells, voice echoing around the small room. "You know what they did to her. You have to."

Jeremy pauses, forehead crinkling at the expressions on our faces. He's scrutinizing them, his head turning back and forth as he dissects every tiny detail. Finally, he says, "You don't know?"

"Don't know what?" *Has he completely lost it?*

He drops Sophie and moves toward me, and I throw my hands in front of me, but he doesn't grab me. He just stares into my eyes. "You really don't know?"

I drop the slack of my chains on the ground with a *clank*. "Dammit, Jeremy. Just spit it out!"

All the tension leaves his shoulders, and he's suddenly much younger. Sad. He slides down to sit on the ground. He gestures for us to do the same and waits until we're all on the same level as if we're back in his living room sipping juice boxes. He has our full attention, and he knows it.

Jeremy hesitates, staring at the stone floor and grimacing as if regretting his choice. He shrugs. "When I broke free of the book six years ago, my mother was still alive. Living in squalor, but alive."

"How is that possible?" Sophie asks.

Jeremy frowns. "What do you mean? The demon doesn't kill you if you break the deal; he makes you wish you were dead. You get so used to living the high life of champagne wishes and caviar dreams that anything less than that is just agonizing. My mother was no different. And in the middle of it all, Dad left her and had her committed to Everling. I guess he got his in the end."

Dan Berg-Nilsen's face flashes through my mind. Did he deserve what he got? Jeremy seems to think so. Anger jumps out at me as I stare into his eyes. Dan was right. He's been with the Great One too long. He's dangerous. Unpredictable.

"Mom went back on the deal. She helped me break out of the book. And her punishment for having a conscience?" Jeremy continues. "For trying to ruin the families' sacrifice? Your parents sacrificed my mother to the demon."

"No." I exhale the word. That can't be true.

"Except the Great One didn't need another servant, so he just devoured her whole. There's nothing left of her. Because of them." Jeremy's nostrils flare, his eyes shining with unshed tears. "I saw the whole show. I guess they had practice with all the animal throats they slit over the years in service of the demon. My mother's death bought them enough time for Carter to reach his birthday. But now, it's time for them to pay up again."

"You're wrong. Our parents loved Caroline. They wouldn't kill one of their own."

Jeremy laughs. "Wake up, Ren! Look around you! They're the same people who banished me to that hell all those years ago. They'll do anything to maintain their wealth. Their power. Mom wasn't a part of their world anymore."

He's right, of course. Here they are again about to sacrifice another kid all because they're scared of having to live in the real world. That's what is at the heart of their actions. Fear. Right beside the classic sin: greed.

"Where were you for the five years after her death?" Sophie asks.

"You'll find out soon enough," Jeremy replies. "Seven months ago, I had my father set up a meeting with your parents and Edmond. Together, we made a plan to trap you both, but I couldn't resist hanging out with you. And man, did I have fun. Being a cat isn't so bad, you know?"

Everything he's said is just barely sinking in. My thoughts skip over the mention of an "Edmond" for the time being and come to a screeching halt at "cat." That damn cat…was *Jeremy*? "*You*?!" I spit out, trying to form the right words. "All this time, that was *you*?"

I knew there was a reason the cat made my skin crawl. It makes sense. The reason he kept disappearing, his ability to leave the book at the same time as me and follow me into another.

Sophie is equally thrown. "*You* were *Hercules*? I put you inside my coat!"

I want to wring the guy's skinny neck. What the hell was the point of that? To have some fun watching us fail?

"I can't lie, Soph. That was a highlight." Jeremy winks and jumps to his feet. "But none of that matters right now. Time's a-ticking." He fishes a pocketknife out of his jeans and flicks it open. Sophie recoils as he steps toward her.

"What are you doing?" I say, rising simultaneously with Sophie.

"You may want to stay still, Sophie." Jeremy points the knife at Sophie's legs and plunges the knife down. Sophie stiffens, closing her eyes.

I tense, too, but the knife doesn't tear into her. It hits the duct tape holding her legs together. Jeremy slices through it and unwraps the rest of it, crumpling it up and dropping it to the floor. He grins and drops a key into Sophie's lap. She takes it almost immediately, chest heaving with adrenaline, and sets to work on the chains around her wrists.

As she works on freeing herself, Jeremy cuts into my own duct tape.

I grab his wrist. "You helped me remember who I was. When you were the cat, I mean. Didn't you?"

He hesitates, then smiles softly. "Side effect of being around a demon for years. You learn a few tricks."

"But why help us? You thought we had something to do with

your mom's death. Why would you want to wake us up?"

Jeremy's done with my tape, and he offers me a hand. I ignore it and get to my feet on my own.

Jeremy shrugs. "I didn't know about Carter when I put you in your books. I knew I needed your help to save him."

Sophie and I exchange a look, and I know she's having the same thought. We're expecting Jeremy to laugh in our faces, but he doesn't. His expression is serious. What is he playing at?

"You think I'd let those bastards do the same thing they did to me to some other kid? Besides, if their empire crumbles, I get my vengeance. It's a win-win."

I'm not ready to trust Jeremy. Far from it. But he's our only shot at saving Carter. As we follow Jeremy to the door, Sophie weaves her fingers through mine. I'm glad she's here. I could never do this alone.

"Let's go save the kid," Jeremy says.

I stop at the book with our names on the cover. It's useless now except for one aspect. It's the only thing left of Eve other than her driver's license still tucked inside my pocket. The book contains the story of her last moments. The least I can do is carry it with me. I pick up the book and follow Sophie and Jeremy out of the room.

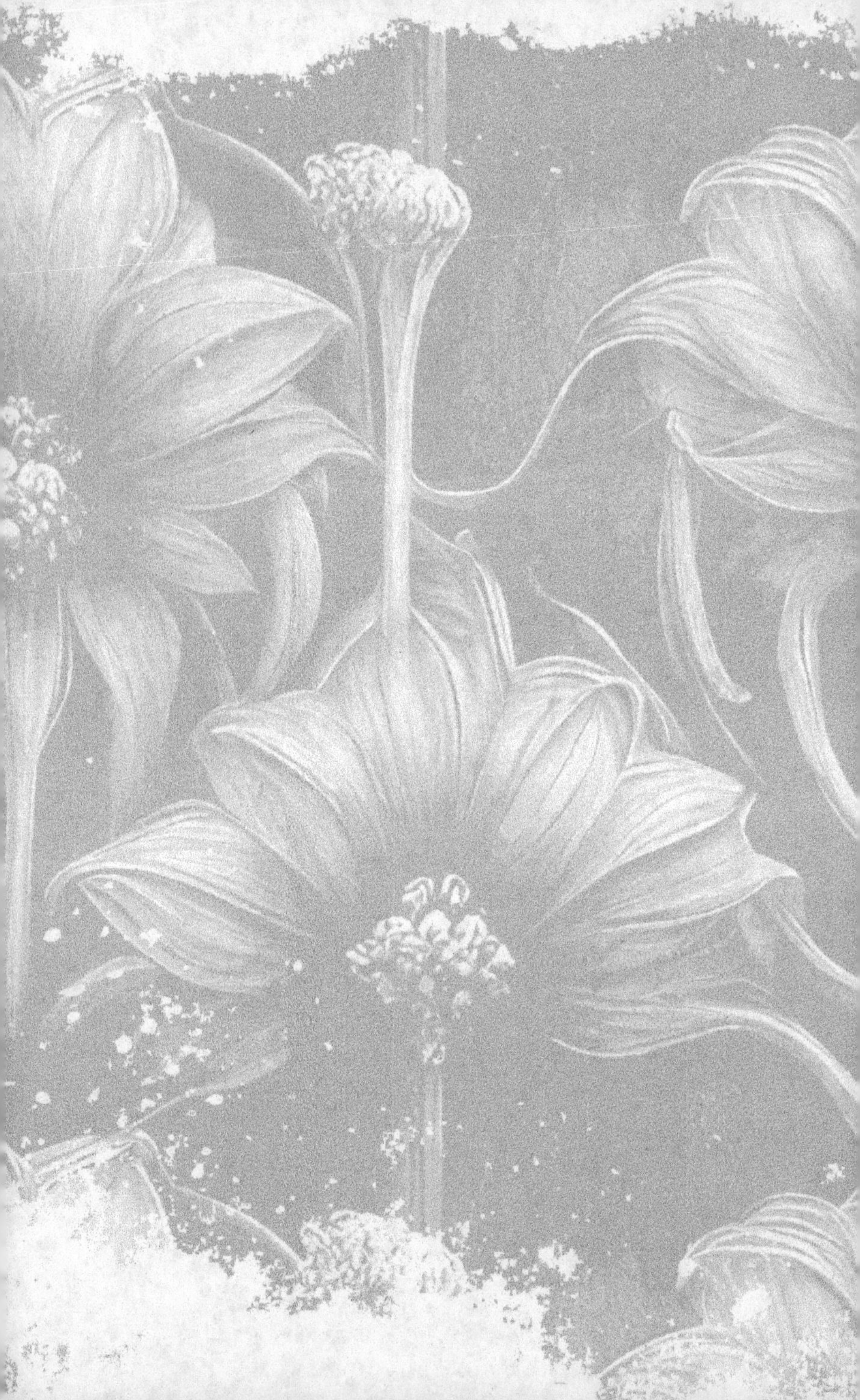

CHAPTER FORTY-TWO

JEREMY BERG-NILSEN

The stairs and door from the dungeon spit us out into a greenhouse. It was our favorite room as kids. It was an Amazon rainforest when we needed it to be. Even Narnia once or twice. We would play hide and seek here, ducking behind bamboo and ferns, laughing when we'd get caught in the sprinkler system. It was also my mother's favorite room. Her pride and joy. When I couldn't find her in our sprawling estate, I'd head straight here, and she'd be talking to the plants or humming to herself.

The sun burned bright on those days but never seemed to burn me before. Now, I don't dwell in here. What little plants remain have long since withered and died, neglected, their mother gone. I know how they must've felt. Abandoned. Confused. Angry. Or maybe that's just me projecting.

Regardless, the atmosphere here is no longer cheery and promising. The moonlight, especially tonight, casts an eerie glow on the greenhouse, leaving everything haunted.

Ren and Sophie follow me into the open space, their eyes darting for booby traps or tricks. I can almost read their minds. Are they remembering the days of hide and seek, too?

"Why does it smell like gasoline in here?" Ren whispers.

I lift a shoulder. "Probably because I poured gasoline in here."

"WHAT?"

I place a finger to my lips. "Basically, every room the others won't be in for the ceremony is doused in it."

We form a small huddle in the middle of the room. It's connected to the rest of the house and surrounded by glass, but the others won't be near here at this time. And all of the guests have long since left. I glance at my watch.

11:44pm.

They'll be donning their purple cloaks right about now. I wonder how flammable they are. That's a happy image.

"*That's* your plan?" Sophie asks. "Burn it all down?"

"Why not? There's nothing but bad memories here."

"That's all well and good, but how are we going to get Carter away from them? We don't have long, do we?"

I shake my head. "No, we don't. It's 11:44."

Sophie gasps, and Ren places a hand on her shoulder.

"We've got time," Ren says.

"Barely." The word escapes my lips, but I'm not the one who says it. It comes from deep within me. From *him*. I've made the stupid mistake of glancing at my reflection, accidentally accessing the demon.

No, not now.

I clench my jaw and fall to my knees, closing my eyes and tilting my head as if that will help beat him back. I open my eyes briefly, and Sophie and Ren take a few steps back.

"What's happening?" Ren asks as Sophie says, "What's wrong with your eyes?"

I force him back into his box, using all the will I have. Something I developed over the months, adapting. Edmond's screams pierce every part of my thoughts, and I think he'll kill me from the inside. But he's contained. For now.

That done, I take a minute to get my bearings, heaving with effort as I rise. Sophie and Ren each take two more steps back. I force a smile, hoping it looks carefree.

"Whelp, I guess the cat's out of the bag."

Sophie swallows hard. "Those eyes—"

"It won't happen again," I say, my palms up. "I've dealt with him, I promise."

Ren's brow furrows. "'Him?' Could someone fill me in here?"

Sophie clutches Ren's arm, digging into her skin. "He's not Jeremy," she says, eyes still on me.

"Wrong," I reply.

"You can't talk your way out of this one." Sophie points a finger at me. "I remember you. You were there that night I almost lost my mind. You went after me, made those horrible shadows. Those *screams*."

Is she going to cry? the demon's voice pipes up. *Spare me.*

I ignore him and step forward. "Yes, I was physically there that night, but that wasn't me. It was him. The demon that took me. He's inside me."

The demon snickers.

Shut up.

Ren carefully unlatches Sophie's grip on her arm, brushes it as if trying to get rid of soreness, and says, "Talk fast. The truth. Now."

"That can't be true. You're lying."

The demon expands his billowy frame to appear larger than usual. "I lie about many things, but not about this. Your parents condemned you to a fate worse than death. Never-ending darkness with me as your only companion. Not to worry. There is a way out."

The demon circles me.

"How?" I ask, barely holding back a whimper.

"Give me your body," the demon says, smiling wide.

"My body?"

The demon ruffles my hair and clothes. "I can't possess an unwilling vessel. I need you to hand it over willingly."

"I'm not giving you my body. That'll never happen." I jut my chin out.

The demon chuckles. "Never say never, little one."

"My family is coming for me."

He laughs louder. "Your family are the ones who put you here in the first place. Remember?"

"Says you," I say, but my voice cracks.

"Perhaps I should let you ruminate a bit. Really get a sense of your predicament."

"No. Please don't go."

But the demon is gone, leaving me to the silence that yawns ahead of me. In all directions.

"Even though the voice was odd and wrong," I continue, "I didn't want to face the unending darkness alone. I welcomed the company, but I never gave in to his demands until—"

"Until?"

"My mother died. I just wanted revenge."

"So you let him take over your *body*?"

"It seemed reasonable."

"What part of that is reasonable?"

"And that's everything?" Sophie asks.

I hesitate. "My mother didn't die before I said yes to the demon. She died *after*."

Ren narrows her eyes at me. "I don't understand. You said your mother's death is what pushed you to give in."

"It was, but it was a trick. It was a vision of the future, not the present. And to top it off, the demon said she made a deal with him, and that's why she died. I caused her death by saying yes to Edmond."

Sophie grabs my arm. "No, Jeremy. Please don't blame

yourself. It was the demon. He tricked you."

I wipe my eyes and sniffle. "But I fell for it. Anyway, whatever I said to you when you escaped the book, that wasn't me either. That was Edmond. I have no memory of any of that. It's how it usually is when he takes over."

Usually. Not always. You remember that night. Don't you, Jeremy?

"How are we supposed to trust you when you're working with a demon?" Ren asks.

"I'm not. I have him handled. He's locked away."

"For now."

For now. Edmond thinks the words at the same moment Ren says them. I shudder.

"He could break out at any time," Ren continues.

"We're running out of time," I say, checking my watch. 11:49. "I'm your inside man and your best chance at saving the kid. But you two need to do the planning from here on out."

"Why?"

"The demon's in me, remember? He knows what I know. He'll do whatever he can to make sure the sacrifice goes smoothly."

Damn right.

After a beat of listening to the wind tap on the greenhouse's windows, Sophie steps forward. "Ren, I know what to do."

"Edmond, are you joining us?" someone calls from another room. The three of us jump out of our skins.

"That's my cue," I say with a bow. "And remember, trust me. You can trust your parents, too. They tried to take Carter away."

Ren's face pales, and she grabs our arm. "You're telling me this *now?*"

"Would you rather I never tell you?"

Ren scoffs.

"What? Isn't this a good thing? Your parents aren't psychopaths like you thought. I thought you'd be happy."

"Happy? Where are they now? You said 'tried.' Were they caught?"

"They're fine. Don't do anything stupid, pussycat." I wink.

ALLISON IVY

"Don't ever call me that again."

Thonk. A planter shatters over my head, dirt cascading to the floor. And darkness overcomes me.

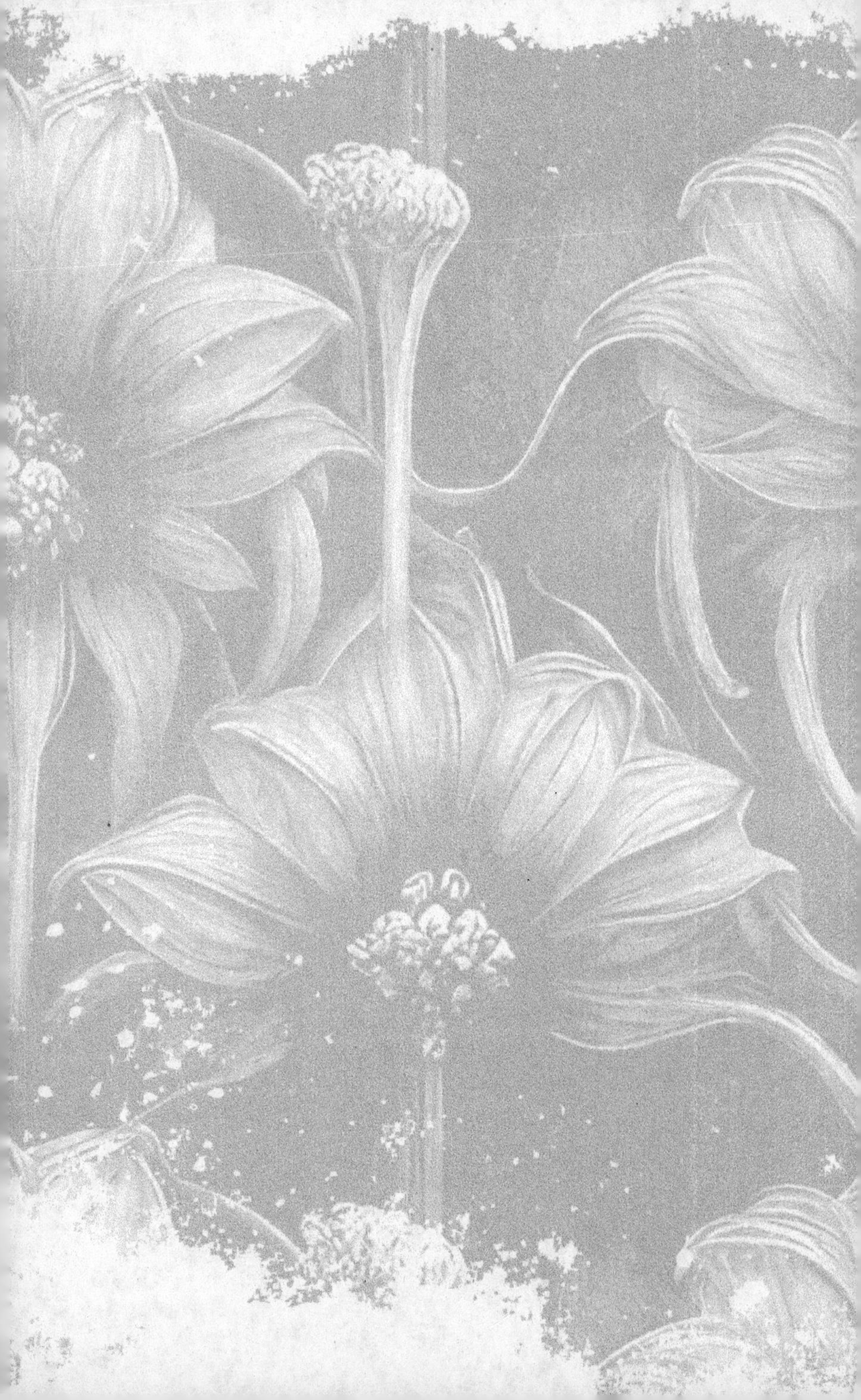

CHAPTER FORTY-THREE

SOPHIE VANGUARD

With Jeremy unconscious, Ren turns to me. "What the hell, Soph?"

She's expecting an answer and a full-fledged plan, no doubt. It's not full-fledged. More like half-fledged. But it's all I've got. I tamp my guilt down deep. *This was the right thing to do.* But Ren's looking at me like I'm dangerous.

"We can't trust him," I say.

She can't blame me. Jeremy's a wild card. We have no idea what he's really thinking. If he even told us the whole truth back in that room. If it was even him talking to us. What choice did I have?

"I don't trust him either, but hello to the violence."

I shrug. "I guess he brings it out in me."

"Not to self: Never piss Sophie Vanguard off." Ren lifts Jeremy's arm to check his watch. "It's 11:54."

My heart skips as she looks to me for the next step. Right. A plan. What is it again?

"Do you think Jeremy was telling the truth about your parents?"

"I don't know. Má always said after Jeremy's sacrifice, she

would never participate again, but—" She shakes her head.

I know what she means. How can we be sure? And they still reap the benefits from their deal. They're not "living in squalor" like Jeremy's mother had.

"We have to assume they're not on our side," I say. "That may change, but I can't be taking chances where Carter's involved."

Ren nods. "What are you thinking?"

"We have to get the book."

On the long walk to the living room, I'm hyperaware of my surroundings. *Rising cortisol in times of extreme fear.* My brain volunteers the random fact without warning. The wallpaper shows every bit of its age, peeling and yellowing. I run my hand over it, and it practically breaks under my touch. This isn't the grand manor I remember. Jeremy—or, more likely, Edmond—must've disguised how rundown it is to keep up appearances with the others. Now, minutes from the sacrifice, there's no need for pretense. He has them where he wants them.

Jeremy's confession flits through my mind. After all Jeremy's been through, to have to witness someone using your body to kill someone you love? I can't imagine it. I can't let my family give Carter to that evil.

By the time I reach the living room, the group of them are chanting. I hide in a crevice at the doorway, out of sight for now.

There's Lien and Đài Ly positioned on the opposite side of the coffee table. Across from them are Mom and Dad. And there, in the same spot where Jeremy stood eighteen years ago, is Carter. Draped in purple.

My blood runs cold. We're too late. How could this happen? Was Jeremy's watch wrong?

Lien holds up a hand, and they all fall silent. "Wait. Do you smell something?"

INKED IN BLOOD AND MEMORY

"Something's on fire," Đài says.

He's right. Smoke billows from the greenhouse. Ren's right on cue. Their heads turn to the doorway, and I hold my breath.

"It'll have to wait. We're too close to midnight. We can't risk missing the deadline."

"Sylvia's right. We get one shot."

They continue to chant.

Wait.

They're not chanting the summoning spell. It's different. If I hadn't studied it so well when I was younger, I might think maybe I don't remember it after all these years. But I know what the spell sounds like, and this isn't it.

The clock on the wall reads 11:56. What could they be chanting that would be worth cutting it so close to the deadline?

Ren pokes her head in from the other entrance as black smoke billows from the open book in Mom's hands. She's unfazed as two hellhounds bound out of the pages and growl in my direction. But Ren's parents have caught sight of their daughter, and I think, *It's over*. They'll turn her in and find me, and Carter will be lost.

"Sylvia," Đài says, and I prepare myself to help Ren. But instead, he says, "We must switch to the summoning spell."

Mom holds up a hand. "We know you're here, girls. Come out now and surrender, or I give the word, and you're dogmeat."

Would she really do that? Sic ferocious dogs on her only daughter?

I honestly don't know. She was fine sending a Minotaur into the book with me.

"You have until the second hand of that clock," she points at the clock behind her, "reaches the 6."

It's creeping toward 3.

4.

5.

Mom sighs. "*Circumspicio*."

The hounds set out at a determined pace, noses to the ground and growling.

My mother hasn't used the kill command, but who's to say she won't use it when the dogs find me? How far can I make it before they take me down for good? Not far enough.

Ren reaches my mother and knocks the book from her hands. It sails past the dogs and lands with a *thud* a few yards from me as my father grabs Ren from behind. She struggles, but Dad has locked her arms in place, and he's the strongest person I know.

11:59.

I step around the corner and inside the room, outing my position to the two dogs, but I'm moving before they look up from the ground. I dive for the book even though it may get me bit. I make it there first and sweep it into my hands, simultaneously calling forth my hazy knowledge of Latin.

I flip the book open and shout, "*Ad fontes*."

The hellhounds whine and disappear in a cloud of black smoke that rushes back into the book in my hands with such force I almost drop it.

My triumph doesn't last.

A hand plucks the book from my grasp, and a flash of yellow eyes wink at me. Jeremy/Edmond brings the book to my mother.

A flicker of a smug grin hits Mom's face. "Thank you, Edmond."

My dad grits his teeth, using all his strength to keep Ren contained, checking the clock. "Midnight, Sylvia. Let's go."

They begin the sacrifice chant. Or rather, my parents begin the chant. Ren's parents, though, have fallen silent. Mom and Dad cast looks at them but continue chanting. They won't be deterred.

"Carter, run!" I rush forward to grab Carter, and at the same moment, Edmond or the Great One or whatever the demon's name is rises from within Jeremy, who falls to his knees.

The demon's rising blasts me back, and I land hard on the wooden floor.

Amidst perplexed expressions, the demon grabs Carter's wrist. My brother's scream is heart-wrenching as the demon lifts him off the coffee table, prepared to suck him into the book.

INKED IN BLOOD AND MEMORY

That's when Lien and Đài grab Carter's ankles, Lien on the right and Đài on the left.

"Sophie!" Carter yells.

Jeremy uses Mom and Dad's confusion to his advantage. They and Ren have also fallen to the ground, and Jeremy tackles Mom, ripping the book from her hand and tossing it blindly behind him.

As Dad pulls Jeremy off of my mother, Ren catches the book and furiously flips through it, and I realize what she's doing. I grab the book from her and scan the pages to find the spell we need. It's close to the back, right? My fingers fumble through the thick pages until, finally, I find it.

The Lys aren't strong enough to keep hold of Carter, and the demon pushes them back with renewed energy and anger. They fall to the ground, and Carter is defenseless.

Ren takes over for them, and Jeremy joins her.

I begin the spell as Mom and Dad split up. Mom strides toward me, high heels clicking as Dad moves to stop Ren and Jeremy. But Đài has recovered and blocks his way. Đài is much smaller than my father, and I don't have much time. I don't know if my Latin will pass the test.

I dodge my mother and sprint to the other side of the room as words spill from my mouth, some of which I haven't read in years. But they must be working because the demon shrieks and drops Carter, fixing his yellow eyes on me instead.

"Change your mind about making a deal, Sophie?" Edmond snarls. He's a cloud of smoke with no mouth in sight. It's eerie.

Ren casts me a questioning look, and shame hits me square in the chest, the Latin stuck in my throat.

"What does he mean?" Ren asks, hands still on Carter's wrists. This isn't the time for this. Not when my little brother's soul quite literally hangs in the balance.

Instead of playing along, I return to the spell on the page in front of me. Three more lines. I read them out, and that's all it takes. The spell is complete. Edmond has no choice but to return to where he came from, which is Jeremy.

In a rush of black smoke, the force of the demon knocks Jeremy back, and he falls to the floor once again, unconscious. I wince. He's having a rough night. I was wrong about him. My friend is still in there. No matter how angry he was at us, he came through.

The greenhouse isn't the only room on fire. Ren has followed my instructions and destroyed a few more of them on her way here.

Smoke and fire punch a hole in the already worn and flimsy ceiling of Berg-Nilsen Manor just as I reach Ren, Jeremy, and Carter.

A rafter falls, knocking Lien and Đài close to the door.

"Má! Ba!" Ren calls, but the flames tower over us. There is no way to get to them. "Get outside!"

"No, Ren!" Đài says.

"Not without you!" comes Lien's voice.

"I'll be fine, I promise. You have to trust me. Go!" Carter climbs down from the coffee table, but before I can reassure him, Mother wails and rushes me, and we both go down.

"You selfish, ungrateful girl!" Her face shows more emotion than I've ever seen from her. Her eyes dance with rage, made even more terrifying by the blazing fire.

She rips the book from my hands and knocks me back, returning to her husband's side.

Relief floods through me when I see Carter is safe, clinging to Ren. He's scared and confused but unharmed.

But the relief is short-lived when I see what my father has wrapped in his bicep.

Jeremy's neck.

CHAPTER FORTY-FOUR

LY THI REN
12:02AM

Roger tightens his grip around Jeremy's throat, who tries to pull the man off him, but it's no use. He's a scraggly twenty-something, and the other is a well-toned, beefy man.

"Let him go," I say.

"Or what?"

Touché. I'm not as skilled as my book counterpart. I don't have the fighting ingrained in my being, but I'm not about to give up on a friend.

Sylvia opens the book and flips through it, and I can only imagine what kind of conjuration she has in mind. Carter clings to me.

"You need to go," Jeremy says.

"No," Sophie says, "We're not leaving you again, Jeremy."

A tear runs down Jeremy's cheek as something changes in his eyes. "I love you guys, too."

He moves before we can do anything, placing his palm on the page Sylvia's decided on. The book glows, and with a *whoosh*, Jeremy and Roger disappear into it.

Sophie and I cry out as the book falls to the ground with a *thud*, and the surrounding flames already lap hungrily toward it. It'll be completely consumed in a matter of minutes.

Sylvia stands obstinate in the midst of it all. You'd never know the love of her life was just sucked into the equivalent of hell. She eyes Carter with a cool, steely glare and holds out an expectant hand. "Hand him over. Now."

"Never," Sophie says, moving Carter behind her. "Give it up, Mom. Look around you. You have no more cards to play."

Desperation flickers in her wide eyes, the only emotion she shows. "You don't know what it's like, Sophie. How *hard* it is just to stay afloat and keep a family together. Worried about if you're going to be able to pay the next bill. You haven't lived in the real world, Sophie. You don't know."

And she does? She's never had to struggle in her life. She's a Haglen, after all.

"Millions of people do it every day. You don't see them turning to devil worship," I say, checking in on the book at our feet.

Sylvia juts out her chin. "They would if they had the chance."

"Give it up, Sylvia," I say, pointing to the clock. "See? It's past 12:01. It's over."

Sylvia's face crumples. Her lips quiver as a vein pulses in her pale forehead. "No."

Sophie holds out her hand. "Come with us, Mom. *Please*. We can start over."

"I'd rather burn." She backs away from us, closer to the flames invading the room. A rafter falls in between us, and the fire spreads to it almost immediately. Sylvia is trapped, but despite all she's done, Sophie reaches toward her as I cover Carter's eyes.

I snatch the book up as the ceiling above Sylvia collapses, and she disappears.

Sophie moves to help her, but I stop her. "It's too late, Soph. We have to go. We have to get Carter out of here."

With nothing more we can do, Sophie takes Carter by the hand

and follows me out of the room.

The front door to the Berg-Nilsen estate is inaccessible. Flames have completely engulfed the wood. My eyes dart to each window, but every one of them is blocked in some way or another. My lungs burn as the air fills with smoke.

Sophie pulls the neck of her shirt up to cover her nose and mouth and instructs Carter to do the same.

"Get low to the ground!" I yell above the inferno. We all crouch and clasp hands, forming a chain as we move forward on the only path we can—toward the staircase.

It's so hot, I can barely think. Sweat pools at my back and forehead as I struggle to see through the fire and smoke.

Somewhere above our coughing, Má and Ba's voices ring out. My ears perk up. "Má! Ba! Where are you?"

"I hear them, too. They're outside."

"You're sure?"

Sophie nods behind her makeshift mask. "They're safe."

We make our way up the staircase, pulling Carter in close between us, away from the growing flames. What seems like an eternity later, we make it to the second floor and have one option—the spiral staircase to the third floor.

We arrive to chaos. Books, ever the outstanding kindling, have fed the fire, but the right side of the room stands untouched.

There, miraculously, a window looks out at the lake below, unobstructed. But we don't have much time. "There!" I point it out, and we run to it.

Beside it, Jeremy's satchel lays on an armchair piled with books, and I grab it and tuck the two books inside.

Briefly, I wonder about my own book with William and Adeline. I still don't know if they were real, and part of me feels obligated to go look for it. But everywhere I turn, the fire has taken over. Wherever the book is now, it's too late to save it.

Sophie grabs my elbow. "Ren, we're at least three stories up; there's no way we can jump that."

"Got a better idea?"

She doesn't reply.

I open the window and feel a rush of adrenaline as I look down, already formulating a plan. *This is going to be fun.*

With one look at Sophie's expression, I reel in my excitement and focus on her and Carter. They both look terrified.

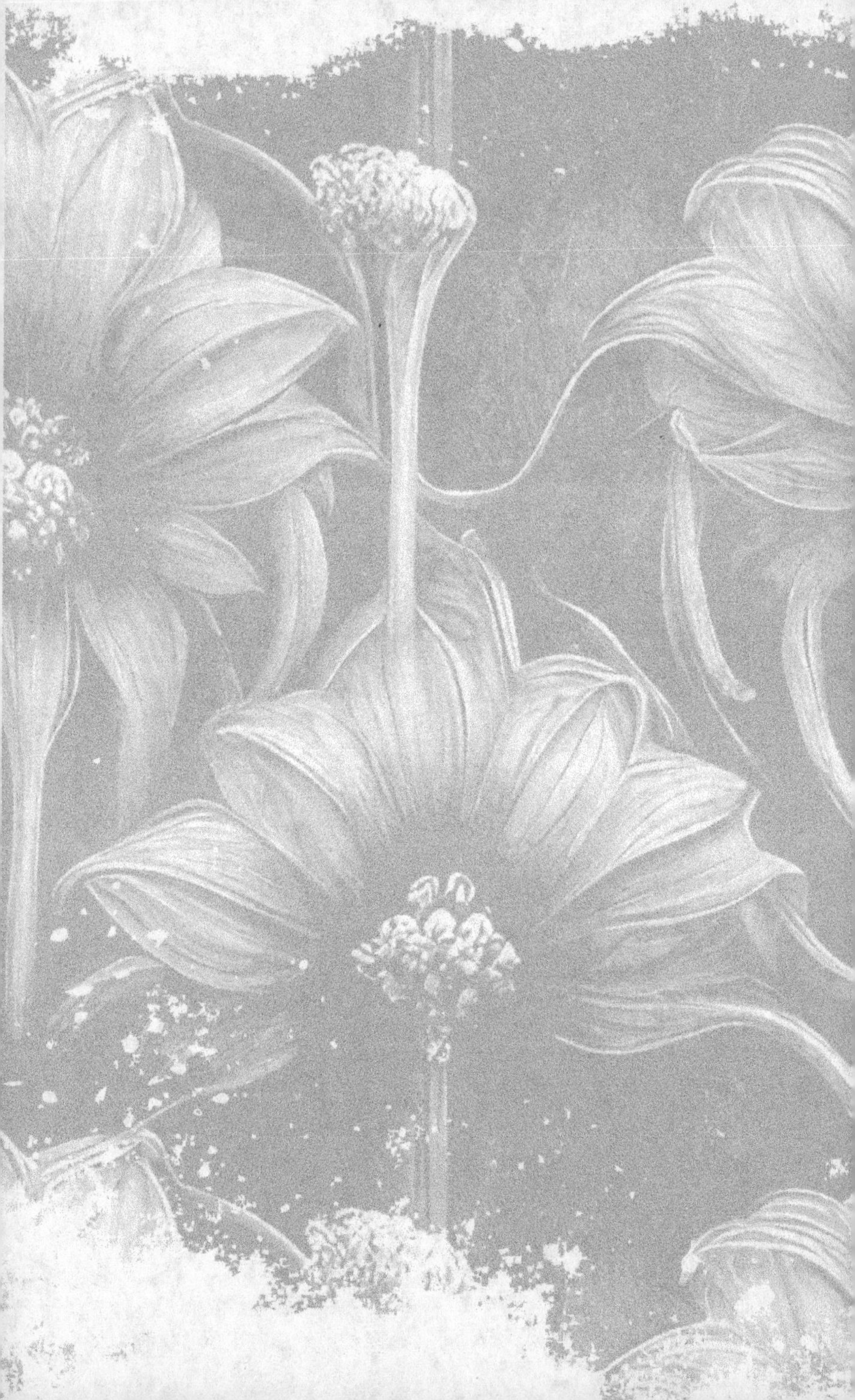

CHAPTER FORTY-FIVE

SOPHIE VANGUARD

I'm terrified.

During my many months of reading to pass the time, the term *l'appel du vide* or "the call of the void" popped up. It's the overwhelming need to jump when faced with a high ledge. I've never had that need, and as I sat digesting the phrase, I could not wrap my head around someone feeling this. Now, I realize I'll never have that feeling because I'm staring into the dark water below us with no urge to jump. The Berg-Nilsens' private lake waits for us.

Swimming in it as a kid, it seemed pretty deep, but that was when we were under four feet tall. And we never jumped into it from the top floor of the house. No matter how much Ren wanted to.

"Who has a lake around their house?" I ask of no one in particular, mainly to fill the silence. Otherwise, I'll lose it.

The windows on the floor below us burst outward, and the flames lap at the cool December air. Movement from across the water catches my eye. Ren's mother has fallen to her knees as her father looks on. They'd surprised me back there, helping us save

Carter.

The roof of the floor below juts out a few feet. It's a balcony. One look at Ren tells me she's seen it, too. Hope surges through me.

"It's so high," Carter murmurs, his voice trembling.

I pick Carter up and shift him to my hip. He clings tightly to my neck, his eyes squeezed shut. "I know, buddy, but we can't stay here. We're going to try to get a little lower. I need you to be brave, okay?"

He nods.

"I'll go first, and you follow," Ren says before inching onto the roof.

"Hold on tight," I tell Carter, and he clutches my neck even tighter. Traveling across a roof is awkward, even without a kid holding on to you. I move as slowly as I can, expecting my foot to slip out at any moment. My every thought is of us falling over the side and missing the lake completely. After an agonizingly long descent, we finally make it to the gutter.

"Ren?"

"Here. I'm ready."

I place a hand on Carter's back. "Okay, I need you to trust me. Can you do that?"

Carter nods, his body trembling under my palm.

"I'm going to pass you down to Ren, okay? She's right underneath us."

"No!" Carter hugs me, trembling even more now.

"Hey, I know it's scary. I know. But Ren is right here. I can see her right now. She's not going to let you fall. Right, Ren?"

"Never, Carter."

With a bit more coaxing, Carter agrees to the plan. He unwraps his arms from my neck and his legs from my hip, and I lift him over the edge of the roof. He drops about a foot before Ren's arms catch him, and she sets him down on the balcony.

Behind me, the fire has reached the same window from which we had escaped. The flames lick at the cool night air.

INKED IN BLOOD AND MEMORY

As Ren celebrates with Carter, trying to keep him as calm as possible, I turn on my stomach and swing my legs over the edge, lowering my body until my arms are fully extended. I hate not knowing how far I have to drop, but it can't be too much of a distance. With that thought, I let go and touch down a millisecond later. I breathe a sigh of relief and high-five Carter, who's quiet but seems proud of himself.

We don't have much space on the balcony as the fire is here as well, lapping at us, waiting to feast. Ren and I peer over the iron railing to the lake below while Carter is short enough to look through the bars. It's less of a drop now, but it's still a pretty big jump.

I'm first up to jump the barrier and sit precariously on the railing. The fingers of my right hand dig into the iron as I white-knuckle it. Ren places Carter back on my hip and then joins us.

"Can you do me a favor, Carter? Take off my glasses."

He does.

"Good. Now, I need you to fold them up and hold onto them. You're going to keep them safe for me. Can you do that?"

He nods, obeying, and I kiss his head. I'm not sure who's shaking more now.

"We got to go." Ren holds out a hand, and I take it.

"Hold your breath," I instruct Carter. He uses his free hand to hold his nose shut. I hold him as tight as possible as Ren descends and pulls us with her.

We fall
and fall
and fall
into the water below.

We emerge from the water, drenched but alive and all in one piece. I swim with Carter still clinging to me until we're close enough to the lakeshore that he breaks away from me and swims the rest of the way himself. Ren is already there and pulls him to his feet. They run to the grass farther away from the house, and I follow close behind, my clothes sagging with the extra weight of the water. Icy air hits me.

"You okay, little man?" Ren asks, tussling Carter's hair. The bag with the books inside is still safe on her shoulder, if dripping wet. I wonder briefly if the water has any effect on them, but I have no plan to open them any time soon to find out.

Carter giggles from his spot on the hillside. "Can we do that again?"

Ren shakes her head.

"Kids, man," she says.

Maybe he won't turn out as traumatized as I thought. I wring the water out of the hem of my shirt as best I can before collapsing on the grass. Carter crawls up to lay on my left side, handing my glasses to me.

"Thanks, dude." I put them on as Ren joins us on my right.

The Berg-Nilsen manor burns in front of us, sirens on the horizon. The estate looks exactly like its book counterpart minus the hedge maze in the back.

Above us, the night sky is in full bloom. I wish I knew what constellation I'm looking at.

Ren laughs in spite of it all, and I turn to look at her. "This would make one hell of a book."

"I guess if we were still trapped in one, this would be the official last page."

Ren gives me a once-over, no doubt taking in the curves of my body underneath my soaked clothes before pulling me close.

"Nah," she says. "It's just the first chapter."

ABOUT THE AUTHOR

Author of *The Dragon and the Double-Edged Sword*, Allison Ivy writes under a pen name and edits for others in her spare time. She grew up reading a book a day (mostly *Goosebumps*, *Fear Street*, or the works of Christopher Pike). Allison graduated from Penn State with a B.A. in English and a Creative Writing certificate. A Pittsburgh native, she currently lives in Pennsylvania and listens to far too many show tunes and DVD commentaries. Find her at:

www.allisonivybooks.com

linktr.ee/allison_ivy

ACKNOWLEDGMENTS

Inked in Blood and Memory is truly the book of my heart. The characters and settings have been with me for years, waiting for me to share them with the world. If you're like me, the horror genre is often a comfort or an escape from reality. I hope this book offered you an escape of your own.

J.V. Hilliard, your words of encouragement and support were appreciated immensely. To Samantha Gove at Raven's Wing Editing Services: Thank you for going over *Inked* with a fine-tooth comb and ironing out the inconsistencies. Your input was invaluable.

To my aunt for being one of my greatest cheerleaders. Thank you for reading the early draft and spreading the word about *Inked*. You've read through a lot of the subpar moments of *Inked* and continue to support me through every publishing endeavor.

Thank you, Mom, Dad, and the rest of my family for all of your help throughout the years. Even though this book isn't exactly in your genre, I hope you find things about it you like.

J.P., you offered so many incredible solutions to the plot of *Inked*. Thank you for taking the time to talk me through each and every one. Beyond that, thank you for believing in me when I thought I'd never be able to write my way out. I'm forever grateful.

Teresa, Lorna, Jean, Jen, and Cyara: thank you for all your kind words and excitement.

Finally, to all my ARC readers, reviewers, and others who have picked *Inked* up on a whim or offered kind words or spread the word about it over social media: Thank you from the bottom of my heart. Self-publishing is a risky venture, and I'm so glad you took a leap of faith on *Inked in Blood and Memory*.

Allison
August 2024

Printed in the USA
CPSIA information can be obtained
at www.ICGtesting.com
LVHW031757051124
795791LV00013B/334